MT.

D0267070

G...ts
of time obs............................—early
research! Now she spends her days fantasising about
...ous men and their love-lives. Annie has been a
...er all her life. She also loves travel, long walks,
od company and great food. You can contact her
annie@annie-west.com or via PO Box 1041,
arners Bay, NSW 2282, Australia.

ith two university degrees and a variety of false
areer starts under her belt, **Michelle Conder** decided
satisfy her lifelong desire to write and finally found
er dream job. She currently lives in Melbourne,
ustralia, with one super-indulgent husband, three
lf-indulgent but exquisite children, a menagerie of
er-indulged pets, and the intention of doing some
m of exercise daily. She loves to hear from her
ders at michelleconder.com.

Also by Annie West

Revelations of a Secret Princess

Royal Brides for Desert Brothers miniseries

Sheikh's Royal Baby Revelation
Demanding His Desert Queen

Also by Michelle Conder

The Italian's Virgin Acquisition
Bound to Her Desert Captor
The Billionaire's Virgin Temptation
Their Royal Wedding Bargain

Discover more at millsandboon.co.uk.

CONTRACTED TO HER GREEK ENEMY

ANNIE WEST

CROWNING HIS UNLIKELY PRINCESS

MICHELLE CONDER

MILLS & BOON

First Published in Great Britain 2020
by Mills & Boon, an imprint of HarperCollins*Publishers*
1 London Bridge Street, London, SE1 9GF

Contracted to Her Greek Enemy © 2020 by Annie West

Crowning His Unlikely Princess © 2020 by Michelle Conder

ISBN: 978-0-263-27816-3

MIX
Paper from
responsible sources
FSC® C007454

This book is produced from independently certified FSC™ paper
to ensure responsible forest management.
For more information visit www.harpercollins.co.uk/green.

Printed and bound in Spain
by CPI, Barcelona

CONTRACTED
TO HER
GREEK ENEMY

ANNIE WEST

This is my 40th book for Harlequin Mills and Boon!

Celebrations are in order, and thanks:

To the readers who enjoy my stories. You've made my dream of writing romance come true.

To my terrific editor Carly Byrne.

To my writer friends, especially Anna Campbell, Abby Green, Michelle Douglas and Cathryn Hein.

To Efthalia Pegios for advice on Greek.

To my wonderful family.

This book is dedicated to my mum.

CHAPTER ONE

'I'VE HAD ENOUGH, DAMEN. I can't stand it any more. I feel like running away.'

Damen's eyebrows rose. Clio wasn't the sort to run from trouble. 'It can't be that bad.'

Wrong response, Nicolaides!

Even before she flashed him an outraged glare, Damen realised his mistake. With a mother and two younger sisters, he had a healthy respect for feminine temper. Clearly this was serious.

'Oh, can't it?' She shook her head and her diamond drop earrings swung. 'He's not just badgering me, but Mama too. It's his only topic of conversation. I don't dare show my face or call Mama because it sets him off again.'

She hefted a shuddery breath and Damen was horrified as he watched tears well. He'd never seen his cousin Clio cry. And though they were only second cousins, they were as close as siblings.

Clio's chin wobbled. 'It's Cassie's wedding soon but I'm not sure I can face going to it. My own little sister's wedding!'

Damen's gut churned. Clio was hurting and *he* was responsible. He should have realised—

'All my father does is rave about how *I* as the eldest should be marrying first. How you and I are a perfect match and how selfish I am not settling down with the man who's decent, honourable and suitable in every way.' She bit her lip and slanted him a glance. 'Of course, he never mentions how suitable your fortune is.'

That flash of humour didn't ease the dark cloud settling over Damen's conscience.

This was no joke. Manos was a difficult man at the best

of times and he could make life hell for Clio and her whole family.

Damen grabbed her hand, felt it tremble and cursed himself for putting her in this situation. Once Manos got an idea it was almost impossible to shift it.

'I'm sorry, Clio. This is all down to me. I should never—'

'*Don't* go all macho and say it's your fault, Damen Nicolaides! I know you're used to shouldering responsibility for everyone, but you're not solely to blame.' She sighed. 'We both are. You think I haven't enjoyed going to all those A-list parties with you? You think I haven't been networking like mad, building up a list of potential clients for my business?'

'It was my idea.' Because he'd tired of fending off women who wanted more from him than a mutually satisfying fling. No matter how often he said he wasn't in the market for the long term, they thought they could change his mind.

With Clio as his semi-regular date things had been much easier. His occasional lovers were more accepting of the fact he wasn't shopping for a wife.

A cold shiver started at his nape and crawled down his spine at the word, chilling each vertebra as it went.

Gentle fingers squeezed his hand. 'You did nothing wrong, Damen.'

He focused on Clio's earnest face and wondered if she was talking about this issue with her father or the past, when clearly Damen *had* been to blame. Typical of Clio to try to absolve him.

She'd stood by him when he'd really needed it. She deserved better than this mess.

'Okay, let's agree neither of us were at fault.' They were adults, entitled to socialise together, even if they weren't and never would be lovers. 'That still leaves the problem of your father. We have to find a way to disabuse him of his expectations without him blaming you.'

Clio pulled her hand away, smoothing it down the silk dress she wore for today's celebration.

'I tell you, I'm running away. To Tierra del Fuego.'

Damen heard despair beneath that light-hearted tone.

'Do you even know where that is?'

'Okay, then, the Arctic Circle. I'll branch into interior design for igloos.'

Despite himself, Damen laughed. His cousin could do it too. She was a talented designer, up for any challenge.

Except getting herself out of this mess. It would take more than Clio's word to convince Manos she and Damen weren't an item. Especially with the prize of Damen's vast fortune in the equation. Which it always was.

That was one of the prime reasons he'd resorted to 'dates' with his cousin, to stave off the women angling to snare a rich husband. A Greek billionaire with no wife and a healthy cash flow despite the recent economic troubles was a catch. One in his early thirties with a full head of hair and all his own teeth was a rarity.

'Forget the igloos and leave this to me.'

'You have an idea?' No mistaking the hope in her tone.

Damen nodded. 'The beginnings of one. But give me time to sort out the details. Trust me, I'll sort Manos.'

Relief eased her tight expression. 'Thanks, Damen. I should have realised I could count on you.'

Twenty minutes later, Damen stood beside his best friend, Christo, who was to marry today. Christo was checking his phone, leaving Damen free to admire the panoramic view of the sea off Corfu. But Damen ignored the vista, instead surveying the guests gathered in the villa's garden.

What he needed was a woman. And quickly.

A woman to play the part of his lover long enough to persuade Manos that Damen and Clio had no future together.

If he attended the upcoming wedding of Clio's sister, Cassie, with a striking new girlfriend in tow, that would dent Manos's hopes. If Damen kept that new girlfriend with him for a couple of months, his very public companion...

But which woman?

Someone single. And attractive, for Manos was no fool. There had to be a sizzle of desire between Damen and his new companion.

But Damen needed someone who wouldn't see this as an opportunity to angle for a real relationship. A woman who wouldn't try to win his affections and carve out a place for herself in his life.

'Relax.' Christo's voice interrupted his thoughts. 'I'm the one getting married, not you.'

Damen flashed his old friend a smile. 'And marrying the same woman twice. That's some sort of record.'

Christo shrugged and spread his hands. 'The first time I had no idea how much she meant to me. This time everything is perfect between us. I just hope you find a woman like Emma one day. A woman who's the centre of your world, the love of your life.'

Damen's smile solidified. As if he believed in that any more! For others, if they were extraordinarily lucky, but not himself. He'd lost his naivety a decade ago.

Ruthlessly he yanked his thoughts from the events that had changed him, and his family, for ever. Today was a joyous day, not one for dwelling on mistakes and tragedy.

Damen retrieved two glasses of champagne from a passing waiter and passed one to his best friend. 'Here's to you and your lovely Emma. And,' he added when they'd both sipped their wine, 'here's to me finding my own perfect woman.'

One who was attractive, intelligent, amenable and, above all, expendable.

'You look stunning, Emma.' Steph finished pinning the antique lace veil in place and stepped back. She'd never seen her best friend so happy. She positively glowed.

Emma grinned. 'You've seen the outfit before.'

It was the one she'd worn the first time she married

Christo, before she deserted him on learning he didn't love her. So much had happened since, but miraculously, in that time Emma and her Greek billionaire husband had sorted out their differences. They were so much in love it almost hurt to look at such joy.

'Hey, Steph, what is it? Are you sure you're okay?'

Instantly guilt crowded in. Emma was too sharp. She'd taken one look at Steph when she stepped off the plane at Corfu Airport and asked what was wrong. Persuading Emma that she was fine, just tired after the trip from Melbourne, had taken all Steph's skill.

Steph refused to mar Emma's big day with her woes. She'd find a solution to the fix she was in, though every avenue she'd pursued so far had proved a dead end. She'd just have to try harder.

Because this trouble didn't affect her alone. She suppressed a shiver.

'Of course I'm okay! Can't I just be a little emotional, seeing you so radiant? You look like a fairy princess.'

For a second she read doubt in Emma's expression before it was ousted by another smile. 'I *feel* like one! Pinch me so I know this is real.'

Steph didn't pinch her, but she did hug her, hard. 'I'm so happy for you, Em. You deserve this after all you've been through.'

'If it's a matter of deserving…' Emma stepped back, shaking her head and clearly intending to say more, but Steph stopped her.

'Come on, Em, it's time to get this show on the road.'

Emma gasped when she saw the time and turned to the door in a flurry of long skirts. Steph twitched the veil into place and followed her out into the warm Greek sunshine.

It was a glorious day in a perfect setting. The garden of the gracious old villa made a wonderful wedding venue, with the stunning blue-green sea as a backdrop. But what made the event so special was the sight of her dear friend committing herself to the man she loved.

Yet now, as Steph mingled with the well-wishers after the ceremony, she couldn't concentrate fully on this wonderful occasion. Not because of her own worries. They'd still be there later, crowding close again soon enough.

No, the buzz of discomfort came from *him*. The man who, every time she turned, was watching her. Even as he chatted with, it seemed, every female under forty at the reception.

Steph could trace his progress through the crowd, since he left behind a trail of starry-eyed women.

But not her.

Because the dark-haired man standing head and superb shoulders above the throng was Damen Nicolaides.

Snake.

Lowlife.

The man who'd conned her into making a fool of herself.

She felt sick when she thought of it.

She couldn't believe how simple it had been for him. Steph might be impulsive but when it came to men she'd learned almost from the cradle not to trust easily.

So why had she forgotten her hard-won lessons the moment Damen Nicolaides crooked his finger? She who'd never allowed herself to be swayed before by masculine charm and a sexy body.

Because she'd made the mistake of believing Damen was different. That he was loyal and caring. Which it appeared he was, for those he genuinely valued. Anyone outside that charmed circle had to be wary. For he was also devious, calculating and utterly ruthless.

The memory of that evening in Melbourne still haunted her when she let her defences down or when she was tired. Which was often, these days, as worry kept her awake most nights.

And why, oh, why had she allowed herself to be wrong-

footed by yet another plausible, smooth-talking male, even after her experience with demon Damen?

In her weaker moments Steph toyed with the idea that in succumbing to Damen's charm she'd somehow destroyed her defences and her judgement. Obviously it was now fatally flawed when it came to the opposite sex.

From now on she'd have nothing to do with them. It was safer that way.

At least with Damen it was only her feminine pride that had been bruised. Which led inevitably to thoughts of the catastrophe facing her back in Australia.

Anguish churned her insides. Suddenly she wasn't in the mood for celebrating.

Steph spied a path leading away from the villa. Picking up her long skirts, she followed it, only stopping when the sounds of celebration grew muted. She was at the top of a low cliff looking over a horseshoe beach of perfect white sand. The breeze brought the mingled scent of cypresses and the sea, and Steph drew a steadying breath.

She'd head back soon. Just take a few moments to recharge her batteries and overcome her maudlin thoughts. This was Emma's special day and Steph intended to be there for her.

'You're not enjoying the party?'

The voice slid through her like melted chocolate, smooth, rich and compelling. To her horror Steph felt something deep inside ease and loosen.

As if she'd been waiting for this.

She'd avoided speaking to Damen Nicolaides. Yet she'd know his voice anywhere. Not merely because she'd earlier heard the deep tone of his murmured conversation with Christo, but because she still heard him in her dreams.

Steph clenched her jaw and stood straighter. So he had a great voice, deep and luscious. She knew better than to be taken in by that.

'I wanted a breather. Some time alone.'

If she stared at the picture-postcard view long enough surely he'd get the message and leave.

Instead she heard the crunch of measured footsteps on gravel.

'Direct as ever, Stephanie.'

Steph bit her lip, hating the way that softening sensation spread, as if the man only had to speak and her female hormones got all fluttery and eager.

Just because no one else called her by her full name. Or made it sound like an invitation to sin.

Heat flared in her veins and shot to her cheeks.

'Then perhaps you'll take the hint and go back to the party.'

His only answer was a huff of amusement that rippled across her tight shoulders and nape. Instead of retreating, he stopped behind and to the side of her. She couldn't see him in her peripheral vision but sensed him. It was an awareness she couldn't explain and didn't want to.

'Here, I brought you a peace offering.'

A hand appeared before her, broad, olive-skinned, perfectly manicured. It held champagne in a crystal glass.

Steph was about to refuse when he continued. 'I thought we could toast the happy couple.'

It was the one thing that could persuade her to accept the drink. Did he know that?

Of course he did. He was smart, this man. Cunning. Steph recalled how easily he'd made her dance to his tune.

And you're only giving him more power now by letting him see that still bothers you.

Steph reached for the glass, careful not to touch those long fingers. She drew a deep breath, reluctantly inhaling that faint scent she remembered from before, a woodsy, warm, appealing aroma. Recognition skittered through her, a spurious sense of rightness. She ignored it and turned.

'To the bride and groom.' She lifted her glass and swallowed. Then took another long sip to ease the sudden dryness in her throat.

Up close he didn't look like a snake. He looked as handsome as ever. Honed cheekbones and a squared jaw that gave him an aura of determination. Long, straight nose, a sensual mouth and eyes of forest green that seemed to glint in the afternoon light. Dark hair that she knew to be soft to the touch.

Her fingers twitched and the glass jerked in her hold. Quickly she dipped her head and took another tiny sip.

'To Emma and Christo,' he murmured. 'May they be happy together for the rest of their lives.'

He drank and Steph found herself watching his throat work. As if there was something innately fascinating about the movement. When she lifted her gaze it meshed with his and awareness jolted through her.

No, no, no. Not awareness. This wasn't like last time. Dislike. Scorn. Disdain. Any of those would do.

'Thank you for the drink,' she said politely, as if to a complete stranger. There, that was better. Treat him like a stranger. 'Now, I'd better head back. Emma—'

'Is surrounded by excited friends and family. She can do without you a little longer.'

Steph's eyebrows rose. 'Nevertheless, it's time I returned.'

'I'd hoped we could talk.'

'Talk?' What could they possibly have to discuss? 'We have nothing to talk about.'

Was it her imagination or did that strong jaw clench? The gleam in those remarkable eyes dimmed and Steph had the impression, suddenly, that something serious lurked behind his air of assurance.

'About Melbourne—'

'There's nothing to discuss. It's in the past.'

'It doesn't feel like it. You look at me with hostility, Stephanie.'

Her fingers curled around the stem of the champagne glass as she fought the impulse to throw the rest of her drink over his too-handsome face.

Except she wouldn't make a scene at Emma's wedding.

Her eyes rounded in disbelief. 'You're surprised by that?'

'I apologised.'

'Oh, and that makes it all right, does it?' Steph waved her hand and vintage champagne arced through the air, splashing onto the ground.

'I did what was necessary to help my friend.'

'You *kidnapped* me!' Steph jammed her finger into the centre of his chest.

'Only a very little kidnap. Christo was desperate, wondering where his bride had disappeared to on their wedding day.'

'That's no excuse. She sent a message saying she was safe. Besides, you can't blame Emma for leaving when she discovered the real reason he'd married her.'

Slowly Damen shook his head. 'They've made their peace now. But that week Christo was mad with worry. I had to help him locate her. And you,' suddenly he leaned towards her, his free hand covering hers and capturing it against his chest, 'you knew where she was.'

'You *assumed* I did.' Steph kept her eyes on his face, rather than that broad chest where his heart thudded strongly beneath her palm.

'It was more than an assumption, Stephanie. It didn't take a genius to work out she'd had help disappearing so completely and quickly. I could see you were uncomfortable keeping quiet about Emma's whereabouts. I knew if I could just get you alone and persuade you...'

The heat in Steph's cheeks turned scorching hot, exploding in fiery darts that shot through her whole body. She ripped her hand from his grasp and stepped back.

'Is *that* what you call it? Persuasion?' Her breath came in sawing gasps that didn't fill her lungs.

Dull colour scored his sculpted cheekbones but Steph felt no satisfaction that she'd actually dented his ego or his conscience.

She was too busy remembering that it wasn't Damen but she who'd made the first move that night.

Exhausted from a long week at work, she'd had no excuse to refuse Damen when he arrived saying he had a lead on Emma's location. He'd asked her to go with him to persuade her back to her husband. Steph had known Emma was in Corfu, since she'd made Emma's travel arrangements. But she couldn't admit that. So she'd gone with Damen, only to doze off on the long drive out of the city.

When she'd woken the car had stopped and Damen was leaning towards her, his breath warm on her face. Half-awake and unthinking, she'd reacted instinctively and lifted her hand to his face. He'd stilled and Steph could have sworn the atmosphere turned electric with mutual need. Then his arms were around her and she was arching into him as he kissed her with a thoroughness that unravelled everything she thought she knew about desire, and every defence she'd ever erected.

Her hands had ploughed through that thick, soft hair with a desperation that betrayed an attraction she'd tried and failed to suppress. All week she'd seen Damen, handsome, caring Damen, support his friend and Emma's family, checking on them all, leaving no stone unturned in the quest to find Emma.

It was only when they'd finally left the car for the deserted beach house that Steph discovered the truth. She'd been walking on air, her blood singing in her veins. Until Damen admitted why he'd brought her to that isolated place.

He'd hold her there till she told him where Emma was, for days if necessary. Even then she hadn't believed him. Thought he actually had a romantic rendezvous in mind. Till eventually she'd reached for her phone and he'd told her he'd taken it from her bag in the car and locked it away.

He hadn't been leaning towards her to wake her, or to steal a kiss. He'd been reaching into her handbag, palming her phone so she couldn't call for assistance.

And when she'd reached for him?

Well, why look a gift horse in the mouth? He must have decided that softening her up with a little seduction would make it easier to get to the truth.

Steph shut her eyes, trying to blot out the memory of that night. Of how she'd betrayed her yearning for a man who didn't care for her. Who'd callously used her attraction to him for his own ends. No doubt he'd silently laughed at her gullibility.

'Stephanie?' A firm hand gripped her elbow. 'Are you okay?'

'*Don't.* Touch. Me.'

One staggering step back and she came up against a cypress tree. Instead of sinking against it she stood straight and stared up into green eyes dark with concern.

He was a good actor. Last year in Australia she'd believed he was as attracted as she.

The worst of it was that to him it had merely been a *little* kidnap, since Christo had phoned soon after Damen's revelation with news he'd discovered Emma's whereabouts. Her abductor had then apologised for his 'drastic action' and driven her home, politely seeing her to her door in a painful parody of a date. All the time she'd squirmed at how she'd revealed her feelings for him. Feelings he didn't return. Feelings he'd callously used.

Steph had felt about an inch tall.

Like all those times when her dad had failed to show up, despite his promises. Because something had cropped up that was more important than spending time with his girl.

'I wanted to apologise.'

Damen's deep voice held a husky edge that might have sounded like guilt. Except Steph would rather trust a crocodile that claimed to be vegetarian than she would this man.

'You've done that before.'

Wide shoulders lifted. 'It obviously didn't work.'

'Work?' Her gaze slewed back to his face and she took in his serious expression.

'You haven't forgiven me.'

For a long time his eyes held hers, then she looked beyond him to the bluer than blue sky and the scented cypress trees. 'You can't have everything.'

She was *not* going to absolve his outrageous behaviour.

'Yet you haven't told Emma what happened.'

Unwillingly she turned back to him. 'Emma had enough to deal with. And later...' She shrugged. 'There was no reason to tell her. Especially as you're her husband's best friend. Why put her in the impossible position of disliking you when she'll have no choice but to see you regularly?'

'Is that how you feel? You dislike me?' Again that echo of something Steph couldn't identify in his tone.

Regret?

Probably more like curiosity. Steph was fairly certain most people approved of Damen Nicolaides, given his looks, charm and stonking great fortune.

She breathed deep, steadying herself. It was time to end this. 'I was brought up to be polite, Mr Nicolaides. But clearly you're too thick-skinned to get the message.' Steph wondered if anyone, particularly a woman, had ever said no to him. Had they all fallen victim to his charm? 'The answer is yes, I dislike you.'

To her chagrin he didn't react. Not even a flicker in that sharp green stare. Clearly her words had no impact on his monumental ego.

Her chin hiked higher. 'I'll be happy if I never have to see or speak with you again.'

That was when she saw it. A stiffening of muscles, drawing the skin tight across the hard planes of his face. A flare of imperious nostrils. A twitch of the lips. And those eyes…despite their cool colour they burned for a second with shocking heat.

A moment later Steph was left wondering if she'd imagined his reaction. He looked as he always did, effortlessly urbane and totally at ease, as if his only worry was deciding whether to summon his jet for a jaunt to Acapulco or Monte Carlo.

His mouth stretched into a smile that made Steph's thudding heart skip. It was a crying shame that the man should be so formidably attractive when he was such a louse.

'That's unfortunate. I was hoping to get to know you better. Spend some time together.'

'Together?' Steph couldn't believe it. Did he really think she'd be sucked into falling for his macho charisma again? Couldn't he comprehend how thoroughly she detested him? 'You have to be joking. I wouldn't spend time with you if you offered me a million dollars.'

A heartbeat's silence, a tic of pulse at his temple, just time enough for Steph to wonder how far her strident words had carried. She was turning towards the path back to the wedding when his voice halted her.

'Then how about two million dollars?'

CHAPTER TWO

THE WORDS WERE out before Damen could think about them. But even as they sank in, he felt a surge of satisfaction.

Because finally Stephanie looked at him with something other than disdain?

Or because instinct told him the offer, despite being instinctive, was pure genius?

He'd wanted a woman who was single, attractive, clever and short-term. Stephanie met his requirements exactly. The fact she didn't like him only made her more perfect.

Except for that niggle deep in Damen's belly when she looked at him like he was something unsavoury.

Then he felt guilt. Regret.

And, he admitted, indignation.

He knew he deserved her anger, understood he'd hurt her. But how could he have stood by and watched his best friend go crazy with worry, knowing Stephanie Logan held the answers he needed?

He'd tried everything he could think of to get the truth out of her but she'd withstood all his appeals for help. When those failed he'd acted decisively to end the farce that she didn't know where Emma was. His motives had been laudable. He'd done it for the best, to give Christo a chance to find his bride and sort out their problems.

Yet it was true Damen had been too taken up with getting answers to consider his actions from Stephanie's perspective. Until she'd looked at him with those huge brown eyes full of hurt. Even her subsequent lashing temper hadn't erased the memory of her embarrassment and pain. That night Damen felt emotions he hadn't felt in a decade or more. Since he'd faced his father that fateful night.

Damen had intended to see her again, to make things

right between them, except there'd been a business crisis that needed his personal attention and he'd had to leave.

Or maybe it was easier to walk away and not face what she made you feel.

'If that's your idea of a joke I don't appreciate it.'

Stephanie swung away, her loose, dark curls bouncing. She'd had short hair in Melbourne. Short and severe, yet somehow the boyish style had emphasised the feminine allure of features that should be merely ordinary.

Watching those glossy curls swirl around her head, Damen recognised she was anything but ordinary. How could she be when she was so vibrant? The air around her crackled with energy and an inner force lit her features whether she was sad, happy or furious.

And when she kissed—

'It's no joke.'

That stopped her. She slammed to a stop and turned to face him. Her chin hiked up as if she had a chance of meeting his gaze on the same level. Yet, though she was far shorter, somehow she managed to look down that petite nose at him. One eyebrow arched and her velvety gaze turned piercing.

That was better.

Her anger he could handle. It was the shadow of hurt he'd seen before that discomfited him.

As if he, Damen Nicolaides, could be swayed by a tiny brunette's emotions! He regularly played hardball at the negotiating table with competitors, contractors, unions and regulators.

The idea was laughable. And yet...

'Obviously you're not serious. You'd never pay two million dollars to—'

'Spend time with you?' He stepped towards her, but cautiously, not wanting her to dash off in a temper before she heard him out. 'In fact I do mean it.'

She shook her head, her forehead wrinkling. 'How much have you had to drink?'

Damen felt his mouth stretch in a grin. 'Barely anything. I'm stone-cold sober.' Far from being insulted, he enjoyed her directness. Only his close family and Christo treated him like a real person these days. Most others were busy trying to get on his good side.

'It can't be a pick-up line because I know you have no interest in picking me up.'

Her voice was cool but the streaks of pink across her cheeks betrayed emotion. Instantly Damen was swept back to that night outside Melbourne. How delicious she'd been in his arms. How delectably flushed and aroused.

'So what's your game? Are you trying to make a fool of me again? Did you enjoy it so much you've developed a taste for it?'

She looked like she could spit fire, arms crossed, empty wine glass beating a tattoo against her bare arm. In her slinky green dress she looked like an angry sea sprite.

Damen felt a tug of desire. He had vivid recollections of how her initial, tentative caresses had grown demanding and surprisingly addictive.

He forced himself to concentrate.

'Come on, Stephanie. I'm not like that. You know why I did what I did.' Enough was enough. He'd inadvertently hurt her but she made him out to be some sort of sadistic manipulator. 'I've said I'm sorry. I'll do what I can to make amends for what I did.'

'Good.' She inclined her head regally. 'You can leave me alone. That will do nicely.'

With a flounce she spun away. The long dress flared out around her legs, drawing attention to her tiny waist. Damen's fingers twitched as he remembered the feel of her slim, restless body against his.

'Don't you want to hear about the two million dollars?' he said silkily, crossing his arms. One thing he knew. There were few people who'd spurn the chance to get their hands on that sort of money.

Naturally she paused. Money talked. Damen told himself he wasn't disappointed that she was like all the rest. He was pleased, because he needed her.

'I can't believe you're serious.'

'Oh, I'm serious.' He'd do whatever it took to bring peace to Clio and her family. Two million was nothing compared with their wellbeing.

'Okay, then.' Again that chin hitched high. Her eyes narrowed to suspicious slits. 'What do you want?'

'You.' He watched her stiffen and hurried on. 'Or, more precisely, your company in public.'

'In public?'

What had she thought? That he'd pay for her in his bed? His jaw tightened. He'd never paid for sex and he didn't intend to begin now. His voice was steely as he answered. 'Of course in public. This is a PR exercise, nothing else. I'm not proposing we become lovers.'

Inexplicably, though, his stomach clenched as her head jerked back and her cheeks turned pale.

As if he'd insulted her.

It reminded him of her bruised look that night in Australia after their kisses in the car. When she discovered he'd taken her there not for seduction but to demand the truth about Emma's location. He'd hurt her and clearly he wasn't forgiven.

The look in those liquid dark eyes when she'd woken to discover him leaning across her, slipping the phone from her bag, had been one of delight. Not surprise, but welcome. As if there was nothing more natural than the pair of them together.

For a few minutes Damen had forgotten why they were there and fallen under her sensual spell. It had been surprisingly potent and he'd been shocked at the depth of his response. The extent to which she distracted him from his purpose.

Ignoring a sharp pang that felt like guilt, Damen spoke. 'I need a woman to act as my companion, my girlfriend, for the next few months. And who'll keep the secret that it's a pretence. That's all.'

'That's all?' Her eyes rounded. 'What happened? You can't get a girlfriend? Have all the women in Greece finally seen past the smiles and the charm to the louse behind the mask?'

Now she tried his temper. A temper Damen was barely aware he had. For years everything in his world had gone the way he wanted it to. Except for the trying tendency of women to see him as a matrimonial prize.

Damen's chin lifted as he stood straighter. Stephanie's expression stilled, her eyes growing wary as she sensed his anger, yet she didn't retreat.

With enormous restraint Damen refused to take the bait. Stephanie's dislike of him meant she was perfect in this role. She'd never hanker for more from him than his money.

'We're not discussing my personal life, except to say that I don't have a lover at the moment. You wouldn't be stepping on anyone's toes.' She opened her mouth, no doubt to say something he didn't want to hear, so Damen kept talking. 'I need someone who can give the *appearance* of being my girlfriend.'

'Why?'

'Does it matter?'

'Of course it matters. No woman worth her salt would get involved in such a crazy scheme without knowing why. It sounds shonky. You're asking me to lie.'

'As I recall, it's not the first time you've done that.'

Her cheeks pinkened and despite his impatience Damen found himself intrigued as fire flashed in her eyes. He couldn't remember any other woman who telegraphed her

emotions that way, or who regularly managed to get a reaction from him.

'That was different! I was protecting my friend.'

'As I was protecting mine.'

Her breath exhaled in a slow stream as she clearly fought
for control.

'Okay, I'll bite, Mr Nicolaides. Tell me more.'

'Damen.' He stifled a sigh. He sensed he'd wait till Hades
froze before she willingly used his name. That should please
him, more proof that she had no scheme to become his girlfriend for real, yet he was chagrined. He wasn't used to
being summarily rejected by a woman. Especially a woman
who still…intrigued him.

He digested that. It could be a mistake, asking her to do
this when he wasn't totally immune to the appeal of those
big brown eyes or that trim figure.

Plus it would be problematic getting involved with Emma's best friend. He could do without the repercussions.

But if this scheme was to work he had to act now. Cassie's
wedding was soon and this masquerade had to seem plausible. The earlier reports filtered to the press and to Manos
that Damen had a live-in lover, the better. Anyone who
knew him would understand how momentous that was, for
in Damen's world the words 'live-in' and 'lover' never existed together.

'I want it to appear for the next month or two that I'm
committed to a woman.'

She shook her head, curls swirling around her face. 'But
why? As a decoy while you have an affair with a married
woman? Am I supposed to keep her husband off the scent?'
Her mouth pursed.

'No!' Where did she get these ideas? Did she think he
had no honour? 'I'd never touch another man's woman!'

Stephanie's expression didn't change. It was a new thing
to have his word doubted. Damen didn't like it.

He raked a hand through his hair, frustration rising.

'Someone has the idea, the completely wrong idea, that I'm planning to marry…a particular woman. I need a pretend lover to convince them they're wrong.'

'You led some poor female to believe you were serious about a relationship and now—'

'No!' Damen blinked as he realised his voice had risen to a roar.

He *never* shouted. Nor did he explain himself. His pride smarted and his chest felt tight with anger and frustration. Suddenly Stephanie Logan's suitability for this masquerade lessened. She had a knack for provoking him that no one else had.

'I haven't misled any woman. The woman in question has no interest in marrying me. It's her family that wants the marriage, primarily because of my fortune.'

'Now, that I can understand.'

Her tone implied no one would want Damen for himself, only for his money. That rankled. Especially as it cut too close to the truth.

The murky past raised its ugly head but he'd had years to practise avoiding painful memories. Ruthlessly he shoved thoughts of the past away.

And found his lips twitching.

A month with Stephanie Logan would whittle his ego down, that was for sure.

If he could get her to agree.

Had he ever met a woman so ready to think the worst of him?

'Listen, the woman and I are friends only. However, her father has other ideas and he's bullying her.'

'To marry you?'

Damen nodded. 'He's a determined man and he's making her life unbearable. He won't let it rest unless I show him my interests lie elsewhere.'

Did Stephanie's flush deepen or did he imagine it?

'So you *do* want camouflage.'

'Listen, Stephanie. No one will be hurt by this masquerade. On the contrary it will make life a whole lot easier for my friend and her family.'

For long moments Stephanie stared back at him. This time Damen found it impossible to read her thoughts. Was she leaning towards agreement? Wondering if she should ask for more money?

'No one would believe we were together.'

He frowned. 'Because we mix in different social circles?'

'You're saying you're out of my league?' She snapped out the words and he knew he'd offended her. 'Actually, my friends wouldn't believe it because I have better taste in men.'

Her bright eyes and angled chin signalled pure challenge. Strangely Damen found himself suppressing a smile. She was so determined to rile him. It made him wonder what it would be like if she put all that energy into something else. His thoughts strayed into scenarios that would make her blush if she knew.

'Why me?' she asked at last.

Damen shrugged. 'You're single. You've got some time free—Emma mentioned you were on holiday. And I know you wouldn't misinterpret this as a chance to establish yourself in my life permanently. The fact you dislike me is a point in your favour.'

Her eyes narrowed. 'Because any other woman would try to worm her way into your affections?'

He spread his hands wide. 'It's a possibility.'

She muttered something under her breath. The only word he heard was 'ego'.

Damen stiffened.

Did he truly want to tie himself for a couple of months to a woman who despised him? Would she even be able to play the part of besotted lover?

The answer was yes and yes.

Stephanie Logan was the ideal candidate for this masquerade. She was an outsider, unknown to friends or family in Greece. And he could trust her motives to be strictly short-term.

As for acting besotted...they said love was the opposite side of hate. Damen just had to harness all that emotional energy in a constructive direction. The way the atmosphere sparked and sizzled when they were together would convince even a sceptic that they were connected.

'And you don't want to settle down because you're busy being a carefree bachelor?' Her voice dripped disapproval.

'Something like that.'

Damen had no intention of explaining his plan to avoid marriage. He'd never have kids. Eventually he'd pass the family enterprise to his sisters' children. Damen had enough family without creating more. Especially as he'd always wonder if his wife had married him for himself or his money.

'I still don't understand why you asked me and not someone else, but the answer's no. I don't like deception and you're the last man I want to spend time with.'

Damen stared at Stephanie's flushed face, her clenched jaw and those high breasts rising and falling with each rapid breath.

He wanted to seal this deal here and now but he read the warning signs. Stephanie was a passionate woman in a temper, ready to lash out, even if it meant passing up an opportunity she'd later regret.

She needed time to consider the advantages of his proposition.

He had a little time. She was staying at the villa while Emma and Christo went on their honeymoon. And his yacht was moored offshore.

'Don't decide now, Stephanie. I'll come back for your final answer later.' Then, scooping the empty glass dangling from her hand, he strolled back to the party.

* * *

Take your time!

Because the man couldn't accept a simple no! He was so arrogant, so stupendously sure of himself, he made Steph's blood boil.

Thinking about Damen made her pulse skitter and her breath came in hard, short bursts. She remembered him saying she was perfect for his plan because she wouldn't try to worm her way into his affections.

As if!

There was only one worm here and it wasn't her.

But, she remembered as she leaned back on the padded sunlounger by the pool, he wasn't here, was he?

Typical of him to throw out such an outrageous proposition then not follow through. Obviously he was toying with her. She'd known he couldn't be serious. Even a shipping tycoon didn't squander two million dollars on such a farcical scheme.

He made her so *angry.* Angry enough to tell him to his face she had better taste in men than to stoop to him. There was a laugh. Her taste in men was abysmal. Nor had there really been men in her life, not the way he'd think.

Steph hadn't seen Damen Nicolaides since last night when they and the other wedding guests waved farewell to the newlyweds.

From things Emma had let drop Steph suspected they were on their way to Iceland to see the Northern Lights. It was a place Steph longed to visit but now, like all those other places on her travel list, it was out of her reach. She'd make the most of these days on Corfu. It was likely to be her last holiday.

Steph picked up her pen and focused on her list of potential employers, but her heart wasn't in it. She'd already contacted the best agencies and there was no work.

Even when she got a new job, her troubles wouldn't be over. There was the matter of all the money she had to recoup. The wheels of justice turned slowly. By the time the authorities caught Jared, if they ever did, her money would have disappeared. And Gran's too.

Steph's belly clenched as she thought of Gran, so eager to support her only granddaughter's first business venture that she'd put her life savings into it.

If Steph had known, she wouldn't have let her take the risk. She'd never have introduced her to Jared.

Steph shook her head. If-onlys were pointless. Jared, her one-time boss and almost business partner, had skipped the country, leaving Steph with nothing but a debt she couldn't service. And Gran with no way of funding the move to the retirement village she'd planned.

Steph ground her teeth and flung the notebook down.

A steady wage wouldn't rectify her financial problems. It was lucky she'd paid for her return flight to Australia months ago. She had barely enough for a week's rent in a hostel when she got back.

There was one obvious way out of her troubles.

Tell Emma. Her friend and her husband were wealthy. Emma wouldn't hesitate to help.

But the thought sickened Steph. She couldn't leech off Emma. This was *her* mistake. *She* had to fix it. She'd trusted Jared, believed him when he said he was moving the money to put a deposit on their new premises.

Besides, money issues could destroy friendships. Emma and Steph had been best mates since they started high school, when Steph had championed quiet Emma and in return been gifted with the truest friend she'd ever made. She'd never jeopardise that.

Nausea rose as she remembered earlier days when she'd still lived with her mother. Suddenly the kids next door weren't allowed to visit. They'd shunned her. Ugly words had been hurled and a shame she'd been too young to understand weighed her down. Because Steph's mother, battling to support them both on her cleaner's wage, had borrowed from her friend next door. Borrowed money she couldn't repay. The friendship died and they'd had to move again to a smaller flat.

Steph's mother had worked hard but she'd never been able to hold on to money. They'd lived from hand to mouth until Steph had finally been packed off to live with Gran.

Steph grimaced. She'd been determined not to be like her mother. From the day she got her first paper round then worked several part-time jobs, she'd scrimped to save and contribute to Gran's housekeeping.

So proud of herself, she'd been. Confident about this exciting venture with Jared, a bespoke travel company, catering to those who wanted an individualised holiday experience.

It had all turned to dust.

Steph swung off the lounger and shot to her feet. She needed a plan. A way to salvage Gran's savings at least.

A way to get money quickly, not in twenty years.

Two million dollars.

The tantalising echo of that deep voice rippled through her. Damen made his crazy proposition sound almost reasonable.

With two million dollars she could buy Gran a home in the retirement village she had her eye on, with the lake view. There'd be money to start again. To avoid the trap her mother had fallen into, working low-paid jobs to get by.

Steph had loved her mother but vowed to learn from her mistakes. She'd be financially independent and never be taken in by a guy who'd let her down. Like Steph's feckless father, who'd never provided emotional or financial support and then disappeared for ever.

A bitter laugh clogged Steph's throat. Look at her now!

She'd fallen for the double whammy. Jared hadn't romanced her, but she'd believed his plausible talk about a new venture, put her money into it, and lost everything.

It was enough to make a woman crazy. She strode towards the beach path. She needed to work off this agitation then find a solution.

She turned the corner at the end of the villa and walked into a wall that shouldn't be there.

A wall a few inches over six feet tall, cushioned with muscle and smelling of the outdoors and hot male flesh.

Steph's middle turned inside out and a fluttering rose in her chest.

'Stephanie. I'd hoped to find you.'

His smile, a flash of perfect white teeth against olive-gold skin should have made her wonder how much Damen had spent on dental surgery. But she suspected it was all real. Just as every inch of that tall frame was the real deal, lean yet strongly muscled. Wearing cut-offs and a T-shirt that clung to that impressive chest, it was clear his masculine appearance owed nothing to his tailor.

Steph swallowed annoyance. Was anything about the man, apart from his morals, less than perfect?

Damen looked into those sparkling eyes and felt a punch to the solar plexus. Stronger even than yesterday, when the sight of Stephanie, alluring in her long gown, had dried his mouth. Only for a moment, because no woman had the power to unnerve him. He wouldn't allow it.

Yesterday it had been due to surprise. Stephanie had seemed so different with those dusky, clustering curls and formal dress. She'd been ultra-feminine and disturbingly sultry.

And today?

His hands closed on her bare arms as he took her in. The scarlet one-piece swimsuit should have looked demure, but on Stephanie's slender curves...

Damen yanked his gaze to her face. That was when he read something other than the scorn he'd seen yesterday.

Was that distress as well as anger?

He looked past her, searching for the person who'd upset

her, but there was no one. Beneath his hold she was taut, almost vibrating, like a wire strung too tight.

'What's wrong?'

'Nothing's wrong.' Predictably her chin rose and she drew a deep breath that tested Damen's determination not to ogle her trim body. 'Except you've intruded on my privacy.'

It felt like relief to have her snark at him, yet Damen wasn't convinced. There were shadows around her eyes, shadows he hadn't put there. She'd already been upset when she stormed towards him.

Bizarre to feel protective of a woman who despised him, yet…

He released his hold, surprised when, for a millisecond, she swayed towards him. Then she planted her feet as if to steady herself.

'I've come for an answer.' Damen folded his arms over his chest, surprised to discover his heart thudding fast.

'You were serious?'

He held her gaze. 'Absolutely. Two million dollars for a couple of months of your time.'

She swallowed and Damen repressed the impulse to lean closer, pushing his advantage.

'Think of all you could do with the money.' He was surprised she'd delayed. Any other woman would have leapt at the chance straight away.

Stephanie Logan had a contrary streak.

Surprising that didn't deter him.

Her eyelids flickered, veiling her eyes as she gnawed lips he knew to be soft and delicious. He was so focused on her mouth it took a moment to realise she'd turned that bright gaze on him again.

'Okay, you've got a deal. I'll be your fake girlfriend for two million dollars.'

CHAPTER THREE

TRIUMPH WAS A surge of adrenalin in Damen's arteries. A lifting of tension he hadn't been aware of till the weight across his shoulders eased.

Because the way was clear to scotch Manos's wedding expectations.

Because Damen hated the idea of people he cared for, like Clio and her mother, being hurt. Especially when it was his fault.

His thoughts strayed to that terrible time when he'd been the catalyst for the disaster that rocked his family. He yanked his mind from that and back on track.

Stephanie at his side, sexy, provoking, intriguing... Which of course was only important as it made her the perfect person to play his pretend lover.

Damen's thoughts slowed on the word 'lover'. Slowed and circled. Despite her animosity and her insults, she intrigued him as no woman had in years.

Another reason to remember this was purely business.

'But I have conditions.'

'Conditions?' He frowned. Was she going to try to negotiate for more money? She must guess he was desperate or he'd never have made the offer.

'Yes.' She folded her arms and her breasts burgeoned against the top of her swimsuit. Damen breathed deep and concentrated on her face. He refused to be distracted during negotiations. 'I want everything spelled out in a legal contract.'

He released his breath. 'Is that all?' Of course there'd be a contract, including a watertight non-disclosure clause so she couldn't sell her story or details of his life to the press.

'Not all.' She paused. 'I want half the money in advance when I sign.'

Damen saw colour rise up her chest and throat into her cheeks. She swallowed quickly and the pulse at the base of her neck beat a rapid tattoo. She expected an argument. Obviously it was important that she get the funds quickly.

Why? Was she in financial difficulty? Or couldn't she wait to get spending?

Damen was on the verge of asking but stopped himself. He didn't need to know her motivations, despite the urgent curiosity he refused to give in to. This was a deal. Her services for his money.

'Done.'

Her eyes widened and he fancied he read surprise there. And nerves. Why? Because she'd hoped he wouldn't agree? Was the offer of two million so alluring she'd been persuaded despite her better judgement?

Now he was being fanciful.

'One other thing.' Her gaze settled near his ear.

Now he was definitely intrigued. Despite the disparity between them, in wealth, power and physical size, Stephanie always met his gaze.

This condition she'd left till last was vitally important.

'No kissing.'

Finally her eyes locked on his and a sizzle pierced Damen's belly, driving down like a hammering pile driver. Then the connection was severed and she stared at his ear again.

'Sorry?'

'You heard me.' She dropped her arms to her sides then almost immediately refolded them. 'I'll play your girlfriend in public, but I won't kiss you, *and*,' she hurried on as if expecting him to interrupt, 'I won't have you kissing me. No lip locks. I want that spelled out in the contract.'

Damen lifted an eyebrow, intrigued. 'If we're lovers people will expect us to be intimate and show affection.'

Her flush intensified. Damen's curiosity deepened. Was she annoyed or embarrassed?

'Intimate in private. In public there are ways of showing affection without kissing.'

Damen shoved his hands into his pockets. 'I'm paying you an enormous sum. I expect you to be completely convincing.'

'And I will be. I just won't kiss you.'

'For religious reasons? Health reasons? I can assure you you're not going to catch some terrible illness.'

She unlocked tightly crossed arms and spread her hands. 'Because I don't care to, okay? Once was more than enough. I won't repeat that mistake.'

Damen was about to say it hadn't felt like a mistake. In fact their kiss had moved him in ways he wasn't used to.

That in itself was reason enough not to say it.

He frowned. 'Then how do you intend to persuade people we're lovers?'

She made a vague gesture. 'By hanging on your every word. Looking into your eyes. Snuggling up—'

'Snuggling? So we're allowed to touch?'

Stephanie's mouth thinned and Damen suspected she stifled the urge to swear.

'Don't be asinine. Sarcasm doesn't suit you.' She shook her head and those lush curls brushed her cheeks. 'There are ways of signalling attraction and intimacy without—'

'Putting my lips on yours.' He watched her blink and something inside him shifted.

Did this woman have any idea how provocative, how downright dangerous, it was to throw down an ultimatum like that? Especially to the man paying such a price for her company?

It was more than an ultimatum. It was a challenge.

Damen didn't back down from challenges. He won them.

'Prove you can be convincing as my lover or the deal is off.'

Damen saw dismay flicker in that bright gaze. Was she going to renege?

Disappointment stirred.

He'd imagined, after the way Stephanie Logan had once stood up for her friend Emma, defying both him and Christo to keep her secret, and the way she'd lambasted him after he'd abducted her, that nothing could daunt this woman. Now he read something in her expression that made him doubt. Maybe he'd misjudged—

She stepped towards him, so close he caught the scent of sun lotion and vanilla. That vanilla fragrance stirred memories of her in his arms, kissing him with a fervour that shredded his control.

Damen was still grappling with that when a small, firm hand closed around his bare forearm, curling loosely yet seeming to brand him. A shiver of something disturbingly like delight reverberated through him.

Stephanie leaned in, her eyes a golden brown that for a change looked soft and melting rather than distrustful.

He liked that look. Very much.

Just as he liked the way her lips parted as if being close to him affected her breathing.

Damen realised his own lungs were working harder. In anticipation, he told himself. If she couldn't convince as his girlfriend he'd have to find someone else.

He didn't want anyone else.

The unsettling notion stirred then was squashed as Stephanie moved nearer.

Sweetly rounded breasts jiggled a hair's breadth from his arm as she rose on tiptoe. She was so close he felt her warm breath on his face. It should have been a mere waft of air. It felt like a deliberate, sensuous stroke of her fingers. Her lips formed a pout that turned her mouth into an invitation to kiss.

Damen didn't bend his head. He stood, waiting.

He didn't have to wait long. She planted her other hand

on his chest, over the spot where his heart accelerated to a quicker beat. Her fingers splayed, slid across the contours of muscle, then stopped.

She blinked and he had the impression she was as surprised by that caress as he was.

Damen expected her to pull away but she leaned still nearer. Delight surged as those brown eyes locked on his in clear invitation.

'Damen,' she murmured in a throaty voice that belonged in the bedroom. Her fingers walked up his chest. Soft fingertips flirted against his collarbone and his flesh tightened.

Something jolted through him. Delight? Anticipation? Both?

He reminded himself this was a game, a test. It wasn't real. But his body ignored logic. Heat trailed low in his groin.

Stephanie leaned still closer, her full breast warm and intoxicatingly inviting against his arm.

'You have no idea,' she whispered, so close that they breathed the same air, 'how very, very alluring I find...'

Damen inclined his head, drawn to those luminous eyes fringed with lush dark lashes. And more, by the conviction she'd finally put aside her dislike, giving in to the attraction that had connected them from the first.

Her fingers on his lips stopped him just as he heard '... your two million dollars.'

Abruptly she was gone.

Damen chilled. It felt like she'd cut him off at the knees.

He'd issued the challenge. He should have known Stephanie Logan would accept it and shouldn't have let himself get distracted. She wasn't the sort to back down.

Or, apparently, to give up the chance of a couple of million.

His lips twisted. He needed to remember that. No matter how sweet he'd once found her. How he'd respected her loyalty to her friend even as he'd cursed her obstinacy.

She was doing this for money and far more convincingly than he'd thought possible.

An undercurrent of doubt channelled through his belly. His hackles rose.

She'd only done what he'd demanded, prove she could play the convincing lover. Yet, looking into that pretty face flushed with satisfaction, he was irresistibly reminded of another woman who'd been all too convincing at feigning ardour and even love.

A woman who'd almost wrecked his life and who'd been the catalyst for his greatest regret.

'How'd I do?' Stephanie stuck her hands on her hips, looking up expectantly.

Did she expect applause?

Grudgingly Damen realised she probably deserved it. She didn't care for him but he'd insisted on a demonstration of fake affection. It was unreasonable to feel betrayed by how well she'd pretended.

'Well enough.'

She frowned but Damen wasn't going to heap praise on her ability to lie.

The muffled voice of his conscience said he was unreasonable. He'd be lying about this fake relationship too. At least Stephanie was upfront about her motives.

Yet it took an effort to shake off his dissatisfaction as he looked into her features, again wearing that familiar, guarded expression.

'So we have a deal?'

'I'll have the contract drawn up straight away. With the specifications you requested.'

Half the money in advance. And no kissing.

Maybe it was his unsettled mood. Maybe it was annoyance at how she'd dredged up negative memories. More probably it was the way she'd bruised his pride, being immune to him when just months ago she'd been eager for his touch.

Whatever the reason, Damen found himself adding a mental corollary to their deal. He'd stick to their bargain but he'd make Stephanie Logan regret her no-kissing rule. In fact, he'd make it his business to ensure she too felt this tingling dissatisfaction that their affair wasn't real.

He'd seduce her into wanting him again.

You're crazy. You hate deception. Yet you're going to lie for a man you don't even like.

Steph threaded her fingers together, willing the voice in her head to stop.

It's worse than that. You don't like him but you're still attracted, aren't you?

'Stephanie?'

'Sorry.' She turned her gaze back to the tall man whose presence filled the study of Emma's villa. Sunlight streamed through the windows, slanting across those high-cut cheekbones before pooling on the papers he'd brought.

'I said, I had the contract drawn up in English, so you don't need a translator.'

'Thank you.' Surprised at his thoughtfulness, she smiled, despite her nerves.

She should have guessed Damen would think of that. He was thorough. In Melbourne he'd been a pillar of strength for his friend, leaving no stone unturned to locate Christo's missing bride. Damen seemed to think of everything.

Suppressing a shiver, Steph crossed to the desk on reluctant feet. Now it came to the crunch she had doubts.

Except Damen would transfer cash to her account the moment she signed. Cash she'd use to buy a lovely, purpose-built home for her grandmother in the development she had her heart set on.

How could she refuse?

Yet her movements were slow as she took the chair he held out. The contract sat before her, a stylish fountain pen beside it.

She breathed deep but instead of settling her nerves, it had the opposite effect. For she inhaled an attractive woodsy scent that she identified as Damen's. Rich, warm and far too appealing.

Steph shut her eyes and suddenly she was back in the garden yesterday, when Damen had threatened to scrap this deal unless she could play the convincing lover.

She'd felt challenged, daunted and a little too excited at being up against all that magnificent manliness. Her heart had raced and she'd told herself it was because she refused to back down. The prize was too big.

Steph had felt a surge of recklessness and been buoyed up by it. It was a welcome change after so much recent self-blame and doubt. For a few moments she'd felt her old self, confident, decisive and practical. Able to handle anything. Sheer relief at that once familiar feeling of assurance had filled her.

Until she'd closed the gap between them to kissing distance. Then she'd felt like a mouse who'd unwittingly been lured between a cat's paws. The heat in Damen's eyes had slammed into her and she realised she played with fire.

She'd retreated from him and suddenly, it seemed, she'd been wrong. There was no fire in his eyes. No desire. Damen Nicolaides didn't want her. He'd never wanted her.

He'd made that embarrassingly clear in Melbourne.

She'd been relieved at the reminder. Truly relieved.

What she'd seen flash in those stunning eyes was pique. Anger that she could act the part so easily yet remain immune to him.

Well, not immune, but she'd do whatever it took to hide that from him!

'Have you finished reading?' His deep voice came from over her shoulder and her eyes popped open.

'I like to take my time with legal documents.'

Not that that had stopped Jared running off with her money. Cold settled in Steph's bones and she set her teeth.

This deal seemed the only way to recoup what she'd lost, not just the money but her control over her life.

Yet she couldn't ignore the feeling it was a mistake.

But she needed to take the risk to reverse the plight she'd put herself and her beloved Gran in. Playing safe wouldn't help now.

Even if it didn't feel safe, she wouldn't fall for Damen Nicolaides again. She was over him, or almost over him. A few weeks in his company would destroy any lingering weakness. He didn't want her, so what was the risk?

Steph concentrated on the contract, reading each sentence carefully, grateful it was set out in simple terms. Her eyes rounded at the penalties she'd incur if she sold her story, but as she had no intention of broadcasting her time with Damen, that was no problem. She had to decide what to tell Emma, but that could wait.

Her breath eased out. There it was, the payment. Half today and half in eight weeks.

And there was her other stipulation.

No kiss on the lips unless specifically verbally invited by Ms Logan.

What an ego this guy had! As if she'd *ever* invite him to kiss her.

Steph frowned. No kiss on the lips. Surely she'd stipulated no kissing at all? Then she recalled saying 'No lip locks'. She reached for the pen. Should she change it?

'Is there a problem?'

She looked up to see Damen, hands in his trouser pockets, wearing a bland expression she suspected hid boredom. There was nothing in his expression that hinted at attraction. All he cared about was convincing people he had a new lover. It was a business deal, nothing else.

Why quibble over terminology? Over a kiss on the lips as opposed to any kiss? Damen wasn't interested in her kisses.

With a determined smile Steph picked up the pen and signed the contract.

'Excellent.' Damen nodded and drew out his phone. 'I'll organise the transfer of funds.'

See? It was easy and straightforward.

Soon Gran would have the home she wanted and a comfortable nest egg too, and Steph would be free of debt.

So why did her neck tingle with a premonition that this wouldn't be safe or easy after all?

CHAPTER FOUR

DAMEN STEPPED ONTO the main deck of his yacht and paused. He'd searched for Stephanie through half the vessel till a crew member mentioned she was outside. Now he saw her, barefoot and compellingly attractive in cut-off white jeans and a red-and-white-striped top.

Usually his girlfriends wore designer labels and regularly checked their hair and make-up. Stephanie didn't bother with make-up and her clothes didn't come from exclusive boutiques. Yet too often he found himself watching her, unable to look away.

He couldn't put his finger on why she drew him. She was attractive rather than beautiful. Engaging. Appealing.

She leaned out, drinking in the view as they came into Athens, curls lifting in the breeze and every line of her body straining forward in excitement. A smile lit her face.

A smile she rarely turned on him.

A now familiar sensation stirred. It was a mix of appreciation, anticipation and annoyance. Though he'd given her time, choosing to sail rather than fly from Corfu to the capital, she was still guarded around him.

That wouldn't do if Manos was to believe they were lovers.

Besides, her cool distance rankled. He was used to fending off women, not exerting himself to draw them closer.

Maybe Stephanie Logan was good for him. Clio always said he had it easy with women.

Not this woman.

At least she wasn't trying to engage his interest, as so many other women had. Yet there had to be a happy medium.

There'd been a couple of memorable times when her defences had tumbled. Like when they'd stopped off the island of Kefalonia for some snorkelling and a sea turtle had swum by. Stephanie had been so delighted she'd grabbed Damen's arm, her face wreathed in smiles.

For the rest of that sojourn he'd basked in her warmth and enthusiasm, enjoying the camaraderie and, he admitted, her approval as he shared his knowledge about the species and efforts being made to protect them.

That was the way she needed to be with him if they were to seem like lovers. No more tiptoeing around each other.

Damen had given her time. He'd waited long enough.

He stepped into the sunshine and felt a fillip of anticipation as Stephanie swung towards him. As if she was as attuned to his presence as he was to hers.

Her eyes ate him up and answering arousal kick-started in his belly. Then, as usual, her expression smoothed out, turning bland. But Damen focused on that moment of unguarded awareness. Despite her disapproval there was still attraction.

That was what they needed to persuade Manos. Damen intended to tap into it, starting now.

'*Kopela mou!* There you are.' He strolled to her side and wrapped his arm around her, drawing her close.

Stephanie froze, her head swinging up. 'What are you doing?' Her whisper was fierce.

'Beginning our liaison, sweetheart. What else?' He settled his hand on her hip and bent closer, enjoying her little shiver of response. He'd been right. For all her disapproval, Stephanie felt this attraction too. His mouth curved in a lazy smile. 'We're in Athens, or almost, and any one of those vessels you're watching could have curious eyes turned this way.'

His gesture encompassed the traffic in and out of the busy port. 'The *Amphitrite* is well known and there's money in selling photos of an elusive billionaire and his new lover.'

'Photos?' Her eyes widened as she turned to stare at the

harbour. 'You mean the paparazzi keep you under surveillance?' Her voice sounded brittle with shock.

Had he just destroyed an innocent's illusions? But it was better she was prepared for the inevitable media speculation. An unknown Australian, appearing at his side out of nowhere, would provoke interest.

Was that why he'd been so determined it should be Stephanie at his side? To get maximum coverage for this masquerade?

It was convenient to think so but Damen knew his motives were more complex. More personal.

'There's nothing to be scared of. I'll protect you. They won't invade our privacy.' Or they'd suffer the consequences. 'Especially if we provide some photo opportunities.'

He turned, curling his index finger under her chin and lifting her face towards his.

To her credit she didn't shy away, but nor did she look lover-like. If there was a photographer out there with a telephoto lens they would see his companion wary rather than enthusiastic. He needed to remedy that, quickly.

Steph told herself there was nothing to be nervous about in broad daylight on the open sea. Except the idea of hidden cameras trained on them sent tension darting through her. Plus Damen's expression did little to reassure.

He barely touched her, yet the warmth of the skin-to-skin touch felt intimate. It was a lover's caress.

No other man had touched her like this.

There'd been no lovers. Her early experiences, with a stressed, distracted mother and an absent father who never kept his promises had made her wary of emotional intimacy. And from her teens on she'd put in long hours working while her peers partied. The closest she'd come to letting down her guard and giving in to passion had been with Damen Nicolaides.

How he'd gloat if he knew! It would feed his already enormous ego.

'What are you doing?' Was that reedy voice hers?

'Providing a photo opportunity.' His mouth kicked up at one side, driving a groove down his cheek that was ridiculously sexy. Or maybe it was his intense stare that was sexy, as if he was aware of nothing but her.

Steph breathed out slowly, finding calm. The notion of Damen unaware of anything but her was laughable. This was an act for the benefit of the public. The realisation eased her racing pulse.

'You really think there are paparazzi out there?'

He shrugged. 'Probably. It pays to be careful. From now on it's best we act in character.'

In character.

As lovers, he means.

Steph gulped and told herself she could do this. She had to. She'd accepted a great wad of his money and it was currently being used to purchase Gran's new home.

Yet now it came to the crunch, with his body a mere hand span away and his breath feathering her face, the warning voice Steph had ignored for days became strident.

'What is it, Stephanie?' Damen actually sounded concerned, which made her wonder what he read in her face.

She tried to smooth her expression. 'This is tougher than I expected.'

Because in his embrace she felt things she'd vowed she wouldn't. Even knowing this was a charade, it was hard not to respond to the evocative tenderness of his touch and the hint of blatant possessiveness.

That scared her. Steph didn't want to be possessed by any man. She was her own woman. She'd learned never to be reliant and had no intention of forgetting that lesson, especially after the way Damen had made a fool of her.

'You've got cold feet?' His fingers tightened on her waist

and a crease was carved between those ebony eyebrows. 'It's too late. You signed a contract.'

His voice was terse, at odds with the lingering hint of a smile.

The disparity chilled her, sending a shiver scudding down her backbone. It was proof that appearances and embraces could lie. They had before with this man.

'Of course I've got cold feet. I'm not used to living a lie. But,' she said when he opened his mouth, 'I won't go back on my word.'

Especially since she no longer had the money he'd paid her.

'I knew I could count on you.' His voice dropped a notch, burring like rough suede across her bare neck and arms.

That, too, was a lie. That hint of desire in his voice. Yet some fatally feminine part of her responded, secretly thrilled.

Steph swallowed.

She was in trouble. Deep trouble.

But there was no escape.

His face tilted and his hand glided along to her jaw, her cheek, brushing her unruly hair back. She'd been too busy before she came to Greece and a hairdresser had been an unnecessary expense. She wished she'd had her hair cut short again, as strong fingers tunnelled through her curls, massaging her scalp in delicious circles that loosened her tense shoulders.

Her blood thickened and slowed and she found herself leaning into his touch.

Not to convince unseen eyes that they were lovers, but because Damen's touch was magic. Slow, sure and sensual, it mocked her determination to keep her distance.

He'd done this before, pretended attraction when there was none, yet even pride couldn't make her pull away.

If she did he'd realise his touch bothered her.

She was caught whatever she did.

Steph opened her mouth to say something, anything to divert him into conversation, when that arm at her waist tightened and his head lowered.

For a second shock held her still, then her hands went to his broad chest, flat against hot muscle and thin cotton as she tried to hold him at a distance.

She needn't have worried. He stopped a scant centimetre away, but his mouth was at her temple, lips scraping her skin as he spoke.

'Try not to look fazed. We're supposed to be lovers, remember?'

How could she forget?

With an effort that felt shockingly like no effort at all, Steph made her hands slide up his chest. Of their own volition they continued, curling around his neck. It felt hard and strong, the flesh there smooth and warm.

It was like the day he'd insisted she prove she could act the part of his lover. She'd made the first move, pleased with her boldness, until proximity to Damen made her body go soft and eager. As if it had been waiting to get close to him.

'Much better,' he purred against her forehead and to Steph's dismay she felt the words like an unfurling ribbon that trailed down through her body.

'You're not supposed to kiss me,' she protested, far too aware of the graze of his mouth.

The protest sounded limp, but she needed words to keep him at a distance when her body refused to obey her command not to melt against him.

'Hardly a kiss, *kopela mou*.' A pause and then he spoke again, his voice deeper than before. 'You'd know it if I kissed you.'

She would indeed. She had perfect recall of the last time. Of how she'd thrown caution to the wind as their mouths fused and desire had quaked through her.

It had been wonderful and cataclysmic at the same time, leaving the defences she'd spent a lifetime constructing in ruins.

'Not that I will, of course, given our contract.' He paused. 'Not without a specific, spoken invitation.'

Steph licked her lips. She was about to blurt out that she'd never give such an invitation, when instinct stopped the words. It would sound like a challenge and the last thing she needed was to provoke Damen Nicolaides into seeing this as a game of one-upmanship.

'How long do we have to stay like this?'

She hitched a breath, conscious of his torso so close she could almost feel it abrading her budding nipples. Heat drenched her. She told herself it was a hot day and Damen held her too close. But Steph wasn't that innocent. This heat came from deep inside. From the feminine core that gloried in being held by Damen. The part of her that had sprung to life once before in his arms.

That untamed, unthinking woman terrified her. She couldn't let her loose. She had to keep control.

'You make this sound like a chore, Stephanie.' Once more his voice drifted low on her name to a note that settled in her bones.

Steph drew a deep breath then stilled when it brought her breasts into contact with Damen. Did she imagine a change in the tempo of his breath tickling her forehead? A tightening in the clasp of that hand at her waist?

She didn't have time to be sure, for Damen stepped back, just enough to watch her with enigmatic eyes. For a moment she felt as if she were sinking out of her depth. Then his mouth crooked up in that slight smile she was coming to know and enjoy far too much.

'But practice makes perfect and in Athens we'll get plenty of practice.'

'We will?' Steph rubbed her palms together, trying to erase the tingling memory of his flesh against hers.

'Of course. I have business here but we'll go out too. Plenty of opportunities to be seen together.'

It was a timely reminder that this was for show. The closeness, his touch, the way his gaze lingered.

'Will she be in Athens? The woman you were involved with?'

That cleared her head like a shower of ice water. The thought of the woman who was the reason for this charade. No matter what Damen said, she was clearly important to him.

Steph reserved judgement on whether the mystery woman was really just Damen's friend or, more likely, his lover. Yet she felt something akin to dislike for the unknown woman.

Because Damen cared so much for her that he'd embark on this outrageous scheme?

It couldn't be that. Steph wasn't *jealous*.

'That needn't concern you.' His hand dropped and the remnants of that satisfied smile disintegrated.

So she was in Athens. Would Steph meet her? Would she even know her if she did?

She folded her arms and looked straight back at that narrowed green stare.

'This masquerade won't work if you're secretly meeting a lover on the side. Someone's bound to find out—'

Damen shook his head and said something sharp in Greek. Steph didn't need to understand the language to hear scorn and impatience.

'How many times do I have to tell you she's not my lover? I don't have a lover!' His voice rose as he made a dismissive gesture. 'The only girlfriend I have is you, Stephanie.'

This was the second time she'd provoked an unguarded response from Damen. Steph told herself she shouldn't be pleased at puncturing his formidable self-assurance. At seeing emotion flare in those heavy-lidded eyes. Yet she was.

The sight made her feel less helpless, less a mere pawn caught in his machinations.

'Careful, Damen.' She wagged her finger. 'If there are paparazzi out there, they'll see you scowling at me. That would destroy the illusion you care about me before we start.'

Even if he did look dramatically sexy with those dark eyebrows scrunched and that strong jaw honed tight.

For a second he didn't react. Then Damen surprised her with a crack of laughter, his face creasing into a smile of rueful amusement that tugged at something deep inside her.

'What they'll think is that we've had a spat. But that's okay because it gives us the chance to make up, very publicly.'

His eyes danced and anticipation swirled through her at the thought of making up with Damen.

Till she realised what she was doing and slammed a brake on her thoughts.

She'd assumed a few days on his yacht would cement her dislike but her feelings for Damen were ambiguous. He got to her in a way no other man did. Even the way he insisted on using her full name, lingering on the syllables as if savouring them, unravelled her defences.

Steph leaned on the railing, needing to look at something other than this man who disturbed her so easily. She saw a marina filled with luxury yachts. Some almost as enormous and beautiful as the *Amphitrite*. Maybe there was some billionaire's convention in town.

'Are we staying on the yacht?'

Not that 'yacht' seemed the right word for a ship with its own helipad, cinema, glass-bottomed pool and umpteen guest suites.

Steph had been in awe, until Damen's insistence that she was free to use anything she wanted, and the genuine friendliness of the staff, put her at ease. She'd earmarked a cosy corner of the library as her own and grown used

to the state-of-the-art gym equipment. Playing the doting
girlfriend would be easier if she could retreat to her comfortable stateroom.

'No, we'll head to my apartment.'

'Just an apartment?' She turned to look at him as he
joined her at the railing, trying to hide her nerves. Suddenly
this masquerade felt uncomfortably real. 'You surprise me.
I thought you'd have a posh town house.'

Actually, she hadn't thought about it. The opulence of his
superyacht had been a revelation. She'd known Damen was
rich, but this level of wealth was far beyond her experience.

'Sorry to disappoint.' The curve of his mouth told her
that her jab didn't bother him. 'But in Athens I find an
apartment convenient. I'm sure you'll find it comfortable.'

'I'm sure I will.' If his yacht was any indication it would
be gorgeous and purpose built. He probably owned the rest
of the building too.

'And it's convenient for shopping. I've had a list drawn
up of the boutiques that might be best for you.'

'That's kind.' If a little strange. 'But I doubt I'll be shopping.'

If she had time in Athens she intended to use it to see the
sights she'd read about. Besides, the money she'd got from
Damen had already been sent to Australia for Gran and to
put towards the business debt Jared had left her with. The
business loan still needed servicing even though there was
now no business.

Damen's eyebrows lifted. 'You'll need new clothes.'

Steph straightened, pushing her shoulders back. Her
hackles rose. 'Are you saying I don't measure up to your
exalted standards?'

Damen read the flash of heat in those wide brown eyes and
felt a frisson of awareness.

It was like that each time he and Stephanie argued. Or
touched.

Her pride and contrariness were a nuisance. Yet he relished each clash, revelled in the moments when Stephanie shared her feelings and thoughts instead of keeping her distance.

This was when he felt closest to the passionate woman who intrigued him despite his best intentions.

Logic said she could be trouble. But Damen had been careful and sensible for a long, long time. Would it be so wrong to give free rein to this attraction?

Damen shook his head. 'Charming as your casual clothes are, they won't do. You're my girlfriend now.'

Though if she really were he'd be happy for her to dress as she did.

His gaze dropped to the cropped red and white top that barely reached her waist. She looked feisty, fresh and sexy. He'd found it almost impossible to keep his hand firm on the waistband of her jeans and not let it slide under the loose-fitting top to her warm flesh. Not because he didn't want to but because he didn't want to spook her. She was already jittery.

As far as he personally was concerned, Stephanie didn't need couture clothes. She was alluring whatever she wore. But this was about image.

Predictably her hands jammed onto her hips and her chin tilted. 'Because your high-class friends wouldn't believe we're an item? Are you ashamed to be seen with me as I am?'

'I'm not ashamed, Stephanie.' It was something quite different he felt when he was with her.

Would she feel so confident surrounded by socialites wearing expensive fashions? This wasn't just about looking good for the press but protecting Stephanie from condescension. Not from his friends or family. They wouldn't care, but there'd be others who'd underrate her because of her simple clothing choices. Damen refused to put her in that position.

He sighed. Why must she make this tough? Pride he understood but surely she was eager to get spending.

'Do you have an outfit for a wedding?'

Her brow crinkled. He could almost see her reviewing the contents of the single suitcase she'd brought.

'Your bridesmaid's dress is very attractive—' that was a masterly understatement, given the effect the sight of her in it had on his libido '—but as my girlfriend you'd have something new for the wedding we're attending at the end of next week.'

'You didn't mention a wedding.'

'I'm mentioning it now. And there'll be social events in Athens. The women will wear designer originals, high heels, jewellery, that sort of thing.' He paused. 'Have you got something suitable in your luggage?'

'Of course not. I came for a relaxed holiday on Corfu.'

'Then you'll feel more comfortable with a new wardrobe.'

Her gaze drifted from his and colour rose in her cheeks. 'I can't afford designer clothes.'

Damen stared. He'd just deposited a million dollars in her account. Surely she could afford a couple of dresses?

The silence lengthened and his patience wore thin. Stephanie was playing this part for the money, he understood that, but was she intent on screwing every cent she could from him?

Memories stirred of another woman who'd milked him for cash. And he, young and besotted, hadn't seen her for what she was till it was almost too late.

Damen's jaw gritted, his nostrils flaring in disdain as the woman before him stood silent, her eyes not quite meeting his.

So much for believing her to be difficult but fundamentally honest. It seemed she too was grasping when it came to getting her hands on his money.

He bent in a mocking bow, hiding his disappointment

with a grim smile. 'Then allow me, *kopela mou*. I'll buy the clothes you need. But I reserve a buyer's right to choose.' His smile widened. 'It will be a pleasure, dressing you.'

CHAPTER FIVE

STEPHANIE MET THAT glittering stare and wolfish smile and felt about an inch tall. Damen made her feel like a commodity he'd bought for his pleasure.

He talked about dressing her but the rapacious gleam in his eyes spoke of undressing.

She swallowed the knot of discomfort blocking her throat. He was aiming to unsettle her because she'd annoyed him. Fortunately she was wise to the fact his supposed attraction was a sham.

That didn't make her feel better.

It didn't take a genius to see Damen thought she angled to get whatever she could from this deal. He thought her a gold-digger.

She opened her mouth to explain then stopped. She had no intention of explaining the tangle of her financial affairs to this incredibly successful businessman. If she said she no longer had the money he'd pepper her with questions. The fiasco of her failed business venture, stolen funds and, above all, her grandmother's precarious financial position because she'd trusted Steph—no, she wasn't ready to share all that.

Pride rescued her.

'Thanks, Damen. I'm quite capable of choosing an outfit for a wedding. Though you have the right of veto, since this is your scheme and you know the people.' Anxiety shimmered through her at the thought of parading in unfamiliar finery amongst a crowd of sophisticates, pretending to be someone she wasn't. Steph wasn't and never would be a glamazon. She knew what she looked good in but her knowledge of designer originals was zero. 'Other than that, I'll get by with what I've brought.'

It wouldn't be pleasant. She knew cheap and cheerful

would only go so far when surrounded by elegant and rich, but she'd get by. She'd never see these people again and if they were so hung up on her wardrobe they weren't people she wanted to know.

Damen's eyes narrowed as if her words puzzled him. 'You'll arouse suspicion if you don't dress like my lover.'

Steph raised her eyebrows. 'You expect me to wear a negligee in public?' She had no doubt his women wore silk and lace, enticing and scanty.

Instead of responding in anger, Damen smiled, a slow, heart-kicking smile that made her legs wobble.

How did he do that when she was annoyed with him?

'I prefer my women to be discreet in public. It's a different matter in private, of course.'

Steph searched for a crushing response but he spoke first.

'How about a compromise? Wear your clothes when you're alone but when you're out with me wear something new, which I'll buy. Yes?'

She wanted to say no. Agreeing would cement his belief that she grasped for every penny she could get. But reason prevailed. She'd look out of place if she stuck to her guns. That would only make her more uncomfortable.

Reluctantly she nodded. 'Okay. A couple of outfits.'

The shopping expedition didn't start well.

Steph's heart sank as the limousine stopped in a street that screamed wealth and exclusivity. Damen gestured to a boutique with a single dress in the window, a dress that even Steph with her limited knowledge knew was a couture original. She swallowed. It was so unlike the chain stores she frequented. Appallingly she felt nervous.

Worse, she felt like a complete fraud.

She *was* a fraud. She was embarking on a big, fat lie.

She just hoped no one would get hurt as a result. Despite Damen's assurances she wondered if his female friend truly had no hopes of a permanent relationship. How would she feel when she saw Steph with Damen?

Steph stepped onto the heat of the Athens pavement, telling herself not to be intimidated. Yet a lifetime of scrimping, determined to avoid the financial difficulties that had beset her mother, had its downside. Steph was used to searching for bargains, not dropping a wad of money on the latest fashions.

'Sorry, Stephanie. I have to take this call.' Damen looked at his phone. 'You start and I'll join you.'

Steph lifted her chin, intensely aware that her dusky pink cotton sundress and flat sandals were out of place here. Memories hovered, of early years when she'd been teased by schoolmates about her ill-fitting clothes, cast-offs her mother had found at a charity shop.

But only for a moment. It had been a long time since she let anyone make her feel uncomfortable because of what she could or couldn't afford.

Yet her heart sank as she entered the shop with its plush, pale carpet and hushed atmosphere. Even the air smelled different. Expensive. Two saleswomen turned, poised, elegant and wearing polite smiles that dimmed as they took her in.

Her *'Kalimera'* was greeted with a cool nod from the older woman and a stare from the younger. Stephanie made herself walk further into the store, towards a sparsely populated rack of clothes. She hadn't reached it when the older saleswoman stepped forward, planting herself before the clothes.

'Can I help you with something specific?' She spoke English, clearly pegging her as a foreigner.

Steph told herself she imagined the protective way the woman stood between her and the rack.

'Thanks. I want a dress, but I prefer to browse.'

After a moment the woman moved aside, hovering too close as Steph examined the clothes.

That was just the beginning. Every time she moved,

one of the women shadowed her. When she paused near a display of handbags, all ostentatiously embellished with a well-known couturier's logo, the younger saleswoman deliberately blocked her path.

Steph's eyes widened. She'd told herself she was oversensitive but she didn't imagine this. They thought her a potential shoplifter. Heat filled her cheeks and she was torn between outrage and embarrassment. Outrage won.

She opened her mouth to speak when a deep voice made her turn.

'Stephanie? Is everything okay?'

Damen stood in the doorway, wide shoulders silhouetted against the sunshine. But there was enough light from the overhead chandelier to see he wasn't happy. That chiselled jaw was tight and a scowl marred his handsome face.

'What's going on here?' His tone was peremptory, but his ire wasn't directed at her. Steph watched the saleswomen stiffen and their eyes widen as he surveyed them. It was a look that could freeze at fifty paces.

'Nothing's going on,' Steph said, her voice a little overloud. There was no way she'd buy clothing here. Her skin crawled at how they'd made her feel. 'I can't see anything I want to wear.'

Damen stalked across the room, his gaze now focused on her, and she felt a glow begin deep inside. Long fingers threaded through hers as he stood close and heat spread through her whole body.

'You're sure? If there's something you want…' He waved towards the handbags.

Instantly the younger saleswoman stepped aside, her smile wide but lacking the smug confidence she'd shown before. 'This is a very exclusive range.' Her words tripped over themselves with eagerness. 'We're the only stockists in the country and I'm sure madam—'

Steph interrupted. She couldn't stand that fake friendliness. 'No, thanks. They're not my style.'

Damen looked from her to the other women and then to the leather goods. 'You're right. They're too gaudy. You don't need to wear someone else's name on your accessories to look good, *agapi mou*. Leave them for someone who feels the need to buy attention.'

Steph swallowed a gasp that was part giggle as she saw the other woman's eyes bulge. But it was true. The bags might be the latest must-have fashion but they were little more than advertisements for the designer whose logo was emblazoned on them so prominently.

Damen whisked her outside, not lowering his voice as he promised to take her somewhere with a better selection.

'You don't need to hold me so tight,' she murmured as they marched down the street.

'Sorry.' His grip on her arm eased and he slowed. 'That pair—'

'Forget them. They're not worth worrying about. I was about to leave when you arrived. There really was nothing there I wanted.' She refused to be treated that way.

Nevertheless, she admitted to herself at least, seeing Damen angry on her behalf made her feel good. She didn't need him to rescue her. She could fend for herself. But his protectiveness, for that was what it had been, warmed her.

Especially since Steph had seen their horror at Damen's scathing words and dismissive look. It was clear they'd recognised him or at least his air of authority, a man who expected and got the best.

Which set that nervous feeling going again in her stomach. She still had the ordeal of another high-end boutique to face.

But contrary to expectations she fared better in the next shop. It was just as exclusive with its white-on-white minimalism, stylish décor and vast arrangements of lilies scenting the air. But Steph was welcomed by a woman with a sincere smile. Even better, as well as clothes in the pale shades that had featured in the last place, the hangers also held bright colours.

Steph gravitated towards them, her hand lifting towards a fall of shimmering turquoise silk.

'How about this?' Damen picked up a dress in chic shades of cream and camel.

Steph's 'No, thanks,' coincided with the saleswoman declaring it was the wrong colour palette for her.

Damen suppressed a smile of satisfaction as Stephanie's expression lightened when the boutique owner insisted she should wear bold colours. Soon the pair were nodding, murmuring about cut and colour as they pored over the floor stock.

Clearly she'd got over her apparent unwillingness to get a new wardrobe. He'd thought she would.

Yet Damen was curious about their disagreement on the yacht. He'd sensed her protest about new clothes wasn't just so she didn't look too eager. As if he really had dented her pride.

He settled in a chair and drew out his phone, skimming messages. But he read none, his attention all on Stephanie.

He'd seen her frozen look of dismay in the last boutique and something inside him had given way. He'd wanted to savage the woman who'd put that expression on her face. As much as he'd wanted to hold and comfort Stephanie.

Except her rigid expression reminded him of the way she'd been with him in Melbourne. After they'd kissed. Her look had made him feel like he'd betrayed her. Despite the bigger picture and his need to help his best friend find his missing wife.

Now he felt like he'd done it again. Hurt her.

Why? Because he'd paid her to play a role? He hadn't forced her hand. Or because he'd left her alone with those snobby witches down the street?

Stephanie could stand up for herself. She didn't need

him as a champion. Damen remembered Emma saying her friend was strong and independent, that Stephanie had stuck up for her when they'd been kids together.

Yet his conscience prickled. And something else. Something more than guilt.

Whether he was responsible or not, Damen didn't want to see her look like that again, pale with distress. Her barbs he could cope with. He almost enjoyed them. Her rare smiles ditto. But that frozen look of stunned hurt pierced something behind his ribs.

Fortunately movement from the rear of the boutique distracted him from his churning thoughts. The saleswoman stepped back from the changing room, looking satisfied. She was followed by...

Damen breathed deep and told himself to ignore the strange little jitter that made his pulse uneven.

It was simply Stephanie dressed up. Not in a pretty bridesmaid's gown. In an outfit designed with one aim. To seduce.

He'd seen his share of seductive women. Had bedded them too. Yet the sight of Stephanie in that clinging outfit sent a blow to the solar plexus that hampered his breathing.

It was a jumpsuit. Was that what you called it? That sounded too prim and old-fashioned for this. She wore silky material that wasn't red and wasn't dark pink but somewhere in between. The neckline lifted to a high collar, but her shoulders were completely bare and there was a narrow slit down between her breasts that gave teasing glimpses of her cleavage. A cleavage that seemed unfettered by a bra. The fabric clung to her waist and hips before falling in loose folds to her feet. Feet encased in high-heeled sandals. She looked fabulous. Sophisticated and effortlessly sexy.

Except he knew the high tilt of that chin. He'd learned that pugnacious angle could signal anger or doubt.

Damen got to his feet, his phone falling. 'You don't like it?'

She swung around, drawing a breath that made her breasts rise against the thin fabric. Heat stirred low in his body. He kept his eyes on hers and read what looked like concern.

She bit her lip and lifted those slender bare shoulders.

It was ridiculous. Except for her arms and shoulders she was covered to her toes. Yet the sight of that flesh, looking velvety soft against the contrasting material, seemed more enticing than if she'd worn a bikini.

'I'm not sure.' Her gaze turned to the full-length mirrors at the back of the room and Damen caught an expression that hovered between wistful and worried.

'It might have been made for you, madam,' the saleswoman said. 'That colour is perfect.'

Still Stephanie looked uncomfortable.

Damen cleared his throat. 'I like it.' Too much. Far, far too much. He looked at her in that slinky, flirty outfit and imagined what she'd look like without it. Without anything. 'You don't?'

In the mirror Stephanie's gaze snared his and his throat dried.

'It's not me, is it? I mean, it's beautiful.' She smoothed her hands down the fabric. 'But it's designed for someone more…'

Damen wasn't used to Stephanie tentative or uncertain. She was forthright to the point of driving him crazy.

'More what?' His voice hit a gravelly note as he took in her slightly lost look. 'It's a perfect fit.' Too perfect but he couldn't complain, for that would be admitting the sight of her in it tied his libido in knots. 'You look classy and sexy.'

'I do?' Her eyes widened.

The saleswoman, after a look at Damen, excused herself and headed back to the changing room.

Damen stared at the sultry figure in the mirror. Two hours ago he'd been annoyed with Stephanie and the way she seemed bent on screwing him for every cent she could. What had happened to his anger?

She hadn't asked for sympathy. If anything she'd downplayed that scene in the other shop. Yet her nervous expression made him pause, and not just because she looked good enough to eat.

Was it possible Stephanie doubted herself in that outfit? Surely that was impossible. He strode across to stand behind her. 'What's the problem? Isn't it comfortable?'

She shook her head. 'It feels gorgeous to wear.' Was that longing in her tone?

Damen stepped in, so close the scent of warm vanilla teased his nostrils. 'Then we'll take it.'

'It's not too…?' She made a vague gesture.

'Too?' He was tempted to agree that she looked too disturbingly sexy. He didn't want other men to see her dressed like this. But Damen wasn't stupid enough to reveal that.

Fascinated, he saw a hint of colour at the base of her throat. Her gaze slid to a point in the mirror near his shoulder. When she spoke the words were clipped. 'I've never worn haute couture. You probably need a certain air to carry it off, to be glamorous and…' Her words petered out with a shrug. 'I'm afraid I look like someone playing dress-up, someone who doesn't belong in such clothes.'

Something tugged at Damen's chest. His eyes narrowed. Was she serious? Stephanie always seemed so confident.

He saw that flush rise higher. He doubted even the best actress could blush at will.

'What you look like, Stephanie, is an attractive, desirable woman. The clothes look great on you but that's window dressing. You looked fabulous in cut-off jeans and bare feet.' He paused as she swung to face him. Her velvety eyes rounded.

For a long moment she didn't say anything. Then a smile curled the corners of her mouth and her shadowed expression morphed into one of pleasure. For Damen, standing so close, the impact of her smile was palpable.

'You made me think my appearance didn't meet your exacting standards, Mr Nicolaides.'

Damen shook his head, entranced by the way she smiled with her whole face. He wondered what it would be like to have her look at him that way regularly. Damen liked it. Too much.

'I never said that. I just want you dressed appropriately for the occasion.'

She tilted her head as if trying to read more than his words. Then she nodded once, her manner turning businesslike, that warm glow quenched as if it had never been. 'Okay. How many outfits do I need?'

Steph was incredibly glad Damen had insisted on new clothes, though she hated the idea of him buying them.

There was something suggestive about a man paying for what she wore. As if he'd bought her too. The idea had made her feel grubby at first, until she saw he was right—she was more comfortable mixing with these well-dressed people wearing what she thought of as her camouflage.

At least she didn't look like a charity case.

Steph washed her hands and told herself he paid her to play a part but he hadn't bought *her*. Even if it felt like it on occasions like this, at his friend's party in a spectacular house looking over Athens and the coast.

Damen was as good as his promise, never kissing her, but whenever they were together in public each look, each touch, even the slightly deeper tone he adopted when speaking to her, gave the impression they were lovers.

He was so adept at it sometimes she found it hard to remember it was an act.

The first night, at the cocktail party opening of a new museum wing, Steph had been fazed by his faux intimacy, struggling to play her part and respond in kind.

What worried her now, after more than a week, was how easily she'd grown accustomed to it.

Looking away from her accusing eyes in the mirror of the guest bathroom, Steph busied herself reviving her lipstick.

She should be able to take this charade in her stride now. Damen stuck to their agreement and she was gradually getting used to the bustle of Athens as she explored the sights each day, chauffeured by his driver.

Instead her uneasiness grew. Oh, she was having a ball exploring this amazing city. That was an experience she'd carry for the rest of her days. But the more time she spent with Damen the more he undercut her prejudice against him. Yesterday he'd even come home early to drive her to Cape Sounion to watch the sunset. She knew he'd done it so they could be seen together, yet Steph hugged to herself a secret delight that he'd been prompted by her saying she wanted to see the famous temple ruins.

They spent every evening together and he was not only attentive but also considerate, charming and with a vein of dry humour that appealed too much. Just the sort of man she could imagine being attracted to.

He was too good an actor, she told herself, remembering how he'd feigned interest in her before. When he'd tried to milk her for information.

She put the lipstick away and surveyed herself. She wore the boldly coloured outfit she'd tried on that first day. Its fragile silk clung to her breasts and hips and swished around her legs like a caress.

Crazy how for a couple of minutes in the boutique she'd been racked by self-doubt. As if she were still the scrawny kid in second-hand clothes who never fitted in. She'd thought she'd got over that self-consciousness, the fear of being judged and found wanting. Steph had buried that sense of being second-best with years of hard work and achievement. She believed in her ability to build the future she wanted, to be the woman she wanted to be.

Yet as she'd stood there, wearing this stunning outfit only the rich could afford, she'd felt out of her depth. Suddenly it wasn't just her ability to play this masquerade that she doubted, but herself. Jared's betrayal, her gullibility in being sucked in by a fraud, losing everything she'd worked for, had smashed her confidence. She'd got the wobbles.

Till Damen's words and the look in his eyes reassured her. She remembered the swelling warmth unfurling through her at his male appreciation. He'd told her she was desirable and she'd seen proof in his body language and gleaming eyes.

Steph didn't need a man's opinion to feel good about herself. Nor did she care for people who'd judge her on how she looked.

Yet she was honest enough to admit that when Damen looked at her with that flare of heat, when she *felt* as much as saw his smile as he took in her appearance, it did wonderful things for her bruised ego.

That had to be why she didn't mind those admiring looks from him. Not because she wanted Damen to want her. That would be disastrous. But because it was balm to her wounded soul.

Steph squared her shoulders and opened the door. Music reached her ears, and the hum of voices. She walked down the corridor and into the vast sitting room that could have swallowed her flat several times over.

Knots of people stood chatting and laughing, all elegant, all beautifully dressed. A few, glimpsed through open doors to the next room, danced. Jewels sparkled and the air was rich with expensive scents. But she couldn't see Damen's dark head above the rest.

Her host, a pleasantly ordinary man for a billionaire, caught her eye. 'You're looking for Damen? He's on the terrace.' He smiled. 'Unless you'd care to dance?'

'Thank you but no.' Steph softened her rejection with a smile.

The idea of dancing in these teetering heels terrified her. She loved the way they looked, making her legs seem so much longer, but dancing in them? She'd probably break her ankle and that would be the end of her attempts to be poised and glamorous.

She threaded through the crowd to the huge space where floor-to-ceiling windows were folded back, opening the room to the terrace and gardens.

There were fewer people here but Damen was easy to locate. Steph told herself it was because of his height but she had the disquieting feeling it was more. Even at a crowded event, on the rare occasions they got separated, she always knew precisely where he was. She had the feeling it worked both ways. More than once she'd seen him look up from a conversation, his gaze unerringly catching hers. Steph wasn't sure whether to be flattered or worried by that.

This time, though, he didn't notice her. He stood at the far edge of the paved terrace, away from other guests, and his attention was on someone beside him, his head inclined as they spoke.

Steph started forward then paused, taking in the scene. There was something about their body language, how close they stood. They didn't touch yet it was obvious even from a distance that they shared an intimacy.

Even in the gloom, with her face averted, it was clear Damen's companion was incredibly beautiful.

She was everything Steph wasn't. Tall and effortlessly poised, as if she was used to holding her own at sophisticated parties full of celebrities and the ultra-wealthy. Her hair was blonde and straight, worn in one of those apparently casual styles that combined an elegant knot with sexy wisps around her neck. She wore a strapless gown that revealed endless legs. She was stunning.

Gazing at her, Steph was aware of the unfamiliarity of her high heels. Of the unruly mass of curls clustered around her head. She'd planned to get a haircut in Athens, thinking even a gamine cut was preferable to her natural look, but Damen had forestalled her, saying she looked charming.

Sophisticated and gorgeous beat charming hands down.

Steph hated the little corkscrew of hurt as memories surfaced, of being ridiculed about her appearance, because poverty *looked* different. But that was then and this was now. Steph hadn't been that girl for a long, long time.

Besides, this wasn't a competition.

Damen was merely talking to the woman.

Yet their ease together, the way their heads angled as if they were sharing secrets, made Steph wonder if *this* was the woman he went to so much trouble for. The woman he insisted wasn't his lover.

Steph began walking, swallowing a bitter taste in her mouth.

Damen's head turned, eyes fixing on her.

She felt that stare like the scrape of a blade over her bare arms and shoulders, like a hand sliding, slow and deliberate, over the flimsy silk that covered her body. He made her feel supremely aware of her body in a way no other man had. It was scary and exciting at the same time.

And it infuriated her that, even now, when she'd interrupted him with another woman, Steph was ultra-aware of him. Not out of self-defence, but with that trembling feminine awareness he'd stirred in her from the first. The awareness that had allowed him to make a fool of her.

Steph was mortified at how he could unsettle her. Her skin flushed and her insides rippled with nerves. She was like a silly sixteen-year-old facing the object of her first crush.

When she stopped it wasn't Damen who broke the silence, but the woman who stepped forward with a welcoming smile.

'Steph, it's great to see you again!'

Steph inhaled a scent of cinnamon and roses, felt the

brush of soft skin and softer hair as the woman kissed her on the cheek.

Steph blinked. 'Clio?'

They'd met the previous week on Corfu. The Greek woman was a friend of Emma and Christo's and Steph had liked her.

Her heart dropped like a stone through water.

She'd told herself it didn't matter who the woman was that Damen cared about so much that he'd go to ridiculous lengths to protect her.

But it did matter.

Clio wasn't just gorgeous and sophisticated. From the little Steph had seen and heard, she knew Clio was kind-hearted, clever and nice. The sort of woman a man was drawn to not just for a fling but for life.

Even if Damen didn't want to marry yet, Clio was the sort of woman who'd fit into his world and make him happy.

She was perfect for him.

What Steph didn't understand was the pang of hurt that lanced from her chest to her stomach. A ripping pain that skewered her to the spot and caught her breath.

Almost as if she was envious.

CHAPTER SIX

STEPHANIE WAS QUIET on the drive home. Not relaxed, but humming with tension. Damen could read her more easily now, even when she tried to keep her feelings to herself. She was full of pent-up emotion. Had been ever since she'd seen Clio.

Silently he sighed. Things had been going so well before that.

Stephanie hadn't been brittle in his company any more. She relaxed with him, smiled, and it was easier for them to play the part of lovers. Except for the frustration that rode him as he looked at her pretty mouth, remembered its taste, and his promise not to kiss her.

Until she invited him.

That day couldn't come soon enough.

Looking at her tight features as they entered his penthouse, he saw it was clear today wasn't that day.

The front door hadn't even closed before Steph swung round, her breasts swaying, bright silk flaring around her legs.

'Is she the one? Clio?' Her words were bullet fast.

Damen shut the door and led the way into the sitting room.

'Would you like a drink?' He poured himself an ouzo, for once not bothering with water. He wanted the burn of aniseed fire, hoping it might sear away his annoyance at her probing and the feeling of being on the brink of doing something irreversible. Damen had spent the evening drinking sparkling water because it was increasingly difficult to hold Stephanie close, pretend they were lovers, and not plant his mouth on hers.

'What I'd like is an answer.'

She stood, arms akimbo, head and shoulders thrust back, breasts forward. In the lamplight the silk was like flame licking her body, turning her into a fierce, sexy Amazon.

Damen tipped back his head and swallowed the ouzo in one mouthful. Fire ripped from his mouth down his throat to his belly. But it didn't quench the need vibrating through him. He slammed the glass down and stepped away.

Why had he thought alcohol would help? Nothing would help, except Stephanie in his arms, in his bed.

'What was the question?'

Her eyebrows rose. 'Is Clio the lover you're protecting with this masquerade? Or are you deceiving her?'

'You don't need to know who it is. That's irrelevant. Two million dollars' worth of irrelevant.' Why must she pester him about this?

Dark curls danced as Stephanie shook her head, her mouth drawing into a straight line. 'I won't be party to a scheme that's going to hurt anyone. I *like* Clio.'

'I've told you, no one will be harmed.' Impatience rose. Hadn't he assured her of that, explained why this charade was necessary? 'Believe me.'

Again she shook her head, her expression implacable.

'I can't.' This time she spoke softly, not gently but as if her voice stretched thin. 'Don't you understand? How can I trust you? You're a liar.'

The accusation was a punch to Damen's gut. He stood straighter, words of outrage forming. No one accused a Nicolaides of dishonour.

'Don't give me that intimidating stare! You know it's true. You don't get to be a multi-billionaire by playing nice. Who knows what sort of shady deals you do to make money?'

Damen stared, taken aback. Where had that come from? Simply because he was successful? Did she have something against businessmen?

'You made me leave Melbourne with you because of a lie that you knew where Emma was—'

'Only to get the truth from you.'

'And the next time I see you you offer me money to lie to your friends and family, to all the world for that matter.' Stephanie drew another, audible breath. 'How can I believe you? I need to *know* what's going on. All week I've wondered about every woman we meet. Is this the one? Or that one? Is she hurting seeing us together? I don't want to be party to a scheme to dupe someone. I should never have agreed to it.'

The wrathful words died on Damen's tongue. There was true distress in Stephanie's face and restlessly plaiting hands.

Everything inside him stilled as suspicion stirred.

'Because someone duped you? Hurt you?'

Stephanie's chin shot higher. Her hands clenched and her hunching shoulders pushed back again so she stood tall.

Yet it was there in her eyes. Acknowledgement. Though he guessed she'd die if she thought he could see it.

Damen's next breath was uneven, as if his lungs refused to work. The thought of someone betraying Stephanie, creating that wounded look, made him want to commit an act of violence.

But with that came the sober realisation that she spoke the truth. She had a right to know more. Especially as they were about to head into the lion's den, visiting Clio's family.

Damen was appalled that Stephanie believed him to be dishonest. It went against everything he stood for.

This had to be sorted.

Plus he wanted to find out about the person who'd harmed her.

Damen drew a slow breath. 'Take a seat, Stephanie.'

Steph sank onto a sofa. Her emotions were jumbled. She didn't understand why seeing Clio with Damen had disrupted her fragile equilibrium. Yet the suspicion they'd been, or perhaps still were, together changed everything.

'*Is* it Clio?'

He took a seat opposite, his arms on his thighs as he leaned forward. For a long time he regarded her enigmatically. Then, reluctantly, it seemed, he nodded.

Steph's heart sank.

'Don't look at me like that,' Damen growled. 'It's not what you think.'

He ploughed his fingers through glossy hair that fell perfectly back into place. Of course it did. Everything in this man's world worked the way he wanted. Business, money... Even women he barely knew agreed to put aside their principles to lie for him.

'Clio isn't and never has been my lover. She's like a sister. In fact, since she's nearer to my age, in some ways she's closer to me than they are.'

'You have sisters?' Steph could have done an internet search on his family but she'd felt that the less she knew about him the better. So far ignorance hadn't provided any protection. She was involved, more involved than was safe.

'Two sisters, one studying in the States and one working overseas.' He paused. 'But my mother's in Greece. You'll meet her at the wedding.'

'Not your father?'

Damen's eyebrows arrowed down. 'He died. A long time ago.'

Maybe that accounted for Damen's innate air of authority, as if he was long used to people jumping to do his bidding.

'I'm sorry.' It was an automatic response, yet that frown told her his father's death still evoked emotions.

'Clio and I are related. Her father is my mother's cousin. Manos is a decent man. He was even something of a mentor when I took over from my father.' Steph noted a twitch of the eyebrows as if the memory of that time wasn't easy.

'Perhaps that gave him expectations where there should be none, because of the bond between our families. He's also extremely obstinate. Once he gets an idea he's likely to steamroller people into agreeing with him.'

Not unlike Damen. But Steph kept the observation to herself.

'Now he believes Clio and I should marry. He's a traditionalist and Clio is his eldest, yet it's her younger sister, Cassie, marrying this weekend and that doesn't sit well. He wants Clio to marry and settle down soon. Plus,' Damen spread his hands, 'he'd like to see the Nicolaides money benefit his family. He thinks I've reached an age where I'm looking for a bride.'

Something shifted in Steph's middle. It wasn't a pain but there was definite discomfort. It had to be due to tension. It had nothing to do with the idea of Damen searching for a wife. That was none of her business.

'That doesn't explain why he thinks you and Clio might marry.'

Damen rolled his shoulders as if they were tight. 'Clio and I have an informal arrangement.'

Steph's stomach lurched as she imagined that agreement. Her own experience was limited but she could imagine Damen enjoying a casual sexual relationship with the lovely Clio. She sat further back on the seat, away from the man watching her so intently.

'Not what you're thinking.'

'You have no idea what I'm thinking!'

He shook his head. 'When you're annoyed or offended you purse your mouth and your nose scrunches up. Despite what I've already told you, despite the fact Clio wasn't in the least jealous, seeing you with me tonight, you've decided we're having an affair. We're not.'

His laser-sharp stare dared her to disagree. Steph said nothing, too concerned about his ability to read her so easily.

'Clio is establishing her interior-design business, and

going out with me is a way to network with wealthy potential clients. Plus we like each other's company. I can relax and laugh with her.'

He couldn't relax with other women? It sounded odd, but perhaps wealthy men found it hard to make true friends. Maybe that was why Damen and Christo were close. Each knew the other wasn't angling to benefit financially from their friendship. It struck Steph that living with a fortune had downsides she'd never considered.

'Clio knows I'm just a pretend girlfriend?'

'I didn't tell her and she didn't ask. A party isn't the place for confidences, especially as the aim is to make the world believe you and I are an item. But, as she begged for help last week to get her father off her back, she probably guessed. You're my way of helping her.' He paused. 'I can give you her number if you want, though I suspect she'd prefer not to talk about her family troubles with someone she barely knows.'

Steph blinked, digesting that. It should sound ridiculous. Instead she found it…plausible.

'I see.' He didn't care if she contacted Clio and it was true Clio hadn't seemed disturbed to see them together. It must be a strong friendship for him to go to such lengths. 'But you have no qualms, lying to everyone else, including your mother?'

Damen folded his arms and surveyed her down that imperious nose like a judge examining a prisoner. Once more she felt she was pushing her luck, pursuing this. But she had to know. Despite how easy it was to feign intimacy with Damen, she hated being party to deception.

'I won't lie to my mother. Nor do I want her thinking I'll marry when I have no intention of ever taking a wife. I'll tell her what she needs to know.'

Steph was torn between wondering why Damen was anti-marriage and a prickling of hurt pride at the idea of his family viewing her as expendable. They'd believe he'd picked her up for a short fling. That she wasn't good enough to be considered for anything else.

But she'd been well paid to play that part. She couldn't afford to be offended or embarrassed.

'Satisfied?' His sensuous mouth curled up at one side.

Steph despised the way she noticed such things, responding to his allure. If she didn't, this would be much easier.

Reluctantly she nodded. She still had questions but she believed what he'd said. Why lie? Especially when she could get the truth from Clio.

'Good. Now tell me why you're so ready to believe the worst of me. I admit we got off to a rocky start in Melbourne. But it's more than that. You don't trust easily.'

Steph met that unblinking stare and wondered how many of her secrets this man had read. Most people saw her as bright and friendly and didn't realise how hard she found it to put her trust in others, especially men.

He turned the tables on her, putting her on the defensive.

'Was it a man?'

She couldn't prevent her flinch. Jared's deception was too recent, too raw. But she hid it, she hoped, with a shrug, horrified at how Damen had pinpointed her weak spot so easily. 'Just because I question your motives doesn't mean I have difficulty trusting people.'

He lifted his eyebrows.

'Besides, my past is my own business. It doesn't concern you.'

'So it was a man. What did he do? Leave you for another woman? Or was he married and you didn't know?'

Steph stifled her automatic response, that it was typical of a man to assume the betrayal was sexual. What would Damen say if he realised she'd never been with a man? She learned to be wary of trusting too much. Besides, instead of going out dating she'd spent almost every waking hour working so she could be totally independent.

'You've got it wrong.'

'Have I?' Again Damen leaned towards her and she had the crazy idea those narrowed eyes saw everything she kept hidden.

'Let's just say I've had my fill of unscrupulous people, ready to do anything to get ahead.'

Her words hit home, for Damen's expression turned dark.

Maybe she should apologise, explain that for once she didn't mean him. But that would lead to demands for explanations and she was exhausted. Steph didn't have the stamina for more.

Tonight had been an emotional minefield. She believed Damen's explanation about Clio but that didn't make their situation easier. It seemed more perilous with every hour they were together.

Steph shot to her feet, wobbling a little on her heels. 'I'm tired. I'll see you in the morning.'

Damen stood too. One long stride closed the gap between them.

There it was again, that shiver of awareness racking her body. To her horror Steph felt her nipples bud against gossamer-fine silk.

Did he notice? His eyes held hers but she saw heat flicker in his expression. His gaze dropped to her mouth and it felt like a caress, there on her lips. All night he'd looked at her mouth in a way that made her tremble with expectation. Made her want him to kiss her.

Did he move closer or did she sway towards him?

Abruptly she stepped away, turning for the door, heart pounding in her throat. 'Goodnight, Damen.'

Would he follow? Reach for her? Forget the contract he'd signed and kiss her?

She wanted him to. Wanted it with a self-destructive force that scared her. Her breath snagged as she waited, pulse thundering, for his touch.

But he made no move. She was almost at the corridor to the bedrooms when he spoke.

'Don't forget we leave early tomorrow.'

'I won't forget.'

How could she? She'd barely got through ten days pretending to be his lover and she was about to head to an island wedding where she'd have to play the part to perfection.

The worrying thing was that part of her wished it were true. That they were lovers. She was tying herself in knots trying to quell this attraction.

Steph no longer hated Damen, could no longer rely on negativity to keep her safe. Tonight he'd taken her into his confidence, naming names and explaining facts about his personal life that she sensed he hated revealing.

Yet he'd done it because he accepted she needed to know. He'd heard her qualms and put her needs above his own desire for privacy. That meant a lot. It also changed the dynamic between them.

This attraction she'd tried to conquer was burrowing deeper than doubt or conscience. Alarmingly, it grew stronger rather than weaker the more she discovered about him.

'You're kidding, right? The whole idea of bringing your mega-yacht was so you could stay on it, surely?' They reached the end of the path and Stephanie swung to face him, her eyes sparking.

Damen knew he should be focused on other things, like handling Manos, who, while ostensibly welcoming, was suspicious and far from happy. Or his own mother, who, despite being told the truth about Stephanie, had regarded the pair of them through today's pre-wedding party with a speculative twinkle that spelled trouble. Or even solving the puzzle of who'd hurt Stephanie so badly, creating that deep-running vein of distrust that she used to keep him at a distance.

But he couldn't concentrate on those things. The late-afternoon breeze teased Stephanie's summery dress and played with those dark curls in a way that made him wish he were free to touch her. Not for the benefit of an audience, but for mutual pleasure.

His belly tightened as he imagined her lifting her pouting lips to his.

Her skin was sun-kissed and, he knew, silky soft. The dress, a floaty thing in white, decorated with cornflowers, accentuated her tiny waist and delectable figure. The cornflower-blue sandal straps tied around her delicate ankles kept drawing his attention to her legs.

'Damen? Are you listening?'

'I am.' And looking. And smelling too. For, as well as the salt scent borne off the water a few hundred metres away, he inhaled Stephanie's warm, vanilla perfume. It was wholesome yet sexy and had a direct line to his libido.

Damen shoved his hands in his pockets and looked at the guest house behind her. Set away from the mansion that was Clio's family home, it perched on a low cliff above the beach.

'I'm sure it's comfortable. Clio refurbished it.'

'It's not the comfort I'm worried about. It's the size. It looks small.'

It was. Bright white like most traditional houses in the Cyclades Islands and surely no bigger than a few rooms. The door gleamed blue, matching the pair of chairs on a tiny terrace positioned to take in the view. Pink geraniums frothed from matching blue pots.

It was charming.

And small, very small.

Damen looked away to his yacht moored in the bay. That was where they should be spending the next two nights. In separate staterooms. Instead...

Damen suppressed a frisson of anticipation.

'It's generous of Manos to offer us the guest house during the wedding celebrations. I couldn't refuse.'

'Of course you could refuse. You're Damen Nicolaides! You run a shipping empire. You make billion-dollar decisions.'

He bit back a laugh. 'Thanks for the pep talk. But this isn't business, this is family, and consequently far more complicated and important.'

He thought of Manos's almost bullish attitude as he'd hosted today's pre-wedding lunch for extended family. Of Clio's set jaw and brittle air and her mother's drawn face. Only Cassie, the bride-to-be, had looked happy.

To refuse Manos's hospitality on such an occasion would have been to insult him. Manos had given him helpful guidance in the turbulent time when Damen had unexpectedly inherited Nicolaides Shipping. His family had supported Damen's in that time of terrible grief. Manos's company and personal wealth hadn't fared as well in the last decade as Damen's, not that he'd reveal that on the occasion of his daughter's wedding. But to have Damen, younger, far wealthier and more successful, the relative he'd once helped in a time of crisis, reject his personal invitation…

Damen refused to do it. Besides, a suspicion had grown today that Clio had arranged the invitation to ram home to her stubborn father that Stephanie was Damen's lover, not a casual friend. One thing was certain—this secluded guest house was designed for intimacy.

Stephanie tilted her head as if seeing him for the first time.

'I'd rather stay on the *Amphitrite* too, but I can't insult Manos by refusing his hospitality.'

If it *had* been Manos's idea originally, he'd probably hoped having Damen stay on the premises would be a chance to pressure him into an engagement with Clio.

'Because it would hurt his pride?'

'Something like that.' Damen wondered how he'd let things get so far. How he hadn't realised his relatives had unrealistic expectations of a match.

'Come on.' He opened the door. 'Let's see what it's like.'

It was worse than he'd thought.

Or, depending on your perspective, he realised, better.

Clio had made the place a sumptuous escape. Wide floor-boards gleamed beneath their feet, extending to a wall of windows. From here you could see only sky and the sea, from aquamarine shallows through shades of turquoise to sapphire depths. A soaring ceiling and simple but luxurious furnishings added to the sense of space. As did the lack of internal walls.

The living space swept around the curve of the cliff. Set in a semi-circular alcove to the left, in front of more windows, was a large bath designed for two, a platform beside it holding towels and an ice bucket. On the other side, in a large alcove with its own set of panoramic windows, was a wide bed, dressed in shades of cream, turquoise and blue.

Damen heard Stephanie's breath hitch. She marched past, surveying first the open bathing area then the bedroom that wasn't a room. The stupendous view she ignored. She opened a door, but it revealed only a fridge and a benchtop with a state-of-the-art coffee machine. Another door opened into a walk-in wardrobe. A third led to a bathroom containing only a toilet and a pair of washbasins.

'Two sinks but they can't afford a wall around the bath!'

Damen's lips twitched. 'The open feel is very popular. I'm told it maximises space.'

'And minimises privacy.' Stephanie strode past him, investigating the sofa and chairs placed to make the most of the view. 'There's not even a pull-out mattress.'

Damen's smile vanished as he registered her distress. 'It will be fine. It's just two nights.'

She spun to face him, hands on hips.

'This isn't a joke. If you think for one minute I'm going to share a bed with you—'

'Of course not.' Damen raised his hands. He was too sensible to admit that his first thought on seeing that massive bed and luxurious bath was to imagine sharing both with Stephanie. Stephanie in his arms, warm, willing and eager for his loving.

He repressed a shiver of arousal that arrowed straight to his groin, and kept his expression bland.

'This isn't a trick to compromise you.'

For a taut second she held his stare, then nodded once and turned away. Damen was surprised at the pleasure he felt knowing she believed him. It was a start, a small one, but important. He'd been stunned in Athens to discover how deep her distrust ran.

And the fact that he wanted her in his bed?

He had every intention of achieving that but not by trickery.

'I could sleep on the sofa,' she said.

Over his dead body. What sort of man did she think him? Actually, it was probably best not to go there.

'You have the bed and I'll take the sofa.' Earnest brown eyes met his. 'Don't even think of arguing, Stephanie.' His pride wouldn't let him sleep in comfort while she bunked down there.

Finally she nodded and turned to the bed. 'They've brought our bags from the yacht. I suppose we should freshen up before this restaurant dinner.'

Damen saw her wistful glance at the massive bath.

She'd done marvellously all day, fielding questions from his extended family, playing his devoted girlfriend and doing it well. Stephanie had been attentive and friendly but not gushing. She'd coped with meeting not only his mother and Clio's family but also dozens of distant relatives, all excited and curious to meet his companion, for Damen was notorious for never bringing a woman to any family celebration.

But, while he'd grown more relaxed as the day wore on, Stephanie had become more tense. Her shoulders were set high and her breathing was shallow, as if she was on high alert.

'Why don't you relax and have a bath? We've got plenty of time and I have calls I need to make. I'll go down to the beach to make them and stretch my legs.'

'If you don't mind, that would be great.' Her smile was tentative but genuine and he felt as if he'd won a victory.

She turned and opened the case that his staff had packed and brought from the yacht.

A second later she was scrabbling to pick up the item on top, moving it from his view. But not before Damen saw a black, lacy bra that looked almost see-through in her hands. Next was a skimpy pair of matching knickers, which left him imagining Stephanie wearing sexy underwear and nothing else, posing for his approval as she had at that Athens boutique.

He sucked in his breath so sharply, pain jabbed his ribs. Heat drenched him.

Damen's ease disintegrated. And so did his amusement at her disapproval of this beautiful retreat.

It struck him that she wasn't the only one who'd be grateful for a barrier between them tonight. A convenient wall so he didn't have to watch her sleeping or lie awake calculating how many steps between the sofa and the bed.

Staying here together would be a special form of torture. Not because he couldn't cope with a sofa, but because, much as he wanted to seduce Stephanie, he refused to take advantage of a situation that made her nervous.

He had a long, frustrating night ahead.

CHAPTER SEVEN

THE MUSIC WOUND to a halt but Steph's heart kept pounding a matching rhythm. The traditional music had initially sounded slow, almost ponderous, but it had altered as the dance went on. Or maybe once she'd been tugged into the line of women holding hands, following the bride, she'd begun to notice extra nuances.

She'd been happy to sit at the outdoor table with its flickering candles and watch. She'd been fascinated by the beauty of what seemed simultaneously a simple dance yet at the same time intriguingly intricate. Women of all ages joined the growing line. There was one, iron-haired and sturdy-framed, who danced with the grace of a professional. There was the little girl in plaits, eyes round with excitement as she watched the bride.

Suddenly, without giving her time to think, there was Clio, pulling Steph from her seat, dragging her to join the throng. Steph had stumbled, protested, but the smiles and nods had drawn her in till she found the beat and then, heart swelling with delight, she hadn't wanted to stop. She'd felt not only welcome but also included, a real part of this joyous event.

She'd barely been aware of the men at the tables. This didn't feel like a dance performed to attract their attention, but something done for the participants, especially the bride. She met the smiling faces of the other women and grinned back. They'd all been so kind and friendly.

It had been the same all day. Except for a few women who'd looked at her when she arrived with Damen as if they'd like to claw her eyes out. But she'd received jealous glares like that in Athens. It came with the territory.

Damen's woman. That was how everyone saw her.

The knowledge set up a familiar thud in her chest. A thud that echoed the erratic pulse beat that had kept her from sleep last night.

She must have snatched some rest, for she'd woken scratchy-eyed to find Damen gone, for an early swim, she discovered later. But it felt as if she'd spent most of the night awake, listening to her drumming pulse, thinking how close he lay, how she wanted to go to him.

Would it have been the bravest thing she'd ever done or the stupidest?

All this flirting, the fleeting caresses and searing looks, was undermining her resistance. Logic said it was all for show. Something else, deep-buried and needy, declared those looks, that tension, the sparking heat when they touched, were more than playacting.

If only she had enough experience to know for sure.

The events of the last months had damaged her self-esteem but Steph wasn't by nature a shrinking violet.

She wanted Damen.

She'd given up trying to avoid that truth. The wanting drove her crazy. If the desire was mutual…

Her breath shuddered out. If it was *mutual* she'd be tempted to do what she'd never done and invite physical intimacy. Because surely that would be a way of getting rid of it. Like an itch that needed to be scratched. Because so far it was simply compounding, growing stronger and more distracting almost by the hour.

Except Steph recalled how easily Damen had feigned attraction. She refused to make that mistake twice. It was one of the reasons she'd been horrified to discover they had to share that sybaritically luxurious and far too small guest house.

She was caught, unable to be sure what he felt but unable to escape this increasingly urgent physical attraction.

She swung round to look for Damen. He was still where

she'd left him, but instead of watching her he was in conversation with a group of men.

Steph's heart sank. What had she expected? That he'd be transfixed by the sight of her stumbling through a traditional Greek dance?

He'd spent the afternoon glued to her side. He'd been the one to pick up her filmy shawl when it slid off on the way to the church. She recalled the warmth of his hands as he'd placed it around her shoulders and the whisper of his breath tickling her face as he stood close and explained the wedding ceremony. He'd spent the day playing the attentive lover, showing Manos and everyone else that he was devoted to his new girlfriend. Was it any surprise his attention wandered now he was alone?

'May I?'

Steph swung around to meet melting dark eyes. The guy's smile was wide and friendly and Steph felt none of that jangling hyper-awareness that taunted her with Damen.

What was more, he looked at her with an avid appreciation she knew was real. Today, when Damen had seen her in her stunning new dress, ready for the wedding, he'd smiled and said she looked perfect. But his gaze hadn't lingered the way this guy's did. Damen had seemed distracted, as if he had something else on his mind. Inevitably Steph decided she looked 'perfect' for her role as pretend girlfriend but the sight left him unmoved.

'You'd like to dance? Yes? My name is Vassili. Come.' He held out his hand, his smile widening. 'Let's have some fun.'

Fun. How long since she'd had that? Always at the back of her mind were worries.

Suppressing the need to check on Damen again—she didn't need his approval—she smiled and put her hand in Vassili's. 'My name is Steph.'

'I know. Stephanie. The most beautiful woman here.'

That smile became a beaming grin and suddenly Steph felt lighter than she had in ages. Laughter trailed behind her as he drew her close.

Damen's eyes narrowed as he watched Stephanie dance. Not traditional dancing now. The music was modern, the moves unchoreographed, and it was hard to see her for the other dancers thronging the outdoor dance space. But he glimpsed turquoise silk, that collar of crystals around her throat, bouncing curls and her glorious, uninhibited smile. A smile she never turned his way. Not since what had happened in Melbourne.

His throat dried to sandpaper roughness. He'd returned to the guest house to find her dressed for the wedding. She wore a dress once more in a style that left her arms and shoulders bare, the fabric attached around the neck only by that glinting collar. And when she turned the upper half of her back was tantalisingly bare.

Damen's palms had prickled with the urge to touch that expanse of skin. Or trace the gleaming fabric as it clung and dipped across her curves before flirting out around her legs. It was a dress made to drive a man to distraction.

She was made to drive him to distraction.

After a sleepless night he wasn't putting up much of a fight. All day he'd been on edge, his body hyper-alert as they acted the loving couple. As he leaned close to explain customs or conversations for her. As he endured the torture of Stephanie turning and murmuring to him, her breath an intimate caress.

Even entering the church and placing that gauzy wrap over her bare shoulders out of respect for tradition, only part of Damen's mind had been on the wedding or Manos or curious onlookers. Most of his brain had been cataloguing how very much he wanted Stephanie.

He'd held back, hadn't tried to seduce her in Manos's

home. Now he couldn't remember why that had seemed a point of honour.

She wanted him. He felt it in those tiny hitched sighs of hers, her dazed look when he touched her and the fluttering pulse that betrayed her time and again.

Damen leaned back in his chair, half listening to the conversation about global markets, financial recovery and bad debts. He couldn't stalk across and claim Stephanie. No one would believe he was so besotted with his new woman that he needed to be with her all the time. It would only make Manos suspicious.

Then the dancers parted and there she was, smiling up at her partner, who'd closed the space between them. He leaned in, whispering something, and she laughed.

Damen sat up, catching the rich yet breathless sound as the music faded.

His jaw clenched. He knew the guy dancing with her. He fancied himself irresistible with his ingratiating smile and practised charm. Let him work his charm on someone else!

'Don't you think, Damen—?'

'Sorry, Manos. Let's talk about this later. Stephanie needs me.' He was already out of his seat, stalking towards the dance floor.

She needed him all right, to keep her safe from suave seducers. From men who looked at her in that sexy dress and wanted her out of it. As he did.

Damen kept his eyes on her as he detoured past the DJ, throwing out not a request but a terse command. A loud pop song, just starting, stopped abruptly, making heads turn.

Stephanie turned too, her gaze colliding with Damen's, as he paced towards her. Her mouth, those lips that drove him again and again to the edge of control, opened as if she couldn't catch her breath.

The first bars of a new tune poured through the evening air, soft, slow, resonant with longing.

Damen saw her swallow, the wide circlet of exquisite crystals around her throat catching the glow from fairy lights strung all about.

Then he was there, looking down at her.

'My dance.'

In his peripheral vision her partner shifted his weight, huffed as if to say something, then faded away.

Damen reached out and did what he'd wanted to do all day. He slid his arm right round her back, low across her waist, feeling the exquisite softness of naked flesh against his palm. He pulled her close, snug against his thighs, and took her hand. His breath eased out in satisfaction. Better. Much better.

'What's the matter? You think Manos won't believe in us if we spend half an hour apart?' Her voice was a hoarse croak that lacerated his control. He wanted to hear more of it, throaty and out of breath, calling his name, crying out for release.

'I'm rescuing you from a playboy who thinks he can seduce my woman.' Damen registered the growl roughening his voice and didn't care. He'd had enough.

The familiar ballad swelled around them and they began dancing, circling, barely moving from the spot.

'Was that necessary? You know I'm not going to be seduced.'

Oh, yes, you are.

For sitting there, watching Stephanie with another man, something inside Damen had snapped. Not his patience. Something more fundamental. He didn't want to think about it or give it a name. He was a pragmatist and he knew the time for resisting was over. That was all he'd let himself consider.

Damen hauled her closer, pleased when her body melted against his despite the stunned expression in those wide golden-brown eyes.

Oh, yes. There'd definitely be a seduction tonight. And it would be he, Damen Nicolaides, orchestrating it. Beginning now.

Steph felt as if she was floating as they strolled down the secluded path. The faint sound of music reached her. Damen said the revellers would continue partying into the early hours, but the bride and groom had left and there was no need to linger.

Steph would have liked to linger, swaying in Damen's arms under the canopy of vines and tiny lights. For the first time since their charade began she hadn't given a thought to the lie they lived, for there, in his arms, it hadn't felt like a lie.

She was no fool. She knew it was the romantic setting, the handsome partner, Damen's proprietorial manner, which should have annoyed her and instead made her insides turn stupidly mushy, that created the strange ambience. Plus her own heightened desire.

She sighed. It was time to shake off the romantic illusion. When they entered their guest suite and were away from prying eyes, the masquerade would end. She was nothing more to Damen than the woman he'd paid a fortune to pretend to be his girlfriend. And he…well, he'd still be too potently alluring for her peace of mind but he needn't know that.

There it was, coming into view at last. The retreat they'd share for one more night. Would she lie awake again, wondering how it would be to indulge in a fling? Imagining being with Damen, the only man who'd broken through her wall of caution, awakening her body to desire?

A large moon hung low over the sea and silvery light bathed the scene in magic, making it impossibly beautiful. Something caught in her chest.

'It's been a wonderful day. Thank you.' Steph made to

withdraw her hand from Damen's but he kept hold of her fingers as they stopped on the terrace.

'Thank *you*, Stephanie.' His low voice skated across her skin, drawing it tight. 'I hadn't expected to enjoy today as much as I did.'

She shrugged. It had been a lovely celebration with friendly people. Even Manos, whose fierce, dark eyes had glittered dangerously at first, had mellowed as the evening progressed. Last seen, he'd been laughing with a group of men who'd shed their jackets, rolled up their sleeves and huddled around a table, drinking brandy and talking earnestly.

Steph moved towards the door but Damen blocked her way.

'Damen?' His arm came round her, drawing her close, his other hand still holding hers.

Delight shivered through her and she stiffened. It was one thing to enjoy the illicit pleasure of being in his arms, knowing it was for show, but they were alone here.

'What is it? Can you see someone?' Were they being watched?

His head lowered and for a snatched moment she imagined his mouth covering hers, those wide shoulders curving around her.

But he didn't do that. He'd promised not to kiss her. He'd signed a contract.

That memory stiffened her spine, a reminder that this wasn't real, as his mouth settled near her ear. Yet her eyes fluttered shut as his breath feathered her skin.

'I can't see anyone. That doesn't mean we can't be seen.' He paused. 'Hold me, Stephanie.'

Steph blinked her eyes open, trying to decipher the curious note in his voice. It wasn't an order so much as a request. There was a yearning in that deep voice that—

She pressed her lips together. There was no yearning, just a man speaking softly so anyone near by wouldn't hear. Reluctantly, enjoying every centimetre of sensation and knowing she shouldn't, Steph slid her hands up his chest to clasp the back of his neck.

He felt so good. That warm, woodsy scent tickled her nostrils and she ran her fingers through his thick hair, scraping along his scalp, telling herself she was making this look real for a potential onlooker, ignoring the fierce hunger drilling down through her middle.

A sigh shuddered through him, and then she was trembling too as his mouth moved along her jaw and down her neck. They weren't kisses exactly. Just the brush of his lips as he whispered something in gravelly Greek beneath his breath. The sound carved a channel of need through her, leaving her wide open and gently aching.

'Damen, I think we should go inside.' Because she couldn't play pretend lovers any more. Not tonight. Not when she felt so...

'Excellent idea, *kopela mou*.'

Yet instead of stepping back, Damen took her by surprise, bending to scoop her into his arms. The world tilted. Steph had never been held like this. Her arms went round his neck, hanging tight lest he drop her.

But it wasn't falling she feared. Not really. It was the riot going on inside her body. The jumble of excitement and anticipation, even knowing this was for the benefit of some unseen watcher.

'Do you really think this is necess—?'

'I do. Absolutely necessary.' His voice was as taut as her stretched nerves.

He opened the door, holding her in his arms, and stepped inside. All the while Steph was bombarded with new sensations. The feeling of being in his arms, surrounded by him. The heat where their bodies pressed together. The fact she could hear his heartbeat if she let herself rest her head against him. The awareness of how close his mouth was.

Above all the almost wonderful, almost scary, sense of being totally reliant on his strength.

Steph waited but Damen didn't release her.

'Damen? I can stand. No one can see us.' The massive windows on the sea side spilled moonlight into the large space, but they were private from prying eyes.

Instead of putting her down, Damen firmed his hold.

'Maybe I don't want to,' he murmured. 'Maybe I've been wanting to hold you like this all night.'

Steph's heart jumped. 'Stop it. We're not playing parts now. You can drop the besotted act.'

'And if it's not an act?' Above her his mouth twisted into a hard smile that looked like a grimace.

'What are you saying, Damen? That you've spent the last few hours longing to hold me like this?' It was preposterous, yet Steph heard the wobble in her voice, as if she wanted to believe it.

'That too. But what I really long for is your mouth on mine.' She felt as well as heard his voice rumble up from his chest. 'Your kisses. Your lips have been driving me crazy. *You've* been driving me crazy. Not just today. For weeks.'

Suddenly she was shoving at his shoulders, wiggling her legs, trying to sit up, get down, till eventually he relented and lowered her to the floor.

She felt her shawl slip to the floor but didn't pick it up. Steph backed up a step, far enough to meet Damen's dark eyes. In the gloom they should have been impossible to read. Instead she felt a punch to the solar plexus when she deciphered his expression.

Yearning, that was what she saw, or imagined she saw. A yearning such as she felt.

Except that couldn't be.

'Stop it. We don't have an audience here. There's no need to keep up the act.'

Slowly he turned his head from side to side. 'It's no act. That part hasn't ever been an act with you, Stephanie.'

Her nape tightened and her hands anchored at her hips. 'It was in Melbourne. That time in the car—'

'When we kissed?' His mouth curled at one side into something too taut to be a smile. 'I didn't plan that, you know. But how could I resist when you were so lush and inviting and I'd been trying to keep my distance all week? When we kissed it was like spring after the longest winter. Like sunshine after frost.' He shook his head. 'No, that's not right. It was more like a volcano erupting out of the blue. As if the caldera at Santorini exploded again, turning everything lava-hot. Burning away the world.'

The image branded her, deep inside, in that place where she tried to hide her feelings. He was right. It had been just like that. For her. Not for him. He'd merely been using her weakness against her.

'What's wrong, Damen?' She turned her voice to steel. 'Are you bored? Is it so difficult to go a few weeks without a woman in your bed that you'd even turn to *me*?'

Pain blanketed her chest but she made herself face him. If he knew how she really felt about him she'd be lost.

If she'd expected her lashing accusation to provoke him she was disappointed. 'Actually, I'm very discerning about who I take to bed. I learned the hard way to be very, very choosy.'

The hard way? Steph frowned, wondering what he meant.

'So what am I? A challenge? The one woman who refuses to be seduced by your charm?'

He folded his arms and she wished she didn't notice the way the gesture accentuated the power of his upper body. 'Definitely a challenge, Stephanie. But that's a separate issue. I've wanted you since I met you. The only reason I didn't seduce you that night in Australia was because I had an obligation to find your friend Emma for Christo. And after that,' he lifted his arms wide, 'I'd hurt you. It wasn't the time.'

To her surprise Steph thought she saw shame or at least regret flicker across his face.

'And you think things are different now? Because you're paying me?'

'They're absolutely different, and not because I'm paying you.' He shook his head. 'I never have and never will pay for a woman in my bed. This, what's between us, has nothing to do with money.'

Steph folded her arms across her chest, holding in her madly pounding heart.

'Then what's changed?'

'*You've* changed.' His night-dark eyes pinioned her. 'You've lost that wounded look as if I'm the big, bad wolf. Instead you look at me the way a woman does when she wants a man.'

Steph's chest rose hard on a shocked intake of air.

'You don't deny it.' His voice was soft as a summer breeze, warm as seduction.

'I don't need to deny it. You're paying me a fortune to pretend to be your lover. Of course I look at you…fondly. I have to be convincing.'

'Fondly?' Slowly he shook his head. 'It's more than that. You're not that good an actress.'

Steph's chin shot high. 'You've got an ego the size of the Aegean, Damen Nicolaides.'

'It's not ego, Stephanie. It's facing the truth. The same truth I faced ages ago. I *want* you, Stephanie, and I've given up pretending not to. You want me too.'

'In your dreams.'

'At least in my dreams I get to have you, Stephanie. There you're always willing and eager in my arms.'

Heat saturated her from the crown of her head to the soles of her feet. He dreamt of her? Just as she dreamt of him? Had he lain awake last night too, imagining what it would be like if they shared that big bed looking out over the sea?

'Nothing to say, Stephanie?'

She opened her mouth then shut it. Bandying words with him was too dangerous. Every word he spoke tapped into the secret channel of desire within her that she'd tried and failed to dam.

Damen stepped closer and her chin rose as she held his stare.

'You don't get anything in this life playing safe, Stephanie.'

'But you don't get burned either.' She hadn't planned to answer but then the words were out, revealing things she'd tried to hide. The yearning. The combustible heat within. The weakness.

Yet, instead of triumph, Damen's expression held understanding.

'Sometimes,' he murmured, 'playing with fire has compensations.'

He paused, watching her. Stephanie almost wished he'd reach for her, touch her and make the doubts disappear. Make it simple by stripping away her defences. But he didn't. He met her gaze gravely, not trying to hide his hunger. Not trying to hide anything. The silvery moonlight revealed features stark with longing but not a man who'd try to force her.

'If you're brave enough to take the risk.'

Steph tried to summon outrage, to be annoyed that he thought her a coward, just for being sensible. It didn't work because the pressure didn't come from Damen. It came from inside herself.

All her life Steph had played safe. Working, saving, planning for the future. Keeping herself to herself rather than venture into the wild realms of passion as so many of her peers had done. There'd been no boyfriends, no lovers. Just a man who'd duped her into trusting him, only to steal from her. And now Damen, who turned her inside out so she hardly recognised herself or what she felt.

She'd tried safety and it hadn't worked.

What did she have to lose?

As the thought surfaced the voice of reason screeched inside her brain, listing all the reasons this was dangerous.

For once Steph ignored the voice of reason.

'There's something I want.' Her voice held a strange, flat note, as if her heart weren't racing or her breaths coming in short gasps.

'Anything I can help with?' He didn't move but somehow he seemed nearer, the air thickening between them.

Steph unfolded her arms and let them hang by her sides. 'I'd like you to kiss me. On the lips.'

CHAPTER EIGHT

DAMEN'S BREATH SEARED IN, leaving his lungs overfull yet somehow without enough air to sustain him.

This was what he wanted. What he'd planned to get for so long. Yet, as he looked into Stephanie's serious face with that tiny frown on her brow and lips parted as if she too couldn't get enough oxygen, it wasn't triumph he felt. Or not entirely.

The hammer beat in his blood revealed the depth of his need. He wasn't besting her. This wasn't a contest. He felt almost scared to touch her, as if she'd melt away or change her mind and he'd be left alone, the craving for her eating him up.

Damen didn't let himself hesitate. He stepped in to stand toe to toe with her. Her nipples grazed him and a spiral of hot metal coiled down from his chest to his groin, screwing his body tighter and hotter.

He palmed her bare back. Her flesh was velvety. His other hand ploughed through her curls, tilting her head. She looked up at him with wide, wary eyes. It was too dark to see their golden depths but even in the gloom he felt her scrutiny. As if she didn't trust him to make this worth her while. As if expecting him to let her down.

That spurred him to take his time, though he wanted to plunder her lips till she stopped thinking and gave him everything.

He pressed his lips to the corner of her mouth, teasing them both, telling himself he could withstand a few more moments' waiting. She trembled and something hard inside softened.

Damen gentled his hand on her scalp, slid his mouth along her cheek, peppering tiny kisses along flesh that tasted like vanilla and something far more precious. To the edge of her jawline, to her ear. Slender fingers grabbed his upper arms. He felt rather than heard her sigh.

That was when his patience disintegrated, even as he told himself to go slow. Now he was back at her mouth, tugging her bottom lip between his teeth, hearing her gasp, feeling her fingers dig into his flesh through his jacket. Damen licked that delicate lower lip, savouring a taste of paradise.

He was telling himself to move on, press more teasing kisses along her jawline, when Stephanie slicked her tongue along the seam of his mouth. A second later she fastened her teeth on his bottom lip and nipped hard.

Sensations, raw and hot, shot through him. All thought of slow seduction faded as he gathered her in, hauling her against a body forged hard as steel.

No coaxing now, just a driving hunger that melded their lips, their tongues tangling in a wild dance of eager ecstasy.

Stephanie quivered against him, but not with nerves. Not with her hands clutching so tight it was as if she wanted to climb up him, all the better to devour him. And even though he, from his superior height, bowed her back over his arm, this wasn't about dominance and submission.

Submission! She was anything but submissive. She didn't just kiss with her lips but with her whole, glorious body. She undulated against him, a symphony of female sensuality as her tongue danced in his mouth, eager and erotic.

Still it wasn't enough. The kiss was deep and druggingly arousing, yet he needed more. With a grunt Damen tugged her closer against his arousal. His arm at her waist shifted till he grasped her bottom and lifted her.

Shards of heat shot through him. It wasn't enough. Not with the taste of Stephanie like sweet, wild honey in his mouth and the feel of her eager body against him.

Damen heard a hum of sound, a low, vibrating growl. It took a moment to realise it came from him. A gruff sound of encouragement and demand so primal it startled him.

Nothing about this kiss was ordinary. He'd expected pleasure, anticipated arousal. He'd even spoken to her of volcanic heat, yet till their mouths touched he'd forgotten how devastating it was, kissing Stephanie Logan.

This was elemental. Like a combustible chemical reaction and as inevitable as the sun rising tomorrow.

Damen gave himself up to it, letting the relentless driving force take him, knowing that to resist, even to think, was pointless.

Some time later, he had no idea how much later, he lifted his head enough to allow them both to breathe. His lungs worked like bellows and his brain had ceased functioning beyond *mine, mine, mine.*

He blinked, trying to ground himself, stunned at his loss of control. At his inability to think. As if he were the one out of his depth.

Damen looked into slumberous eyes slowly opening to look up at him, at a kiss-ravaged mouth, those lips plump and pouting, and self-knowledge smote him. He *was* reeling. For the first time he wasn't in command of himself.

He didn't give a damn.

He wanted more. He wanted everything.

Her hand on his chest stopped him when he made to kiss her again.

'Wait. Stop.'

Chest heaving, Damen paused.

'Yes?'

'This feels dangerous.'

Damen suppressed a smile. 'Not dangerous, *agapi mou.* Just a little on the edge.'

Who was he kidding? They were combustible. It was like saying a summer wildfire, scorching all before it, was just a little dangerous.

'I can't think when we kiss.' Her voice was breathless, wondering, and Damen wanted to reassure her everything was okay. That she could rely on him to put the brakes on.

But he couldn't. Kissing Stephanie was like being on a runaway train and never wanting to get off.

He shook his head and straightened. 'You're right. When we kiss…'

He paused, cleared his throat. The man he'd become didn't admit to weakness. He'd forced himself to learn from his past, catastrophic mistake. He didn't hand anyone, especially a woman, the power of holding the truth about him.

It would be easy to step back, murmur something about respecting her desire for caution. Well, not easy, but more acceptable than admitting the truth, that she threatened to undo him.

'When we kiss?' Her eyes searched his, her hands still clutching his arms as if she needed his support to stay upright.

Damen could lie, brush off the truth and walk away. But if he did, would he ever hold her in his arms again? The thought of never kissing her again left him bereft.

'When we kiss,' he growled, 'I don't want to stop. I want you, Stephanie. Completely. Unreservedly. I want you wild, wanton and abandoned. I want to worship you with my body till you scream in ecstasy and barely have the energy to give yourself to me again. And I want to keep loving you till we're both wrung-out wrecks, unable to move.'

Damen's lips twisted into a grimace. So much for keeping the truth to himself. To not handing her power on a plate.

Steph felt the thrill of excitement start in her belly and spread in radiating waves. She trembled so hard surely Damen saw. Yet he scowled down at her as if she'd done something wrong.

He looked so *fierce*. As if he wanted to fight rather than kiss. As if this were some battle between them.

Slowly she processed his words. Not just the shiver-inducing promise of sexual satisfaction but that revealing comment. *I don't want to stop.*

Steph didn't pretend to be an expert about Damen but she knew some things about him. One was that he guarded himself. He thought before he acted, each action planned and scrutinised. He didn't rush headlong into things but considered them, then worked out the strategy that would best suit his needs, like hiring a faux-girlfriend.

He'd even taken a pragmatic approach to his love life, guarding against importunate lovers via his arrangement with Clio.

Yet there was nothing pragmatic about his expression now.

He looked different, his features stripped back as if passion had scoured any softness from his face. Yet Steph felt no fear, just fellow feeling. It was the same for her. As if their kiss had stolen away the comfortable platitudes she surrounded herself with and left only a single truth.

She wanted Damen, and no amount of prevaricating or pretending could change that.

Beneath her palm his heart thundered.

They were equals in this. He'd admitted as much. It wouldn't be safe. It would be wild and ecstatic. But maybe just once in her life she should discover what that felt like. Step off the straight and narrow and let herself go.

It wasn't as if Damen would be around long term, interfering with her life or trying to turn a moment's wildness into something more significant.

The choice was hers.

Steph moistened her lips, aware of Damen's eyes following the movement. It sent a corkscrew of heat twisting through her.

'I'm not experienced.'

His head reared back as if he needed to distance himself and Steph felt a jerk of dismay at that tiny withdrawal. Damen blinked, his eyes narrowing as if wondering if he'd heard right.

'Not *very* experienced?'

Was this a deal-breaker for him? Pride told her if her virginity was a problem, then tough, he'd be the one to miss out. But she wanted him so badly. Couldn't imagine turning back now.

Her chin rose and she focused on a point beyond his shoulder. 'It doesn't matter. Forget I spoke.'

Warm fingers cupped her chin and turned her face to his. 'It matters, *kopela mou*.' He breathed deep, his chest a living wall before her. 'Thank you for telling me.' He paused. 'It's an unexpected…responsibility.'

She opened her mouth to say it wasn't a responsibility, just a physical fact she thought he should know about. But before she could speak his mouth covered hers.

This kiss was different. Not desperate or wild. It was light, gentle, but with no less purpose and no less pleasure. It was a kiss that tasted sweet with promise, heady with longing and as it went on something vital melted inside her. Steph could almost swear she heard music somewhere, beautiful music. But that was impossible.

Heat rose, weaving through her blood, softening her bones. Steph leaned into him, needing his strength to support her, and once more Damen scooped her close.

This time when he lifted his head, breathing hard through his nostrils, there was no looking away, no pretending. He stared down at her and it felt as though he saw her in a way no one else ever had. It should have been scary but it felt right. Steph wanted him to see her, the real her, to be as wholly caught up in this moment as she was.

Damen lifted his fingers to her forehead, smoothing a line above her eyebrows. 'There's nothing to worry about, Stephanie. I promise you.'

She wasn't worried. Well, not much. But there was no need for words as Damen led her to the bed.

'Undress me.' His voice, low as a caress, wound through her as he shrugged out of his jacket and tossed it over a chair. His shoulders looked so broad in that white shirt, gleaming in the moonlight. Her fingers twitched and she swallowed hard, knowing she'd fumble her way through undressing him, revealing her ineptitude and nervous excitement.

What did it matter?

Steph reached for his bow tie, the silk soft to the touch as he undid his cufflinks. Tugging the tie free, she undid the top of his shirt then got distracted by the dark, silky skin she revealed. The pads of her fingers slid across his collarbone, discovering dips and notches, then down to where a smattering of crisp hair dusted his chest. It tickled her fingers and palms when she spread them across that wall of hot muscle.

One brown nipple budded under her palm and Damen's skin tightened as muscles jumped then eased.

Steph looked up to find his gaze fixed, dark and glowing on her as he reefed off his shirt. His hands went to his belt and the thrumming beat of her heart rose to her throat.

Her hands drifted lower, discovering flesh that was surprisingly soft, taut over muscle and bone. Her gaze followed her hands and she discovered he'd shucked his trousers and underwear down to his ankles, standing before her proudly erect.

Steph's throat tightened. He looked impossibly beautiful, impossibly huge. A flutter of nerves butterflied through her middle to settle between her legs, turning into a hot, achy sensation that made her shift restlessly.

Damen said nothing, just stood with his arms at his sides, waiting.

Steph anchored one palm on that flat abdomen and dragged her other down, fingertips touching the thatch of dark hair then reaching his heavy arousal. To her surprise it felt like silk over solid heat. Tentatively she curled her hand around him, sliding gently right to the tip.

A sound like the wind soughing through trees penetrated the silence. It took a moment to realise it was Damen, sighing in pleasure, his eyes glittering through narrowed slits.

She repeated the movement, feeling a rising power, and this time he moved, thrusting into her hand, his hips tilting to follow her caress.

'You like that.' It should have sounded stupid. It probably did sound naïve. Yet Damen didn't laugh. The tendons in his neck stood proud and the muscles in his arms and chest bunched as if he forced himself into immobility.

'I do. When you touch me I feel…' He shook his head, his mouth a grimace as Steph let her other hand dance, feather light across his abdomen, grazing one hip, then down, then up again.

She saw what it cost him to stand while she looked her fill, exploring. She watched his pulse judder, saw the sheen at his throat as if he was burning up. Damen was a strong man, used to wielding authority, making things happen. Yet he held himself still, giving her time to adjust. Giving her power.

Because she'd told him she was inexperienced. Because he knew she was nervous as well as excited. Suddenly she wasn't nervous any more. Not enough to wait, at any rate.

She dropped to her knees before him, scrabbling to find first one gleaming shoe then another, helping him out of them and his socks till he could step free of his clothes and stand naked before her. She lifted her eyes, drawn once more by the uncompromising shape of his erection. Would he—?

Damen's hand closed around hers, drawing her up.

He didn't say anything, simply reached around to the back of the halter-neck collar of her dress and flicked it undone. Steph blinked, her arm automatically lifting to hold the bodice up while Damen dragged the side zipper open. Then his arms dropped and he stood, waiting.

Steph's heart thundered as she released the fabric, felt it slide free, down her breasts, stomach and thighs, to land with a plop around her feet.

Damen's chest rose mightily then sank again before he lifted one hand, brushing across her breasts. He teased her nipples with a barely there touch that sent shocking jolts of heat shooting to that needy place between her legs.

'And your shoes.' His voice was a whisper of sound, barely audible over her pulse.

Steph reached for his arm, clutched as she lifted one foot and fumbled at the buckle, drawing off the high heel. Then the other. Now she stood before him, naked but for panties of skimpy lace.

She drew a deep breath, registering a new scent in the air, not the evocative scent she associated with Damen but something headier, slightly musky.

Arousal. That was what she smelt in the air thickening between them. It was what she felt pounding through her blood, heating her body till she glowed.

Eyes on Damen's, she hooked her thumbs under the lace at her hips and dragged it down, letting it pool at her feet.

His gaze tracked down, zeroing in on the dark V between her legs, and his mouth crooked up at one side as if in approval. He lifted his hand, palm up, and Steph put hers in it, feeling relief and excitement as his fingers folded around hers. Fire skated from their linked hands all the way up her arm then down, down, deep inside. He led her to the bed, drawing her down beside him so they sat side by side.

It wasn't what she'd expected. She'd supposed that once naked they'd be in each other's arms, kissing, letting nature take its course in a flurry of urgent excitement.

Instead the line of Damen's jaw looked almost grim in the spill of moonlight.

'I want to make this good for you, Stephanie. You'll need to tell me what you like and what you don't.'

'I don't know.' Steph swallowed, feeling suddenly gauche.

Damen shook his head. 'You will soon enough. Promise me,' he paused, 'if you feel uncomfortable, tell me and I'll stop. At any point. Agreed?'

She nodded, suddenly alarmed at the possibility he might

expect more than she knew how to give. She thought of stories she'd heard about sexual kinks and—

'Don't worry, *koritsi mou*. All you have to do is enjoy yourself. Okay?'

Steph nodded. She hated feeling like this, with no clue. So she lifted her palm to his shoulder, feeling a frisson of response in the shiver that passed through his big frame.

'What I'd really like,' she said, her voice hoarse, 'is to kiss you. To lie against you naked and kiss you.'

The serious expression around his eyes eased and the smile he sent her was pure devilry. 'Since you insist.'

Then, before she had a chance to register movement, she was flat on her back on the mattress, with Damen lying half above, half beside her, his shoulders wide against the streaming moonlight.

Steph sucked in an urgent breath, full of that heady scent of Damen and sex. It lifted her breasts against his chest and everything inside stopped for a second in sheer wonder at how good that felt. But there was more, far more. The scratchy friction of his hairy leg, hot as it slid over hers. Hard fingers pushing through her hair, holding her still as his mouth lowered to hers.

This time his kiss stole her breath instantly. For they were together as never before. So close, touching everywhere. The furnace-like heat of his tall frame, even the way his arms caged her as he propped himself above her, taking some of his weight, all added to the amazing intimacy.

Soon that expectant stillness vanished, obliterated by the need for more of what Damen gave her. His hard body against hers, his hands moving knowingly, his mouth… Oh, his mouth. That earlier kiss had been a mere prelude to what he did now, drawing her to the edge of ecstasy with his mouth on hers till she writhed, eager for more.

Strong hands clamped hers, lifting her arms above her head.

'What—?'

'It's okay. We just need to slow things a little. I don't have many condoms with me and they need to last the night.' He nipped the sensitive place between her neck and shoulder, making her gasp.

'That's not slowing things. That's…' Her words ended with a sigh as Damen worked his way up to her ear, kissing, nipping, turning her to jelly. Yet before she could catch her breath he moved down her body, settling between her thighs as if he belonged there and capturing her breasts in his hands. His breath was hot on first one nipple then the other as he blew across them, watching them rise to aching points.

'Please, Damen.'

He lifted his head. 'You don't like this?'

Steph shook her head. 'I do. Too much.'

'Then relax, and I'll show you how much better it can be.'

That was the start of what she thought of later as exquisite torture. Damen worked his way around her body, drawing wild responses from the tiniest caresses. And all the time she heard his voice, deep enough to shudder through her bones, asking if she liked this, or this. When the truth was she liked it all. Too much. Each new caress, each press of his lips or stroke of his hand drew the tension in her tighter.

Till finally, with a gleam in his dark eyes, he sank once more between her thighs. It took just the touch of his tongue, a single, sliding stroke, and Steph shattered in a piercing explosion of pleasure. Light burst in a rainbow of colour behind her eyelids, the breath seized in her lungs and her body stretched taut, racked by aftershocks that gradually diminished, leaving her dazed and boneless.

Finally she opened her eyes. There was Damen, his gaze fixed on her, his face intent, as if there was nothing more important than her pleasure.

Steph's mouth curled up in a breathless smile. 'Before you ask, I *did* like that.'

His answering grin was the sexiest thing she'd seen, perhaps because of where he lay, his broad shoulders between the V of her legs.

'Good. Let's do it again.'

Steph lifted herself on one elbow, a protest forming on her lips because of course she couldn't possibly climax like that again, not now she was totally sated.

Except it seemed Damen knew her better than she did. This time he used tongue, lips and teeth to ease her back into that state of frantic need, while his long fingers explored and delved, making her arch off the bed as that tightness gathered again, sensitive nerve endings singing with excitement.

All through it, Damen held her gaze.

That, his knowing look, the dark, hungry gleam that caressed as surely as his hand and mouth, was what turned her to mush. Stopped the protest that had formed in her mouth. Why would she want to stop anything that felt so wonderful?

That time when she came Steph screamed, her fingers clutching the thick hair on Damen's head, her eyes locked with his. Her cries took ages to die, morphing into something like a sob as finally he prowled his way up her body and she could put her arms around him, clutching him close.

She squeezed him tight, wrapping her leaden legs around him, burrowing her face into his shoulder, drawing the spicy hot scent of him deep inside. In the pulsing quiet everything seemed to slow and centre. Steph felt as if she'd discovered a new world, a place she'd never known existed. Because of Damen.

Eventually there was movement as he rolled over, taking her with him so she lay straddled and boneless across his tall frame.

For a long time they lay like that, unmoving, till finally Damen stroked his hand down Steph's spine and, to her surprise, she felt herself arch into him.

'Are you ready for more, Stephanie?'

'More?' Blearily she lifted her head but his meaning

was clear as he shifted and she felt the slide of his arousal against her core.

Of course there was more. He'd given her orgasms and it was only fair he should claim his own. Yet as his hips tilted and Steph felt the press of that iron and silk shaft between her legs, she didn't feel as exhausted as she had before. Instead she was…excited. Her breath caught deep in her chest as Damen's hands brushed her breasts, then sank to her hips.

Experimentally Steph slid against him and was shocked by the white-hot bolt of heat that shot through her.

'I like that,' he growled, his voice barely recognisable. The sound of it, rough and hungry, made something dance inside, some feminine part of her that revelled in the idea of Damen on the edge. 'Do you?'

For answer Steph moved again, more deliberately, bracing her hands on his shoulders, concentrating on his flesh gliding against hers. 'I do.'

In the gloom she caught his grin, or was it a grimace? 'Good. Then take me.'

It took Steph a moment to digest his meaning. It wasn't what she'd expected. She'd imagined him propped over her, powering into her, setting their rhythm.

But this was the man who'd taken an age pleasuring her, leashing his own desires to make her first time good. More than good. The wetness between her legs, the melting sensation there, told its own story. Now he let her set the pace. How much easier could he have made it? If there was going to be pain, she sensed it would be fleeting.

Besides, she decided as she wriggled back a little, despite her climaxes, Damen had left her with an aching emptiness inside. An emptiness she wanted him to fill.

She rose onto her knees then gingerly reached for him, finding him already sheathed. His fingers clamped tighter around her hips.

'Like this?' She centred herself over him, watching him nod, seeing his mouth pull back into a flat line as she slowly sank. It was the weirdest feeling, a stretching sensation that made her pause, panting.

Steph waited for him to tell her to keep going, to pull her down with those large hands, but he simply waited, watching, till the slight discomfort faded. She tilted her hips and, as if in response, Damen lifted up from beneath in a long, slow glide that stole her breath.

'More,' he urged in a voice of gravel.

Steph blinked. There was more? How was that possible? She longed to find out. Steadying herself on his shoulders, she bore down till they were locked together with him buried deep inside.

She blinked, astonished at how easy it had been and how remarkable it felt. Except Damen's hands on her hips were urging her up. She followed the prompting, then blinked as he tugged her back down while he tilted his pelvis and thrust.

The sensation was amazing. It felt...

Steph gasped a shocked breath and repeated the movement, more smoothly this time, meeting the angle of his thrust with her own, then feeling the aftershock ripple through her like the shadow of an earthquake.

'Damen. Please, I...'

Her body began to shake, those worn-out muscles trembling as pleasure rose. Not like before. This was bigger, deeper, tugging at her soul as well as her body. She felt them moving as one, then moving in counterpoint, making the most remarkable magic between them.

That was how it felt. Magic.

Like the most profound magic in the world. Steph felt bigger than herself, part of something wondrous.

Maybe it was the way Damen held her eyes as they made the magic together, or the press of his hands so possessive at her hips. The thrusting caress of his body within hers, circling in a way that shot showers of flaming sparks through the darkness at the edge of her vision.

Then she heard it, Damen's voice, but not his voice. A low growl of triumph and wonder as he called her name and thrust high. Suddenly she was falling to meet him, the whole world bursting into flames around her, consuming her, cradling her in a fiery embrace that became Damen's embrace, his arms tight round her, his breath caressing her cheek, holding her to him as ecstasy took them both.

CHAPTER NINE

DAMEN WATCHED HER SLEEPING. It had been late when finally they'd collapsed, sated, in a tangle on the sheets. For hours after that he'd lain there, unable to sleep, his brain racing as he surveyed the woman curled so trustingly in his arms.

He didn't do post-coital cuddles. He didn't invite lovers to spend the night. Not in ten years. Not since Ingrid.

He waited for the familiar shudder of revulsion at the name but for once it didn't come. Probably because he held Stephanie warm and limp in his embrace.

Last night had felt like a turning point and he'd spent the last couple of hours inventing plausible reasons for that.

Because she'd been a virgin.

Because he'd wanted her for so long, longer than he'd ever wanted and gone without a woman.

Because, although he'd paid for her presence in his world, she'd made it clear that she gave her body as a gift that had nothing to do with the contract they'd negotiated or the masquerade they played.

Because her innocence and forthrightness were a combination so heady it made her different to any other woman he'd let into his life.

Because he'd *let* her into his life. He'd explained the reasons for their masquerade, explained his relationship with Manos and Clio, he who never explained himself to any woman.

He sensed that last came closest to the truth.

Damen had let Stephanie in, not just to his bed, but under his guard in ways that hadn't been apparent till too late.

Now, watching the sun rise over the Aegean, the pink and apricot dawn light changing to a clear blue sky, Damen wasn't concentrating on the work he'd do later from his yacht, or the discussions he'd have with Manos. He was thinking about how and when he'd have Stephanie again. Whether she'd be sore from making love and whether he should back off for a day and whether he had the resolve to do that if she needed space. Whether she'd enjoy it if he took her from behind, and how she'd feel about spending the whole day naked in his bed.

He scrubbed his palm over his face, trying to erase the erotic fantasies that crowded his brain.

Every time he tried to think about the next few weeks, even the next couple of days, he circled back to Stephanie naked beneath him, above him, before him. Stephanie caressing him. How would she feel about using her mouth on him?

She sighed and stretched voluptuously, her lips soft against his chest, her legs sliding around his, sending his temperature soaring and his libido into overdrive.

Damen waited, breathless, for her to wake. Instead she sank more deeply against him as if he were her own private pillow. Her even breathing was a caress against sensitised flesh. The sight of her pink nipple, trembling invitingly with each rise of her chest, was designed, surely, to taunt him.

Carefully Damen slid from the bed, propping a pillow under her arm and cheek, telling himself he didn't really want her to wake. Because Stephanie would wake full of questions.

Questions he had no desire to answer.

Questions about how their relationship would change now they were lovers.

Loping to the wardrobe, Damen gritted his teeth. The answer was simple. There was no change. Not in any material way. They'd go on as before except—here he allowed himself a satisfied smile—that when they were alone they could indulge their taste for passion. He was pretty sure after last night that Stephanie, so sensual and passionate, would be eager for that.

But that would be only in the privacy of their bed. Nothing else was different. She wasn't his girlfriend. There'd be no long-term relationship, no matter how phenomenal the sex.

Damen grabbed swim shorts and a towel. He'd take an early dip and give her some privacy when she woke. She'd appreciate that.

And it would signal that nothing significant had altered. She was smart. She'd understand he wouldn't make promises he had no intention of keeping. Promises that might lead a woman to believe in happy endings.

No fear of that with Stephanie, despite the surprise of her virginity. She was here solely for the money. She'd made no bones about that. She wouldn't start dreaming of a wedding ring just because they'd enjoyed sex.

Which meant, he realised as he dragged the shorts on, that she really was the perfect woman. Sexy, passionate and short-term.

Damen smiled and let himself out into the sunshine. It was going to be a glorious day.

Where was she?

Damen stalked along the path to the main house, his brow knotted as he scanned the terrace where last night guests had danced till late. It was empty and tidy too, as if an army of helpers had cleared away last night's detritus.

She must be here. There was no other possibility.

When he'd returned to the guest house it had been empty, the bed tidy, Stephanie's bag packed beside it. But there'd been no sign of her. Only the lingering aroma of coffee in the air, making his nostrils twitch.

Damen had returned warily. He'd enjoyed his morning swim, then, since it was early, had swum to the *Amphitrite* to put in an hour's work on the computer. An hour had become two but he'd known Stephanie would be exhausted after last night. *He'd* been exhausted, but so energised with his brain on overload, rest had been out of the question.

Besides, he admitted to a lingering doubt about whether she'd see their situation with quite the same clarity he did. Women could be emotional and it would be no surprise if, the morning after losing her virginity, Stephanie was a little clingy.

He should never have had sex with her, not after discovering she was still innocent, sexually at least. But abstinence had been impossible by the time he'd tasted her lips.

He'd returned to the guest house wondering if he approached an emotional battleground.

Only to find that, far from clinging unbearably, Stephanie had deserted him!

Pain arced through his jaw and he realised he was grinding his teeth.

He didn't want her clinging but he didn't expect her to disappear. What if he'd wanted to discuss this development in their relationship? What about laying out new ground rules? Had she no consideration?

He pushed open the door to Manos's home and followed the sound of voices.

Steph looked up from the laptop as Clio offered another plate of goodies. Baklava this time, dripping with sweet syrup. 'Truly, I couldn't eat any more.'

'Nonsense. You worked hard helping out, which you shouldn't have done, being a visitor.'

'I was glad to help. It was nice to be involved.'

She'd arrived at the big house to find Clio, her mother and Damen's mother putting things to rights after the caterers had finished the heavy work of clearing up.

It had been a relief to see Clio's warm smile, and accept her offer of breakfast with the three women in the massive kitchen.

Steph had felt so very alone this morning.

She'd told herself she was being overly emotional. Of course she hadn't expected Damen to be there, waiting to share breakfast with her.

Or hold her in his arms as he'd done last night.

She'd woken to unaccustomed aches in places she'd never ached. Not badly, just a gentle throb that reminded her of how they'd spent the night.

It was stupid to want those strong arms holding her close to the comforting thud of Damen's heart. Stupid to long for his hoarse endearments in Greek that melted her insides, for that sense of oneness that had transformed a physical act into something wondrous.

Steph should be grateful he'd left early and she'd had the guest house to herself. There'd been no stilted morning-after conversation. She'd been able to take a leisurely bath and make strong, sweet coffee to help banish the lingering wisps of fantasy.

Because it had been fantasy. A night of glorious passion in the arms of her perfect lover.

But now it was a new day. The passion was gone and so was her lover. Damen wasn't perfect and nor was she. She'd made the massive mistake of giving in to desire, telling herself she could enjoy simple sex then walk away.

Now she realised there was no such thing as simple sex. Not for her, and not with Damen.

'Try it at least,' Clio urged. 'Mama made it to a family recipe.'

Steph took a spoonful and glorious flavours exploded in her mouth. 'This is stunning.'

From the other side of the kitchen Clio's mother beamed. 'I'm glad you like it. It's the least I can do, especially as you're doing me this big favour.' She nodded to the laptop in front of Steph on the marble island bench. 'If I can get away for a little while, maybe even persuade Manos…' She shrugged. 'You have no idea how much that would mean.'

Steph looked at the worry lines marking the older woman's face and remembered Manos's dark eyes flashing with suppressed temper yesterday. Damen had said Manos would make his whole family's life miserable if he didn't get his way. It seemed he'd been doing just that. Even beautiful Clio looked tired and drawn.

Suddenly Steph was glad she'd agreed to Damen's scheme to rescue Clio from her father's machinations.

But she could do more. 'I think I've got the perfect place for the quiet holiday you wanted. It's in a scenic part of Italy, not crowded with tourists yet gorgeous and utterly peaceful. I found it for clients recently and they loved it.' She turned the laptop.

'Is that a convent?' The women crowded close.

'Yes, but the accommodation is luxurious. It's a guest house in the grounds and no tourists are allowed, only the nuns and their guests. There are views to the lake and mountains plus a walled courtyard full of roses.' Steph scrolled through photos, pleased to see her audience's excitement. 'It's a short walk to town, where there are restaurants and a supermarket if you want to self-cater.' Manos might be wealthy but his wife enjoyed cooking.

'The comforts of home,' Clio murmured, 'without the stresses.'

Her mother nodded. 'It looks amazing. How did you know about it?'

'It's what I do. I'm a travel advisor and I specialise…specialised in tailoring unique holiday experiences. Mainly at the luxury end of the market.'

'Specialised, past tense?' Clio asked as the two older women focused on the photos. 'What happened?'

Steph shrugged. 'It's a tough time in the travel industry. Lots of people don't think they need professional help when they can trawl the internet themselves.'

Clio tilted her head, as if considering. 'But if you were working at the luxury end of the market…?'

Steph met her questioning gaze and finally nodded. It

wasn't a secret really, even if she didn't usually like discussing it. 'I came unstuck in a business venture.'

'Oh, rotten luck. The business model wasn't sound?'

Steph knew Clio was running her own start-up company and didn't take offence at her direct question. 'Oh, it was sound. Sadly my partner wasn't.'

She turned as Manos and Damen entered the kitchen, Manos speaking Greek and gesturing emphatically.

Steph's skin prickled as she met Damen's unblinking green stare.

Last time he'd seen her they'd been naked in bed.

She sat straighter, wishing she had more than palazzo pants and a slinky top to keep her safe from that heated gaze. He only had to look at her and her skin heated to a fiery blush.

Could everyone tell? Did they all know that she and he…?

Belatedly she stopped her runaway thoughts. Of course no one else knew she'd given Damen her virginity last night. Or that she'd spent hours learning how dangerous a patient, generous, potently desirable man could be to her equilibrium. As far as the world was concerned, she and Damen were already lovers, even if Clio suspected otherwise.

Steph drew a breath and tried to tame her racing pulse. She nodded to both men. 'Good morning. Have you come to join us for coffee?'

The morning tested Damen's patience.

He wanted, desperately, to get Stephanie alone. He'd told himself he needed to clarify with her that nothing had changed, that she had no expectations beyond their contract. Yet to his chagrin it seemed there was no need. She treated him with a casual friendliness that should have pleased him, yet instead irked.

Or maybe he wanted to get her alone so they could revisit some of last night's more spectacular moments. Since waking he'd been unable to concentrate fully on anything but the memory of her satiny skin, her sighs of pleasure and the exquisite delight she'd offered him.

But every attempt to be alone with her was thwarted. By Clio and her mother offering food and coffee. By Manos, eager to talk business. By the interested gleam in his own mother's eyes as she looked from Damen to Stephanie and back again, clearly wondering if there was more to their relationship than he'd let on.

Obviously he wasn't the only one to notice Stephanie's delightful blush when their eyes met. It was the only hint that anything had changed between them.

Such as him taking her virginity in the night.

That knowledge throbbed through him every time he saw her looking cool and exasperatingly sexy in jade-green silk and those wide, floaty trousers that made him think of veils and beds and sex.

Damen considered himself a modern man, not hung up on old traditions. Yet to his surprise, the knowledge he'd been Stephanie's first lover branded itself on his psyche. He felt...engaged. Protective. Possessive.

He wanted to haul her away to somewhere private where he could keep her for himself.

Which didn't make sense when he'd already told himself nothing had altered between them.

By the time they finally finished their goodbyes, late in the afternoon, and headed for the yacht, Damen's patience hung by a thread.

He should have been pleased that Stephanie didn't attempt to talk on the walk to the beach, or the short trip to the yacht. There were no fluttering eyelashes, no hand on his arm as she leaned close to whisper in his ear. None of the tactics previous lovers had used to manufacture an illusion of emotional intimacy. Instead she seemed interested in everything but him. The colour of the water. The view of the island. The silver flash as a school of fish passed them. Even her phone, as if she had urgent business to conduct.

Which reminded him. Her partner. Who was that? He'd caught the phrase as he walked into the kitchen. He'd been listening to Manos but, as usual, when Stephanie was near, Damen's attention veered straight to her.

Who was this partner? He couldn't have been a lover, since only Damen could claim that role. Yet dissatisfaction niggled. He needed to know more.

When they stepped onto the deck Damen took Stephanie's arm and guided her into the privacy of a sitting room. For an instant she looked as if she'd protest, but only for an instant. She must realise there was no point trying to avoid this discussion.

He waited till the door was closed and Stephanie stood by the window, as if drawn to the view of the island.

Damen was drawn to the view of her. Utterly alluring despite the tight set of her shoulders. Was she going to make trouble after all?

'Are you okay?'

It wasn't what he'd planned to say. It surprised her too, for she swung to face him, eyes wide.

'Of course. Don't I look it?'

What she looked was sumptuously inviting. Her slender curves showed to advantage in that outfit and her skin had a healthy glow.

Was she embarrassed? Nervous under his scrutiny?

Her chin lifted and her eyebrows too, as if challenging him.

'You look fine.' Her eyes narrowed and he hurried on. 'More than fine.' Damen cursed his sudden inability to articulate. 'We need to talk.'

Did he imagine that Stephanie tensed? Her mouth drew into a flat line, as if she didn't want to hear what he had to say.

'Go on.'

Damen stuck his hands in the pockets of his jeans. Did he start by finding out how she felt physically after last night? Or come straight to the point and reiterate that their agreement hadn't changed?

He opened his mouth and heard himself say, 'Tell me about your partner.'

'Sorry?' She definitely stood straighter this time, arms curving around her waist in a defensive gesture.

So the guy *was* important to her. Damen had sensed it. 'Earlier today you said something about a partner. I want to know about him.'

'Why? He has nothing to do with this…us…' She made a wide, arcing gesture.

'I don't want any loose ends that might complicate things. We've still got six weeks together and I don't want any murky surprises.'

Steph bit her lip. Murky surprises. That was one way to describe Jared. He'd wrecked her life and even now she couldn't be rid of him. Not with Damen standing there like the lord of all he surveyed, demanding she lift the lid on her private life.

Disappointment was a swirling, bitter pool in her stomach.

What did she expect? That after last night Damen would turn to her with affection in his eyes? Or at least softness?

That he'd want to be alone with her to make love again? Because, like her, he felt bound together by this spell, even when they were surrounded by others?

Except it wasn't making love, it was sex.

Yet every time she'd met his eyes today she'd felt a great whump of emotion slam into her, like the roar of a bonfire igniting in a rush of flame. Heat trickled through her at the connection they shared, the connection no one else seemed to have noticed.

She was deluded. There was no connection. Last night

meant nothing to him. She wouldn't allow herself to be so pathetic as to reveal how much it had meant to her.

'You needn't worry. He's out of my life. I'll never see him again.'

'Nevertheless, I need to know.' He paused, expectant. Finally he added, 'I'll treat what you tell me in confidence. I just need to know nothing from your past will derail our... arrangement.'

Clearly her word wasn't good enough.

Steph bit back the words of hurt cramming onto her tongue.

But a look at Damen's set jaw and hard eyes told her he wouldn't back down. Besides, what did it matter? She was past the stage of caring what he thought of her gullibility. She'd laid herself wide open to him last night, not just physically, but emotionally too, and he didn't give a damn. There'd been no tenderness today, no acknowledgement. Nothing.

It left her feeling hollow. Which was good, because the alternative, to feel upset that he took what had happened last night for granted, would put her in an untenable position.

Suddenly Damen's lack of sensitivity felt like a blessing in disguise. If he didn't care then she didn't have to either.

'What do you want to know?'

He blinked and for a moment she could almost believe she'd discomfited him. Only for a moment.

'Everything. Who he is, what he is to you. What he did.'

Steph swallowed, her throat gritty. 'Not much, then.'

Yet had locking the past away like a shameful secret helped her deal with it? It wasn't as if she'd done anything wrong. Besides, with the money she was earning from Damen she had the power to undo the damage, financially if not personally. It would take a long time to trust again.

She swung away towards the bank of windows. Already the island was slipping away, the big yacht gathering speed as it headed for open water.

'His name's Jared and he was my boss. He managed a travel agency in Melbourne, though he didn't own it.'

'Just your boss?'

Steph frowned at the terse question but didn't bother turning. She kept her eyes on the creamy arc of sand that fringed the bay and the bright sparkle of sunlight on water. A couple of seabirds wheeled, pale against the brilliant blue sky.

'I looked on him as a mentor. Later he was my business partner.' She swallowed a bitter tang.

'You went into business together?'

Did he have to sound so surprised? 'I'm excellent at what I do. I brought in more business than anyone else in the team. Travel is my passion.' She paused, 'Well, other people's travel. I haven't done much myself.'

'You're a travel agent who hasn't travelled? I thought that was a perk of the job, trying out fabulous holiday destinations.'

Steph shrugged. 'I've travelled in Australia but not overseas. There was never time. I was always working.' Putting money aside for a secure future. 'Exploring the world was my dream. I almost went to South America but Gran got sick and...'

She stopped. He didn't need to know about Gran's cancer scare.

'So you became partners. In a new agency?'

Steph nodded. 'It was to specialise in bespoke, luxury travel. That's what I'm good at.' What she'd *been* good at. Who knew if she'd work in that field again?

Damen didn't say anything, just waited, and suddenly Steph wanted this over. 'We signed an agreement, pooled our resources, secured a loan and...' She stepped closer to the windows, putting out her hand to the wall of glass. 'He was going to put a deposit down on our new premises but instead he disappeared.'

'He had an accident?' Damen's voice came from just

over her shoulder and she turned to meet his stare. It was steady and unemotional.

'No accident. He simply took off. He cleared out the money we'd borrowed, the money I'd put up, even…' She stopped then shrugged. It was strangely cathartic telling the tale. Why not continue? 'I'd introduced him to my gran. What I didn't know was that he persuaded her to invest a chunk of her savings.' Steph dragged in a deep breath. 'The police are looking for him.'

Dark green eyes bored into her. 'That's why you wanted cash up front.'

He didn't sound happy. He sounded disapproving, as if she'd done something wrong, instead of being left high and dry by a fraudster.

Steph folded her arms again. 'It is. You have a problem with that?'

His brow furrowed. 'You should have told me.'

'Why? So you could lecture me on financial risk?' A flicker of familiar flame shot through her. 'I did everything right, everything by the book. How was I to know Jared would run when he got the cash?'

She shook her head. 'No, don't answer that. I'm sure you'd tell me I should have checked his background better, should have somehow divined he was a crook. Even though he had no criminal history.'

Steph swung away and stared at the fast-receding island. Would they return to Athens now? To days spent alone then evenings where Damen showed her off like a trophy? She shivered and rubbed her hands up her arms.

'Is there anything else? If not I'd like to go and lie down. It's been a…tiring couple of days.'

She felt him behind her, so close his warmth seeped into her. Even now, with her nerves jangling, she had a fantasy that he'd lean forward, put his arms around her and hold her close. Tell her he was sorry about what had happened with Jared. Tell her he was sorry they hadn't spent the day together because what he'd wanted, more than anything, was to be alone with her.

Because last night had been special.

She was special.

'Stephanie, I—'

'No!' Those couple of syllables didn't reveal any of the tenderness she'd come to crave last night. 'Not now. I need to rest.'

She spun on her heel and marched to the door. She'd had enough of men, and of Damen Nicolaides. She needed time alone.

CHAPTER TEN

DAMEN JABBED THE PUNCHBAG. Left, left, right. The quick blows should relieve the tension grabbing his shoulders and chest.

Not tonight. He'd been in the gym for forty minutes and was still wound too tight.

He turned away, unlacing the boxing gloves and scrubbing his face with a towel.

The problem was Stephanie and the nagging feeling he'd done the wrong thing.

He should have trusted his instincts. Not the familiar voice of caution that urged him to keep his distance, but the one that wanted to sweep her into his arms and his bed and keep her there.

He'd made a tactical error keeping his distance. It was clear she didn't want anything to do with him. He'd missed his chance for more intimacy. Strangely though, that wasn't the worst. The worst was knowing she was hurting and he was part of that hurt because he'd let her down.

Clio would say he felt this way because of his managing personality, because he'd shouldered responsibility for his family and the vast empire that was Nicolaides Shipping at a young age. Damen wasn't so sure. This felt different.

Stephanie wasn't family, yet he felt...

Damen shook his head. Better to stick to facts than feelings. Fact one. Last night had been phenomenal, and instead of thanking Stephanie, and looking after her when he guessed she was physically sore and possibly feeling out of her depth, he'd left her at first light then found excuses to keep away.

Fact two. She'd more than fulfilled her part of their bargain. Not only had she played her part in public but today she'd gone beyond what was necessary, helping Clio and her mother with this idea of a luxury retreat in Italy and even charming Manos. He hadn't seen his aunt look so relaxed in ages.

Fact three. Stephanie wasn't a gold-digger, eager for his money. She'd needed cash to make good money stolen from her and her grandmother.

Pain tore through Damen's belly as he imagined how she'd felt, discovering her business partner was a thief. That everything she'd worked towards was gone, and her grandmother's savings too.

Damen remembered his annoyance at having to pay for Stephanie's wardrobe in Athens and felt his skin crawl. He was so used to assuming people were avaricious he hadn't considered any other option.

That was one thing, at least, he'd rectified. He'd transferred the other million dollars into her account and discreet enquiries were being made in Melbourne to ensure that would cover the business loan she'd mentioned. Technically it wasn't Damen's debt and yet he felt he owed her.

He wasn't used to feeling guilty, as if he'd done the wrong thing. There must be something he could do to make it up to Stephanie.

Damen raked the towel around his neck then stopped, an idea forming.

She wanted to travel. It was her dream. He recalled all her outings in Athens to museums and ancient ruins, to markets and landmarks. She'd spent every moment of her free time exploring the city. No doubt she'd spend the next six weeks doing the same. Unless Damen changed his plans.

A smile eased across his face as he reached for the ship's phone.

Next morning Steph woke alone.

Of course she didn't miss Damen!

Yesterday she'd hoped for even a shadow of the intimacy they'd shared. Instead Damen had interrogated her about her past as if he was more interested in Jared than their lovemaking.

Even so, her thoughts were all of Damen.

Till she opened her curtains.

Steph stared, dumbfounded, at the view. She recognised it, of course, though the iconic vista, known the world over, was usually from above, looking down to where she was.

Beyond the window the sea was the rich blue of lapis lazuli. Rising from it were cliffs of deep ochre red and dark grey, frosted along the top with a canopy of white buildings, bright in the sun.

Santorini.

She breathed deep and blinked. From here she could make out a zigzag track up the slope that she knew was popular with tourists who paid to ride donkeys along the steep, cobblestoned road. She thought of the honeymoons she'd booked here for clients, the luxury hotels with terraces that seemed to hang out over the cliffs, the perfect venue for cocktails as the sun sank into the sea. The marvellous frescoes that had been discovered at the other end of the island, remnants of an ancient civilisation that had been shattered by a massive volcanic eruption. The fabled Atlantis, some said.

Steph almost danced with excitement as she dressed and hurried from her room.

Only to skid to a stop when she found Damen emerging from his stateroom at the same time.

'You look well,' he said. 'You had a good rest?'

It was crazy to feel a flicker of exultation at the sound of his voice. The man was just making polite conversation. Yet the impact of that deep tone and his penetrating forest-green stare was real.

'I did, thank you.'

He nodded but didn't move. His brows twitched together

and Steph had the curious idea that he hesitated, as if he wasn't sure how to proceed.

Damen Nicolaides, hesitating? Not possible. Yet, instead of turning away in search of breakfast, Steph waited, heart thudding high in her throat.

He reached a hand towards her then dropped it, the furrow deepening on his brow.

'I owe you an apology, for yesterday.'

Steph felt her eyebrows lift.

His gaze drifted away then slewed back, pinning her to the spot. 'I should have been there in the morning. When you woke. What we shared was...'

Steph held herself completely still, waiting.

'... Phenomenal. And I didn't even thank you.' Again his hand rose, this time to the back of his neck, as if the muscles there were tight.

They couldn't be as tight as Steph's. She didn't want a post mortem of that night, not if it entailed this stilted conversation. Two nights ago intimacy had seemed right, perfect. But now...

'I don't need your thanks.' She turned away, preferring not to meet that searching stare. 'You're not obligated to me.'

'Stephanie.' This time his voice was urgent. He stepped close, hemming her in. 'Please listen.'

Reluctantly she turned back. Damen met her gaze steadily. 'I'm trying, very badly, to apologise.' He spread his hands. 'What we shared was special. So special it threw me. Yesterday I didn't behave well. I should have checked you were okay and—'

'Of course I was okay. It was just sex.' Her voice was too strident, as if she tried to convince herself as well as him.

'Nevertheless, I apologise for deserting you. I went off to do some work but that's no excuse for poor behaviour.'

Stephanie wished the carpeted floor would open up and swallow her. Which was worse, Damen thinking she was so fragile she needed him by her side because she'd surrendered her virginity, as if she were some Victorian maiden? Or the decadent thrill of excitement stirring inside, hearing him admit what they'd shared was special?

Because that would mean she felt the same. That she wanted more of what she'd tasted that night in Damen's arms. The idea terrified her.

'Apology accepted.'

For a long moment Damen said nothing, his stare far too unsettling.

'Why are we at Santorini?' she said quickly. 'I thought we were returning to Athens.'

Damen drew her arm through his, leading her away from the staterooms. Steph tried not to react, though the feel of his arm on hers made her nerve endings jitter and heat pool low inside. 'I changed my mind. I can work from the *Amphitrite* a bit longer. You might as well see some of the islands while you're in Greece.'

Steph rocked to a halt. 'You came here for me?'

She frowned, trying to fathom what was going on. Damen didn't change his schedule for her. *She* fitted into his world.

'What do you want, Damen?' Carefully she slipped free of his hold. 'Why are you doing this?'

Because he wants more sex.

And that's good because you do too.

Ruthlessly Steph stifled the voice in her head. She had more self-respect than to give herself to him just because he'd arranged a treat. Even if it was a wonderful treat. Even if she wanted him as much now as she had two nights ago.

Damen tilted his head as if to get a clearer view of her face. 'You're helping me enormously, performing this charade, and you went further than you needed to yesterday, helping Clio and her mother. They really do need to get away and you've got them excited at the prospect.'

Steph shrugged. 'It wasn't difficult. It's what I do.'

'But you didn't *need* to. You did it because you're a nice person.'

Strange how those simple words resonated like the most lavish praise.

'I wanted to do something for you. You said you'd never had the chance to travel and here we are on the Aegean. It seemed selfish to sail back to Athens before you'd seen more of the islands.'

Dazed, Steph stared up into that handsome face. Every time she felt she understood Damen Nicolaides he pulled the rug out from under her feet.

'Come on.' He reached for her elbow and led her down the wide passage. 'The sooner we eat, the sooner you can explore.'

They stayed at Santorini for two days and to Steph's surprise Damen took several hours off from his work each day to accompany her ashore. Steph thought he'd be bored doing tourist things, seeing ancient frescoes, clambering up and down meandering streets and stopping every few metres as she found yet another spectacular view. But never once did he reveal impatience, though he admitted he preferred visiting when the crowds were thinner.

From Santorini they cruised east, calling at Astypalaia, Kos and Symi. Steph explored quaint towns, museums and ancient ruins, and swam in crystal waters. She'd never felt more relaxed and enthralled. Each day brought new discoveries, stunning vistas, friendly people and fascinating places.

It also brought hours with Damen, not at some exclusive party, but hand in hand as he led her through narrow streets, drank thick Greek coffee in the shade of vine-covered pergolas and told her about his country.

What surprised her most was that Damen seemed at home in such simple surroundings, far from the trappings of enormous wealth. And the fact that she enjoyed being with him. Enjoyed it too much to maintain a proud distance.

Back on the yacht they dined on deck, eating sumptuous meals perfectly prepared, and watching the sun set in a glow of tangerine over the dark sea. Each night, as they sat in the candlelight, it became harder for Steph to recall why she was angry with Damen.

Especially when she discovered he'd paid the second instalment of her contracted fee. Because, he said, he trusted her to make good on her contract and act the part of his lover for another six weeks. And because he didn't want her to suffer any more because of Jared's theft. He'd been concerned to learn about the joint loan they'd taken out and her ability to service the repayments.

It was amazing how wonderful it felt to have the burden of the lost money completely lifted from her shoulders.

His gesture rocked Steph. She'd thought Damen a man who'd stick to the letter of their agreement. She'd never expected such generosity, or trust.

No one in her life had shown such faith in her. With two exceptions: Gran and Emma. Steph understood how rare it was.

That action by Damen, extravagant and unexpected, confused her. It was too big a gesture. It evoked a raft of emotions she struggled to contain. Emotions she didn't know what to do with.

It would have been simpler if Damen had made a move on her, assuming that she'd agree to have sex again, partly because, as he said, it had been phenomenal, and partly out of gratitude.

Instead she was flummoxed to find he treated her like an honoured guest. He was charming and attentive but didn't press for intimacy. When they were ashore he played the part of lover in public with his arm around her waist, or feeding her delicacies from his plate, or whispering in her ear.

Steph got almost used to it. What she couldn't get used to was the way Damen's arm would drop from around her once they boarded his yacht and there was no need for a public display of affection.

What did that say about her?

It had been a week since they'd shared a bed. A week during which she'd gone to sleep each night recalling how magical that night had been. Her mind tortured her with steamy erotic dreams that left her wide awake in the early hours, heart pumping and body aching for fulfilment.

Damen had done that to her.

Except Steph knew that wasn't right.

She'd done it. She'd opened the Pandora's Box that was sexual desire. She'd chosen to seek physical release with Damen and now she bore the consequences. The fact that he was an amazing, generous lover only compounded the problem. If he'd been selfish in bed, a total disappointment, it would have made things so much easier.

Instead the memory of him, them, drove her crazy.

She wanted him. Badly. It was worse now she knew what she was missing. Especially spending this time with Damen, seeing the best of him, enjoying every day to the full. Even the casual brush of his arm against hers sent a thrill of wanting through her.

They emerged from deep shadow and walked out into the heat bouncing off the cobblestoned square. Automatically Steph turned around and stared back up at the thick, crenellated towers soaring up against the blue sky.

'My first visit to a castle.'

'I guessed.' Damen's voice was soft in her ear.

She turned to find those deep green eyes crinkling in amusement.

'There wasn't a centimetre of it you didn't examine. Especially the mosaics.'

He was right. She'd taken hundreds of photos. The Palace of the Grand Master of the Knights of Rhodes was a stunning building. It mightn't be filled to the brim with antiques but she'd strung out their visit, poring over every detail.

Steph's lips twitched. 'You're right and you've been so patient. I owe you. What would you like in return?'

Just like that the amusement faded from his eyes, banished by a hot glitter that sent fire curling through her blood. Steph's breath snagged and her heart pounded high and hard as if it tried to leap out of her chest.

Steph knew that look. She'd seen it the night they'd gone to bed together. And every night since in her lonely bed as she relived the thrill of being naked with Damen.

She licked dry lips, his gaze following the movement. The way he watched her was so…intimate, she felt it as if he reached out to trail his fingers across her mouth.

Abruptly he looked away, surveying the streets leading from the palace into the old town of Rhodes. It was a reminder that they were in public. She noticed some phones and cameras turned their way.

Had that look on Damen's face been for show?

She couldn't believe it. When they were out together Damen smiled at her but never once had she glimpsed that hot, hungry stare that turned her insides molten.

'I'm ready for a cool drink.' His hand closed around hers, sending a quiver of excitement through her. Steph curled her fingers into his and let him lead her, not down the main street but into a picturesque alley that was blessedly cool, with high stone buildings on either side. Beaten copper pots hung outside an artisan's workshop, gleaming even in the shadows.

Damen led her down the lane, taking a side turning and then another, till they were in a street so narrow Steph could almost touch the walls on each side. Then on their left was an open door, a small, shaded courtyard with rush-bottomed chairs and tiny tables.

Minutes later she was sipping gratefully from an iced glass. But the cold drink didn't quench the heat that had erupted at Damen's blatantly possessive stare outside the palace.

It was a warm day, even in the trellised shade, even with the icy drink. But not that hot. The fiery heat came from within. She put her glass down and turned to Damen. Predictably he was already regarding her, his gaze steady but unreadable.

'What's wrong? You're not enjoying yourself now.'

The man was too perceptive. He saw things she preferred he didn't.

No, that wasn't right. Steph couldn't lie to herself any longer. She liked it when they were both on the same page. When it took just a look and they were in agreement. It happened increasingly as they spent time together and she discovered Damen was far more than a bossy tycoon. He was a man with a sense of humour, with patience and much more.

'It's not that. Visiting Rhodes is the best. I've wanted to come here for so long. And it's every bit as wonderful as I thought.'

'But?'

Steph's pulse thudded as she held his eyes.

She could prevaricate.

Or she could trust her instinct.

'Perhaps there's something else you'd like even more than exploring a medieval city.' He paused, his eyes glittering like shards of precious gems. 'I know there's something else *I* want.'

'What do you want, Damen?'

He leaned close. 'To kiss you on the lips. To take you in my arms. To make love to you.'

Steph's breath escaped in a sigh that felt like relief. 'I want that too.'

The words were barely out when he stood, drawing her up beside him, tossing some money onto the table.

His mouth curved into a smile that threatened to unstring her knees. 'Then what are we waiting for, *agapi mou*?'

* * *

If he'd cared about such things Damen would have been annoyed at his total lack of cool as he strode through the winding streets of old Rhodes, back to the harbour. A couple of times Stephanie almost had to trot to keep up, but she didn't complain. Far from it. Her eyes glowed in anticipation, and whenever he glanced at her beside him it was all he could do not to scoop her up in his arms and break into a run.

She was so deliciously alluring. Damen couldn't believe how lucky he was.

They made it back onto the yacht in a breathless rush that made him feel like a reckless teenager. Except that wasn't quite right. Oh, the rampant lust was there, but beneath it was something else. Caring, admiration, something deeper than he'd felt in his youthful testosterone-fuelled amours.

Damen didn't release her hand as they marched through the yacht to his stateroom. The door swung shut and he turned to face Stephanie.

Her breasts rose rapidly as if, like him, she had trouble capturing enough air. Her eyes were wide with a saucy excitement that drilled heat straight to his loins.

'You wanted to kiss me.'

'Yes.' His voice emerged as a rasp.

'I wish you'd hurry up. It's been so long.'

Beneath her bodice Stephanie's nipples peaked in invitation. His body tightened.

'I want more than that.' Why he held back he didn't fully understand. To be sure she needed this as much as he did? He couldn't be the only one to feel this desperation. 'I want everything. Once I touch you…' He spread his hands.

Stephanie smiled. A sultry smile that lifted the corners of her mouth and shimmered in her gold-toned eyes. It was bewitching. So must Circe have smiled on Odysseus, luring him. It was hard to believe that a week ago Stephanie had been a virgin.

Damen's hands cupped her cheeks as he took her mouth, plundering deep into her sweetness, sealing her lips with his.

It was everything he remembered and more. He was only dimly aware of their surroundings as he backed her across the room till her legs touched the bed and he tumbled them both onto it.

Stephanie was all satiny limbs, ardent mouth and soft, eager body. Her fingers ripped at his shirt as he shoved her skirt up.

The next moments were a blur of building excitement. His shirt came off, and then his belt. Stephanie's lacy underwear came away in his hand with one forceful tug. The sound of it ripping fed a frenzy for completion that he only just managed to leash.

'Condom,' he gasped, forcing himself to move away.

Stephanie's hands were busy with his trousers as he reached for the bedside table, tearing a packet open with his teeth. Seconds later, sheathed, he settled between her bare legs, her skirt rucked up beneath his bare torso, her eyes heavy-lidded in anticipation.

She was glorious.

Damen made himself pause, hefted a breath that felt like agony as his lungs heaved.

A hand between her legs confirmed she was ready. He palmed her thigh, smooth and supple, and lifted it high. She lifted the other one too, hooking it over his bare hip, and something dived deep in his belly. It was a swooping sensation that heralded the end of his control.

Damen lowered his head and took her mouth again, glorying in the way she opened for him, like a flower to sunshine. He tilted his hips, finding the spot he needed and moving slowly, inexorably, alert to any sign of discomfort. Stephanie gasped against his mouth, lifted her pelvis and wrapped her legs tight around his hips, locking him to her.

He had a moment to glory in the perfection that was

their joining. But only a moment. For he needed to move, withdraw and glide back again, harder this time and faster.

Stephanie's breath expelled in a soft *oof* of air against his lips as her hands clawed his bare shoulders.

Another thrust, this time met by a perfectly timed lift of her hips that sent flickering sensation from his groin to his spine and up to the back of his skull where his skin pulled tight. Everything pulled tight.

'Stephanie,' he growled, turned on even by the sound of her name on his tongue.

Her palms lifted to his cheeks as she put her mouth to his and bit his lower lip.

Liquid heat seared him, incinerating control.

He gathered her close, angling till he felt Stephanie's giveaway judder of response, then thrusting home again and again until she broke apart in his arms and he fell with her into the vast, consuming wave of ecstasy.

Damen held her tight, thoughts disintegrating under that powerful onslaught.

As he slowly came back to himself, Damen had enough sense to roll onto his back so as not to crush her. He took Stephanie with him, cradling her.

It took a long time for his brain to crank into gear. When it did he was torn between satisfaction and consternation.

Because he was certain of one thing. He wanted more than six weeks with Stephanie. Their allotted time wouldn't be nearly enough to make the most of this explosive attraction.

Inevitably his mind went to Ingrid, who'd seduced his younger self with sex and a display of affection that had been as false as her promises.

Ingrid, who'd made him dance to her tune, all the way, almost, to the altar.

As ever, his thoughts slewed away from that. There'd be no altar, no marriage in Damen's future. That was the one thing of which he was absolutely sure. The very thought made him break into a cold sweat. Because tangled with that thought was the memory of the tragedy he'd created, which affected his family to this day.

Damen wasn't certain what this connection to Stephanie meant for his well-ordered life, but he wasn't stupid enough to ignore something so profound. So pleasurable.

His lips curved in a lazy smile as he smoothed his hand over her damp, flushed skin and she arched beneath his touch, her sated body responsive even now.

So it was settled. He'd keep Stephanie with him beyond the term of their contract. He'd talk to her about it later. As soon as he worked out the terms of a new arrangement that would satisfy them both.

CHAPTER ELEVEN

STEPHANIE'S PULSE THROBBED so fast and hard she put a hand out to the door jamb, steadying herself. She was light-headed, but only, she assured herself, because she was nervous. More nervous than she'd ever been in her life.

One slow breath. Another.

They didn't help much.

Nothing would help, till she could dismiss the suspicion that had gnawed at her the last few days.

She'd left Rhodes in a rosy haze of delight. Stephanie had barely been aware of their surroundings, so wrapped up was she in Damen. Even his apology about returning to Athens for necessary meetings hadn't punctured her happiness.

They took several days sailing to the capital and spent most of the time together. When Damen worked, Steph caught up on her sleep. Which was just as well, since Damen usually woke her with the devil in his eyes and seduction in those clever hands.

Increasingly Steph wondered where this relationship might lead. For, great as the sex was, it *was* a relationship. That, more than anything, was what had taken her unawares. Sexual compatibility she'd been prepared for, but this…this was more.

They talked, sharing information about themselves, often small things, it was true, but it felt as if she was finally coming to understand this complex man and he her. He even told her about his sisters, clearly proud of their achievements. They laughed and found pleasure in each other's company, even when they were too exhausted to make love. Or when she was. Damen had a stamina that astounded her, but he tempered it with concern for her wellbeing, as if she were still an untried innocent.

Innocent! Her mouth tightened as she surveyed the sitting room of his penthouse. It was designer-elegant with sculptures and other artworks that could have graced a museum. The morning view over Athens was stupendous and even the floral arrangements cost more than she'd spend in a week on food in Melbourne.

What she and Damen shared felt wonderful, so wonderful she didn't want to question too closely where it might lead. As if by doing so she'd tempt fate to end it. Yet in the cold, hard light of day some might look at this arrangement and say he'd bought her company.

Steph's stomach clenched and nausea stirred.

No! That wasn't what this was.

This relationship was about mutual attraction and respect. Despite the money he'd paid her for the charade, in their *real* relationship they were equals. Each giving freely of themselves. Neither expecting nor demanding anything long term.

Long term...

Another unsettling swirl of nausea.

Steph straightened. It was time to scotch the anxiety that had been nibbling away at her since she realised her period was late.

She looked at the pregnancy kit she'd bought from the chemist down the road as soon as it opened. It was just a precaution. The chances of pregnancy were ninety-nine point something per cent against, since Damen had used a condom every time.

Of course it would be a false alarm.

'I gather congratulations are in order.' Christo's voice on the end of the line didn't sound congratulatory. It sounded terse.

'Sorry?' Damen turned his back on the now empty conference table and strode to the windows looking out on the sea, darkening as the sun set. The headquarters of Nicolaides Shipping faced the harbour of Piraeus, a reminder of the company's focus and the source of its vast wealth. 'Are you back from your honeymoon already?'

'No. But Emma will be concerned when she reads the reports so I thought I'd get the story from you first.'

Damen frowned. 'You've lost me. What story?'

'You don't know?'

'Christo, I don't have time for guessing games. I've got my hands full with major negotiations.'

He rolled his shoulders. That last meeting had been long and trying, but his plans to re-establish his firm's shipbuilding capacity in Greece might finally come to fruition. In his father's day all that had moved offshore to places where costs were cheaper. Damen was determined that at least some of that work would return to his own country, his contribution to the local economy.

'You and Stephanie. You're in the press.'

'Is that all?' Damen smiled as he thought of Stephanie. Persuading her to be his companion was surely his most brilliant idea.

Manos had backed off. Clio was ecstatic. But most important of all was Stephanie herself. He couldn't recall the last time a woman had made him feel so good. So full of anticipation just at the thought of seeing her at the end of the day.

He'd known she was special from the start. The attraction between them was explosive and showed no signs of diminishing. He liked spending time with her out of bed too. She was bright and fun and genuine and he wanted her to stay in Greece past the end of their contract. He wasn't foolish enough to expect what they had to last. Damen knew not to expect permanency. But for the foreseeable future...

'All? You don't sound fazed.'

'Of course not.' He made himself focus on Christo. 'Stephanie...' He paused. He preferred not to mention the money she'd accepted from him. Christo might get the wrong idea about her. 'She agreed to stay with me for a couple of months. To play the part of my girlfriend. I was getting heat from another quarter to marry and you know that's impossible.'

'Is it?'

Damen frowned. Christo was one of the few who knew the details of his past. Though even he didn't know it all. 'Of course. You know I'll never marry.'

Christo muttered something that sounded like a curse. 'You're saying the latest reports aren't true? I can tell Emma the gossip online is wrong?'

Damen hesitated. Their relationship might have begun as a charade but it was more now. Damen planned to ask Stephanie to stay with him, past the expiry of their agreement, until their passion died a natural death. Something that burned so brightly must destroy itself eventually. But there was no reason they shouldn't make the most of it while it lasted.

'Stephanie and I…enjoy each other's company.'

'And?'

'Isn't that enough?' No doubt gossip was ramping up because Damen didn't have live-in lovers. He valued his privacy too much and didn't trust women not to get the idea they could worm their way into his life permanently. But Stephanie was different.

'So you're sharing a bed. All the world knows that, except Emma, so far. She'll get her hopes up about the pair of you when she finds out. But this new rumour…'

'What new rumour?' Damen frowned. Why were they wasting time discussing paparazzi gossip?

'You really don't know?' There was a strange note in his friend's voice. 'Then it's unfounded gossip. I knew you'd never—'

'Never what?' Damen spoke through gritted teeth.

There was a pause, long enough to hear his pulse beat once, twice, three times.

'Get her pregnant. A story broke today that you're expecting a child together.'

Shock jabbed Damen, before reason took over. He laughed, assuring his friend that the gossip-mongers were inventing a story where there was none.

His good humour lasted until, trawling through so-called news reports, he saw a photo of Stephanie on the street outside his apartment, smiling directly into the camera. Below it, the article said:

An excited Stephanie Logan, Damen Nicolaides' girlfriend, confided it was early days, with the pregnancy only a few weeks along.

Stephanie felt trapped. She didn't want to go out after what had happened on the street this morning, when a man had shoved a camera in her face. But nor did she feel like asking if Damen's driver could take her sightseeing.

Not when her world had just turned upside down.

Pregnant. She was pregnant with Damen's child.

Even now, hours after seeing the pregnancy test results, she couldn't process it.

How could she be pregnant? Yet she'd heard stories about people who'd conceived despite protection.

Her hand crept to her abdomen. Was it true? Was a new life forming there? She told herself she wouldn't be certain till she'd had the test confirmed by a doctor, yet she *felt* different. When she crossed her arms her breasts were sensitive. That, combined with her late period, had sent her scurrying to the chemist.

It had been embarrassing, explaining to a stranger what she wanted, but she'd needed help to find the kit and translate the instructions.

Maybe she'd done it wrong? Maybe it was a false positive?

She was clutching at straws.

Steph planted her hands on the railing of the penthouse terrace and tried to still her whirling thoughts. She had no plan for the future. All she felt was shock.

And a tiny seed of what might be excitement.

Because, no matter how unexpected, there was something thrilling as well as terrifying about the prospect of a baby.

She narrowed her eyes against the glare of late sun on the pale city.

All her life she'd told herself she wouldn't make her mother's mistakes. She'd be independent financially and emotionally. No struggling as a single mum to make ends meet. It was true that, thanks to Damen's money, she was able to repay the money she owed, and her gran's money, and have some left for herself.

But she'd still be a single mother.

An unemployed single mother. Despite the cushion of cash in her account, she'd have to find a job eventually.

Steph dragged in a deep breath, filled with fear.

It wasn't simply fear about the burdens of bringing up a child. Selfishly it was as much about herself and Damen. About what this news meant for them. She hadn't let herself hope for permanency with him. But the prospect of losing him now made her feel hollow with pain.

This news would end their idyll.

She wrapped her arms around herself. Was it selfish to worry about that when she should be worrying about the new life inside her?

The undeniable truth was that Damen *mattered* to her, far more than she'd let herself believe. *They* mattered as a couple. What they had was so fragile, so new, yet it felt profound. Not like a fling at all.

For her.

But for him?

'Enjoying the sunset?' Damen's voice reached out from

the shadows, curling like a lasso around her middle and drawing tight.

Steph swung round, a relieved smile tugging at her lips. Despite her nerves, despite everything, she felt better now Damen was here.

What did that say about how far she'd come from the fiercely independent, fiercely distrustful woman who'd arrived in Greece last month?

Steph feared it said everything.

The way she felt about Damen—

'Nothing to say, Stephanie?' He stepped further onto the terrace, the sunset burnishing his face to stark bronze. He looked like an ancient warrior, proud and relentless. A shiver scuttled down her spine.

This wasn't the lover she'd known the last few weeks.

It wasn't even the managing billionaire who'd expected her to fall in with his outrageous plans.

Steph looked into blazing eyes that nevertheless made her bones frost. This was a stranger. A man she didn't know. Something almost like fear stirred at the base of her spine.

'Damen. I didn't expect you yet.' He'd mentioned late meetings.

'I found I couldn't keep away.' His lips curled at the corners, but instead of forming a smile his expression looked more like a grimace.

'What's wrong? Has something happened?' She walked towards him, thinking of his mother, of Clio and the others she'd met at the wedding. Or maybe he'd had bad news about one of his sisters.

'I thought you could tell me.' He paused, his brow drawing down in the middle. 'Have you got news for me?'

'How did you know?' She goggled up at him, stunned.

'Call it a hunch.'

Steph frowned. She'd told nobody. Even without the time difference from Greece, she couldn't talk to Gran about this yet, or Emma, who was still on her honeymoon. First she had to come to grips with the news. And talk to Damen. She hadn't looked at her phone all day, worried that if she started searching for information on pregnancy she'd scare herself silly.

'A hunch?' She shook her head. 'How—?'

'What's your news, Stephanie?'

Dubiously she stared at him. Every sense told her something was wrong. He couldn't know about the baby. Yet...

'You might want to sit down.'

Instead he simply folded his arms over his chest. His body language worried her. She told herself she was upset, misreading his non-verbal cues.

'Okay, then.' She drew a slow breath. 'I took a pregnancy test this morning. And it appears I'm pregnant.'

Nothing. Not a word for two whole beats of her heart.

'Appears?'

Steph frowned. He didn't look surprised.

'I *am* pregnant.' Now it came to the crunch she was sure of it. 'Though I'd like to check with a doctor.'

'How very convenient.'

She blinked and it was as if the movement dragged the scales from her eyes. For now she read Damen's expression. Anger laced with disdain.

At *her*!

Her head reared back. 'It's not my fault. You can't think I engineered this. There were two of us having sex.'

Making love, that was how it had felt, but she couldn't say that, not when he looked at her with fury in those glittering eyes.

A chill iced her to the marrow. Steph stepped back till she came up against the railing. Horrified, she told herself not to cringe. She'd done nothing wrong!

'You were the one to handle protection.'

If anything the reminder only stoked his anger. His eyes narrowed and his jaw tightened. It was a wonder steam didn't come out of his ears.

'You really think I'm so gullible?' His words were soft but tinged with menace.

Sternly Steph reminded herself Damen might be furious but he wasn't dangerous.

'You might not want to believe it, Damen, but it's true.' She stared up at him, refusing to be cowed by that pulsing anger. 'You might not like the surprise but I'd thought you a better man than to react like this.'

His hand sliced the air dismissively. 'Stop now. I know this is a con.'

'Sorry?' She'd expected surprise, but nothing like this.

'I know you've contrived this. You should stop while you're ahead.'

Abruptly, gloriously, it was Steph seeing red. Contrived, indeed! Did he think she'd engineered a lie to—what? Trap him into a long-term relationship?

Steph gasped as the pieces clicked into place and she realised that was exactly what he thought. The monstrous ego of the man!

It didn't matter that mere minutes ago she'd realised she…cared for him much more than she should. That the idea of ending their affair tore at her heart. She'd like to slap him for his egotistical arrogance.

Steph swung away and marched inside.

'Don't walk away from me! We haven't finished.'

Too bad. Steph refused to stand there, an unwilling target for his poisonous barbs.

She strode to the bathroom off the master bedroom, swiping the test result off the marble counter. When she turned it was to find Damen filling the doorway. He was a tall man, broad-shouldered and well-built, but anger seemed to make him even bigger. Steph didn't care. She crossed the space and shoved the plastic into his hand.

'What's this?' But his eyes were rounding as he spoke. His olive-gold skin paled a couple of shades.

'Proof.' Steph folded her arms tight across her heaving chest. 'I went to the chemist and bought a kit.'

But Damen was already shaking his head. 'Of course you've somehow got hold of a positive result. The bluff wouldn't work otherwise.'

'Bluff? I don't understand.'

His steely gaze captured hers. 'You really are a good actress, Stephanie. First class. But I know this is a lie. Otherwise why leak the news to the press? You're trying to force my hand.'

She shook her head. 'You're not making sense.' Had he had an accident? A blow to the head? But no, he looked pulsing with vibrant energy.

For answer he pulled a phone from his pocket, thumbed the screen and held it out to her.

Shock Baby Revelation for Nicolaides CEO!

That was as far as Steph got, as the words began to run together. But that was enough. That and the photo of her taken this morning.

A trembling began in her knees, turning into racking shudders. Her stomach, empty because she'd been too agitated to eat lunch, lurched. The room swayed, or maybe it was her.

Big hands grabbed her arms, half hauling, half lifting her across the room and onto the deeply cushioned seat beside the sunken bath. Damen forced her head down between her knees and slowly the awful sick feeling receded.

'Let me go.' She shook him off. 'I'm not going to be sick.'

Yet horror lingered at the back of her mouth. Steph took her time, breathing slowly, confronting the fact that her precious secret had become fodder for a sleazy press story. Eventually she realised that must be why Damen had come back looking like some merciless god seeking vengeance.

But how…?

'How did they get the story if you didn't tell them? Why did you smile for that photo if you weren't colluding with them?' His voice was hard but she saw something like concern in his assessing eyes, as if the sight of her weak and upset bothered him.

'I didn't. I smiled at the doorman to your building. He's always so friendly and today he helped me, directing me to a chemist. But as I came back to the apartment some guy with a big camera got in my way just as I was saying hi.'

She lifted the phone still clutched in her hand. Yes. It made sense. That was when the photo had been taken. By the man in the T-shirt of bilious green.

Steph frowned. 'It was him!'

'What is it? What did he do?'

Damen hunkered before her. He didn't touch her but he was so close his body heat blanketed her. She shivered, suddenly aware of how cold she felt.

'Stephanie?'

Muzzily she looked up into those brilliant eyes. If she didn't know better she'd say he looked worried. Except that would mean Damen cared when instead he thought she'd constructed a hoax and sold her story to the press.

'You think I went to the media with a story that I was pregnant? Why? For the cash they'd give for a scoop? Or to force your hand into a long-term commitment? Because you wouldn't kick me out if I was pregnant?'

Her voice was a shallow rasp but he heard her and his expression told her everything she needed to know.

Wearily she held out the phone to him then leaned back in the chair, closing her eyes. She didn't want to deal with the media stories or Damen.

'Tell me about the man, Stephanie.' His voice was soft, persuasive yet still compelling.

She wanted to yell at him, demand he leave her alone, that he go and take his massive ego with him. But she didn't have the energy. All day she'd been wound so tight and now she felt totally undone.

'Stephanie, talk to me.'

He palmed her cheek with a warm hand just as he'd done when they made love. It sent pain arrowing through her, a jab to the heart. She wrenched her head away, snapping her eyes open to glare at him.

'Don't. Touch. Me.'

Something ripped across Damen's expression, something she couldn't name and didn't want to.

'Please, Stephanie. Tell me about the man.'

She sighed. She was tempted to let him work it out himself but what was the point?

'The man with the camera, who took the photo. He wore a distinctive green T-shirt. He was there in the chemist when I was.'

'Did you talk to him?'

'No. I just spoke to the pharmacist. I needed help finding a pregnancy kit and getting instructions on how to use it.' She paused, frowning. The other guy had browsed for something in the next aisle.

'Did you tell the pharmacist anything else?'

'I didn't give him my name or yours, if that's what you're thinking.' She paused. 'I did ask if it would work in the very early stages of pregnancy because I couldn't be more than a few weeks along.'

Damen's expression changed, hard lines marking his features.

'What?'

'That's what they wrote in the press, that the…pregnancy was in the early stages.'

'So maybe they got that from the pharmacist or the man with the camera.' She sat straighter. 'They certainly didn't get it from me. I was hoping it was a false alarm, that I wasn't really pregnant.' Her voice dipped on the word as the enormity of the situation hit her. 'If I was going to tell someone it wouldn't be the press, no matter what you think.'

'I believe you.'

'Sorry?'

Sombre eyes met hers. Damen held his phone out to her. 'Is this the man you saw?'

She peered at a grainy photo. 'Different clothes but that's him.'

'He's paparazzi. He's been hanging around since we got back to Athens. Security moved him on but not effectively enough. He probably followed you from the apartment building.' Damen drew a slow breath. 'I owe you an apology.'

'You do.'

'I'm sorry, Stephanie. I shouldn't have doubted you. I should have known better.'

'You should.' It had hurt terribly that he'd jumped to such a vile conclusion about her. 'I thought we were beginning to know each other.' That had been the worst part. That he knew her now, or should, yet still he'd thought the worst.

Damen's mouth flattened, but then he nodded. 'You're right.' He drew a deep breath. 'I've spent a long time learning to be suspicious, especially of women. It's a hard habit to break. I can't tell you how sorry I am.'

Steph wanted to know why he was suspicious of women. But this wasn't the time to pursue it. She felt appallingly light-headed. Shock, she supposed.

It was as if he read her mind. 'Would you feel better lying down?'

She nodded but before she could stand Damen slid his arms around her and lifted her high against his chest. Steph didn't need to be carried. But her legs felt like overcooked pasta and, despite everything, it was comforting to rest her head against his shoulder. She didn't even protest when he took her to the master suite. She'd fight that out with him later, when she had more energy.

Damen laid her on the bed and took her shoes off, pulling a light blanket over her. It was like when she was a child and Gran had taken care of her when she got ill. Except she wasn't a child and Damen was nothing like Gran.

Then he confounded her by pressing a kiss to her brow.

'Rest now. The doctor will be here soon.'

'Doctor?' She scrambled up onto one elbow.

'You said you'd like to see a doctor. I'll feel better too. You're as white as a sheet.'

Steph lay back and watched him march out of the room. He meant it. There was concern on that wide brow and in his clenched jaw.

For her wellbeing?

Or because he needed to know for sure if she was pregnant?

To her dismay Steph discovered she wanted it to be for her. Because that would mean Damen cared.

It was dangerous, wishful thinking, the sort that could get her into trouble.

Except she was already in as deep as it went. For though she smarted at Damen's suspicions and wasn't in a forgiving mood, she'd realised something today that changed everything.

She'd fallen in love with Damen Nicolaides.

CHAPTER TWELVE

DAMEN STARED INTO the darkness. It was well past midnight and he needed sleep. Tomorrow there'd be vital negotiations and decisions. Yet sleep eluded him.

His brain raced, sifting the day's events. Confirmation from the doctor that Stephanie was pregnant, and, despite his fears at seeing her so weak, essentially well. And the unholy mess he'd made of things, shattering the trust he'd built with Stephanie.

Distrust came naturally to a man who'd been pursued all his life by those wanting a piece of his wealth. It became his default mode after Ingrid and her scheme to marry him, not for love, as she'd made him believe, but for money. The fact that fiasco—his fault for being gullible—had resulted in his father's death...

Damen's chest cramped as memories rose. But he didn't allow them to tug him into that black vortex of regret. He couldn't afford to, not with Stephanie's news. He needed to focus on the future.

His arms tightened around her, soft and trusting in his embrace. She was burrowed against him, head under his chin, her arm around his waist. It was all he could do not to wake her and lose himself in her sweet, welcoming body.

That moment this evening when she'd shied from his touch as if it were poisoned, when she'd looked at him with hurt branded in that shimmering stare...

That had pierced him to the core.

He deserved her disdain. Yet he hadn't been able to keep away. There'd be hell to pay tomorrow when she realised they'd shared a bed.

She'd been asleep when he'd entered, curled in a ball as if to protect herself from forces beyond her control. Damen had tasted guilt, like chilled metal on his tongue, knowing he was responsible for her distress.

He'd come to check on her, concerned despite the doctor's reassurances. But he'd been unable to walk away when she looked so vulnerable.

It had felt natural to strip off and get into bed, purely so he could be sure she was okay in the night. When she'd turned to him in her sleep…as she had every other night recently…of course he'd cuddled her, doing his best to assuage the hurt he'd caused.

But their closeness brought no relief.

Instead it magnified the size of their problem.

He grimaced. How skewed were his priorities to see a child as a problem?

It wasn't that he didn't like kids. It was that, after Ingrid and his fatal error in judgement, he'd known he'd never have children.

Now he would. He tried to imagine a child with his nose or the trademark Nicolaides stubbornness. Instead he saw a little girl with curls and golden-brown eyes. Stephanie holding her.

His breath snagged. Excitement stirred. A thrill of delight. And possessiveness.

He knew without a moment's doubt that he wanted this baby. Would do everything to care for and protect it.

Did Stephanie even want the child? The thought of her terminating the pregnancy made him break into a cold sweat.

Surely that wasn't likely. He couldn't imagine Stephanie taking that step.

What, then? The child was his too. He wanted to be part of its life. No. More. He wanted to be a full-time father. His family was close-knit and family ties were an ingrained part of him.

Damen had to persuade Stephanie to stay in Greece and

raise the child together. Or, if that wouldn't work, let him raise it without her.

His mind darted from one possibility to another. He could offer her money to relinquish the baby.

Right. As if that would work.

Stephanie had taken his money once but only because of her financial distress. Offering money now would set her against him. She wasn't avaricious. She was grounded, honest, honourable. She'd make a great mother.

He doubted she could be bought.

Did he even want to try?

Pain rayed through his jaw from grinding his teeth.

He needed Stephanie here, with him. Their baby deserved to have both parents.

But there was nothing to bind Stephanie here, to guarantee he'd have his child permanently.

Another contract? Without the lure of money, what could he offer to persuade her to stay?

What would cement his role as a full-time father?

He refused to consider being in his child's life for half of each year or just for holidays.

Could he appeal to Stephanie's maternal instincts? Persuade her two parents were better than one?

Stephanie shifted and Damen relaxed his hold, all the time searching for something that would bind her and their child to him.

There had to be something. If not money, then…

He grimaced as he tasted a familiar sour tang.

There was one way to secure a permanent role in his child's life.

The one thing he'd vowed on his father's grave to avoid.

Marriage.

Damen's breath whistled from his lungs and his heart set up a rough, catapulting rhythm. Nausea churned and his skin prickled as a decade of self-disgust and regret scoured him.

He couldn't do it.

There had to be another way. He had all night to find an alternative. Anything but that.

'Ochi, Baba. Ochi!'

This time Steph caught Damen's husky words. Before they'd been just a hoarse mumble of Greek. His head turned and he flung an arm across the bed.

She'd woken as the mattress moved beneath her, only to discover it wasn't the mattress but Damen. She'd been lying across him, cosily curled up in his big bed.

The room was dark and she blearily wondered how they had come to be sharing when she realised Damen was in the throes of a nightmare. He was scorching hot, as if with fever, his legs shifting restlessly as if trying to run.

She sat up and he instantly rolled away, clawing the bedding, his voice urgent, shoulders heaving.

Steph knew distress. This was real, and, despite her earlier anger, seeing him like this made her heart turn over.

Damen was controlled and strong. Even in anger he was composed. Only when they made love—

No, she wasn't going there.

'Damen.' She grabbed his shoulder, slippery with damp heat. 'Wake up.'

He turned, flinging out an arm that caught her on the elbow. He mumbled, and in the gloom she saw his ferocious scowl.

'Wake up. You're having a nightmare.' She put her other hand on his cheek, feeling bristles scratch her palm. It reminded her of the nights they'd slept together after hours of…no, not lovemaking, but sex.

She knew this man intimately, or so she'd thought. Till he'd stalked in tonight like an avenging angel.

Yet his fury hadn't lasted, had it? Only a few minutes into their argument and he'd been hunkering down before her, concerned and gentle.

Steph shook him harder. She refused to make excuses for appalling behaviour. How dared he accuse her of selling stories to the press?

Except she remembered goggling at Clio as she recounted the lengths women had gone to to snare Damen Nicolaides. Bribing hotel staff so they could wait, naked, in his bed. The short-lived paternity suit by a woman who, it was soon proved, had never even met him.

She leaned closer. 'Quick, Damen. You need to wake up!'

His eyes started open. For a long moment he stared blindly up at her. Then his hands curled around her shoulders.

'Stephanie? What is it? Are you all right?'

He sat up in a rush, his gaze darting around the room as if searching for a threat, then coming to rest on her. Those strong hands stroked down her arms.

'What is it? Are you ill? What can I do?'

And just like that, Steph's righteous indignation faded. He'd done wrong but he did care. Really care.

'Stephanie, tell me!' His urgency tugged at her heartstrings. Ridiculously she found herself blinking tears.

'I'm okay. It's you. You were having a nightmare.'

His grip tightened around her wrists. His chest rose on an audible, uneven breath.

'A nightmare.'

'You were thrashing around. It must have been a bad one.'

'Was I?' His voice sounded flat. He dropped his hands and she felt suddenly bereft. 'I apologise. I didn't mean to wake you. You need rest.'

This wasn't about her. He'd been so tortured. 'Do you have nightmares often?'

'Never.' He dragged a hand across his scalp in a gesture she knew signalled he wasn't as in control as he wanted her to believe.

'And this time?'

Damen's voice hadn't merely been agitated. He'd sounded as if his heart were being torn out.

'I don't recall.' He turned and retrieved the pillow that he'd pushed off the bed, leaving her staring at bare shoulders and the streamlined curve of his spine.

So very strong and yet, it seemed, vulnerable.

Curiosity rose. What did he dream that distressed him so? Something to do with their baby?

'I apologise for waking you, Stephanie. Shall we try to sleep?'

He had the decency at least not to lie down and assume she'd spend the rest of the night with him. He sat, hair tousled, big frame tense, watching her.

She should move to another room. Or demand he go.

She had a right to privacy.

Except she craved the comfort of Damen cradling her as much as ever.

She wanted to bridge the gulf between them, not widen it.

Silently she nodded and lay down. Damen drew a light cover over them both and sank onto the pillow beside her.

'I promise not to disturb you again.'

How could he promise that? The only way to prevent another nightmare was to stay awake all night.

She opened her mouth to ask him about it, then stopped. He wouldn't answer her questions. He'd made that clear.

But he had revealed something. She knew very little Greek but she knew *ne* was yes and *ochi* was no. She'd also heard Clio's sister calling her father *Baba*, which Steph assumed meant Dad.

Damen had been dreaming of his father, shouting, 'No, Dad, no!'

Something about his father stressed him unbearably. Something one of them had done or not done?

Was the nightmare triggered by today's news?

Steph wrapped her arms around her middle and rolled away to stare, wide-eyed, into the dark.

* * *

'I keep telling you, I'm perfectly fine. Yesterday was an aberration.' Steph saw a pulse tick at Damen's jaw but eventually he nodded.

Damen's concern was pleasant but she didn't need cosseting, or being told to rest when what she wanted was exercise. A walk or maybe a swim. After yesterday's fiasco with the paparazzi she'd content herself with a swim in the rooftop pool.

'Aren't you going to work?' They'd slept late and now lingered over breakfast on the terrace. Usually Damen had left for the office by now.

'Not today. We need to talk.'

Looking into that handsome face, tight with tension, Steph felt her stomach dip.

'I'm having the baby,' she blurted. She'd spent yesterday examining every option and knew that was non-negotiable.

'Good.' His mouth eased into a smile. 'I'm glad.'

'You are?'

Crazy that her heart thumped at his approval, or maybe just at the sight of his smile. Surely loving someone didn't make you so completely vulnerable to them? Steph was still her own woman. That wouldn't alter.

'Absolutely. Family is important. Of course I want this child.'

His starkly possessive tone simultaneously thrilled her and made her skin prickle with apprehension.

'*Our* child.' This baby wasn't his alone.

'Exactly. Our child, our responsibility.' He nodded and offered her more fresh orange juice. 'It's early, I know,' he said, 'but have you thought about the future?'

'Of course.' She'd peppered the doctor with questions about pregnancy, about diet and vitamins. Beyond that loomed the scary prospect of childbirth and motherhood. Steph didn't have much experience with babies. She had a lot to learn.

'So have I.' He paused. 'I have a proposition.'

Steph looked up from her bowl of yoghurt drizzled with honey and nuts to find him watching her closely. His smile had gone and he looked as serious as she'd ever seen him. More than serious. Grim.

Something inside plunged. Her defences rose. After yesterday she'd thought her trust in Damen had hit rock bottom. Surely he wasn't going to disappoint her again. She didn't think her bruised heart could bear it.

'A proposition?' She sat straighter, breathing carefully to slow her racing heart. 'You're not going to propose buying my child from me, are you?'

Damen inhabited a world far removed from hers. He had incredible power and money.

Damen's hand closed around her fist. '*Our* child needs both of us, Stephanie. You and me together. As its mother, you hold a very special place no one else can fill.'

Steph sank back in her chair, relief filling her. She'd got him so wrong.

Excitement rippled through her. He'd called her special, said their baby needed them both.

Tendrils of hope wound through her. She loved this man and she knew he…liked her. He was attracted. Now he spoke with respect in his voice about her being special.

Was he beginning to feel a little of what she did? Not love, but perhaps one day he'd assess his feelings and realise—

'What's your proposition?' She needed to hear, not try to guess.

Steph told herself to be calm, not to expect too much. Yet she couldn't stifle a jitter of excitement.

'That you stay in Greece, with me.' He halted, surveying her closely.

Had he registered her suddenly indrawn breath? At least he couldn't feel her fluttering pulse.

'You want me to live in Greece?'

'With me, Stephanie.' His thumb stroked the tender flesh at her wrist. Maybe, after all, he was aware of her runaway heartbeat. 'I want to marry you.'

She froze, unable to speak or even, it seemed, breathe. Her chest tightened from lack of oxygen as she stared across at Damen.

He meant it. She'd never seen him look so serious. In fact, he was frowning. New lines bracketed his mouth and his jaw was a study in tension.

Steph swallowed but couldn't dislodge the blockage in her throat.

This was when he'd tell her he didn't want to lose her. That she'd come to mean so much to him. That together, with time and a common cause in bringing up their child, they might find love.

Steph waited.

Damen's eyes met hers but there was a curious blankness in them, so different from the heat she was used to, or the charming devilry. The lines around his mouth became grooves, carving deeper as she watched.

Was he nervous? No. This wasn't the expression of a man holding his breath as he waited his beloved's response.

'You don't look happy at the idea.'

His shoulders lifted. 'This is a serious matter. It's not about happiness but doing right.' Then, as if reading her expression, he added, 'Happiness will come through our child.' He curved his lips into a smile but it didn't reassure. His face looked tight, painfully so, as if the stretched lips made his face ache.

Disappointment tasted bitter on her tongue. Disappointment and dismay.

She'd imagined that a proposal of marriage would be a happy event.

Not this one. Not with the would-be groom looking as if he tasted poison. Even his golden tan had paled. He looked almost unwell.

A proposition, he'd called it. Not a proposal.

As if this was a business deal.

'Why marry?' she eventually croaked.

Damen looked down to their joined hands. 'Many reasons. Above all, to do what's best for our baby. Children thrive in a stable home, loved by their family. We can give the baby that. I will love our child with all that I am, and I believe you feel the same.'

Piercing green eyes snared hers and Steph nodded. Already she felt protective of this new life. Soon, she guessed, it would become love.

'If we marry we can give it the support and stability it needs. We can support each other, and our families will too. Your grandmother, my mother and sisters. I'll fly your grandmother to Greece as often as she likes. Who knows, she may even settle here once you're living in the country.'

Steph tried to imagine Gran in Greece. It was generous of Damen to think of her, to realise Steph would want her support.

'I want the best for our child, Stephanie. Sharing the burdens and joys of parenthood is not only fair but also the best outcome for all of us.'

It sounded as if he was speaking about a commercial merger, not a family.

'I know it's a big thing to move to a new country. But we'll visit Australia often. If you want to pursue your business here, I'll back you, give you every support. Plus we'll travel.' His hand squeezed hers. 'That's your dream. I can make that happen. We'll go wherever you want.' He stopped and she saw calculation in his expression. 'That's the benefit of marrying a wealthy man. I can provide whatever you want.'

Except love.

Except being wanted for myself, not because of my baby.

A great hollow formed in her middle, expanding wider

and deeper till it felt as if she was nothing but a narrow layer of flesh over gaping emptiness.

Questions crowded. Why did he want marriage so badly when he must know he'd already have rights as a father? What if it didn't work? What if Damen fell in love with someone else? For as sure as her name was Logan, he wasn't in love with her.

Soon, she knew, the hurt would start.

It was starting now as she stared into a face set with determination yet almost gaunt with...what? Damen looked ill.

His proposition sounded like a company merger.

A merger he doesn't really want.

As soon as the thought rose Steph knew it was right.

He offered marriage to stake a claim for complete access to the baby.

'You really want this child,' she murmured and had immediate confirmation from the flash of excitement in his eyes.

'Absolutely!'

Steph's insides churned in distress.

He wants the child but not you.

He doesn't want marriage but he'll go through with it to secure his baby.

'I'm sorry, Damen, I—'

'Don't make up your mind now!'

'I was about to say I need time to think.'

'Fine. Excellent.'

But it wasn't fine and it certainly wasn't excellent. Steph's heart had cracked and she feared that soon it might just shatter.

CHAPTER THIRTEEN

DAMEN HAD LEARNED to rein in impatience. Even as a CEO he occasionally had to bide his time, wait for the right moment to seal a deal.

This was one of those times. Stephanie was coming to terms with her pregnancy. She wasn't her usual bright, forthright self. Even allowing for shock and the life changes she faced, he worried at her lacklustre mood.

His own mood was best not examined. He got through each day focusing on what needed to be done.

He'd begun searching for a family home. An island within commuting distance. Somewhere with a private beach and large garden. Stephanie might like overseeing the renovations. Or perhaps they'd build. That could be the project to drag her out of the doldrums.

Damen devoted himself to persuading her to accept him by showing her how good life would be for her here.

He spirited her away for an overnight stay on picturesque Hydra. In Athens he took her not to crowded social events, but to his favourite restaurants where the food was exquisite and the ambience delightful.

Knowing her interest in his country's culture, he organised a special night visit to the Benaki Museum, a jewel in the crown of Athens' attractions, where the curator led them on a private tour. For the first time in days Stephanie was animated, inspecting exquisite ancient gold jewellery, hand-stitched traditional clothes and embroideries, art works and other treasures.

He thought about buying her lavish gifts, jewellery and clothes, a car, but decided to wait. He sensed gifts wouldn't sway her.

But what would?

What would make her say yes?

After days of Stephanie avoiding meaningful discussions, the time had come. Damen needed an answer. He was strung so tight at the looming prospect of marriage that it felt as if he might just snap. He barely slept and when he did he was haunted by dreams.

He found her burrowed into the corner of a sofa, a magazine on her lap.

'We need to talk, Stephanie.'

Her head came up as he took a seat opposite, and that was when Damen saw the phone at her ear.

'I have to go, Emma,' she said into the phone. 'I'll call later. I'm fine, truly.' She ended the call, eyes wary. 'What is it, Damen?'

Her eyes were shadowed. She didn't appear like a woman excited to spend her life with him.

His gut clenched. He didn't want marriage either, yet he *needed* it. He *had* to persuade her.

'You haven't given me an answer.' Damen made his voice gentle. He even managed an encouraging smile.

She stared back with unwavering eyes. Her gaze drilled right through him.

'You don't really want to marry me.'

Damen sat taller. 'Of course I do! I proposed, didn't I?'

The words were less than persuasive but she'd caught him off guard. He felt himself floundering.

'That wasn't a marriage proposal, it was a business proposition.'

Was that where he'd gone wrong? Did she want flowers and candles? The trappings of romance? He delved into his pocket and brought out the ring box that had weighed him down for days. He should have produced it earlier.

He was extending his hand when she shook her head and jumped up from the sofa.

'No! Don't.'

Damen frowned. She sounded distressed, as if he'd offered her an insult instead of an honourable proposal.

He shot to his feet.

'Stephanie. *Koritsi mou*. I *do* want to marry you. To make a family for our child.'

Vehemently she shook her head 'That's just it, Damen. You're only interested in the baby. You're not even interested in sex, just fussing over me because I'm carrying your precious heir.'

He stepped forward, the ache in his chest easing. Is that what worried her? 'I've been putting your needs ahead of my own. I—'

'It's more than that.' She heaved a deep breath. 'For days I've watched you. Just as I watched you when you made your…proposition. And one thing is absolutely clear. You don't want to marry me. You looked sick to the stomach when you proposed. Even now you're unhappy. You're not an eager bridegroom.'

That was what made her hesitate?

For the first time ever Damen wished he could lie with ease. Over the years he'd become adept at hiding his feelings, but when it came to marriage the very thought scraped him raw.

'I do want to marry you, Stephanie.' Couldn't she hear the urgency in his voice?

'No, you want control over our baby. You don't want me to leave with it.'

Damen's breath snared. If she knew that, then why hadn't she walked away? She wasn't happy but she hadn't left. Which meant he had a chance to get what he wanted.

His brow corrugated. He was fumbling in the dark, missing the clue that would unlock this situation.

'This isn't about control, Stephanie. This is about caring, building a future.'

She folded her arms, the gesture both protective and defiant. 'But you don't really want marriage, or me.'

Damen's jaw jammed. They were going in circles. Of course he didn't want marriage. The very word was associated in his mind with tragedy and guilt. But he'd do what was right.

'Stephanie...' his voice sounded stretched too thin '... you're wrong. That's exactly what I want.'

'Prove it. Explain why you never intended to marry. Tell me what happened to make you look sick whenever you mention marriage.'

'I don't—'

'I need the truth, Damen. Don't you see?' Her mouth crumpled, her distress stabbing him. 'How can I trust you when there's a problem but you won't acknowledge it? How can I spend my life with you? Be honest and I can decide what to do. Tell me what happened to you.'

Her words shook him to the core.

It was one thing, an appallingly difficult thing, to speak of marriage. It was another, he discovered, to share the secret that darkened his soul.

Yet if he didn't she might leave and never come back.

He dragged air into constricted lungs and gestured to the sofa. 'You should sit.' He waited till she was settled then forced himself to follow suit. What he really wanted was to walk away and not have this conversation.

'I almost married once.' His tone was clipped. 'I was twenty-two and in love. Ingrid was...' he paused '...perfect.' He breathed out the word.

'Or so I thought.' He caught Stephanie's sombre stare. 'She was beautiful and engaging. Clever, great company.' Great in bed.

At least he'd thought so. Now he had trouble remembering sexual pleasure with her. His mind was too full of Stephanie.

'What went wrong?'

'My father advised me to wait but I was young and impatient, so sure of myself.' His next breath felt like millstones grinding in his chest.

'You ignored him?'

'I listened but I wasn't convinced. Then, a week before the wedding, I found her phone. Not her usual phone but a spare I knew nothing about. I picked it up thinking to leave a surprise message but I was the one to get the surprise.'

Damen looked away, his thoughts a decade in the past.

'I found messages between her and her boyfriend.'

He heard a gasp.

'I thought it was a joke but I couldn't let it go. I dug deeper. It turned out she had a boyfriend when she met me. Our great romantic love was a calculated scheme to get their hands on my money. Even with a prenup there was a sizeable profit to be had if she left me after a year. Plus anything she'd managed to siphon off in the meantime.'

Ingrid had been good at that, convincing him to splash the cash on her. On things with a solid resale value, like jewellery.

'She was going to marry you then take your money to her lover?' Stephanie's tone was breathless.

'Exactly.' He darted a look her way.

'But she didn't get it…you.'

'I dumped her five days before the wedding.'

'Good! You were well rid of her.' The spark in Stephanie's eyes might have cheered him in other circumstances.

'That's not all.' Damen looked at the doors to the terrace. The impulse to escape was almost unstoppable. But she needed to hear this. 'My father called me into his office. He was…severely disappointed.' Damen's mouth twisted, remembering his normally placid father's tirade about staining the family honour and what a disappointment his only son was.

Damen looked down at his linked hands, the movement pulling the muscles in his neck too tight.

'He wouldn't let me explain, just launched into a diatribe

about how I wasn't fit to bear the Nicolaides name. How close he was to disowning me for dishonouring my fiancée and creating a scandal. I, being young and proud and hating that I hadn't taken his original advice, just stood there, getting angrier and more outraged. How dared he berate *me* when Ingrid was a liar? How could he take her part without asking my side of things? I didn't rush to disabuse him. I let him rant, knowing he'd have to eat his words when he learned the truth.'

'But he calmed down when you told him.'

Damen lifted his head. His body felt leaden, each movement ponderous. Even sucking air into his chest was an effort.

'No.' Damen swallowed. The knot of terrible emotion rose from his chest to his throat, threatening to choke him. 'Before I'd even started explaining he collapsed. The scene brought on a massive heart attack. He died before the medics arrived. I tried CPR but...'

Damen looked into Stephanie's pale face but it wasn't hers he saw.

'He died because of me. I'm to blame for my father's death.'

He sucked in a breath that didn't ease the cramping pain in his chest.

'Of course I feel sick when I think of marriage. It makes me remember a death that could have been avoided. My actions destroyed my father and my whole family paid the price.'

Stephanie reeled. Damen's anguish shattered her lingering anger and disappointment. He looked like a man crushed under an impossible weight, his features stark with pain, his voice unrecognisable.

She stumbled up, her instinct to comfort him. She couldn't bear to see him so tortured. But she'd only taken one step when Damen flung out an arm to ward her off.

She stopped, heart contracting. That gesture said so much. About his hurt. And his ability to hurt her, more, it seemed, every day.

'Damen, you can't take responsibility for your father's death. There must have been an underlying condition—'

'Didn't you hear what I said?' He shot to his feet but turned away, not towards her. His shoulders hunched as he shoved his hands in his pockets. 'It happened because of my actions. There's no changing that.' He paused. 'So now you know. Are you satisfied?'

Steph stared at that proud, handsome profile set in obdurate lines. Her heart bled for him. Yet the taut way he held himself confirmed his mind was closed.

For one heartbeat, then another, she stood poised to go to him. Comfort him.

Till he turned his back as if to stare at the city view. The discussion was over.

Finally Steph stumbled from the room. With each step she ached for Damen's touch on her arm, the sound of him calling her back.

There was nothing.

Hours later she sat in the shade of a spreading tree in the ruins of the city's ancient marketplace. Before her was a marble temple but she didn't see its beautiful symmetry. Instead she saw the anguish in Damen's eyes, heard the rasp of guilt and regret in his voice.

He believed he'd killed his father. It seemed the terrible events of that time, his fiancée's betrayal and guilt over his father's death, had melded in his mind. He saw his marriage plans as a catalyst for disaster. No wonder he'd planned never to marry.

That explained his nightmares, calling out to his father.

Sympathy knotted Steph's insides. She'd hung on to disappointment because she sensed his proposal was reluctant.

Now indignation and anger transformed into pity. What a burden Damen carried!

She wanted to wrap her arms around him and comfort him. She wanted the right to be at his side.

She loved him.

Instead of happiness the knowledge brought pain.

At least now she understood it was the idea of marriage itself that sickened him.

It wasn't anything personal.

That was the problem. None of Damen's plans for her was personal. He didn't want *her*. He wanted their baby. Tying her to him in marriage guaranteed that.

She doubled up in distress. It would be cruel to abandon him, knowing the past tortured him. But how much crueller to her child to stay, living a lie that might end in heartache for everyone?

Could she accept his proposal and hope marriage might lead Damen to love rather than to boredom or dislike?

Or should she make a clean break?

'And so,' she paused to twist her goblet of sparkling water, 'I've decided to go home, to Australia.'

The words pounded into Damen like sledgehammer blows.

He wished he hadn't eaten his delicious dinner. It curdled in his stomach.

'But I'll stay till the end of our two months.' Her lips formed something approximating a smile. 'I'll honour our contract.'

Damen shoved his chair back from the table, the legs screeching on the flagstones of the rooftop terrace. But instead of shooting to his feet he reached for Stephanie's hand.

Touching her silky skin eased his rackety heartbeat.

It had been an emotional day. He'd plumbed the depths with his admission. Yet in the face of this the burden he'd carried for a decade faded towards insignificance. He'd learned to cope with guilt. He sensed he wouldn't cope with Stephanie leaving.

The world blurred as his heart beat too fast and the edges of his vision blackened. He saw her eyes widen.

Damen focused on keeping his hand gentle on hers while the rest of his body went rigid.

All except for that bit of him deep within that crumbled at her words.

Stephanie leaving him.

The thought was unbearable.

Stephanie living on the other side of the world. Taking their baby.

He'd be reduced to seeing his child for, at best, six months a year. As for Stephanie… He imagined cursory conversations as the child passed from one to the other. They'd be strangers, living separate lives.

That odd feeling intensified. As if bits of his organs, his bones, broke away. Roaring white noise filled his head. Reality reduced to the racing thrum of his heart and the hand so soft and unresponsive beneath his.

Arguments to make her stay formed in his head. Inducements that only extreme wealth could buy.

Yet, as he looked into those earnest eyes, read the downward turn of her mouth and the fluttering pulse beneath his hand, Damen knew he was beaten.

Nothing he could offer, neither money nor privilege, would buy her company.

Devastation filled him.

Yet he had to ask. 'Is there anything I can do to change your mind?'

Her mouth crimped at the corners as if she bit back an instinctive response. For a second her eyes blazed more gold than brown. Then they shuttered.

'Nothing.'

CHAPTER FOURTEEN

DAYS LATER, DAMEN stood before his mother in the comfortable sitting room of her Athens home.

His world had tilted on its axis since Stephanie had forced him to reveal his dreadful secret, then declared she was going back to Australia.

Her decision had left him, for the second time in his life, feeling utterly powerless.

Who could blame her for choosing to go? Why would she tie herself to a man who'd killed his own father?

The pain wrapping around his chest worsened daily, as if unseen bonds tightened with each passing hour.

Now Damen had one more trial to face. He couldn't make things right for his father or for Stephanie, couldn't convince her to stay. Yet the unquiet past still haunted him. He'd been a coward in not speaking the truth before. It was a truth he owed his mother.

Yet speaking the words, watching comprehension dawn on her beloved face, made his heart break.

'Damen, no! It's not true!' Her voice shook.

Damen stood his ground, hands clasped behind his back.

'I'm sorry, Mama. But it is. Ten years ago I told you a sanitised version of what happened.'

He moved towards her as she scrambled from her seat, taking her trembling hands.

'You were distraught. I didn't think you'd cope with the whole truth. That *I* was responsible for *Baba's* death. Later...' he sighed. 'Later I was a coward. I couldn't bear to hurt you even more.'

'Foolish, foolish boy.' To his amazement she leaned against him, letting him embrace her. His heart catapulted against his ribs. He'd feared her reaction. Yet still he was gripped by a terrible tension.

His mother leaned back in his arms, her eyes locking on his. 'You're wrong. You didn't kill your father.' Her voice cracked and she squeezed his arm.

Damen shook his head, pain shafting through his soul. Of course his mother didn't want to believe it.

'I'm sorry, Mama.' His breath lifted his chest. 'I didn't listen to him earlier when I should have. Then, that final day, I let him rant because I was too proud, too hurt that he blamed me.'

'He wasn't himself,' she answered. 'He was stressed about the business—'

'That doesn't excuse me.'

His mother shook her head, her expression wistful. 'Your father was a good man but he wasn't himself. He was... scared.'

'Scared?' Damen's head reared back. He couldn't believe such a thing of his father.

'I wanted to tell you but he was adamant. He was scared for the business. Times were tough and you were relatively inexperienced. He had faith in you,' she said quickly, 'but he feared you had a lot to learn if you had to take over.'

'But—' He stopped when she raised her hand.

'He was moody, seeing disaster everywhere, which wasn't your father.' Her expression was wistful. 'You know how positive he usually was. But the doctors warned his health was bad and told him to step back from work. He'd already had two heart attacks.'

'Two heart attacks?' Damen goggled. How had he not known?

'I'm sorry. I wanted him to tell you and your sisters but he refused. They were mild attacks but he was told to work less and get more exercise. He promised he would but instead he put in extra hours, wanting to fix some problems before he handed over to you.'

'He never mentioned me taking over. Never mentioned being ill.'

'He was going to talk to you after the wedding.' She dabbed her eyes. 'He wanted to hand Nicolaides Shipping to you in good shape, but with the economic troubles...' She shrugged. 'You weren't responsible. He'd promised to reduce his hours but he was obsessed with fixing the business first. I tried to persuade him—'

'It's not your fault, Mama.'

'And it's not yours. You said he was ranting. You know how out of character that was. The stress got to him, the worry he wouldn't be around to support you and your sisters.' She bit her lip. 'If anyone caused the attack, it was him. Ignoring medical advice.'

His mother blinked back tears and Damen pulled her close, murmuring words of comfort.

His head spun. If what his mother said was true...

Of course it was. She'd never invent something like that.

It didn't excuse his stupid behaviour, putting his pride first, but it changed so much. Gave a new perspective. The revelation of his father's physical and mental state suddenly made sense, explaining his unusual behaviour. It didn't absolve Damen but already the dread weight of guilt eased.

Maybe now he'd learn to cope better with the past.

Was it possible he might even move on from it?

Steph smoothed her hands down the red dress, avoiding her eyes in the mirror. She was afraid her reflection would reveal her pain. Damen had said they were going ashore for a special party. Hopefully this bright colour would divert attention from the smudges beneath her eyes that concealer hadn't quite covered.

She put on the wide silver bangle Damen had given her in Rhodes. The piece was funky and pretty. She'd seen it in an artisan's shop and when Damen bought it for her she'd felt trembling excitement as if she was on the brink of a thrilling new part of her life.

Her breath shuddered. Thrilling, yes, with single motherhood and a broken heart. Not what she'd hoped for.

She'd fallen for a man so damaged by his first love that he was incapable of loving. Or at least loving her. Maybe one day he'd love again, but she'd be gone. She couldn't live with the little he offered. Duty. Responsibility. Never love.

Two weeks ago in Athens she'd announced she was leaving and for a few moments she'd thought there was hope. That he *did* care for her and would fight to keep her. Instead Damen accepted her announcement with soul-destroying equanimity.

All she could do was hope to get through their contracted time with dignity.

Fifteen minutes later she and Damen were on a small island. It was beautiful. Even the water in the bay was jewel-toned. Ahead was a gracious old house. Pale yellow walls, terracotta tiles, long windows with white shutters. It looked charming.

Steph drew a deep breath scented by the sea and wild herbs.

'Who lives here?' She looked for evidence of a party but all was silent.

'It was built a long time ago by a famous admiral.' It was the first time Damen had spoken since they left the yacht and his deep voice trawled through her like honey-dipped silk. 'He was a pirate too, according to the stories. You like it?'

'It's gorgeous.' Easier to concentrate on her surroundings than Damen, close beside her but distant in every way that mattered.

How was she to get through the next weeks? She couldn't leave. They had a deal. It wasn't his fault she'd made the error of falling in love.

Steph's heart squeezed.

They reached the front door and Damen opened it. 'After you.'

Steph stepped into the hallway, blinking after the dazzling sunshine. They were in a square foyer with an elegant curving staircase.

'This way.' Damen ushered her into a sitting room, the furnishings beautiful but worn.

More silence. There were no voices. No clink of china or glass. She looked out to Damen's yacht, moored in the bay. There were no other boats.

Her spine prickled with belated warning.

Steph swung around to find Damen close. His distinctive scent wafted into her nostrils. Her yearning grew. How was she to pretend not to care?

'What is this, Damen?'

'It's the house I've bought. I'll use it as my base and commute to Athens when I need to.' He looked around. 'It needs renovation and a sympathetic extension, but when it's done it will be special.'

Steph agreed but didn't want to discuss renovations.

'There's no party, is there? Why are we here?'

To her surprise Damen smiled. It was the first genuine smile she'd seen from him in two weeks and it unravelled her defences.

'This is a kidnap.'

'Sorry?' She must have misheard.

'I'm kidnapping you. I botched my first effort but this time I'm determined to do it right.' The smile faded and suddenly he was standing so close the heat from his body washed through her. 'I'm keeping you on the island till you agree to my terms.'

Steph tottered backwards, her hand at her throat. 'You can't!'

'Watch me.' He looked more sombre than she'd ever known him.

Tears of fury and hurt pricked her eyes. 'You're utterly

ruthless. What do you want, Damen? Another contract? I can tell you now I'll never sign over my baby to you. I'll swim to the next island if I have to.'

'It's not like that.'

'Of course it's like that. If you think holding me here will convince me to—'

'It's not the baby I want.'

Steph's mouth sagged open.

'Not the baby?'

He was so close she had to tilt her chin to meet his eyes. Awareness zinged through her. She tried to stifle it and focus on anger.

'No, I want *you*.'

'You're not making sense.'

'On the contrary, for the first time since we met I'm talking perfect sense.' His glittering eyes held a promise of something that made her heart turn over. 'I've wanted you since the day we met.'

'You had me, remember?'

He shook his head. 'I've never had you, *agapi mou*, not really. Oh, we had sex, and it was amazing. But I want more than your body.'

'Yes. You want my baby.' She couldn't let herself forget that.

'Of course I want our child. Or, I should say I want to share our child. But there's something I want more.'

Steph frowned, not daring to hope.

'I want *you*, Stephanie. Not just sleeping in my bed or sharing responsibility for our child.' He paused and she saw his nostrils flare as if he fought for breath. 'I want you with me because you care for me. Because I care for you.' Another pause. Another deep breath.

'I love you, Stephanie. If you give us a chance, I believe I can make you happy. You might even come to love me too.'

Steph shuffled back till she came up against a sofa. 'You're lying. You don't...love me.' Her heart dipped on the word and she wrapped her arms around her middle to keep the hurt at bay. 'You're cruel pretending to.'

'You accused me of lying before, *agapi mou*, and I regret you had cause ever to doubt my honesty. But I tell you now, on my oath as a Nicolaides, I've never been more genuine. I love you.' He said it again slowly, his gaze pinioning her so she couldn't look away.

'No!' She put out a hand to ward him off, though he hadn't moved. Her palm landed on his chest, her fingers splaying on familiar hard contours. 'You're saying this so I'll marry you and so the baby—'

'Actually, I do want to marry you. I want that more than anything.' Damen's hand closed on hers, holding it against his staccato-beating heart. His eyes gleamed as if lit by an inner fire. 'The thought of losing you has cured me of my horror of marriage. Because I've realised life is too short to waste a moment of being with the woman I love.'

His words slammed the breath back into her lungs. Her head swam.

'I had a long talk with my mother too. I told her about the day my father died. What I hadn't known was that he'd already had a couple of heart attacks. That doesn't excuse my behaviour, but you were right. I was too ready to blame myself. And stupidly I let that stand in the way of *us*.'

Could there really be an *us*? Steph watched him in amazement, trying to process the change in him.

'I want to be your husband, Stephanie. But if you don't want to marry, I'll accept that. Whatever you like, as long as you stay. Give me a chance to show you how good our life can be together.'

Steph blinked, overwhelmed. She wanted so much to believe but she couldn't let herself.

'I was attracted to you from the first. I only left because I thought I'd wrecked my chances with you. Then in Corfu...' He paused and she felt his heart quicken beneath her palm. 'You have no idea how much I wanted you. Even if I hadn't needed a pretend lover I'd have tried to seduce you. Everything about you attracted me. Your looks, your feisty attitude, your sense of humour. Even the way you refused to be impressed by me. You sizzle with energy and passion and I wanted that for myself. I still do. Especially now I've learned what a warm and honest heart you have.'

Steph's breath came in short bursts, warring emotions filling her. His words meant so much, and she desperately wanted to believe them.

'You didn't love me a fortnight ago. You didn't want to marry me.' His unwilling proposal had hurt so badly.

Damen lifted his other hand to her cheek, and to her shame she didn't have the strength to shy away. If anything she nestled closer.

Damen's pupils dilated. His fingers moved in a tender caress.

'That's just it. I *did* love you, though I hadn't let myself think in those terms. Because I'd loved Ingrid and that led to heartache and tragedy.'

'It wasn't your fault!' She'd felt helpless, watching Damen grapple with his demons. 'Stop blaming yourself.'

'That's what my mother says.'

'She's right.' Steph hoped never to see such anguish as she'd seen in Damen's eyes that day.

'I'm glad you think so. She also told me I was a fool if I let you go without telling you how I feel.'

Steph's eyes widened, hope rising.

'But I was going to tell you anyway. I can't let you go because I love you. Not as I thought I loved Ingrid, with a boy's infatuation, but deeply, with all I am and all I hope to be.' His voice deepened on the words. They sounded like a pledge. '*S'agapo,* Stephanie *mou.*'

'Oh, Damen.' She blinked back tears. 'How am I supposed to stay strong and resist you when you say that?'

'I want you to be strong, *asteri mou.* To be the independent, gorgeous woman you already are. I just don't want you to resist *me*.' His voice cracked and her eyes widened. 'Stay with me. Things were good between us and they can be even better. Look in your heart and give us a chance. Maybe you'll come to love me too.'

The last of Steph's resistance crumbled. She'd taken chances and made mistakes. But this wasn't a mistake.

This was the man she wanted to build a life with. A man who'd wrestled his demons and emerged wanting her. A decent, caring, wonderful man who deserved a second chance.

In the end the words slipped out easily.

'I already love you, Damen. That's why I've been miserable, thinking all you cared about was our baby.'

She felt the crash of his heart at her words.

He must have seen the truth in her face, for he smiled. That soul-lifting smile that made her heart beat double time.

'You love me.' His voice held wonder and satisfaction.

His arm looped around her waist, pulling her to him.

Steph went willingly.

'And you love me.' It was there in his eyes, his embrace, in the very air they breathed.

'Let me show you how much.' His arms were strong yet gentle as he scooped her up and headed for the staircase and the bedrooms above. 'I'll never tire of saying the words, *agapi mou*, but I want you to be absolutely sure of my feelings, and actions speak louder than words.'

In the end he convinced Stephanie both with words and potently persuasive actions.

EPILOGUE

A COOL BREEZE ruffled the cypresses but the sky was cloudless and the day perfect.

Damen's gaze traversed the garden from the villa, across the terrace where friends and family clustered. The steps to this garden by the sea were bright with potted roses and other flowers in shades of red, Stephanie's favourite colour. Red ribbons decorated the arbour where he stood with Christo.

Damen didn't care about decorations. Nor witnesses, though he was glad his family was here. His sisters gossiped with Clio. Manos and his wife chatted with friends and kids raced in circles, laughing as parents herded them to seats. His mother sat with Stephanie's grandmother and the friend she'd brought from Australia, a tall, white-haired man. From the older man's expression when he looked at Mrs Logan, Damen guessed there'd be another wedding soon.

'Emma's done a fantastic job preparing for today.' Damen mightn't care about decorations but he wanted today perfect for Stephanie.

'I'll tell her you said so,' Christo responded. 'She'll be thrilled. Even more thrilled than when you said you wanted to be married on Corfu.'

'It's a special place for us.' Where he and Stephanie had met again, argued and struck sparks off each other, and agreed to become pretend lovers. Now they were so much more. 'Besides, the renovations aren't finished at our villa.'

'You can have the christening party there.'

Damen met his friend's grin just as the string quartet began playing a familiar tune. His heart shot straight to his throat, beating hard and fast.

He turned and his breath stopped.

She was even more beautiful than he remembered. He hadn't seen her since yesterday, having stayed aboard the yacht while she spent the night with Emma.

Damen's throat dried.

Stephanie's hair shone like ebony and she carried red flowers before her small baby bump. Her gown was deep cream, wide across the shoulders but fitted across the breasts and falling in folds to her feet. The pearl and ruby necklace he'd given her glowed against her skin. She looked as elegant as a princess, as delicate as a fairy. She was his dream of heaven.

Then she was there, before him. Her eyes shone golden brown, her smile turned him inside out.

Damen took her hand, lifting it to his mouth. The scent of vanilla and Stephanie, of happiness, filled him.

He whispered in her ear, 'You're absolutely sure?' He'd suggested that they marry after the baby was born, a gesture to prove he wanted marriage because he loved her, not to secure their child.

'I'm sure.' Her eyes flashed. 'I can't wait to be your wife. I love you, Damen Nicolaides, and I mean to have you.'

Damen grinned as his heart filled. 'Have I mentioned I adore a woman who knows what she wants?'

Ignoring custom, he swooped down to kiss her lips. Instantly she melted, his fiery, adorable love.

The sound of Christo clearing his throat finally penetrated and reluctantly Damen straightened. Stephanie's eyes shone and a tantalising smile curved her sweet lips. Damen took her arm and turned to the celebrant.

Could any day be more perfect?

And this was just the beginning.

* * * * *

CROWNING
HIS UNLIKELY
PRINCESS

MICHELLE CONDER

To Heather, the international twin,
for so many years of love, friendship and laughter.

And all the times you stopped outside a bar
to see who was inside!

And to Charlotte, my editor.
Without you this book would not be half as good.

CHAPTER ONE

CASSIDY CHECKED THE prospectus in her hand against the one on her computer screen and felt her stomach sink to her toes.

She had given him the wrong one.

She was doomed.

She would be fired.

This was it.

After a day that had started out badly and only got worse as it had progressed, it would be the tip of the iceberg.

She hadn't had a day as bad as this one since her father had moved her and her sister out of the small parish in which they had grown up during the middle of the night all those years ago as if they had been criminals. They hadn't been, but for a while they had been treated like they were. And she'd contributed to that, hadn't she?

But beating herself up about past mistakes wasn't going to help her now.

If she didn't fix this, her meticulous boss would be heading to an important meeting in Boston the following morning to finalise the capital investment they needed for a major project with the wrong information. That would be eight months of painstaking work down the tubes. After the unexpected bombshell her sister had dropped on her this morning that had set off her day from hell, it was the last straw.

And she had no one to blame but herself. She should not have let Peta's unexpected news derail her as much as it had, and she could either sit here and feel sorry for herself or she could get on and fix it.

And she still had time, she noted, checking her watch.

She double-checked the updated version of the document, ensuring that the right figures were in the right place this time, and hit the print button.

Of course the printer ran out of paper halfway through but that was to be expected. It should be one of Murphy's laws that when a day started out badly you should just go back to bed and pull the sheet over your head.

Her forehead throbbed as she recalled how she had barely been awake when one of her eleven-year-old twin nieces had come careening into her bedroom with the news that their mother was getting married. Her mother, and Cassidy's sister. The one who had moved in with her after she had hit rock bottom again. The one who had sworn off men after she'd become a teenage mother and been dumped by the twins' father before they had even been born.

Peta had come into her room after that with a sheepish grin on her face and a diamond ring on her finger.

'I wasn't sure how to tell you,' she'd said, half grimacing, half smiling. 'Dan completely surprised me with his proposal and he wants me and the girls to move in with him right away. Not that we will,' Peta had rushed to assure her. 'Not until you find another place to live, or a flatmate, because I know you can't afford the rent here on your own.'

Shell-shocked, Cassidy had just looked at her. 'You're engaged?'

'I know, right?' Peta had stared down at her ring with a stunned but delighted expression. 'I can't believe it either but… He's so special, Cass. And he even wants to adopt the twins.'

A lump had formed in Cassidy's throat at that. The twins were hers! She had been at their birth, she had helped her sister raise them, she had taken Amber to the emergency department when she'd broken her arm and Peta had been stuck on the other side of the city at work. She had been the one to read stories to April to take her mind off her twin in the operating room while they'd waited.

Dan was… Dan was… He was a nice guy, a lovely guy, but marriage?

In hindsight she should have been more prepared for it. Her sister was one of those uniquely beautiful people that made others do a double-take.

Like her boss. Prince Logan of Arrantino.

They moved through life on another level from the more ordinary folk like herself, turning heads and breaking hearts as they went.

It had always been that way. Growing up, the boys at high school had only ever shown an interest in Cassidy to get an introduction to her sister. It was something she had grown so used to that even now she always questioned a man's hidden agenda before accepting an invitation to dinner. Not that she'd had many of those since the last guy she'd dated, who had only wanted her for her study notes. After the disastrous incident in high school, which she refused to think about, she really should have known better.

Just once she'd like to meet a man who wanted her for her body. Was that too much to ask?

An image of her boss leapt into her head and she immediately banished it. The only reason he would ever want her body was to bury it after he murdered her for making so many errors today.

First by putting through a phone call from a teary ex, hoping for a second chance, instead of the CEO of their law firm, and then for mixing up the restaurant where he was supposed to meet a client for lunch. She'd confused the luncheon date with one he was scheduled to have the following day and he'd been twenty minutes late as a result.

Now this debacle… She stacked the copies of the prospectus carefully on the table. The last thing she needed to do was to drop them as she raced down the stairs to the copy room and set about binding each one into a shiny booklet.

At this time of the evening the office was basically empty, most of her work colleagues at the bank having already gone home, so she was alone with her self-recriminations.

Which she was eternally thankful for.

The thought of having to make polite small talk with a colleague, or returning home before she could paste on her face a genuinely happy smile for her sister, was too much right now. Not that she wasn't genuinely happy for her sister. She was. She was just afraid of what it meant for her.

Afraid to face a future without seeing her family on a daily basis. Afraid to face a future with no one special in her life ever. She could almost see herself now, an unmarried woman with a shawl around her shoulders to keep out the chill, and a dozen feral cats fighting over bowls of cat food.

Her throat thickened. She and her sister were a team. They had been ever since the twins had been born when Peta had only just turned seventeen, and Cassidy eighteen. With their mother having walked out two years earlier, and their father struggling to keep his head above water, Cassidy had become the rock everyone leaned on. Which had been fine with her. She liked helping out, and she had never been the kind of person who walked away when the going got tough.

Glad that she kept up her fitness routine, she took

the stairs two at a time as she returned to her office and dropped the glossy prospectuses on her desk, automatically reaching for her phone to dial the courier service.

Then she hesitated.

It would be her luck that the courier either didn't show up or had an accident and the prospectuses ended up at the bottom of the Hudson. Not only would that be an environmental hazard, it would mean she could still be sacked for stupidity.

Being hired as Logan's EA a few months out of college two years ago had been an amazing coup and she'd pinched herself for months afterwards at having landed such a lucrative role.

She knew she had only got it because she had been in the right place at the right time and the HR manager had been desperate. Otherwise she wouldn't be where she was today. Working in a job that she loved for a man who was called a business genius by anyone who mattered. He was a commanding force who stopped at nothing to get what he wanted. Which had intimidated the heck out of her when she'd first come to work for him, but which she'd been advised not to show.

'His previous EAs left because they either couldn't keep up with the demanding workload,' the fastidious HR manager had informed her as they'd marched down the hallway for her interview with her boss, 'they were intimidated by the fact that he's a prince and second in line to the throne of Arrantino, or they fell in love with him. Any of these three will have you out the door in seconds.'

Down to the last few dollars in her bank account Cassidy had assured the immaculately groomed manager that love was so far off her radar it didn't even register as a blip. On top of that she'd held down two jobs and still come out top of her class during her senior year at high school so she knew nothing else other than hard work.

Cassidy stared at the ten prospectuses she'd just wrapped in brown paper. Her boss's apartment was only a fifteen-minute brisk walk away and she had delivered things there before. So why not now? She could use the time to contemplate what she would say to her sister when she got home. And she'd also be more relaxed knowing that she'd rectified her mistake and her boss had the right material for his meeting.

Maybe she would even be lucky enough to find his apartment empty so she could swap the incorrect prospectuses with the new ones without him even knowing. Now, that would be a coup she could smile about.

Feeling better than she had all day, she slipped into her suit jacket, grabbed her handbag, and jabbed the lift button to take her to the ground floor.

Being mid-July, Fifth Avenue was teeming with sun-burned tourists wearing ill-fitting shorts and weighed down with *I Heart New York* shopping bags.

Weaving in and around them with accustomed dexterity, Cassidy didn't notice that the sky had turned leaden until a large raindrop landed like a burst water balloon right in the centre of her precious parcel.

Groaning with acceptance that this just was not her day, she ducked under a striped shop awning with a couple of women dressed for a night out just as the heavens really opened.

Another drop of water dripped onto her forehead and she barely batted an eyelash as she swiped at it with the back of her hand, glancing up to see a hole in the awning. At this rate a lorry would speed past, hit a puddle, and finish the job. It would only be fitting.

'Excuse me,' one of the women ventured. 'My app's

stopped working. Is Broadway left or right from here? We're late for a show.'

'Left,' Cassidy directed, wishing that getting to Times Square for a musical was the biggest worry on her to-do list right now. In fact, she couldn't remember the last time she'd done anything light-hearted or fun. Who had the time for such frivolities?

Shrugging out of her jacket, she wrapped it around her parcel and hunted around for a cab. Of course the Avenue was gridlocked in the sudden downpour with not a yellow cab in sight.

Resigned to her fate, she stepped out into the deluge, knowing that if she didn't move soon she wouldn't make it home before dark. She only hoped that her boss appreciated her dedication when it came to bonus time.

By the time she made it to his landmark building she was a sodden, out-of-breath mess.

The doorman did a double-take when he saw her and rushed to hold the door open as she dashed inside. 'Evening, Miss Ryan.'

'Evening, Michael.' She paused to catch her breath, her heart racing a mile a minute. 'Is the boss in?'

'Yes, ma'am. He came in an hour ago.'

'Great,' she said glumly. No chance she could hide her mistake, then.

Since he hadn't responded to her earlier text, she used her personal pass to access his penthouse apartment and waited for his private lift.

A sudden attack of nerves hit her as the lift ascended to the top floor. She'd been here on numerous occasions before to drop things off, but she'd never been here when he'd been at home. The thought of seeing him on his home turf made her feel a little jittery, but perhaps that was just a residual feeling from a day she couldn't wait to see the back of.

Arriving in his state-of-the-art apartment with three-hundred-and-sixty-degree views over Manhattan and beyond, she stepped carefully from the elevator so she didn't slip on the marble floor. It was a gorgeous space, the interior designer who had remodelled it having used light wood grain and endless yards of glass to create a home that was boundless and warmly inviting.

Conscious that she was soaking wet, she moved stiffly into the immaculate open-plan living area and called his name. When she didn't get an answer she glanced outside the windows, momentarily captivated by the sunset over heaven-bound skyscrapers. She exhaled slowly, taking in the magnitude and peace of her surroundings. She could see the congested traffic in the distance, the mad dash of pedestrians trying to get to their next destination, and it almost felt surreal in the stillness of Logan's apartment.

After a day that had not let up from morning till now it was like being cocooned in cotton wool, safe from the frantic beat of a city that never slept. A welcome reprieve.

And then suddenly that reprieve was shattered when she felt the air shift behind her. Knowing that it could only be her boss, she gripped her jacket-wrapped parcel tighter and turned, letting out a short gasp when she was confronted by the sight of him. Sweat-soaked in a singlet top that did little to disguise his wide shoulders and ripped torso and tiny gym shorts that hugged his strong thighs, he was a spectacular display of blatant male power and vitality. He had earbuds inserted and she could hear the pounding music from where she stood.

For a moment she couldn't speak, her body frozen by the impact of over six feet of bronzed, honed muscle glistening with athletic prowess. Of course, she'd guessed that he was well built beneath his custom-made business suits but her imagination hadn't even come close to the real thing.

Logan's eyes did a slow perusal down her body and she was so out of sorts she felt her insides start to heat up, her heart pumping hard again as if she was still outside, rushing to get out of the rain.

She swallowed heavily, horrified to note that her body was reacting to the sight of him in a way that transcended the professional boss-employee relationship. It had been the same reaction she'd had on first meeting him behind his big desk in a tailored suit and a very bad mood. He hadn't smiled at her then either, testing her mettle by reading her every reaction to his questions with thickly lashed deep blue eyes that were dangerously intelligent.

It was the same look he was giving her now, only this time she didn't feel half as successful at hiding her emotions, something she generally considered one of her superpowers after a childhood fraught with upheaval.

A superpower she had employed within the confines of his office that very first day to hide how attractive she'd found him, concentrating instead on how fortunate she had been to even have the chance at such a prestigious job, and how desperately she had needed the money. It had also helped that there was the somewhat minor—but pivotal—point that a man who already had everything the world had to offer would not give a woman such as herself a second glance.

A bead of water rolled from her forehead down her nose and onto her top lip. Her tongue sneaked out to capture it and Logan's blue eyes darkened, his nostrils flaring as his gaze lingered on her lips. Cassidy felt a surge of sexual awareness so deeply within her body it shook her to the core.

She was like a startled impala facing a hungry lion, with nowhere to run, and she suddenly felt less annoyed at the women who regularly called his office, trying to win a second chance with him, and more sorry for them. If he ever swept her up in those massive arms she wasn't certain she'd want him to let her go either.

Fortunately the scowl that crossed his face was a timely reminder that the chance of him ever sweeping her up into anything was less than zero.

Squeezing her soggy jacket tighter against her chest, she knew that she had to do something to sever this strange connection between them before she embarrassed herself.

But before she had the chance, Logan reached into his pocket and killed the music on his phone before yanking the earbuds out of his ears. 'What are you doing here, Cassidy? And why are you dripping all over my floor?'

They had started using their first names after about six months of working together when he had complained that he felt like she was always about to deliver bad news when she addressed him as Mr de Silva, but now her name sounded strangely intimate on his tongue.

'I...' She crushed the moment of madness she'd just experienced and lifted her chin. 'I need to give you the prospectuses for your meeting tomorrow morning.' She unwrapped the jacket in her arms and held out the package but he didn't move to take it.

'I already have the prospectuses for tomorrow.'

Cassidy grimaced and with her free hand brushed at the rivulets of water rolling down her neck. 'Actually, you don't. You have the wrong ones.'

'Wrong...' His eyes scanned her from head to toe again, a scowl darkening his blue eyes. 'You're drenched.'

'Sorry.' She glanced down to find that her blouse was so wet she might as well have not been wearing one. With a squeak of alarm she crossed her free arm over her breasts, only then realising how terrible she must look in general.

His scowl deepened as he plucked her sodden jacket and

the package from her hand and disappeared down the hallway, returning a moment later with a towel.

'You know where the bathroom is,' he bit out, keeping
his eyes above her neckline. 'Use it.'

'Actually, I don't,' she said, rubbing her arms from the
chill that was either coming from him or the air-condi-
tioning. 'I've only ever dropped things off before and left.'

Clearly annoyed to have his peaceful night invaded, he
strode down the hall, impatience evident in every taut line
of his hard body. 'Here.'

He pushed open the door to a bathroom and Cassidy
gratefully disappeared inside.

She nearly let out another squeak at seeing blotches of
mascara pooled beneath her eyes and straggly bits of her
hair sticking to her ears and neck.

The ruined woman in the mirror was not the impeccably presented one she had turned herself into since leaving
Ohio and it was yet more confirmation that she should not
have got out of bed that morning.

Taking a deep breath, she skimmed the towel beneath
her eyes and wiped her face and neck. Then she unpinned
her hair and searched in her bag for her hairbrush. Not
finding it, she had a vague memory of Amber asking if
she could borrow it the night before. Cursing her beloved
niece, she finger-combed the mass of tangled waves and
tried to re-pin her hair. Unfortunately the rain had made it
curl in every direction so she gave up, letting it hang past
her shoulders. She shivered in the air-conditioned bathroom
and groaned anew when she realised that her bra was vis-
ible beneath the downlights.

Terrific.

She pulled her blouse away from her skin and wondered
if it would look odd if she walked out holding it like that.

Deciding that she'd have to brazen it out, she tilted her

chin and exited the bathroom. She'd get her coat, wish her boss goodnight, and head off to face the next disaster. It couldn't possibly be any worse than this one.

Peeking into the living room, she caught sight of her boss outlined against the New York skyline, his hands on his hips. The clouds had parted and late sunbeams shone down on the newly washed buildings, gilding them in gold and silver.

But it was the gorgeous view inside the room that held her attention more. Tall, broad-shouldered and lean-hipped, with long, muscular legs and dark blond hair that gently curled against his strong neck, he was the epitome of sleek male power in the prime of life. He might be a cold-hearted workaholic but he was pure perfection to look at.

Against her wishes her heart rate quickened once again and, unwilling to get caught staring at him a second time, she turned away to hunt for her jacket.

Logan turned to find Cassidy scanning the room and looking more like something the cat would drag in than his usual efficient EA. All day she'd been off and now she even looked it. Her usually perfect up-do a cloud of chestnut waves, her wet blouse the texture of tissue paper, and just as revealing, and her face clean of make-up. The only thing familiar about her was her glasses, ones she'd adjusted further up her nose with her little finger when she'd caught him staring at her. A nervous gesture he'd only ever seen now and then.

His office ran like clockwork thanks to her. But the woman standing in front of him looked like she should be about to do a strip tease before ending up in his bed.

Wondering when his libido had regressed to the point that a woman in a wet shirt could turn him on, he strode out of the room and returned with one of his sweatshirts.

'Unless you're planning to enter a wet T-shirt competition after you leave here, you'd better put this on.'

Her eyes didn't quite meet his as she took it from him and slid it over her head, her thanks muffled by the fabric.

The sweatshirt was miles too big, falling midway down her thighs and draping over her hands, but it did the job of turning her from shapely to shapeless as required.

He didn't know what had happened today but it had all started when he had arrived at his office to find that Cassidy wasn't there. Always on time, and with his morning coffee ready for when he walked in, she had been noticeably absent. Not only had he been required to make his own coffee but he'd had to field two visits from junior staff asking for information he didn't have. Then his COO's assistant had stopped by to make an appointment for him to meet with her boss and had tried to linger.

When Cassidy had finally arrived, blaming the subway, she'd been harried. At first he hadn't noticed because she'd appeared as well groomed as always in a black suit and white blouse, her auburn hair pinned back into a French twist. She'd worn it like that on her first day and had never deviated from the style. It had annoyed him at first because it was always the same, but then he'd come to appreciate her consistency. Not to mention her efficiency.

But she hadn't been efficient today. Following up one unexpected mistake with another and another until he'd almost asked her what was wrong.

He hadn't because the last thing he wanted to do was to encourage personal interactions in the office. He did not want to give her any ideas that might change the nature of their working relationship. Something that had happened with more than one EA in the past.

In his experience people were rarely as they seemed on the outside and yet he was sure that his EA was exactly as she seemed: an intelligent, quiet, sensible woman who had incredibly sultry lips. And vivid, velvet-green eyes. He'd noticed both right away, and nearly hadn't hired her because of his reaction to them, but his HR manager had convinced him that she was perfect.

And she had been.

Perfect.

Until now.

She glanced at him and adjusted her glasses again. 'I know you're busy so if you tell me where my jacket is, I'll get out of your hair.'

'Not before you explain why I left the office with the wrong information, you won't.'

She sighed heavily, her chest rising and falling with the effort. 'I was hoping you wouldn't ask.'

Logan raised a brow at her evasive response, another clue that his EA had left the building and had been replaced by a woman he didn't know.

'Relying on hope is a waste of time and since we don't always get what we want I'll ask again.'

She glanced at her hands before raising her little chin as she looked at him. 'I gave you the draft of the prospectus that was the one before the final copy.' She opened her hands in front of her in a conciliatory gesture. 'I'm not sure how it happened. I did text you to let you know I would be stopping by but clearly you didn't get it.'

'Clearly.' He tried not to be annoyed at her incompetence but he was. 'But I could have collected them from the office in the morning.'

'You have an early flight to Boston and I didn't want to put you out.' She gripped her fingers together. 'It's been a horrible day and I'm really sorry for mucking up.' Her hands lifted in a helpless gesture. 'I'm not myself right now.'

She could join the club. If his unwanted physical reaction to her was any indication, he wasn't himself either. Which was why he needed to retrieve her jacket and send her on her way. About to do exactly that, he frowned when his phone rang. Pulling it from his pocket, his frown deepened when he saw his brother's name flash up on the screen.

Given that it was the middle of the night in Arrantino, it couldn't be good news and he pressed the answer button.

'What?'

His blunt greeting was met with a touch of humour. 'Have I caught you at a bad time, brother? You're not with a woman, are you?'

'Yes.' Before he could think better of it his eyes raked over Cassidy again. She tucked a strand of her hair behind her ear and the innocent gesture sent a raw bolt of primal lust roaring through his blood. Closing it down with iron-clad self-control, he turned away from her and corrected his answer. 'No.'

'Good. Have you got a minute? I have…something to tell you.'

Hearing the hesitation in his brother's voice sent an icy shiver of dread down his spine, driving all thoughts of his EA's legs from his mind. 'What is it? Have you been to the doctor? Has—?'

Logan stopped, unable to voice the fear that his brother's teenage leukaemia had returned. Leo had fought the illness bravely but Logan doubted he would ever fully recover from seeing his brother so weakened by the disease. Neither would he forget how powerless he had felt in the face of something he couldn't control.

'No. It's nothing like that,' his brother assured him. 'Well, not entirely. It's just that…' The pause on the end of the phone took ten years off Logan's life. 'I've decided to abdicate. Which makes you the next King of Arrantino.'

CHAPTER TWO

LOGAN'S EYES NARROWED on the darkening sky that stretched for miles outside his window, not sure he'd heard his brother correctly. 'Abdicate?' He ploughed his hand through his sweaty blond hair. 'What the hell are you talking about?'

'An…*issue* has arisen.' His brother sounded pained. 'It wasn't supposed to be like this, to be splashed across the news, but… You know how this works. We live in a gold-fish bowl. I wanted it to come out differently but that opportunity has passed.'

'You're not making a bit of sense,' Logan growled. 'Cut to the chase and tell me what's going on.'

'The long and short of it is that Anastasia and I have formally broken up and I'm stepping down.'

'Divorcing your wife is not a reason to abdicate,' Logan said. Especially when divorcing that scheming little preda-tor was the best thing Leo could ever do for himself and his country. The woman had played both of them like a finely tuned instrument five years ago, latching onto the brother who would make her Queen in the end. She had caused a rift between the two of them when Logan had tried to warn Leo against marriage. But her beauty had blinded Leo, and Logan suspected that his brother had also been heav-ily influenced by his duty as King. Their mother had been in Leo's ear about the need to produce an heir for months before Anastasia had turned up on the scene and the notion had taken root. Unlike Logan, Leo had always tried to do the right thing, rarely questioning his royal duties. Until now, it seemed.

'No, it's not,' Leo agreed. 'But having an affair that has made headline news around the world is.'

'Damn.' Logan swore under his breath. He had never had any hard evidence of Anastasia's affairs, but perhaps she had gone too far this time and finally shown his brother her true colours. 'What has Anastasia done now?' he asked, not even trying to mask the disgust in his voice.

'It's not Anastasia. It's me. And strictly speaking I haven't had an affair because I haven't consummated the relationship yet, but I was photographed kissing another woman and the press are playing it that way, so what does it matter? Mother has hit the roof. The world's press are trying to draw comparisons between myself and Father and are desperate to know who my new love interest is… It's bedlam over here.'

Still processing the fact that his brother was seeing another woman, Logan braced a hand against the window, his muscles rigid. He had no doubt that his mother had hit the roof.

They had all lived in the shadow of their late father's damaging affairs and she had been hurt the most. Both he and his brother had hated his father for it so the fact that Leo had let this happen was shocking enough. The fact that he wanted to abdicate unthinkable.

'Just keep a cool head,' he advised, already working out how he was going to handle the crisis. 'And don't do anything rash. Like abdicate!'

'Too late,' Leo stated without any humour in his voice. 'And actually it's not a rash decision. I made it a month ago. I've just been sitting with it to make sure it's the right one to make.'

'A month ago? Why the hell didn't you call me earlier?'

'Because if it wasn't right I didn't want to bother you. And I knew you'd try to talk me out of it.'

'Damn right I'd have tried to talk you out of it. I wasn't born to be King, you were. And I don't want the job!'

'I had a feeling you'd say that but if you really don't want to do it then we can pass the throne to Ped—'

'Do not even go there,' Logan warned, his throat burning with fury. 'Pedro wouldn't know the first thing about running a country and we both know it.' Their cousin was a surfing maniac who preferred the beach to the boardroom and little else. Except maybe women.

'Yes. But I can no longer fulfil the role. The woman I'm in love with is a single mother who hates the spotlight and—'

'In love?' Logan pushed away from the window, suddenly conscious that Cassidy was still standing in the middle of his living room, nibbling on her lower lip. Dragging his gaze away from those even white teeth, he refocused. 'Are you serious?'

Leo laughed self-consciously. 'I know you think love is little more than sentimental tripe, but it's not. This woman is wonderful. Amazing. I had no idea I could feel this way and all I want to do is protect her and her daughter.'

All Logan wanted to do was stop his brother from doing something stupid. Like abdicate. Because there was no way he wanted to be King. He'd never overly enjoyed the pomp and ceremony and the constant attention that went with royal life, and he really hated the comparisons that were made between him and their late father. As the son who looked most like the old man he'd always borne the brunt of that kind of attention and he'd hated being likened to a man he didn't respect. A man who had chosen to put everything in life—his job, his passions, and his baser instincts—ahead of the welfare of his family and country.

Their father had been a master at manipulation and both he and Leo had gone from loving him to fearing him to turning away from him and, finally, to loathing him. Especially when his affairs had become public knowledge, hurting their mother and embarrassing them all.

And now Leo had fallen into the same trap. Being caught with a woman who wasn't his wife. No matter how innocent it had been, it was still a big deal.

'Just…' He heaved out a sigh. 'Just don't do anything yet. Don't make any solid decisions while you're emotional. And definitely do not put out any statements.' His mind was already turning, working through ideas of how they could stem the fallout from the scandal his brother had inadvertently created. 'I'll be in Arrantino by nightfall. Morning your time.'

'If I'm not here to greet you, I'll make sure Margaux is completely up to speed on what's happening.'

'I don't want to speak to your private secretary,' Logan growled. 'I want to speak to you.'

'I'll try.' Logan could already hear that his brother was distracted.

Ringing off, Logan took a moment to stare into space. King? There was no way he wanted to become King. It was a poisoned chalice he'd always been glad he'd never had to take on.

Cassidy cleared her throat, her gaze taking in her boss's flexed shoulder muscles as he steadied his breathing.

She'd never seen him so disturbed before, and she felt an unexpected shaft of compassion for him. She had felt like she'd had her life turned on its head this morning, and now it seemed like his was about to do the same thing.

He turned toward her, his expression steely. 'How much of that did you get?'

Feeling awful that she'd overheard any of it, she shrugged diffidently. 'Your brother intends to abdicate and you don't want to be King.' *You also think love is a waste of time, and you don't seem to be a fan of your brother's soon-to-be ex-wife.*

'That's pretty much it. Throw in a divorce, a woman on the side, and a hungry pack of journalists and you've potentially got a national crisis.'

'Wow. And I thought my morning had been bad. What are you going to do?'

'Talk him out of it.'

Cassidy sighed. 'You always seem to know what your next move is. One of the things I admire most about you is your ability to make a decision on the spot. I wish that was one of my superpowers.'

'Superpower?'

'Things I excel at.'

'Your superpower is running my office. Which I'm going to need you to get on top of right away because we need to fly to Arrantino. Tonight. Hopefully we're only looking at a twenty-four-hour turnaround but you'll need to rearrange the rest of my week in case it's not.'

'Okay, right.' She frowned. 'I'll send an email to postpone tomorrow's meeting in Boston. Then first thing tomorrow I'll see what can be delegated and what has to be rearranged. Do you want me to call Ben to reschedule the flight?'

'I already sent him a text requesting that we fly out as soon as he can log a new flight plan.'

'Okay, then I'll…' Cassidy paused. That was the second time she'd heard him refer to both of them. 'We?'

'Yes.' Logan checked an incoming text on his phone. 'I need you to come with me.'

Cassidy blinked as her brain slowly processed his words. 'But I can't go with you.'

Logan's head snapped up. He looked at her as if she'd never said no to him before, perhaps because she hadn't. 'Why not?'

She thought about the conversation she still needed to have with her sister, and her obligation to take care of the twins two evenings a week while her sister studied at night school. 'I have obligations. Commitments.' She smoothed her hand over her sodden hair. And if this trip did by chance go longer than twenty-four hours her sister wouldn't be happy. Not with her final exams about to start.

'Yes, you do have commitments. To me. And right now I need you.'

'You need me to run your office, which I can do better from New York.'

'I decide where you're best fit to serve me, Cassidy, not you.'

Up until now Cassidy would have said that she didn't have a temper, but she was so exhausted from all the issues she'd had to contend with today that she could feel it rising. And not once in the time she had worked for him had he ever spoken to her in such an imperious tone. It made her think of a spoiled, rich prince getting everything he wanted. Which no doubt he had done.

Having grown up in the opposite of the lap of luxury, she couldn't even imagine how it would feel to have every one of your needs met whenever you desired it. Unfortunately her boss didn't share that experience. Which was no doubt why he showed so little emotion whenever one of his ex-girlfriends rang up begging for a second chance. Which he never gave. Once you were off Logan de Silva's list of intimate contacts, you were off. From what she had seen, he was a man who cared very little about anything other than winning his next billion-dollar deal, and she sometimes envied him that because she cared too much about everything.

'Well, I'm sorry but I can't just drop everything to be at your beck and call. When I first started working for you I explained that I would need advance notice if you ever needed me to travel with you.' Which so far he hadn't. 'And leaving to go halfway around the world in five minutes hardly counts as even short notice.'

'And might I remind you,' he said with lethal softness, 'that when you signed on as my EA I explained that I pay above and beyond the average wage because I specifically require you to be at my beck and call, and you were more than happy with that at the time.'

The dark look in his eyes made her feel hot and bothered. She was still uncomfortably aware that he was standing in front of her half-naked, her eyes constantly drawn to the pelt of dark hair that curled over the top of his singlet. She couldn't seem to stop herself from imagining how he would look naked.

She was also uncomfortably aware that what he said was true. But all she could think about was how she was going to tell Peta that she wouldn't be around this week when her sister had to take her final exams. It must be another one of Murphy's laws that when something horrible happened, it happened at the worst possible time.

Silence stretched between them with such savage intensity it completely took the wind out of her sails. She'd never been good with confrontation, which was why she was so good in her role as peacemaker in her family. It was her other superpower, along with her ability to compartmentalise situations and move on.

Knowing by his expression that he wouldn't take no for an answer, she grimaced. 'You're right, I did agree with your requirements when I took the job, but...' She faced him as one might face an angry lion in a small enclosure without a whip or a chair. 'I'll have to make a call first. Peta needs me more than ever this week.'

Logan came toward her, all power and languid grace, and for a moment she didn't think he was going to stop. Her eyes widened as she was assailed with the unexpected vision of him wrapping one of those large hands around the back of her neck and drawing her up on her toes to kiss her. Heat travelled swiftly up through her body, making her tingle in all the wrong places.

Breathless, she waited for what would no doubt be the kiss of her life to happen, but of course it didn't. He stopped an inch from touching her. 'As I said, so do I.' The look he gave her could have cut glass. All signs of the vulnerability she had glimpsed when he'd been speaking to his brother had completely disappeared. 'And my needs take precedence over Peter's. I'll have Gordon drop you home so you can shower and change and then I'll collect you in an hour. Be ready.'

His gaze flicked slowly down over her body and back up and Cassidy became very conscious that she must look like the Wicked Witch of the West with her hair drying in clumps and wearing one of his sweatshirts that was miles too big for her.

Then he was gone, leaving her to stew in silence.

She wondered if he was ever like this with his dates. But if he was they wouldn't be crying on the end of the phone when he broke up with them, they'd be rejoicing.

Like this he was domineering and exacting. There was only one way and that was his. Usually she didn't mind it. Usually she went with it.

Usually when she didn't feel like her life was falling apart at the seams. It made her want to tell him just where he could take his demanding attitude and what he could do with it when he got there. Which would shock the heck out of him because, while he encouraged her to give him her opinion on matters of business, he would never encourage her to outwardly defy him.

And she was sure if that ever happened he'd be the juggernaut he always was, speeding over whatever roadblocks were in his way like a souped-up supercar. Cassidy, by comparison, was more like a moped, dodging life's pitfalls as best she could with only one cylinder.

Logan stepped into the shower and doused his head under a stream of hot water. He didn't know what had shocked him more, the fact that Cassidy had said no to him or that she had a lover called Peter.

A shaft of something akin to jealousy speared through him and he knew why that was. She was the best EA he'd ever had. There was no way he wanted her falling in love, getting married, going off to have babies and leaving him.

Was she already in love with the guy? Is that why she was so keen to leave on time two nights a week and baulked at working weekends?

He thought about the way her bright green eyes had widened as he'd invaded her personal space. For a moment he'd been overcome with the urge to keep going and power her back against the wall until he had her flattened against him, and the intensity of that urge had been the only thing that had stopped him.

Had she felt the inconvenient chemistry between them?

Had she wanted him to claim her?

Logan swore softly and stuck his head back under the stream of water, turning it to an icy blast.

He had not found himself at the mercy of his baser instincts since he'd learned that giving in to passion and losing control was what had nearly brought his father unstuck. It was certainly what had eventually broken them as a family. Even calling themselves a family was a stretch. They'd been an institution that had performed for the public like trained seals, both parents putting duty ahead of everything else.

And he wouldn't ruin things with the best EA he'd ever had by confusing desire with a heightened state of adrenaline. Which was all that had been.

First the shock of finding her in his apartment like a half-drowned kitten and then being confronted with all that gloriously wild hair he'd itched to bury his fingers in. Who knew she'd been hiding that from the world?

Did she hide it from Peter as well, or just him?

Why do you care?

Irritated to find his mind once again charging down a path he had no intention of allowing it to go, he put the brakes on all thoughts of Cassidy's unruly appearance. It had happened, but it was over.

The sooner he saw her again in her usual sedate office attire the sooner he could forget he'd ever seen her any other way.

Professional. Sensible. Unflappable.

So no more imagining himself peeling open her lacy bra. No more wondering if her hair would be silky soft beneath his fingertips. And definitely no more arousing himself by wondering how her body would fit against his as he pressed himself into her.

Like now.

Cursing again, he pulled on jeans and a pullover and questioned his instinctive decision to take her with him to Arrantino. Perhaps she would be better staying back here in his office, taking care of business while he was gone.

But as soon as the thought formed he discounted it. The fact was he needed Cassidy with him because he had no idea what he was about to face, or how long he'd be gone. He was hoping it would only be a twenty-four-hour turn-around. Fly in, drum some sense into his brother, say hello to his mother, and fly out. Simple. Easy.

But if for some reason simple turned to complicated it would be far more efficient to have Cassidy with him than sending urgent messages to a different time zone and wondering how long it would be before she processed them.

But for that to happen she had to be completely on her game. She had to be back to her usual measured self.

And for that matter, so did he.

In her own words it had been a horrible day, capped off with a horrible night. His current adrenaline rush had nothing to do with Cassidy and everything to do with his brother's announcement that he wanted to abdicate. He wouldn't, Logan would see to that, but it had thrown him. Put him in in a heightened state of awareness. Like a warrior of old about to go into battle. All his senses were switched on and that was the only reason he had felt any form of arousal for Cassidy.

Feeling as if he had everything in hand again, he organised a change of clothes for himself and texted his driver to see if he'd returned to pick him up. The sooner he got to Arrantino and back, the better.

CHAPTER THREE

CASSIDY HAD TO jiggle her key in the lock a bit to open the old door of her clapboard rental and when she did she found the twins doing their homework on the coffee table, watching the latest reality singing show.

They waved an absent-minded hello, their eyes glued to the TV, as Peta came out of the kitchenette, wiping her hands on a dishrag. 'You're late tonight. I was getting worried.'

'Sorry. I sent a text.'

'An hour ago.' Peta followed her into the bedroom. 'Is everything okay? You look like you've just climbed out of someone's bed. And whose sweatshirt are you wearing?'

She had almost forgotten the shirt and blushed even though there was no reason to. 'It's Logan's.'

'Your boss?' Peta frowned as Cassidy reached into her closet and pulled her ancient suitcase down from the shelf. 'Why are you wearing your boss's shirt, and where are you going?'

'Arrantino.'

'For how long?'

Cassidy glanced over at her sister's disgruntled expression as she quickly folded a work blouse into her suitcase. 'I don't know. A day or two.'

'A day or two?' Peta frowned. 'I need you to take care of the girls this week. I'm in the middle of my final exams.'

'I know.' Cassidy hated that she was putting her sister out, and she genuinely loved taking care of her nieces. 'I thought maybe Dan could do it if I'm not back. Or Miss Marple across the hall.' Not that the twins liked her very much, other than when they deliberately confused her by pretending to be each other. 'I'm really sorry, but there's nothing I can do.'

'There is.' Her sister slapped her hands on her hips. 'You could say no.'

Cassidy thought about reminding Peta that her job as Logan de Silva's assistant was the only reason they could afford to pay their current rent, and the reason Peta had been able to attend beauty school while paying for her twins to get a decent education, but didn't. She didn't want Peta to feel guilty about Cassidy providing for them financially when she genuinely loved her job, and her sister and her twin nieces even more.

'You don't say no to Logan de Silva,' she said.

'Then quit. You initially took the job in the bank because it paid so well, but you're not really utilising your project management degree to the fullest. Maybe you should put some feelers out to see where that can take you.'

And one day she would. She'd move on from this job and expand her professional scope but that time wasn't when she might have to trawl through real-estate ads looking for a new place to live.

'You know your boss says jump and you say how high?' Peta added. 'And you still haven't explained why you're wearing his shirt.' Her sister gave her an assessing look. 'There's nothing going on between you, is there?'

'Of course not!' The very idea was a joke. 'I'm wearing his shirt because I got caught in the rain.'

'Thank God.' Peta exhaled a relieved breath. 'I don't want to see you get hurt.'

The fact that her sister thought she would be the one to get hurt in such a preposterous scenario stung a little. 'Maybe he would be the one left broken-hearted,' she said loftily.

'Get real.' Peta laughed, folding a skirt Cassidy had placed on the bed and adding it to her suitcase. 'He's a prince and a billionaire. I think we both know who would come out worst if anything did happen between you.'

And that stung a lot. It wasn't as if she harboured any secret illusions where her illustrious boss was concerned. She knew he was out of her league. And really she wasn't even sure she wanted to meet anyone. The few times she had dated had been a disaster she didn't care to repeat.

But for Peta to also just assume that she wasn't capable of attracting a man like Logan if she actually wanted to hurt more than it should. She'd sustained her sister in every way that she could over the years and a little bit of support in return wouldn't go astray.

'Lucky I'm not that foolish,' she said, blindly grabbing underwear from a drawer.

'Just be careful,' Peta cautioned. 'I've heard the way your voice changes when you talk about him and it worries me. You've been so content to do his bidding since you started working for him and I've sometimes wondered if you're not a little bit in love with him, Cass.'

'In love…?' Cassidy zipped her suitcase closed with a little more force than necessary. 'That's absurd.' She wasn't in love with her boss. If she was ever going to fall in love she wanted it to be with someone she had half a chance of being with, not with a prince who had an appetite for supermodels. Being five feet five and homely, that wouldn't be her.

She sighed. How did things change so quickly? Yesterday she'd gone to work, stopped at the dojo where she practised martial arts for two hours twice a week and helped the twins with their maths homework after dinner. Her private life ran as seamlessly as her professional life and she was happy with it. There were no complications and no nasty surprises waiting around the corner.

Peta gave her a look. 'Your problem is that you're always too willing to help the underdog and it will come back to bite you one day.'

Cassidy laughed and shook her head. 'If there is one thing Logan de Silva cannot be described as, it's an underdog.'

'I was speaking metaphorically,' Peta dismissed. 'But he plays to your sense of obligation and I don't want him to take advantage of you.'

Perhaps he wasn't the only one who did that, she reflected, instantly contrite at the unbidden thought. Her sister was beautiful and wilful but she was also loyal and loving.

'Just don't be a pushover,' Peta continued. 'You deserve more for yourself. You deserve to have a life other than work and me and the twins. It's something to think about.'

Cassidy felt her hackles rise at the underlying message in her sister's tone. 'I have a life. And I love taking care of my nieces.'

'Yes, but you don't have anything else.'

'I don't need anything else,' she said, struggling not to feel testy at her sister's insistence. 'Look, I can't stand here and argue with you right now. I need to grab a shower, change, and do my hair before he arrives to collect me. And, yes, I know that makes me a pushover in your eyes but...'

Right now she didn't feel as if she had any choice. Logan had made it clear that she had to go with him and unless she was prepared to lose her job—which she wasn't at the moment—she could hardly defy him.

A shiver went through her as she recalled that moment

in his apartment when she'd seen him standing there half-naked, dripping in sweat. It was as if she'd never seen such a thing before. She had. Plenty of times at her dojo.

The last person she wanted to find attractive was her boss. And hopefully the feeling was an aberration, the result of stress, and would be completely gone by the time she joined him in the car.

Noticing that Peta was still watching her with a frown on her face, Cassidy lifted her chin. 'I'll be fine. I'm always fine.'

But half an hour later, as Dan carried her case to the front door, she didn't feel fine.

'Don't worry about the girls,' he said, giving her shoulder a light squeeze as he leaned down to kiss her cheek. 'I'll look out for them while you're gone.'

Cassidy murmured her appreciation as she handed Logan's driver her suitcase. She especially didn't feel fine as she followed Gordon down the short walkway and climbed into the back of the town car. She felt more of a pushover than ever.

Her sister's comments kept replaying in her head, particularly the one about her being secretly in love with her boss, as she glanced over to find him sprawled in the back of the car like a disgruntled model wearing faded jeans and a knit sweater that hugged his muscular frame. She really wished that he didn't look so good because she couldn't deny that the flashes of sexual chemistry she'd felt in his apartment earlier had seriously unsettled her. Particularly since they hadn't gone away as she'd hoped. It was as if seeing him half-naked had revealed a deep-seated desire inside herself she hadn't even known she possessed. And she needed to close it down. Now.

Despite what Peta said, she was happy with her life. She

didn't need anything else, and she wasn't about to jeopardise her job by making the fatal error of creating more out of this unwanted attraction to her boss than actually existed. Today was just one of those days and tomorrow she'd be back to normal. Until then she'd grit her teeth and focus on work.

'Why are you wearing a suit?'

His voice was low and smooth in the confines of the darkened car.

Cassidy glanced at him. 'Because we're going on a business trip.' And, in her view, clothes maketh the person.

Growing up in a small, conservative parish, you soon learned that the way you dressed mattered a lot. She knew what it meant to be gossiped about and turned into an outcast. After their mother had deserted them Peta had become a bit of a wild child, running with the wrong crowd and falling pregnant by the town rebel at sixteen. The townsfolk had gone from supportive to vitriolic, and in the blink of an eye the Ryan girls were bad news. Then Cassidy had inadvertently added to their newfound notoriety in a way that had seemed to solidify her family's reputation in the eyes of their town.

She still remembered how devastating it had felt to walk down the street and know that everyone was whispering about you behind your back. Their father had lost his job, having to find work in a nearby parish, leaving her and Peta alone for long periods of time.

Finally they had moved and things had slowly improved, but with twin babies to clothe and feed, they had all gone into survivor mode. During that time Cassidy had vowed to step out of the mould she'd been placed in so that now, when people met her, they saw the smart, capable woman that she was and not the downtrodden girl she had once been.

'It's late,' Logan said, dragging her mind out of the past

she'd left behind. 'And we'll be flying all night. I don't expect you to be uncomfortable.'

'I won't be.' And even if she was she'd never let him know.

Wondering if she was going to get anything right today, she pulled her tablet out of her bag to check her emails. What she needed to do was think of this unexpected trip to Arrantino as a godsend because it would give her a chance to work up a plan and think clearly about her next move.

Because no matter how much she hated the thought of it, her sister was moving out and Cassidy had no clue as to what she would do next. She couldn't afford to live alone, but the thought of getting a new flatmate depressed her. What if the person she chose turned out to be a weirdo? Or what if things didn't work out between Peta and Dan? Perhaps she should remain alone in case her sister and the twins needed to move back in again. The whole situation made her feel vulnerable and rejected—two emotional states she worked very hard to avoid.

Just as she had worked hard to help her sister out, upgrading to a larger place when Peta and the twins had moved to New York so she could be on hand to support them. Peta had barely been able to make ends meet since the twins had been born and as Cassidy had been finishing an online degree at Colombia, it had made sense for them to all move in together.

But she really wanted to ask Peta if she was sure about Dan. After she'd had the twins Peta had vowed to never trust another man again. She'd devoted herself to bringing up her girls and giving them a stable life and, okay, maybe it had been short-sighted to think that Peta would never meet another man again, but Cassidy had believed her when she'd said she was done with men. They had even joked that if there were any good men left in the world they wouldn't come near the Ryan sisters.

'Are you planning to turn that on, or just stare at it the whole time?'

Cassidy blinked, embarrassed to discover that she had become so engrossed by memories of the past that she had yet to turn on her device. 'I had an argument with Peta,' she admitted with a slight grimace. 'It's distracted me.'

Logan's brow climbed his forehead. 'Over you coming with me, I presume.'

'Yes.'

'You did explain that it's just business.'

'Of course,' she said briskly. 'But apparently I'm always putting work ahead of my social life. It's unhealthy.'

'Peter sounds a little demanding. I hope this isn't going to interfere with your work.'

'Not at all.'

Although hadn't Peta's announcement about her engagement been the thing to put her in a spin in the first place?

Logan must have noted something in her expression because he scowled. 'You had better be sure because I need you to be your usual self while we're in Arrantino.'

'I know you're referring to how many times I mucked up today,' she said, 'but that was out of the ordinary.'

'I want ordinary.'

Well, if there was an annual award for Miss Ordinary she'd win it uncontested. 'You've got it.' She gave him a tight smile.

Despite the lateness of the hour, Republic Airport was busy and noisy as Gordon drove the car straight onto the tarmac. A light plane was about to land, and a jeep sped out of a nearby hangar to greet it. Another plane was set to take off and closer at hand a small black helicopter sat like a squat beetle, its rotors suddenly whining and whipping up the air around them.

Cassidy ducked her head against the downdraught, moving quickly toward the set of airstairs connected to Logan's private plane. Strands of her hair had come loose from the downdraught and she pushed them back, missing one of the steps as she did so.

Logan immediately clamped his strong hand around her elbow, sending a bolt of sensation up her arm.

Disturbed by even that small touch, Cassidy thanked him and quickly scrambled to ascend the stairs.

Taking in the plush leather interior in one quick glance, she settled into one of the armchairs by the window, buckled her seat belt and handed a customs official her passport to check.

Once they were cleared to fly, Logan took the seat on the other side of the glossy table from her.

Ignoring the way her heart sped up, she scrolled through her boss's schedule and fired off a few quick emails, cancelling the most obvious meetings.

Then she worked through the various emails on her tablet. So far there were none relating to the scandal in Arrantino, but Cassidy knew that it was just a matter of time. 'Once we're airborne we'll need to go over my schedule for the week and decide which meetings to delegate and which ones to cancel.'

'I've already worked that out,' she said without looking up. 'I'm just not sure what to do with the stakeholder meeting for the new Westgate tunnel development on Thursday morning. It's still two days away so we can wait, but I don't want to cancel at the last minute because there's a very real chance that the Peterstone Organisation will get cold feet and pull out before then.'

Which would undermine the whole process, not to mention render all the work they had done winning over the relevant Australian government agencies over the last eight months to be the front runners to win the bid to build the new tunnel. It was a ten-billion-dollar deal, but they needed the equity that the Peterstone Organisation was looking to invest to cover the debt. She knew it was an important deal to Logan because it would launch the Arrantino bank into a whole new market.

Everyone had said that he wouldn't be able to pull it off, which had only made him work harder, and she'd hate to see all that effort go to waste.

'If they pull out because I can't make it then they pull out,' he said dismissively. 'The future of my country is more important than one deal.'

Knowing he was downplaying how disappointed he was at the prospect of losing the coup, she nodded. 'I'll draft a response and put it on hold until you've had a chance to speak with your brother.' Her fingers flew effortlessly across the keyboard, only pausing when the plane set off down the runway.

Cassidy glanced out the window and gripped the armrests with both hands.

'Are you a nervous flyer?'

Unaware that Logan had been watching her, she glanced up, a wide smile curving her lips. 'No.' She sounded breathless, a warm buzzing feeling in her stomach as the jet rocketed down the runway. 'I love flying. Particularly take-off. I've only ever flown once before and I don't want to miss a single part of it.'

Peta had won an all-expenses-paid trip to Cancun on the radio after arriving in New York and for one blissful week she, Peta, and the twins had soaked up the sun and sipped mocktails by the swimming pool. It had definitely given

Cassidy the travel bug, but since then she'd had little time or money to set aside for holidays.

Suddenly the plane lifted off and her stomach bottomed out. 'Does it always feel that way?'

'I don't know,' Logan said with a frown. 'I barely take any notice any more.'

'Well, I definitely want to experience that again.' She released a rushed breath, and then coloured when she noticed the frown on his face. 'Sorry. You're probably used to travelling with women who are a lot more sophisticated. Shall we get back to work?'

'Actually, it's probably best if you turn in and get some sleep. There's a bedroom at the rear of the plane. You can use that.'

Cassidy could feel the weight of the whole day bearing down on her and she groaned softly when she mentally went through the clothing she had packed and realised that she had been so distracted by her discussion with Peta that she hadn't packed anything to sleep in. In fact, the only thing other than suits and clean underwear she had packed was her dobok, and she'd only grabbed that because it had been lying on the end of the bed freshly laundered. She hadn't even packed a change of shoes.

As if sensing her frustration, Logan glanced up from the reports he had spread out on the table. 'What's wrong?'

Reluctant to go into the specifics, she shrugged lightly. 'I forgot to pack something to sleep in.'

His eyes caught and held hers for a moment. 'I have plenty of shirts on board, you can use one of those.'

'No, that's fine.' She already borrowed an item of his clothing today and it was more than enough. 'Just tell me how many hours are left in this day.'

'Two.'

'I think I'm going to sit here and count the seconds before I move again. I swear I must have walked under a ladder or a black cat crossed my path this morning without me noticing it.'

His brow quirked. 'You're superstitious?'

'No.' She sighed heavily. 'But how else do you account for a day like today?'

Logan's lips curled into a rueful grin. 'You roll with it.'

That is exactly what her sensei would tell her to do.

'Easy for some,' she said despondently. 'I'm not a roll-with-it kind of girl.' She never had been and she never would be. 'I'm more the pull it apart, analyse it to death and put it into a plastic food container kind of girl. That's why your office runs so well.'

And maybe why her love life sucked. She'd discovered on the few dates that she'd had that men generally didn't appreciate being picked apart so that their motives were laid bare. Unfortunately for them, Cassidy didn't like being used so it inevitably turned into a lose-lose situation.

'My office hasn't run quite so well today,' Logan drawled.

'I know. And again I'm sorry about that. I had a few things on my mind.'

'Such as?'

Cassidy blinked with surprise, absently noting the granite-hard line of his unshaven jaw. She had never seen him as anything other than clean-shaven in the office and she couldn't stop herself from wondering if it would be hard or soft to the touch. 'You really want to know?'

'If it means I have my EA back then I do.'

For a moment she had thought that he'd actually been interested in her as a person and now she felt…disappointed. Wondering whether to tell him or not, she decided that he had asked and, knowing him, he'd likely push until she answered anyway.

'My sister told me that she's getting married and it threw me out all day.'

Logan frowned. 'You don't like her partner?'

'No, I love him. He's great…but she… It's just taken me by surprise. And on top of that she needed me to look after my twin nieces this week so she's not happy with me for leaving.'

'Can't she find someone else?'

'I'm hoping she can, but really I look after them all the time so we've never had to rely on anyone else on a regular basis.'

'All the time?'

Seeing his surprise, she shrugged. 'Pretty much. But I'm always happy to do it. I love my nieces.'

'I'm sure you do. But it sounds like your sister is taking advantage.'

Having felt guilty for thinking the same thing herself once or twice, Cassidy jumped to Peta's defence. 'She's had a hard time. She was a teenage mother and the twin's father bailed before they were born. She didn't have a lot of help and it was really hard for her.'

'I have no doubt. So who did help out?' he asked shrewdly. 'You?'

'There wasn't anyone else. Our mother had left two years earlier, and our father sort of lost the plot. He became depressed and started gambling…' She bit into her lower lip as she remembered how worried she and Peta had been that something would happen to him. That fear had been realised when a few years back he'd died after his car had collided with a tree.

'Logan, I'm pretty sure you don't want to hear any of this.' And she was shocked to find that she was seriously at risk of blurting out her long, sordid history, including her own awful indiscretion, and she never talked about the past to anyone, preferring to leave it long buried. 'I promise that once we land I'll be back to normal. In fact, I'll start now. I'm going to sit here and work all night then my lack of packing won't matter.'

'You can't do that. We'll arrive just before lunch Arrantinian time tomorrow and I need you fresh. If you don't sleep you'll suffer jet-lag.'

'I'll be fine.'

Logan sat back in his chair, regarding her steadily. 'I didn't know you were this stubborn.'

'I'm not stubborn.'

'Cassidy, if I have to order you into the bedroom, I will.'

Cassidy's eyes went wide. She blushed, even though she knew there was no reason to. Still the devil on her shoulder whispered to her that she should ask him what he would do if she disobeyed and the heated anticipation that shot through her sent her flying to her feet.

'Fine. I'll use the bed. But I'm not borrowing a shirt.'

Not waiting for his response, she grabbed her bag and suitcase and went in search of the bedroom.

Logan released a slow breath after Cassidy headed out of sight and scrubbed his hand over his face.

He was very glad that she hadn't taken up the offer of his shirt. Just the thought of her in that and nothing else had been enough to send his blood pressure sky high again. But what would she be wearing instead? Her underwear? Nothing?

Cursing beneath his breath as his body responded with predictable urgency, he ripped the cap off the nearest water bottle and guzzled the liquid to cool himself down.

When Cassidy had stepped into his car dressed in a suit, and with her hair fastidiously tied back, despite his questioning of her, he'd breathed a sigh of relief that his normal EA had returned, but she kept doing things that threw him off centre.

Like her excitement over the plane taking off. She'd been right when she'd said she'd come across as unsophisticated. None of the other women he dated would have ever shown such a natural reaction, always carefully considering how they looked before opening their mouths, and to his disbelief he'd found himself enjoying Cassidy's uncensored delight.

He'd enjoyed her smile even more. It had transformed her face from attractive to stunning and he'd been unable to look away. It was as if he'd never seen the woman smile before and with a frown he realised that he couldn't remember a time when he had. Not like that, anyway. She came to work, she did her job, and then she went home. It was the way he liked it and the way he wanted it to remain.

Wondering if she was as innocent in other matters as she was in flying, Logan gave himself a mental dressing down. He recognised that he was probably only seeking a distraction from thinking about his current problems, but his EA was off limits. Besides, she already had a lover. The tall, well-built guy who had kissed her goodbye in her doorway. So not that innocent after all.

His jaw clenched at the thought of her with some unknown man, and he didn't like the way that affected him either. Cassidy could be with ten men and it wouldn't have anything to do with him.

Reminding himself that he might be his father's son but he most definitely did not behave like him with his employees, he forced his mind to forget Cassidy's sweet smile and instead think about the more important issue of what he was going to say to his brother after he arrived in Arrantino.

He also reminded himself that Cassidy's childhood was none of his business and that he did not get personal with his EAs. Personal equalled complicated and complicated equalled trouble. All he needed to know about Cassidy was whether she was fit enough to do her job, not how she had coped with all the difficulties she had obviously faced.

He rolled his shoulders and felt the muscles in his back bunch and release. Maybe his sudden interest in her was not only to do with shock, but because he didn't want to think about going home. Going home to face the restricted life of a sitting monarch.

Not if he could help it.

It was enough to sometimes feel that he was like his father, a man who had always been in control of his surroundings—Logan certainly didn't want to return and take up the same job that he had held. But he also knew that he'd do anything for his brother after watching him battle so much to be well. It left him in quite a dilemma.

Unbidden, his gaze shifted to the rear of the plane. To Cassidy. He scrubbed a hand over his face, resigned to the fact that it was going to be a long night.

CHAPTER FOUR

ARRANTINO WAS BEAUTIFUL.

Cassidy couldn't take her eyes off the landscape she could see from her vantage point in the plane as they were coming in to land. High mountains and deep green valleys and villages dotted outside the main city, which looked to have a wall running around the perimeter and a river winding through it. Not that she could see it all, but she could see that it was nestled on the coast and the sand looked like a ribbon of gold against the deep blue of the Mediterranean.

A blue the exact shade of Logan's eyes.

Not that she should be thinking about his eyes. Or any other part of his anatomy, for that matter. Today was a new day and it was going to be the exact opposite of the day before.

To her surprise she'd managed to sleep most of the night in the hugely comfortable bed and she was showered and dressed for success, as the twins would say.

In the end she'd slept in her knickers and blouse and it had been okay. With any luck Logan would sort out this issue with his brother quickly and they'd be back home by tonight New York time before she even needed to launder anything.

She wondered what was behind Logan's staunch determination that he would not be King. She could guess that some of it had to do with the fact that he didn't want to change his life and maybe he didn't want to move back to Arrantino, but his comment that he wasn't king material had made her curious.

If anyone was king material, in her mind, it was her boss. He commanded attention and respect wherever he went, without even trying, and people lined up to get his advice. Admittedly that advice was usually business related but she didn't believe for a second that his keen intelligence was limited to running a bank. Especially since he'd completely turned it around in the five years he'd been at the helm and lifted it from just another boutique investment bank into a global concern. His reach into the Australasian market was the last bastion he had to conquer and she knew he wouldn't rest until he had, and he would because he worked harder than any person she'd ever met before.

His determination was a formidable force and she was only glad it was his brother who had to face it and not her.

The image of him stalking toward her in his apartment building as he'd told her that his needs took precedence over Peta's sent a hot, shivery sensation down her spine, pooling low in her pelvis. Which did not bode well for the business-as-usual front she planned to adopt.

The last thing she had ever wanted was to find her boss sexually attractive and for those few moments, and a few afterwards when she'd caught the look in his eyes, that was how she had felt.

And it didn't seem to matter that he was exactly the kind of man her dear father had warned her and Peta away from when they had hit their teenage years. Men who were too good looking for their own good, and expected everything to drop into their laps. Cassidy wasn't sure if Logan expected it, or if it just happened because of who he was, but there was no doubt that it did happen. Her sister's question about whether she was in love with him returned like a bomb. But she wasn't in love with Logan, just her job.

A job she relied on too much to ever put it in jeopardy by developing feelings for her boss. Her world had fallen apart before, and now, with her sister throwing in the curveball of her impending marriage, it was more imperative than ever that Cassidy keep at least one aspect of her life the same. Because while most people could deal with change relatively easily, the whole concept of it made her want to run for the hills.

Feeling skittish about what lay ahead, she went online on her laptop and did another check on what was being reported, to find that not only was news of the King's affair being bandied around but the breaking news was that he planned to abdicate as well.

Cassidy knew how much Logan would hate this new development. How much he would hate being critiqued and analysed by the world's media. And no doubt it would make his conversation with his brother that much more difficult. But would it make the King more or less inclined to abdicate? And what would that mean for her if Logan did become King? Would she keep working for him? Would he want her to? Would she want to?

Not wanting to think about any of that, she shoved all thoughts of her family and the changes afoot in her life to the back of her mind and concentrated on the information in front of her. From what she could see, the palace had not yet commented on the growing crisis, but in her estimation they would need to do so soon. Already the London Stock Exchange had responded to the news of the King's imminent abdication with a downward turn of Arrantinian stock, and no doubt New York would follow suit when it opened.

In addition, the paparazzi were trying even harder to

find out the identity of the petite brunette seen in the King's arms and Cassidy was only glad it wasn't her.

She knew how it felt to have everyone talking about you behind your back and she never wanted to go through that again.

Wondering where her boss was now that they were so close to landing, she looked up to see him walking toward her.

Freshly showered and shaved, with his honey-blond hair scraped back from his forehead and wearing a crisp navy suit with a pale blue shirt that highlighted his olive skin, he looked like a man who could give a woman a night of endlessly hot sex.

And since when did she start her mornings thinking about sex, endless or otherwise?

She swallowed heavily, and sternly reminded herself that wide shoulders and a powerful physique were the least important attributes that made a man desirable. A caring nature and a good sense of humour were far more favourable.

Unfortunately those traits didn't even rate as he sprawled in the seat opposite her like a model, his brilliant blue eyes scanning her face as he picked up the espresso the co-pilot had not long since delivered. 'What's wrong?'

'Why do you think something is wrong?' she parried.

'You're staring.'

'Oh, I...' She sucked in a deep breath and forcibly shut down the disastrous attraction she was struggling to get on top of. There was the much more pressing issue of the conjecture surrounding Leo's abdication to inform him of. 'I think you need to brace yourself.'

Logan stretched out his long legs beneath the table, taking up most of the space. 'Just give it to me straight.'

'The media have picked up the story that Leo is thinking of abdicating, pretty much the whole world now knows.'

Logan didn't move a muscle as he looked at her, his thickly lashed gaze narrowing dangerously. 'Perhaps next time I say give it to me straight, don't listen.' He let out a frustrated breath and massaged his forehead. 'Anything else?'

'Arrantinian stock has fallen four percent in London this morning and there's intense speculation as to whether you will become King or not.'

'Let them speculate.' The dangerous look in his eyes deepened and he suddenly pushed to his feet and paced around the cabin. 'It's what they do best. Lying in wait for one of us to slip up.'

Cassidy grimaced. 'Todd Greene is also one of the journalists on the story.' And she knew how her boss would take that news and he didn't disappoint, cursing volubly under his breath.

Todd Greene had been searching for dirt on Logan for three years now. Ever since Logan had insisted that he be fired from a respected newspaper for writing a salacious story about an actress Logan had dated that had ended with her checking into rehab. Todd had struggled to find work after that and as a result he had promised that he'd get Logan back. So far he'd come up empty.

'From his article I get the feeling he's either in Arrantino or on his way,' she added, frowning as she scanned an article questioning the King's health.

'What is it?' Having noticed her hesitation, Logan's interest sharpened to that of a sword tip.

'I'm not sure. There's something here about your brother's illness returning.'

She glanced up in time to see a flash of pain cross her boss's face. 'It hasn't,' he said woodenly. 'Leo is fine.'

Cassidy knew very little about his brother. She'd never had any inclination to delve into Logan's royal history so she hadn't. But she knew all about what it felt like to have people whisper about you behind your back and she wouldn't wish it on anyone. 'What did he have?'

Logan arched a brow at her question. 'You mean you haven't done an Internet search on my background already?'

'No.' She could sense his anger from across the enclosed space and some deep-seated part of her wanted to reach across the small distance and sooth him. 'Should I have done?'

He gave a harsh bark of laughter. 'No, but it's not a secret. Leo had leukaemia as a teenager.'

'Oh, that's terrible.'

'Yes, it was.' Logan dragged a hand through his hair. 'But it was a long time ago. I rarely think about it now, but at the time…' His eyes took on a shadowed hue. 'It was pretty ugly. I took a leave of absence from school for a few months to be with him and basically ran amok, dodging the palace tutors and entertaining Leo as much as I could during his weaker moments.' He shook his head as if to clear the memory. 'You do not want to challenge me to a game of Monopoly,' he said. 'I'm an expert.'

Always having assumed that her boss was as coldhearted as he was rumoured to be, she was moved to discover once again that, at least where his brother was concerned, he was anything but. 'I'll keep that in mind,' she said, her tone softening as she added, 'That was really nice of you…to stay with your brother, considering how you must have been feeling at the time.'

'It wasn't *nice*.' As if rejecting her sympathy, his voice turned hard. 'It was *necessary*. My parents were unavailable to give him the care that he required. Someone had to step up and I was glad to do it.'

'I understand completely.'

And she did. She'd stepped up many times since Peta had become pregnant and she wouldn't change a thing either.

Something passed between them as he looked at her. Some level of understanding that went deeper than anything they'd ever shared before.

'Do you think you should take a seat for landing?' she offered, unsure how to deal with the unexpected connection between them, as well as being aware that they were perilously close to landing.

Logan glanced out of the window and surprised her by resuming his seat again. When the plane lightly touched down on the tarmac Cassidy felt a whole new bundle of nerves jump around inside her stomach.

In a short time she would be meeting Logan's family and she'd never felt her small-town roots as keenly as she did right now.

'So when I greet your brother I curtsy and call him Your Majesty—is that right?'

'Yes.' He stood up and straightened his shirt cuffs. 'Though you needn't worry about mucking up your greeting. I think my brother has bigger issues to face.'

'I know. But I don't want to get it wrong.' The last thing she wanted to do was draw attention to herself. 'And I curtsy to your mother as well.'

'Yes. And since she was Queen she is still referred to as Your Majesty.'

'Okay,' Cassidy said, a look of concentration on her face.

Logan gave her a faint smile. 'It's not like you to be nervous. You weren't when you met me.'

'Of course I was nervous.' She shot him a quick look. 'It was a job interview and I really wanted the job.'

'You hid it well.'

'Another of my superpowers.'

He gave her a bemused smile. 'How many do you have?'

'Not many. I think that's the last one.'

He shook his head as if there was something about her he couldn't fathom, and placed his hand in the small of her back to indicate that she should precede him toward the doorway.

Flustered as much by the small gesture as the warmth of his hand, she barely registered when two imposing men in sharp black suits stepped into the plane. For a moment she thought they were being hijacked and then they nodded at Logan.

'Your Highness.' They greeted him in unison and Cassidy's eyes widened. Should she be calling him that now? 'The car is here.'

'Thank you.' Logan gestured for her to precede him and as soon as the bright sunlight blinded her she came to a dead stop. She hadn't realised he had followed so closely behind her until she felt his breath fan the nape of her neck when he spoke.

'What is it?'

'Just...the sun.'

Feeling gauche again, she sucked in a deep breath, her eyes following the cavalcade of black SUVs lined up on the tarmac like hyphens on a page. Aware that she hadn't moved and that Logan was waiting, she collected herself and descended the stairs as if she did this sort of thing every day of the week and twice on Sundays.

Cool, Cassidy, she reminded herself. *Remember to be cool and to not look like Dorothy straight out of Kansas at everything you see.*

Highly attuned to her boss's every movement as the cars headed off in formation, Cassidy saw Logan's jaw harden as he read an email on his phone.

'More problems?' she asked quietly.

'Yes,' he said. 'Leo won't be at the palace to meet us. He's taken his new woman into hiding to protect her from the media fallout. He's promised to call me later.' By the disdain in his voice Logan wasn't happy with that idea. 'A press release is already being prepared to confirm his abdication. The palace is in lockdown to contain the fallout from the media speculation.'

'That makes sense.' Cassidy pulled up the stock market app on her tablet. 'Arrantino banking stock has fallen by eleven percent in New York and while that's not catastrophic the reports suggest that the spillover will affect trading in many of the local businesses. On top of that—' she paused, knowing that he wouldn't like this next bit '—the Peterstone Organisation has pulled out of the Westgate deal.'

Logan swore roughly. 'Whoever leaked my brother's plans to the press is going to wish that they hadn't when I'm finished with them. But forget Peterstone. I suspect that they're overcapitalised as it is and the leadership crisis has given them the excuse they were looking for to pull out without losing face. Instead contact the Kellard Insurance trustees. They showed some interest in investing in the tunnel at one point and I know they're still looking for an equity stake to put their pension fund into. It might bridge the gap in time to make the tender deadline.'

Noting down everything he said, Cassidy looked up in time to see their car pass through a large stone archway that separated the countryside from the city of Trinia, Arrantino's major metropolitan and business centre.

'Wow, it's beautiful,' she murmured, her eyes glancing over a city that seemed to perfectly blend centuries-old buildings with brand-new constructions. 'And hardly any traffic. That's amazing for a city with just under a million citizens.'

Logan gave her an amused look. 'That's because the traffic has been cleared for our arrival. Once we're through, this boulevard will resemble Fifth Avenue at rush hour.'

'Oh, sorry.' She turned her attention back to the tablet, embarrassed.

Logan took her chin in his hand and turned her face so that she was looking at him once more. 'Why are you sorry?'

His fingers felt warm and strong and a liquid bubble felt like it burst deep inside her. 'I just keep making mistakes.'

'That wasn't a mistake. You don't know the royal protocol.'

'No.' Her throat felt thick and she swallowed, wanting to move and not wanting to move at the same time. 'It's just a little overwhelming, I suppose.'

Logan's brows arched. 'You'll be fine. This will be all over before you know it.'

Cassidy sucked in a soft, deep breath when Logan released his hold on her, her traitorous skin tingling from his touch. Within moments they were turning into the wrought-iron gates that led to the Royal Palace. The cars rumbled slowly over the wide cobblestoned drive that opened out into a massive forecourt.

'That's my great-grandfather, Javier,' Logan said, noticing her staring at a large statue of a military figure on a rearing horse as the cars stopped at the main entrance to the palace. 'He prevented the French from invading our humble country, thus aligning ourselves more closely with the Spanish, and becoming a national hero.'

'That would explain why Arrantinians speak a version of Spanish.'

'We were part of Spain for a long time before my great-great-grandfather seceded, so we go back a long way with our neighbour. That wasn't the easiest of battles either and you'll see his painting front and centre as you walk through the front doors.

'The palace is amazing. There must be a thousand windows on this side alone. I've seen pictures of it, of course, but in the flesh…'

'It's imposing. But it's meant to be that way. To put off any interlopers who thought we were fair game for a small kingdom, and to make any others envious of Arrantino's wealth.'

'Ah, the shock and awe trick.'

Her lips curved into a smile, but Logan obviously didn't share her humour because he turned away as a footman opened his door.

'Your Highness.'

She tried not to let his abrupt dismissal affect her by reminding herself that she was here to work, not to entertain him, but she wasn't completely successful.

He held his hand out to assist her from the car and Cassidy took it, even though she didn't want to. He gripped her fingers firmly, releasing her as soon as her feet touched the ground as if he felt the same tremor that she did when they touched. Which was probably the most fanciful thought she'd had yet and was evidence that maybe she wasn't as completely back to normal as she would like.

Something to work on.

Turning toward the stone steps, she was just in time to see Logan grin widely at the portly man in a suit and waistcoat standing to attention in front of him.

They greeted each other in Arrantinian before Logan turned back to her. 'This is my assistant, Cassidy Ryan. Cassidy, this is Gerome. He has been with our family for, what is it, Gerome? One century or two?'

'Sometimes it feels like two, Your Highness,' the retainer deadpanned.

He shared a look with Logan that seemed to suggest that right now it seemed like even more.

'Indeed.' Logan shook his head. 'Is my mother about?'

'Her Highness has a meeting with the director of the festival of the arts but she has been informed of your arrival. Housekeeping is preparing your apartments for your return and the King advised that you are to have free use of his offices.'

'Very good. Please arrange for a selection of pastries and extra-strong coffee to be delivered there.'

Now that they were here, Cassidy sensed the huge responsibility that truly faced her boss and she couldn't help feeling sorry for him. Her small problem of having to find another place to live seemed minute in comparison.

'Follow me,' Logan directed, striding through two huge wooden doors that stood about twenty feet tall.

They made their way towards the rear of the palace and Cassidy barely knew where to look as they passed through the vaulted, richly carpeted hallways lined with antique furniture and centuries-old artwork interspersed with oak-tree-thick marble pillars. The feeling was one of peace and serenity and if she hadn't been rushing to keep up with her boss she would have slowed her pace to fit the setting.

The King's formal offices were made up of four rooms, large and airy with French-style windows that overlooked emerald-green lawns bordering the river. The Arrantino mountain range majestically filled in the backdrop, the sky already a blinding azure blue.

The main office was uncluttered and contemporary, a large walnut desk taking up the centre position with comfortable cream sofas beneath French windows, and centuries-old paintings and modern bookcases lining the walls.

This room alone was the size of her apartment back home and it was difficult not to gape.

'Do you want me to use the desk we passed on the way in?' she asked, her tablet in her hand as she prepared to stop gawping and get down to business.

'No. Set up on the sofa for now. I'm assuming Leo's private secretary uses that desk so I'll have another one brought in here temporarily.'

As soon as he spoke a slender woman with the grace of a dancer stepped into the office. With midnight-black hair, red lips and the build of a greyhound, she looked like she belonged on the set of a nineteen-fifties French film noir.

'Welcome, Your Highness.' Even her voice was smoky-soft with mystery. 'The King sends his apologies for not being here to greet you.'

'Margaux. It's good to see you again. This is Cassidy, my assistant. We'll need a desk brought in here. Can you arrange it?'

'Of course, sir. Is there anything else?'

'You don't happen to know the whereabouts of my brother, do you?'

'No. He didn't say.'

Logan's mouth pressed into a flat line. 'I'll want a debrief soon, but I'll let you know when.'

'As you wish. I'm at your disposal.'

Wondering just how much the other woman would be at his disposal, Cassidy caught the catty thought and banished it. Margaux had acted like a consummate professional—just as she needed to do—and she set her phone and laptop on the coffee table while she replied to a new email that had just come in requesting data on a deal they had not long closed.

Relieved to have work to focus on, she emptied her mind of everything else, only stopping to enjoy a delicious pastry and welcome cup of coffee from a team of servants who came and went as discreetly as mice.

An hour later an older woman who was sharply beautiful with styled blonde hair and timeless blue eyes a shade lighter than Logan's entered, almost breathing fire.

'Logan.' She didn't bother knocking as she swept into the room. 'It's good to see you. Leo said that he had brought you up to speed on the crisis.'

Logan bowed in greeting before kissing the woman on both cheeks. 'He's informed me of what he intends to do. I plan to change his mind about it. May I introduce you to Cassidy Ryan, my executive assistant.'

The woman cast Cassidy an appraising glance under which she felt like squirming.

'Cassidy, my mother, Her Majesty, Queen Valeria.'

His mother?

Shocked, Cassidy wobbled to her feet and lowered into what she hoped was a decent curtsy. 'Your Majesty, it's a pleasure to meet you. You have a lovely home.'

The Queen barely gave her a nod, dismissing her out of hand as she turned back to her son. 'Do you know where Leo has gone? He hasn't apprised me of his whereabouts.'

'Not specifically,' Logan said. 'Only that he's taking care of the woman he's currently seeing.'

His mother made a moue of distaste. 'That is so like Leo. He's such an emotional animal.' She shook her head as if that were a very bad thing. 'Don't think for a minute that you will be able to talk him out of his current plan of action. He's very set about abdicating. And so he should be, given the scandal.'

'You only think that because of the past.'

'I've forgotten the past,' she said briskly. 'As should you. The future is all that matters and our country needs you. You can't distance yourself from us for ever, and you will make a great king. You've always been level-headed in a crisis.'

'I don't want the role,' Logan ground out.

'Maybe not.' His mother eyed him, then continued, 'The new modern art wing at the national museum must be opened this afternoon, and then there is a meeting with the cabinet tomorrow. If Leo's not back, you'll need to attend that as well.'

'Isn't there someone else who can open the museum?'

'No. I have a choral exhibition to oversee. And the director of the museum will be expecting someone of senior rank since he's already been promised an audience with the King.'

'Fine. Just tell me that I'm not expected to make a speech.'

'Of course you are. And there's one more issue I need to table.' His mother gave him a pointed look. 'Your future intended.'

Logan shook his head and scowled at his mother. 'I haven't agreed to take over yet,' he pointed out. 'And neither do I have an intended.'

'Which is why I've put together a list of potential candidates for you to consider.'

'Your Majesty.' Logan's voice was dangerously soft, his blue eyes piercing. 'Finding a wife is the lowest item on my list of priorities.'

'I know it is.' His mother arched a brow that suggested that she didn't care a whit what was on his list of priorities. 'Hence the need for someone to take charge in this regard. And before you regale me with your intention to find your own wife, may I remind you that you haven't found one so far and as the King-in-waiting you need to produce an heir. But this time we don't want any outsiders. You must choose someone from our echelon of society who knows exactly what is expected of one in royal life. The monarchy won't survive another mistake or another scandal.'

Logan gave a growl under his breath and ran his hand through his hair. '*If* I am to become King, I'm aware of what my future obligations will entail.'

'Good, then there won't be any issues about it. I'll have Margaux forward the list to your email.'

'I'm sure it will make riveting reading. Cassidy, can you liaise with Margaux to see if Leo had drafted a speech for this afternoon? I may as well start with something that *actually* needs my attention.'

'Of course.'

Cassidy curtsied again to his mother before quickly leaving the room. Frankly she couldn't get out of there fast enough. She was used to being the least important person in the room, but to his mother she had been all but invisible.

'I really don't think you should be calling your assistant by her first name,' she heard his mother say before she had fully closed the door behind her. 'It has a tendency to make them believe that they are closer to you than they really are.'

'Cassidy is my employee. That's all she has ever been and all she ever will be, and she knows that.'

'I hope you're right, Valeria replied. 'If she developed personal feelings for you she would have to go.'

'I'm well aware of that. If she developed feelings for me I'd want her to go.'

'Can I help you?'

Caught eavesdropping when she really hadn't meant to, Cassidy jumped. Margaux was watching her with open curiosity.

Logan's comment that she knew exactly what she was to him was a timely reminder that whatever she had been feeling up to now about her boss was completely one-sided.

Which she already *knew*, but there was nothing like having something confirmed to really bring it home.

'The King's speech for the museum this afternoon.' She gave Margaux what she hoped was a confident smile. 'If you have one, can you please forward it to me as soon as possible?'

CHAPTER FIVE

AN HOUR LATER Cassidy had almost convinced herself that she was working out of her own New York office until Logan stopped beside the sofa and she glanced up and then around to see antique furniture and blue and gold flock-covered walls.

Logan's presence here seemed more imposing than ever. His handsome face was grim and Cassidy's belly did a mini-flip to find him standing so close to her.

Clearly his mood hadn't improved from earlier that morning and she once more found herself feeling sorry for him. He'd been fielding calls from New York since speaking to his mother, sorting out issues with the bank and acting as if it was business as usual when it was anything but. At least for her. This palace…his mother…the gravitas that permeated the air was a step up from even the bank's hallowed hallways. Not to mention the information that he was expected to marry someone from a noble family. The thought made her throat thicken because she had never considered that Logan would give up his bachelor lifestyle for anyone. He had always seemed so unattainable and she supposed he still was because although he might have to marry if he became King, it wouldn't be to an ordinary woman like her.

'No contact from Leo yet?'

His voice was calm, but she knew he was growing impatient.

'I'm afraid not.'

His mouth tightened as he rolled his shirtsleeves down over his muscular forearms and fastened his gold cufflinks. 'I've given him your number in case mine is busy and I don't care what I'm doing. If he calls, interrupt me.'

'I will.'

'How have you found Margaux?'

More sophisticated than she could ever hope to be.

'Great. She's very particular and thorough, and she's been very helpful. She forwarded your brother's speech and I've reworded some of the components to make it sound more like you. I sent it to your phone.'

'Then we're good to go.'

'We?' There was that word again and Cassidy pushed her glasses closer to her face with the tip of her little finger. She hadn't anticipated that Logan would want her to go with him on an official visit. He'd been handling royal affairs since he came out of nappies, whereas the most formal occasion Cassidy had attended was her niece's high school awards night.

'Yes. I want you there. I need an update on the Westgate tunnel deal.'

'Actually, I can give you that now.' She swallowed heavily. 'Kellard are definitely interested and I've arranged a tentative video conference with the trustees this Thursday. That way if it all comes off we'll still sign off on the tender bid by close of business that day. Everyone is on standby pending your approval.'

'And this is why I can't do without you.' He gave her a smile that made her breath catch. 'Of course I approve.

We can set it up at the conference room down the hallway. You'll have to clear it with the IT depart—'

'Already done. I'm waiting for the head of IT to get back to me about it.'

Logan nodded. 'Let me know as soon as he does. In the meantime, pull the relevant information together and get any new figures from Accounting.' He glanced down at his phone, frowning. 'What are the Cliff Notes on this speech I'm expected to give?'

'The contemporary art movement in Arrantino and how it has influenced the direction of art on the world stage. There are also some awards to give out to the students who received grants last year.'

'Great. I know more about tropical fish than I do about contemporary art on any stage.'

Unprepared for his sudden display of humour, Cassidy barely kept a laugh from escaping her throat. The last thing she wanted was to find her boss funny, it would only make him more appealing when she was trying to find reasons for him to be less so. 'It sounds quite fascinating, actually. Apparently the light in Arrantino during the summertime would make Van Gogh weep.'

'You're an art buff?'

Cassidy instantly bristled at the implied surprise in his voice. 'When you grow up in a small country town you become curious about everything.'

He cocked his head, studying her far too intently. 'It wasn't a criticism. Where you grow up doesn't define who you are as a person.'

Doesn't it?

Cassidy felt the knot of bitterness well up inside her at how easily the folk of her home town had judged her family as no-hopers after Peta's pregnancy, and then her own drastic miscalculation when she'd tried to win a boy's affection when she had agreed to send him a photo of herself in her underwear… Had she known he was going to share it with his friends…laugh about it…call her a…

She shook her head, the shame of knowing she had been as naïve as to think that one of the most popular boys at school had actually liked her for her still made her feel ill. She'd embarrassed herself and her father and the only good thing about it was that it had no bearing on her life now. No one else would ever have to know. Logan would never have to know.

Turning back to him, she reached for her handbag, feigning a lightness she didn't feel. 'Forget I said anything. Shall we go?'

Logan hesitated, seeming to see something in her expression that he wanted to explore, and Cassidy forced herself to remain poker-faced. It might be a new day but things had still yet to return to normal between them and she knew that was her fault entirely.

Logan frowned as Cassidy kept her attention firmly focused on her phone during the car ride to the museum. Things had yet to return to normal between them and for that he blamed himself entirely. He was just too aware of her for comfort, his senses tuned into her in a way they never had been within the structure of his glass office.

He took in her neat hair and gabardine suit. Her low-heeled shoes. She looked the same as always and yet he couldn't get the picture of her wet and unkempt out of his mind. He couldn't shake the image of that see-through blouse, and during the short nap he'd caught on the plane he'd dreamt of peeling it from her body.

Knowing his sudden obsession with his EA was most likely due to the tension created by his brother's possible abdication didn't help. Neither was clamping down on the thoughts every time they arose. It was as if his body was running on a different track from his mind and for a man used to being in control of himself and everything around him it was concerning.

Deciding that dwelling on it wasn't going to help either, he turned his attention to the speech he needed to give, memorising the key aspects, and only glancing up when the car arrived in front of the museum. Built halfway through the last century, it was one of Arrantino's landmark tourist destinations due to the intricately placed mosaic tiles around the outside.

His great-grandfather had commissioned it. His father had added a wing. Now he was opening another one.

Following in the old man's footsteps?

Not if he could help it. And especially not with Cassidy, whose professionalism was the aspect of her nature he admired most. He'd never ruin that by giving in to his baser desires.

Cassidy lifted her head as if sensing the sudden shift in his mood.

She was good at that, sensing what he needed when he needed it.

The noise from the crowd clustered behind the barriers went wild as his door was opened. Cassidy's eyes widened and he gave her a look. 'Welcome to the other part of my world.'

She peered at the expectant crowd. 'I think every unattached female in Arrantino got the message that you would be here this afternoon.'

Amused by her observation but determined to close down any thoughts of that nature, Logan shook his head. 'Stick close and follow my cues.'

Stepping from the car, he reached back to offer Cassidy his hand before he could think better of it. Once again a tingle of unwanted awareness slid up his arm and his eyes cut to hers. Soft colour winged into her face as she snatched her hand back as if she too had been burned by the brief contact.

Frustrated that even the mildest of touches could set off alarm bells in his head, he was determined to not touch her again. Or ride in a car with her given that her floral scent was still clinging to him.

Intensely glad that the palace security team had kept the hungry paparazzi at bay, he greeted members of the public for five minutes before joining the museum director on the steps to the entrance and heading inside.

'It's an honour to have you here in His Majesty's stead, Your Highness,' the director gushed. 'We hope the King is well.'

'The King is fine,' Logan said. 'You have a good turn-out today.'

'Thanks to your visit. The recipients of the royal grants are very much looking forward to meeting you.'

'And I them.'

Turning to ensure that Cassidy was okay, he turned to find her deep in conversation with various staff members, seemingly undaunted by the pomp and ceremony of the occasion.

As if sensing his eyes on her, she raised her head, giving him a questioning look he translated to mean, *Do you need me?*

Part of him instantly replied that, yes, he did need her, but since it wasn't a part of him that controlled logic and discipline he ignored it, giving a subtle shake of his head and tuning back into the director's descriptions of the innovations that had taken place in the museum since he'd last visited.

There was an air of gravitas to the whole affair and

Logan wasn't sure if it was because his brother's potential abdication was overshadowing the situation or not, but try as he may he couldn't seem to get the young artists who were the recipients of the royal grants to relax and open up about their work with the freedom he would have liked.

Frustrated, he was digging deeper into the motivation of one particularly interesting piece of work when a soft laugh rang out in the quiet room.

Every head turned toward his Cassidy, who had her fingers clamped over her mouth to stifle her mirth. The artist beside her could barely contain her own laughter, and the director of the museum frowned sternly.

But Logan couldn't help moving toward the pair to find out what had made her laugh.

'Want to share?'

'Oh, I'm sorry.' She bit down on her lower lip as she realised that she had an audience. 'It's nothing really. I was admiring Michael's oil painting of snails, only for him to confess that actually they're pastry scrolls.'

'It's a breakfast theme,' the young artist confirmed graciously, 'but you could eat snails for breakfast if you wished.'

'Not the ones in my garden,' Cassidy confessed, making everyone around her smile.

She peeked up at Logan through her long lashes as they moved on to the next piece. 'I'm going to let you take the lead on this one,' she murmured. 'I'm likely to offend someone if I do it.'

'I doubt you could offend a flea,' he observed, finding his gaze riveted to her lively expression.

If he had thought her smile had been stunning during his plane taking off, it was nothing compared to seeing her so open and warm with the people around her.

And her enthusiasm was infectious, relaxing everyone around her.

It was the icebreaker he had been looking for and it completely changed the mood of the tour, replacing the dry discourse over the various pieces into lively, friendly chatter. Logan followed it up with a speech promising more grants in the future and a private moment with the director.

He was wondering where Cassidy had disappeared to when one of the staff informed him that she had ducked into the ladies' room. When she didn't reappear after a few minutes, Logan checked his watch and excused himself to go and find her.

Following the directions to the nearest ladies', he rounded a corner and was nearly knocked over as Cassidy barrelled straight into him.

Instinctively he caught her to him. His body immediately registered the contact of soft, curvy woman, his response to her so primal and inappropriate it left him speechless.

The sweet scent of her hair product infiltrated his senses and he filled his lungs with it.

Cassidy's fingers automatically went to push her falling glasses back up her nose, the move flattening her soft breasts against the solid wall of his chest.

As if she too registered the experience, her wide, shocked eyes flew to his.

It was a shock he shared given the raw bolt of lust that was already turning him hard.

Gritting his teeth against the assault on his senses, he absently noticed that her mouth was mere inches from his and wondered what it was about her that pulled so forcefully at his self-control. It took everything in him not to bridge that gap and lower her to the floor.

'Easy,' he said as she stumbled, his hands clenching her slender hipbones, part of him aware that it would be so easy to slip his hands further around to cup her rounded bottom.

She was tiny compared to him, the top of her head barely reaching his chin. Without her heels she'd be even shorter and he'd have to bend to kiss her.

For a moment, she didn't move, her breathing as laboured as his.

And then one of the catering staff rounded the corner, her startled gasp at finding them standing so close together very telling.

Stepping back, Logan ran a hand through his hair.

Cassidy straightened her jacket.

They both looked as if they'd been caught with their hands in the candy jar and yet nothing had happened.

Nothing other than what had exploded inside his imagination.

'We need to get back,' he said, dismissing the incident as if it had never happened.

Still shaken at having found herself plastered up against her boss with her arms wrapped around his neck, Cassidy remained avidly glued to her phone all the way back to the palace.

Fortunately Logan seemed just as disinclined to engage her in conversation, which was good because if he looked at her she was afraid that he would be able to read the naked desire written on her face if he did.

It was embarrassing really, how badly she had wanted to kiss him. It was as if two years of working together professionally had dissolved into a murky puddle of lust, never to be found again.

Acting as if nothing had happened at all, and maybe for him it hadn't, Cassidy trailed him as he strode into the King's offices. Flicking his cuff, he checked his watch and frowned. 'It's getting late. Perhaps we should call it a night.'

It was getting late, but Cassidy was functioning on New York time and that, combined with her sleep on the plane, meant that she wasn't tired at all.

'I'm going to get a bit more done,' she said, taking a seat at the smaller desk that had been placed on one side of the room for her use while they had been gone. 'You wouldn't believe how many requests for information have been forwarded to me. I swear in this day and age of instant information overload no one can wait for anything.'

'One of the drawbacks,' Logan agreed wearily. 'Not that we have anything firm to report yet.'

She saw the tension in his shoulders and the tight skin around his eyes and her heart knocked against her chest in sympathy. She'd never quite seen him as human before, but there were glimpses of it, like now.

'I'll handle it,' she assured him. 'I want to touch base with some of our larger clients and I also need to get back to a couple of the Kellard trustees who would prefer to speak to you directly instead of reading the prospectus.'

Logan grunted. 'I need to meet with Housekeeping in my apartment. If Leo should call—'

'I know. Come and find you.' Cassidy waved him off, needing some time on her own. 'Will do.'

Logan frowned as he stopped beside her. 'Don't wear yourself out. Your energy level will hit rock bottom at some point.'

Sure that he was right, Cassidy let out a breath of relief as he left the room, feeling like a balloon that had been popped by a pin.

She caught a glimpse of herself in a mirror on the far wall, surprised to find that she still looked the same as she always did. Somehow she'd expected a crazy woman to be staring back at her with wild hair and bright eyes. Because she didn't feel the same. She felt more unbalanced now than yesterday. But that was because everything had changed, hadn't it?

Being here with Logan, knowing her life would be different when she returned… Was it any wonder she was feeling so out of sorts? This was normal. She just needed to compartmentalise—something she had always believed she was very good at due to her messy childhood—and stop reacting physically to her boss.

He hadn't wanted to kiss her back in the museum any more than he'd wanted to kiss her in his apartment the night before. He kissed supermodels and society princesses. He did not kiss ordinary girls from Ohio.

Pulling out her laptop, she sat down behind the new desk that had been set up with an ink blotter and stationery. Everything was fine. Everything was exactly as it should be.

Not sure how convinced she was of the truth of that, she was nonetheless relieved when a staff member knocked and entered the office, wheeling in a covered trolley with alluring silver-domed plates.

'Please tell me you have hot coffee in that jug?' Cassidy said, her saliva glands already salivating at the thought.

'Yes, ma'am. And some sandwiches. His Highness thought you might require some refreshments.'

'His Highness is a god,' she said, without thinking.

The young girl gave her a shy smile. 'He is, ma'am, yes.'

Just for a moment Cassidy wondered what it would be like to be waited on hand and foot, and then recalled the moment Logan had stepped out of the car at the museum and the adoring crowd had surged excitedly against the barriers to get his attention.

It had been like something out of a Hollywood film.

Logan had waved and smiled and as soon as he'd neared the museum the small delegation of staff had subtly straightened, standing to attention, wide smiles on their faces in anticipation of meeting him. Cassidy had noticed that he often had that effect. Whenever he entered a room the atmosphere buzzed with palpable electricity, his self-assurance a cloak that caused everyone else to defer to him without even realising that they were doing it. His very presence commanded respect from those around him. But it was even more pronounced in Arrantino, where his importance was beyond question.

A little overawed, she had found herself standing straighter as well, but of course Logan didn't bat an eye-lash, completely relaxed and at ease, and accepting the fawning attention with unquestioning self-confidence. And why wouldn't he? This was the life he had been born into. And no doubt the attention would be even more servile if he did become King.

She wondered if the attention had something to do with why he didn't want to become King and then reminded herself that she was not going to be curious about him. It only served to make her more aware of him as a man, instead of as her boss, and she was very afraid that if she continued down that road she'd never be able to get off it.

Turning to work to ground herself again in reality, she opened the first email. Now that most of the business world had learned that Logan was in Arrantino, and not at the helm of the bank as usual, she was inundated with frazzled clients demanding to know what was happening.

It was a diplomatic minefield and she relished the chance to navigate it because if there was one aspect of her life she was confident in it was her ability to do her job. Only she suddenly wondered how much longer she would have the job.

If Logan did become King he would no doubt want someone who was conversant with royal issues as his assistant. Someone like the lovely Margaux. Which meant that Cassidy would be out one place to live and one job. The thought landed like a sickening thud in her stomach. Not only would she be finding new accommodation, or a housemate, when she returned to New York, but she might be looking for new employment as well. For someone who saw change as akin to death, she couldn't think of anything worse. It was as if some unseen force had taken hold of her life and shaken it up as if she were living inside a snow globe.

Glad when a new email landed in her inbox, she opened it to find that it was the list of marriageable young women his mother had promised to have her aide send through. Well, if that wasn't enough to ground her in reality, nothing was.

Work, she reminded herself as she felt the weight of all the turmoil around her weighing her down once more. *You're here to work so get on with it.*

Forty-five minutes later her phone rang from an unknown number.

CHAPTER SIX

'GOOD AFTERNOON, MISS RYAN. It's Leo, Logan's brother. I can't seem to get hold of my brother and I only have a short window to speak with him. Do you happen to know where he is?'

'Yes, Your Majesty.' Cassidy tried not to feel overawed, the King's deep voice reminding her of Logan's. 'I believe he's in his apartment. If you wouldn't mind holding I'll take the phone to him.'

'Thank you.'

Pushing to her feet, Cassidy slid her heels back on and dashed out the door. Having no clue where to go, she approached a nearby footman and asked for directions.

'I'll take you there myself, ma'am. This way.'

Sensing the urgency permeating every cell of her body, the young footman didn't waste time, wending his way up a grand staircase and along a richly decorated hallway until they reached a set of ornate cream doors.

She fervently hoped that Logan hadn't gone anywhere else because she knew how important this call was to him and wondered why he hadn't picked up his own phone.

'This is it, ma'am, His Highness's apartment.'

'Thanks.'

Cassidy checked that the King was still on the phone and gave the young footman a grateful nod as she knocked on the door.

Smoothing back her hair, she waited for Logan to tell her to enter and when she didn't hear anything she tried the handle, suddenly nervous as the door clicked open.

Telling herself that there was nothing to be nervous about, she stepped inside, her eyes widening at the sheer opulence of the room.

It was so stately and handsome she half expected Elizabeth Bennet to come wandering out of one of the rooms at any moment.

Feeling a sense of *déjà vu* at having once again entered her boss's private sanctuary unannounced, she moved further into the apartment, fervently hoping that she wasn't going to be confronted by muscles glistening with sweat and vitality from an intense workout. Assuring herself that the same situation was as likely to happen as—

'Oh, my God!'

Cassidy's hand flew to her stalled heart as she came face to face with her boss in the middle of the parquetry hallway.

This time he wasn't wearing anything as bad as gym clothes. This time it was much worse because the only thing he was wearing was a towel tied low around his lean hips, his ripped torso and corrugated-iron abs so much more delicious than her imagination could have conjured up.

'Please, tell me that this is a bad dream,' she groaned, a liquid heat unfurling low in her pelvis as she stared at the sleek perfection of his hard body.

In the process of rubbing his hair dry with another towel, Logan came to a complete standstill and stared at her.

'It's not a dream, bad or otherwise. Is that for me?'

Incapable of coherent thought, Cassidy had no idea what he was talking about.

'The phone, Cassidy.' Logan's voice was dark and low. 'Is it for me?'

The phone? The phone?

Appalled, she remembered that she had the King on the line and held it out to him as if it were a baton she needed to pass on to the next competitor in a relay. 'Yes, yes, it's for you.' Her heart was racing like a runaway train as he prowled toward her. Plucking it out of her hand, he told her to wait for him before he disappeared back down the hallway.

Feeling like the survivor of a car crash, Cassidy didn't move for a good few minutes, not wanting to do anything that might bring him back.

Then she took a deep breath, absently noticing a tray of fresh glasses and a silver jug beaded with moisture.

Suddenly parched, she poured herself an icy drink and thought about rolling the glass across her sweaty forehead to cool herself down.

Fortunately, drinking it had the desired effect and she felt her heart rate start to return to normal, only to sense Logan pad up behind her. Just her luck that his phone call would be so short.

She didn't turn to face him, pretty sure that if he was still wearing the towel she'd resign on the spot. Because how could she possibly go on working for him and not picture him naked every time she saw him?

'That was my brother.'

'I know.'

'I was in the shower when he tried my cell.'

Cassidy took a gulp of water. 'I kind of got that.'

Logan shifted behind her. 'Are you going to look at me or stand facing the wall for the rest of the night?'

Hearing the irritation in his voice, she slowly turned and automatically scanned his body for clothing. Fortunately he'd changed while he'd been speaking to the King, and was now dressed in a T-shirt and sweatpants as black as his mood.

'I'm really sorry for walking in on you like that,' she said softly. 'Had I known—'

'Forget it,' he dismissed. 'It's becoming a habit I'm getting used to.'

'Well, I'm not,' she squeaked indignantly. 'And I can assure you it will never happen again. I'm going to return your private key card as soon as we get back to New York because I'm never going into your personal space again unless you're with me, or not there at all.'

Logan raked a hand through his still wet hair. 'That's not something you'll have to worry about in the future because I'm not returning to New York.'

'Oh.'

Knowing exactly why that would be, and seeing the weight of it in the tense line of his shoulders, she watched as he stalked to a minibar between a set of shelves and poured himself a healthy dose of something amber. Probably Scotch.

'Want one?'

He held up his glass and Cassidy shook her head. In the office she knew what was expected of her. She knew her role. Now, without the separation of Logan's oak desk and surrounded by metres of glass, everything was different. She was different. And so was he.

She also knew that if Leo had given up the throne, Logan wouldn't be happy. He hadn't wanted his life to change, but he was too honourable not to step into his brother's place if that was truly required. After all, this was the man who had sat by his brother's bedside while he'd been sick as a teenager.

In an attempt to get them back on track, Cassidy tried to focus on work. 'I take it from that comment about not returning to New York that your talk with your brother didn't go so well.'

Logan barked out a laugh. 'That's a polite way of putting it.'

'What did he say?'

'He's enamoured of this woman. Elly Michaels. She's an archaeologist and as my brother is a keen artefact-collector they've been bonding over five-hundred-year-old ceramics since they met six months ago. Apparently she makes him smile even when she's not there.'

Logan said the last with a healthy degree of derision but it made Cassidy go soft inside. 'Oh, that is so sweet.'

Logan's brow rose in mockery. 'Sweet? To be at the mercy of your emotions? I took you as far too sensible to take that view.'

She was sensible now, but she hadn't always been. Neediness had made her stupid and she'd never forget the disappointment on her father's face when his good girl had gone bad. When he'd discovered she'd sent that photo. And she had vowed to never succumb to the feeling again.

But she couldn't deny that, when her guard was down, like now, she felt something akin to that with her boss. Having refused to view him as anything other than her boss for so long, she didn't know why she was finding it so hard to switch back to that now, but she was.

Cassidy grimaced. 'I usually am, but…to find someone special like that is very rare.'

'You don't have to convince me of that. I'd go so far as to say non-existent.'

And she supposed she could guess as to why that was if his father had cheated on his mother so often.

'But tell me,' he continued softly, almost challengingly, 'does Peter share your romantic outlook on life?'

'I don't know if I'd go so far as to call my outlook romantic,' she said carefully, knowing that maybe, possibly, if she gave free rein to her deepest desires, it might come close. 'But Peta is definitely that way inclined.'

Her sister had always loved the idea of being in love and even the twins' father bailing on her hadn't been able to squash that side of her nature completely. Hence Dan…

'Lucky you,' Logan drawled in a tone that, had he been any other man, she would have said was jealous. 'To find a man who matches you so well.'

'Man?' A frown formed between her eyes. Then realisation dawned. 'I think we might have our wires crossed somehow. Peta is my sister.'

'Your sister?' Logan looked at her as if she had sprouted an extra head. 'Then who the hell was the guy who kissed you in your doorway when I picked you up?'

'That was Dan. My sister's fiancé.' She shook her head. 'Seriously, we've talked about Peta's reaction to my coming here… How could you think that she was a…a what? A lover? A boyfriend? I haven't dated in years.'

'Easily.' The arrogant gleam was back in his eyes. 'You're a beautiful woman. Why wouldn't I believe you were seeing someone?'

He thought she was beautiful?

'Because we work so closely together,' she said, flustered by the unexpected compliment. 'And I know every woman you date because I have to inevitably buy them goodbye gifts.'

'Clearly I don't know half as much about you. Why haven't you dated for so long?'

'Because I haven't been asked.' She felt her face burn under his intense scrutiny. 'But even if I had, I'm not interested in dating anyone.'

Not at all enjoying having the focus on a part of her life that was such a dismal failure, she mentally searched for a distraction. 'You know what I do when I'm upset?' she said with Mary Poppins–like enthusiasm. 'I do something physical.'

A cynical smile twisted his lips. 'What are you suggesting, Miss Ryan?'

Whenever he addressed her like that she thought of sex and it took a lot to remind herself that he wasn't thinking the same thing. Only this time he was. But that was because he was moody and looking for an argument. And she was directly in the firing line.

'Not that kind of outlet,' she managed. 'I meant exercise. For me that's taekwondo, but for you I know it's running.'

His eyes gleamed speculatively as he considered her. 'How good are you?'

Cassidy frowned. 'That wasn't an invitation to spar with you.'

'I didn't take it as one.' Dark lashes lowered to conceal the compelling blue of his eyes. 'That's why I'm issuing one of my own.'

'But you don't even practise taekwondo,' she said on a rushed breath, her mind frantically searching for some way she could get out of this diplomatically.

Unfortunately Logan had his juggernaut expression in place. 'I know karate. It should make for an interesting session.'

Cassidy shook her head. 'There's no way I can spar with you.'

'Afraid I'll hurt you?' he asked softly.

No, she was afraid she'd have to touch him, and she had enough brain cells still working to understand a bad idea when she came across one. 'It wouldn't be appropriate.'

That arrogant gleam returned. 'Why not? We're not working right now. And even so… I don't care about what's appropriate. I care about doing something I want. And what I want is to find out what my EA is made of.'

If she had to answer that, she'd say jelly. 'This is not a good idea.'

'Duly noted.' Logan's grin turned wolfish. 'Now go and suit up.'

Her *sister*?

Logan was stunned. How had he got that so spectacularly wrong? And why did finding out that she didn't have a lover make him feel so much better than before? It wasn't as if he cared if Cassidy had someone special back home and, really, it changed nothing between them.

Even if he had the freedom to explore the sexual spark between them, he wouldn't. Not only did she work for him but she was the kind of woman who would inevitably want more from him. The kind he tried to stay away from.

Still, he was aware that on some level he was playing with fire by inviting her to spar with him. Especially when he saw her walking toward him in her white cotton dobok and matching black pants, her long hair pulled into a plait that trailed down the centre of her back like a silky horse's tail. She looked younger like this, her lovely face and clear eyes so guileless he could see just how nervous she felt.

And she probably had good reason to feel that way. He wasn't exactly himself right now.

Finding out that Leo would not reconsider his abdication, making him the next King of Arrantino, had shaken him. He still wasn't convinced that his brother giving up the throne for a woman was the wisest course of action, but he'd kept his own council this time. Leo had accused him of being over-protective in the past, but having sat by his brother's bedside while he'd gone through months of chemotherapy had been painful to watch. Then having his marriage fail… Was it really being over-protective to want to prevent someone you loved from experiencing pain?

Because what if this Elly woman turned out to be just another version of Anastasia?

Grabbing two bottles of water from the refrigerator, he joined Cassidy. She looked stiff and uncertain as she glanced up at him, her green eyes brighter without her glasses.

'You're not wearing your glasses?' he asked, not recalling a time he had seen her without them before.

'No. I generally need my glasses for work because I suffer from eye strain, but I don't need them all the time.'

Something else he hadn't known about her.

He led her downstairs to the gym and pushed open the door, wondering how many more secrets she had that he had yet to uncover.

Uncover?

He frowned. He didn't want to uncover Cassidy's secrets.

Her plait swished as she walked ahead of him beckoning him to wrap his fist around the thick length and tug on it until her mouth was under his. There was definitely one secret his body was keen to uncover but he forced his mind not to go there. She was out of bounds.

The gym wasn't empty. Two palace employees who looked to be in the middle of a workout were there, but Logan wasn't in the mood for company and levelled a look at them both.

Mumbling a formal greeting, both men collected their gear and left through the second door.

Cassidy turned to face him, her slender brow arched as she toed off the soft slippers provided for palace guests. 'You made them leave.'

'Yes.' He placed the two water bottles on the bench against the wall, completely unapologetic.

'You didn't have to do that,' she said. 'We're only going to be using the mat.'

Logan lifted a brow. 'Oh, did you want an audience when I soundly beat you, *Miss Ryan*?'

A soft blush touched her cheeks as she shook her head. 'I may look small, *Mr de Silva*, but I've beaten men larger than you before.'

Her beguiling gaze raked from his broad shoulders down over his powerful thighs and he actually felt a shiver move across his skin.

As if she had no idea of the effect she had on him, she gazed at him steadily from across the mat. Which was probably for the best.

Obviously feeling the swirl of his shifting emotions, she tilted her little chin up at him. 'So what happens now?'

Making the decision to switch his brain from sex to sparring, he toed off his runners and moved to stand in the middle of the mat. When he had offered to spar with her it had been out of a genuine need to let off some steam and, okay, a small amount of curiosity to see her in action. Knowing that she held a senior black belt had only elevated that interest. 'Now we spar,' he said.

Aware of every move she made, he noticed the moment she hesitated. 'Actually, I meant about you becoming King. What's the process?'

'A notice will go out tomorrow.' She stepped back from him and stretched from side to side, bending to touch her toes to warm up.

Logan told himself not to watch. 'The coronation will be on Friday.'

'Four days from now?' She straightened and rolled her slender shoulders. 'Why so soon?'

'To avoid any more fallout for Arrantino and to ensure that the focus is on the future. Not the past.'

'That makes sense.'

Having finished her stretches, she came to stand directly in front of him, her subtle scent reaching out to ensnare him. When he didn't immediately move, her eyes flickered to his warily. 'You know we can still change our mind about this.'

'Too late.' He overrode his sensual response and bowed to her. 'I'm already having fun.'

And he was. Seeing another side to Cassidy was far more interesting than contemplating how incredibly his life was about to change.

'I'm still not used to seeing everyone bow and curtsy to you as they have been today,' she murmured. 'Does that mean I'm supposed to as well?'

'Only when you first see me in the day.'

'Oh, sorry. I forgot this morning.'

'Next time it will be ten lashes at dawn,' he promised, bending his knees to take up the traditional karate stance. 'Shall we?'

Her green eyes gleamed as she observed him and he knew that she was relishing the opportunity to spar with him as much as he was with her. A dark thrill raced through his body at the prospect that he might have met his match.

Cassidy took up a similar pose, tracking his expressions and movements with the confidence of a seasoned practitioner.

Logan breathed in through his nostrils, once more picking up the scent of flowers and musk.

Which was when she struck, moving her arms in a quick series of blocking moves before sweeping his legs out from under him.

She laughed as he lay sprawling at her feet, the sound light and musical. Not at all put out by her getting the jump on him, he leapt lithely to his feet.

'Like that, is it?' he drawled softly.

She laughed again, dancing away from him lightly.

'First rule of combat. Never underestimate your opponent,' she advised, clearly delighted in her small victory.

Feeling alive and invigorated, Logan pulled a few light moves on her, impressed with her technique and her agility. Not that he seriously thought he was at risk of being defeated when she was so light he could lift her up with one hand tied behind his back.

'How is it you know taekwondo?' he asked, as he blocked another lethal combination of moves.

'My father insisted that my sister and I take self-defence lessons when we were younger, and I became hooked.' She threw in a high kick that he dodged. 'They offered lessons at our local YMCA and I used it as a break from reading.'

'Bookworm, were you?'

He used the question to distract her, and it worked because she wasn't ready as he forced her back on the mat and rolled her over his arm and sent her to the floor.

Pink with exertion, she jumped gracefully to her feet, scowling at him. 'You deliberately distracted me. And, yes, I'm boring if that's what you were getting at.'

'Boring?' With that mouth, and those eyes? 'You're turning out to be the least boring woman I know.'

His comment was followed by a serious of twists and kicks that had him roll off to the side rather than find himself face planting on the mat. She arched a brow, a smug grin curving her lips. 'You won't get me with fake compliments.'

Fake?

'I don't do fake.'

She gave him an uncertain glance and he used the momentum of her being on the back foot to use a series of kicking moves that were a combination of two different forms of martial arts, taking her by surprise as she tumbled again.

'That was illegal,' she complained, facing him.

'No, it wasn't. I practise Krav Maga as well.'

Cassidy rolled her eyes. 'Naturally you would know the most aggressive forms of martial arts.'

'Of course.' Logan shrugged. *Basic Prince Training.*

'Really? I would have thought that basic prince training would involve how to be demanding and get what you want.'

Logan grinned at the playful dig. 'That's *Basic Prince Training Part Two.*'

Laughing, she threw in an illegal move of her own, but Logan was primed for it, flipping her onto her back and straddling her waist with his strong thighs.

They stared at each other, both panting hard. Logan wanted to lean down and take her soft mouth with his own and almost did, but she pushed him back and he rolled to his feet.

'Why don't you want to be King?'

Not sure if she was trying to distract him again, he dismissed her question. 'Too much responsibility.'

'Meaning that you don't want to talk about it.'

He should have known she was too smart not to see through his flippant answer. 'Correct. Water?'

She took the bottle he offered and twisted the top, guzzling down a healthy amount. 'It always seems so glamorous,' she mused. 'You live in a fancy palace, you have servants at your beck and call, you can go whereever you want, people want to meet you and be with you, and you get to raise awareness on important issues.'

Logan drank deeply from his own bottle. 'Apart from raising awareness on important issues, the reality is very different. It's a life that is rarely your own. You're at the mercy of the press waiting for you to step out of line, you attract people who are interested in power and diamonds and not necessarily in that order, and you have no privacy. You don't have any secrets. It's frustrating.'

Cassidy's brow shot up. 'You like having secrets?'

'No.' His teeth ground together. 'I like having a life that's not built on a house of cards.'

'Are you saying that yours was?'

Accustomed to being surrounded by people who devoured gossip about him, and usually knew more than they let on, Logan found himself wondering if she was being straight with him. He'd had every psychological game played on him by women trying to make their position in his life permanent that he immediately questioned her sincerity.

Was he really so jaded?

Because there was nothing in Cassidy's expressive green eyes to suggest that she was anything other than sincere.

'Behind many closed doors life is different from that which we present to the world,' Logan said. 'Mine was no different.'

In fact, when their doors were closed they'd lived a powerless childhood filled with nasty, unspoken grievances between his parents.

'Did you want to talk about it?'

No, he didn't. But somehow her soft invitation drew something out of him. 'My father wasn't quite the man the history books make him out to be. Behind closed doors he had a constant string of affairs. It didn't matter if a woman was married, single, an acquaintance, or if she worked for him, the only prerequisite for him to sleep with her was that she be attractive.' He gave a snort of disgust.

'It was fortunate that cell phones with cameras weren't around during the height of his glory days or it would have been much worse. As it was, the press dined out on the rumours of his exploits for long enough to make my mother check into a Swiss rehab facility for three months. That was the year Leo was diagnosed with leukaemia and my father's response was to head to a hotel with five international strippers.'

'Oh, wow, that's...'

'Water under the bridge,' he said starkly, wondering what had possessed him to reveal so much to her. He stepped back, hoping the physical distance would sever the moment of intimacy that had developed between them.

'I can see now why you don't want to be King,' she said softly. 'Why you don't want to be likened to your father, but it doesn't always have to be that way.' The look she gave him was full of a sympathy he'd never needed. 'If you live congruent to your values and want something different you'll be perfectly placed to create it.' She gave him a faint smile. 'Didn't you say that we don't have to be defined by our past?'

Yes, he had said words to that effect and having them fed back to him made him realise that in this instance he might not practise what he preached. Since he wasn't given to sentimentalising any aspect of his life he had never given it much thought, and he didn't particularly want to now.

'It's poor form to throw a man's words back at him,' he growled. Particularly if those words made sense.

Putting his water bottle down, he came at her again.

She danced out of his way with grace and skill. 'If it's worth anything,' she parried, 'I agree with your mother. I think you'll make an amazing king.'

Logan's heart kicked hard behind his ribcage. Her words *did* mean something but he was unwilling to explore exactly what that was either.

'Are we here to spar or to talk?' he challenged.

He didn't give her a chance to respond, forcing her back

off the mat with a series of manoeuvres he was careful to keep controlled and smooth.

Sensing that he was holding back, she ramped things up with a look of determination he couldn't help but revel in.

Logan fended off her jabs, deliberately flinching as her foot connected with his ribs.

Immediately contrite, she stopped. 'Oh, no, did I—?'

Taking full advantage of her caring nature, he flipped her so that she landed flat on her back with her delicate wrists pinned above her head, his thighs straddling her slender waist to lock her beneath him.

'I win,' he breathed. 'You're well and truly pinned now.'

Cassidy raised her hips beneath him, but that only served to have him press her more firmly into the mat, which was when their sparring session turned to something else entirely.

Both of them went still, Logan's eyes locked on her lips as he leaned over her, Cassidy's eyes dark and uncertain as she gazed back at him.

The demanding ache in his groin pushed at him to do what he had wanted to do since he'd seen her completely undone in his apartment. Take her and damn the consequences.

She moistened her lips with the tip of her tongue, her fingers flexing beneath his hold.

His body throbbed with a powerful hunger that fogged his brain, his fingers burning with the desire to grab the belt at her waist and yank her dobok open so that he could feast on her high firm breasts.

If she made one move, gave him the slightest indication that she wanted this as much as he did, he'd—he'd what? Kiss her? Forget that she was his employee? He'd returned to Arrantino to put out the fires created by his brother's scandal, not to create one of his own.

As if sensing the shift in his emotions, she blinked, tugging her hands out of his hold.

Logan let her take control, rolling onto his back, stunned to realise that for the first time in his life he was not as in control of his actions as he liked to think that he was. That he had actually been closer than ever before to setting aside every one of his principles and doing something he would surely come to regret had he followed through on it. And the consequences would be catastrophic at this point. He was going to be King. Now, more than ever, he needed to reinforce his ironclad self-control—not lose it altogether!

'Yes, you win.'

Her husky agreement broke through the litany of self-recrimination inside his head and Logan glanced up at her, his breathing still uneven. He wasn't sure what he'd won exactly but whatever it was he hoped his sanity was attached.

CHAPTER SEVEN

'Damn,' Logan muttered as the medal he was pinning to his military uniform slipped for the third time. Knowing that he should have taken his brother's advice and used a valet on the morning of his coronation, he glanced in the mirror and realised that the row of medals symbolising various aspects of his new role as head of his kingdom were not in a straight line.

Exasperated, he stalked out of his room and into the living area, his gaze zeroing in on Cassidy, who was standing by the window.

She glanced up from her trusty tablet as he appeared, every hair on her head tightly tied back and her standard black suit obscuring the toned, feminine body he'd spent the last four days trying to forget.

Which shouldn't have been all that difficult given the volume of work he had needed to juggle as outgoing CEO of a major bank and incoming King, but it had still been a challenge.

Now, though, with the big event mere hours away he found his mind straying, and it took considerable effort to stop his mind from returning to their—in hindsight—ill-thought-out martial arts session.

He stopped in front of her, his gaze scanning the neutral expression she wore, as if she'd wiped the memory of how much they had enjoyed themselves from her memory.

Something he knew he should appreciate but for some reason didn't.

In fact, her professionalism only made him want to wrap his arm around her waist and flatten her against him to find out how long it would take for him to bring back that dazed look in her luminous green eyes.

Eyes there were once more hidden behind her tortoiseshell glasses.

'Did you need something?' she asked as the silence lengthened between them.

Yes, you, his libido barked before he could prevent it.

Scowling, he pointed to his chest. 'These medals aren't straight.'

She frowned. 'It's the middle two that are out of place.'

'I know,' he said, arching a brow. 'That's why I'm here.'

She shook her head, biting into the flesh of her bottom lip as she placed her device on a nearby table. 'You'll have to undo your jacket so I can get my hand inside. Otherwise I might prick you.'

Logan felt every muscle in his body tighten as he slowly slid the brass buttons from their moorings, disconcerted when even this simple act felt sexually charged between them.

As if she felt the same current in the air that he did, she refused to look up at him as she carefully slid her slender hand inside his jacket so that it lay against his heart.

Focused entirely on keeping his pulse at an even rhythm, he stared at the top of her glossy head, wishing he'd now done the job himself.

'Are you nervous about today?'

Her unexpected question went some way to lessening the tension between them and he eased out a breath. 'Not especially,' he answered honestly.

Since the last phone call with his brother he'd reconciled himself to what lay ahead and almost felt at peace with it.

Having shocked himself by opening up to Cassidy about his concerns, he felt more at home with the decision. She had been right to remind him that while he might not have chosen this life for himself, he could, in fact, make this role his own. Her observation had helped propel his mind out of the past, where he had been unaware it had been stuck, and into the future where it belonged.

He still wasn't convinced that Leo had done the right thing in giving up his role as monarch, but that wasn't his business any more. His brother had made his choice. Logan only hoped he was happy with it, and that one day the two of them could get back to experiencing the close bond they had once enjoyed.

Cassidy glanced up at him, a faint smile on her lips. 'I won't tell anyone if you are.'

Logan felt bemused by her response. 'I believe you wouldn't. But as you pointed out, I was born to this life. And don't they say what you resist persists?'

Like this nagging attraction that knocked him for six every time he got close to her.

'I don't remember saying that you were born to it exactly.' She readjusted her glasses on her pert nose, and he noticed the pulse at the base of her neck hammering lightly against her creamy skin. 'But I'd be nervous.'

She bent and pinned the last medal in place. 'There.' She quickly withdrew her hand from inside his jacket and he wondered why control was such a difficult concept around her. 'All done.'

'Now this,' he said, holding out a royal blue sash. He knew he could put it on himself, but he found that he was unwilling to end this quietly intimate moment between them.

She took the sash, her throat bobbing as she swallowed. 'Where does it go?'

'Under the epaulette on my left shoulder.'

Stepping closer, she pushed up onto her toes to feed the silk fabric through the epaulette, her breasts brushing his chest as she reached around his waist to grab it.

Logan's breath hissed out through his teeth and Cassidy's face flamed as she quickly secured it by his right hip and stepped back.

'Anything else?' Her tone was harried, as if she couldn't wait to get away from him.

'Yes. Are you coming tonight?'

'To the ball?' Her eyes widened. 'I didn't know I was invited.'

She hadn't been but he wanted her there and he wasn't in the mood to question that sudden decision. 'You are.'

A frown pleated her smooth brow. 'Do employees usually go?'

'No.'

'Then I shouldn't.'

'You should. You've been instrumental in pulling everything together over the last few days. If nothing else, you deserve a night off.'

'Yes.' She grimaced. 'But I was thinking more along the lines of a warm bath and an early night.'

She moved away from him to pick up her handbag.

'You can have a bath any time.' He scowled, frustrated that she was clearly unimpressed by a gesture that felt more right the more he thought about it. 'If you're not there I'll come and get you.'

She shook her head, her expression still slightly harried. 'Can we discuss it later?'

'No.' Logan moved to her side. 'We'll discuss it now.'

'Fine.' She let out a rushed breath. 'I'll come.'

When her eyes flicked around the room, Logan stilled, his nostrils flaring. 'Did you just try to manage me?'

'Yes. No. Maybe.' Her hands fluttered between them. 'You have more important things to think about right now than whether I go to the ball or not.'

A noise from the doorway startled them both.

His mother strode in, her glance going between the two of them with barely suppressed censure. 'I agree with Miss Ryan. You *do* have more important things to think about.'

Cassidy made a quick curtsy but Logan barely suppressed a scowl at the intrusion. 'I disagree. I think Cassidy should attend the coronation ball.'

'Indeed.' His mother's raised brow spoke volumes. 'Well, that is a surprise.'

'Not really.' Logan redid the buttons on his jacket. 'Cassidy has worked by my side for a long time. I want her there.'

'It would hardly be fair to put Miss Ryan in a position that made her feel uncomfortable.' His mother's smile did not reach her eyes. 'Which reminds me, did you receive the list of potential marriage partners I forwarded yesterday?'

'Yes.' In the absence of being able to pour himself a drink at such an early hour, Logan moved to the side table and downed a short black coffee instead. Finding it cold, he grimaced. 'I've had a look at it, but, as I said when I first arrived, marriage isn't high on my priority list.'

'Once today is over, you can bump it up,' his mother said imperiously. 'And in the meantime five of the young ladies on the list will be in attendance at the ball tonight and I expect you to be at your charming best. These women have impeccable pedigrees and no damaging skeletons in their closets.'

Logan watched Cassidy fossick in her handbag as if she was looking for a way to dig herself out of the room. If she found one, he'd join her. Because there was no way he was ready for marriage and he wouldn't be pressured into it the way his parents had pressured Leo with Anastasia.

Sighing, he gave his mother his full attention. 'I won't let you down. But I need to do this my way.'

'I know. I am merely trying to ease your load.' Her gaze softened on his and she squeezed his arm. 'And when this is all done I'm looking forward to walking with you in the garden like old times. For now, I'll see you downstairs a little later.'

Without glancing at Cassidy, she left the room, leaving a cloud of perfume in her wake.

Cassidy glanced across at him, pushing her glasses up onto her nose, and he knew instantly that she wasn't going to accept his invitation to the ball.

'Don't even think about not attending tonight,' he said before she had opened her mouth.

'I don't think it's a good idea and neither does your mother.'

'My mother has just turned my coronation into a match-making event. Who else will bail me out when I need it?'

Cassidy gave him a look. 'You hardly need me by your side to keep a woman at bay. And you should use this as an opportunity to get to know whomever she's invited.'

Frustrated that she was being so stubborn, he glowered at her. 'I don't care about the women on the list.'

'You should.' Her tongue swept out to moisten her lips. 'They're all quite lovely. And very accomplished.'

'Stop echoing my mother's sentiments and stop defying me.'

He did not want to get to know the women on his mother's list. He wanted to get to know Cassidy. A thought that should have sent more shock waves through him than it did.

Her eyes widened as she looked at him. 'Your mother already doesn't like me. If I go tonight she'll like me even less.'

'My mother doesn't know you and has a deep distrust of staff members.'

Her brows drew down with concern. 'Because of your father's affairs?'

'Yes. She's really quite warm when she lowers her guard.'

'Maybe, but I—'

'Should be there tonight.' Logan stepped into her personal space, cutting off her protest. 'Despite what my mother said, it will be fun.'

He didn't want to question further why he wanted her there.

She gave him a baleful look. 'Even if I wanted to attend, I don't have anything suitable to wear.'

'I'll have a gown delivered here by the end of the day.'

'I don't want you buying me clothing.'

Which is what makes you so different from every other woman I've ever come across.

'Do it anyway.'

She sighed. 'You have your juggernaut expression on again.'

'My what?'

She shook her head. 'It's a look you get when you're not prepared to take no for an answer.'

Logan grinned at her slowly. 'Finally we understand each other.'

Cassidy stared at the couture gown hanging on the outside of her wardrobe door. It was a strapless design in mint green covered in a swirl of tiny crystal beads that looked like it would hug every one of her curves before flaring out at her hips to fall gracefully to the floor.

And there was no way she could wear it.

Her phone rang, and she knew who it was without checking the screen. 'I'm not wearing it.'

'You absolutely are wearing it,' her sister replied vehemently. 'It's stunning. And the twins and I want photos of you in it.'

Cassidy rolled her eyes. She'd been on the phone to her sister, talking about Logan's coronation, when the beautiful gown had been delivered and her sister had demanded she send a photo. And not only the gown had arrived but also accessories, and various bags containing an array of casual clothes, nightwear and shoes. How Logan had guessed her size she didn't know, but after having a quick look he'd got it exactly right.

Turning away from the shopping bags, she flopped back onto the bed. The coronation had been long and sombre, the full import of what Logan had now become slowly sinking in over the course of the day. 'I'm not wearing it because I'm not going.'

And surely Logan wouldn't come looking for her. Not with two hundred important guests all queuing to pay homage to the new King.

'What do you mean?' Her sister sounded like she was doing the dishes as she chatted to her. 'Of course you're going.'

'I'm not. How did the exams go this week?'

'I think I did okay. I might have written down the wrong chemical compound for a face peel but I'm sure I passed. And don't change the subject. Why aren't you going?'

Because she had a bad, sneaking, *horrible* suspicion that she was falling for her boss. Just as her sister had warned her not to do.

And really she'd like to blame Peta for putting the thought into her head, but she was too honest with herself for that. The fact was she'd held a faintly burning candle for Logan since the day she'd started working for him. Spending time with him in Arrantino and really getting to know him, she'd come to learn that he wasn't the spoiled, arrogant, uncaring man she had convinced herself that he was.

He cared. Deeply. About his family. His country. It was love that he wasn't interested in and for all her spouting on about not wanting to find someone special for herself, she realised that she did. She did want someone in her life who looked at her the way Dan looked at Peta. She wanted someone to curl up next to at night. Someone who found her interesting and sexy and desirable.

And even though Logan would never be that man, her senses still leapt with excitement whenever he was near, her body switching to high alert in case he touched her again. Hoping that he *would* touch her again.

The other evening when they had been sparring and he'd braced himself over her in a display of masculine strength she had been so aroused, so feverish with need, she hadn't been able to move. All she had wanted was to reach up and pull his mouth down to hers.

Then he'd frowned, as if he'd read every one of her illicit desires and rejected them outright, and she'd managed to push him away. After that she'd gone into lockdown. Using her superpower to hide how she felt from him.

'Cassidy?' Her sister clanged a pot on the stove and cut into her uncomfortable ruminations. 'Why aren't you going?'

Not ready to admit to her sister how right she had been about everything, Cassidy sighed. 'I'm tired. It's been a long day.'

'Oh, fiddle,' Peta said. 'It's not as if invitations like this drop out of the sky every day. Of course you should go.'

'I thought you advised me not to get too close to my boss.'

'Oh, I might have been a bit cranky after you told me you wouldn't be home this week. No, Amber, do not open those cookies, dinner will be ready in a minute.' Peta let out a frustrated growl. 'Sorry, what was I saying? Oh, yeah. I shouldn't have taken my bad mood out on you. But I still hold to what I said. Do not fall for your boss. That would be a disaster. But you definitely have to go to the ball. Your boss has just been crowned King. This is a once-in-a-lifetime situation. You'll be like Cinderella. Who knows, you might inspire lust in someone who turns out to be Prince Charming. You are in a palace after all.'

'I'm not exactly lust-inducing material,' Cassidy said glumly, wondering if the lust Logan had inspired in her on that mat the other night had been at all reciprocated.

'That's only because of what happened with that jerk in high school,' Peta advised softly. 'But that was years ago. You're older now. And you're gorgeous.'

'You might think that but—'

'You *are* gorgeous,' Peta interrupted vehemently. 'But you don't see it. You need to stop hiding yourself away and let yourself shine. And don't pull that face I know you're pulling. You're just afraid to put yourself out there in case you get your heart broken. Well, guess what, kiddo? It might happen. But it might not. And despite what Dad told us, not all men are bastards. I finally found a good one.'

'So things are good with Dan?' Cassidy asked, glad for the chance to redirect her sister's energies toward her new fiancé.

'Fantastic. Now do me a favour. Have a shower, straighten your hair and fully immerse yourself in this opportunity so that you have no regrets.'

Cassidy stared at the ornate ceiling above her head. She knew her sister was trying to be helpful but it wasn't just the jerk from high school that had made her reticent to put herself on the line where relationships were concerned. She just didn't know whom to trust. After her mother had left, and then the guy in college who had only wanted her for her study notes, on top of Peta now moving on... it just seemed that she was destined to be alone. And the only reason she had so few regrets in life was because of caution—not immersion.

Sometimes she wished that she could be more like her sister. Sometimes she wished that she had more faith in herself and a more positive outlook on life, but the thought of being wrong, of being caught unawares was too scary for her to take that view of life.

'When will you get to experience something like this again?' Peta coaxed.

Probably never, if she was being honest. 'I'll think about it. Say hi to the girls for me. I miss you all.'

'We miss you too. In the meantime, be like Alice and make lots of amazing memories tonight.'

'I thought I was Cinderella?'

Peta laughed. 'Be whoever you want. Be yourself. Create your own fairytale.'

'You've read too many fairytales to the twins. Life rarely works out that way. You know that.'

'Yes, but rarely is not never. You can make your dreams come true, Cass, you just have to want them badly enough. This is a once-in-a-lifetime opportunity. And don't forget, send photos.'

Her sister rang off and Cassidy pushed herself into a sitting position. She stared at the beautiful dress that was hanging so serenely on the hanger as if daring her to put it on.

She wondered if Logan had chosen it himself and then berated herself for the fanciful thought. As if he would have had the time, or inclination, to *choose* a dress for her. Likely he had called someone and delegated the task. That's what a sensible person would have done. That's what *she* would have done.

Because deep down she was a sensible person. Sensible and cautious. She thought of her father's voice after her sister had fallen pregnant, wearily telling her that he was just glad he had one level-headed child.

And apart from her one faux pas she had been level-headed. Level-headed and sensible. And a sensible person did not dress up in a gown they couldn't afford and attend a ball they had no right to attend.

But sensible people could also miss out on fun if they didn't take a chance now and then, a rogue voice inside her head taunted.

And she was older now. Wiser. Perhaps it was time to be more proactive in her life rather than reactive.

And perhaps the place to start with that was her job. With Logan now the King, his life was in Arrantino. Hers was in the States. And even if that wasn't the case, it wasn't as if she could work for him for ever. Not with the way she felt about him. Because something had shifted between them this last week and she couldn't seem to shift it back. Just being in the same room with him made her want to touch him and if he should ever guess how she felt she'd die of mortification.

But she didn't have to think about that right now, did she? She had time up her sleeve. Unless Logan wanted it otherwise, she could give it a month. Help him transition into his new role and put some feelers out to recruitment agencies in New York. In the meantime, she'd keep her head down, do her best to get on top of this pesky attraction and think about what she wanted for herself for a change.

Feeling marginally better now that she had a way forward, she found her gaze returning to the designer gown on her cupboard. As if pulled by a magical thread, she pushed herself off the bed and ran her fingers lightly over the gorgeous fabric. The silky material slid through her fingertips like a shimmering waterfall, the crystal beads catching the overhead light and glowing like tiny diamonds.

Once in a lifetime...

She took the dress down and held it in front of her, gazing at herself in the full-length mirror. She couldn't do it. She couldn't attend a royal ball as if she might actually belong there.

So don't think that. Go as a chance to see how the other half live and create some amazing memories. If you're already planning to resign, what's the harm?

Frowning as the rogue voice tempted her once more, she shook her head. Could she really wear a dress like this? It was a dress that belonged to a princess and, no matter how hard she dreamed, Cassidy knew that she would never be princess material.

CHAPTER EIGHT

AFTER WHAT FELT like the longest day in his life Logan would have liked nothing more than to loosen his tie and sprawl on the nearby sofa, maybe stream a rugby game and open a chilled bottle of ale—but that moment was a long way off. First there was dinner for two hundred followed by the ball.

He searched the large drawing room, which was rapidly filling with elegantly attired guests, for Cassidy, wondering if she would show up. He knew the gown he'd chosen on the drive over to Government House for the official handover had arrived because the stylist had sent him confirmation and photos.

Cassidy had been adamant that she hadn't wanted to wear it and she was probably the first woman to ever turn down a gift from him. In his experience his female companions adored receiving trinkets and the more expensive the better. Not that Cassidy was one of his *companions*, but she would look sensational in the green silk. As she would in the matching bra and panties—

You aren't going there, he reminded himself. He had ordered the underwear on the advice of the stylist, not because he particularly wanted to see her in tiny scraps of lace and nothing else.

And if he believed that, he'd believe the moon was made of cheese...

Irritated with his one-track mind, he turned his attention back to his diplomatic advisor's assessment of a recent European summit and what it meant for Arrantino.

He knew he should be concentrating as come Monday morning it would be his job to make decisions on the laws that would serve Arrantino in the future but he couldn't focus.

What would he do if Cassidy decided that not only wasn't she prepared to wear the dress he'd chosen but that she wouldn't attend the ball at all? It wasn't as if she *had* to attend. The only work he would be doing tonight would be to thank his supporters and well-wishers.

Cassidy's official duties had ended when the coronation had come to a close. Since she'd worked above and beyond what was expected of her since arriving in Arrantino, he couldn't blame her for wanting to kick back and put her feet up. But he didn't want her to do that. He wanted her here, with him, and as much as that didn't make sense, denying it would only be lying to himself.

Never before had he had so much trouble keeping a woman to the role he'd predetermined that she would play in his life and it was starting to seriously bother him. Would he be able to work with her as his private secretary in the future? He hadn't mentioned the future role since their sparring session but it made sense for her to continue to work for him. They made an exceptional team. She knew what he needed sometimes before he knew it himself, and she had never been afraid to give her opinion, even if it didn't align with his. He'd come to appreciate that as much as her efficiency in running his office.

But would she want that? Would she want to move to Arrantino? He hoped so. She would be an asset to any company, and if there was one thing he prided himself on, it was that he was an astute businessman.

'Wouldn't you agree, Your Majesty?'

Having only half listened so far, he forced his mind to the current conversation regarding the latest round of trade talks Arrantino had entered into with India, one of their biggest export markets, breathing a sigh of relief when Leo appeared and politely dragged him out onto the terrace.

Swapping his champagne flute for a beer, Leo leaned against the balustrade and raised his own bottle in a toast. 'I thought I'd save you from having to listen to Joaquín pontificating about his exemplary knowledge of world affairs. You'll hear it over and over anyway.'

'Great,' Logan said sardonically, taking a grateful swig of the ice-cold beer. 'There's only so much sucking up a man can take in one day. I don't know how you did it.'

'Patience,' Leo said.

Logan raised a brow. 'Great. Then I'm stuffed.'

Leo chuckled, and slapped him on the shoulder. 'You'll be fine and you know it.'

'Maybe.' Logan knew he would still hate the goldfish-bowl aspect of the role, but the opportunity to address many of the challenging issues facing the world was something he was looking forward to sinking his teeth into.

'How are you holding up?' He gave Leo an astute look, knowing that with everything that had gone on, he couldn't be having an easy time of it.

'Mixed emotions.' Leo grimaced. 'I'm taking Elly and Skylar to Greece on Sunday. There's a dig taking place on one of the islands she's interested in and I thought it would be good to get away. The press haven't let up and she's worried about the impact it might have on Skylar.'

'I'm sure she is.' Logan's cynical heart thumped. He hated the thought that his brother was being taken advantage of yet again. It wasn't anything tangible. But it had happened before with Anastasia, and Leo's more trusting nature meant that it was possible for that to happen again. 'I just hope she's on the up and up.'

'Don't go there,' Leo warned, his chest expanding. 'I know you're just being protective, which is why I haven't bloodied your nose already.'

'I hope you're right.'

'I am,' Leo said. 'Elly isn't like Anastasia but, regardless, you really need to stop judging women from the jaded view that they're only out for all they can get.'

'I don't.' Logan gave a mocking grin at his brother's arched brow. 'Okay, perhaps I do. It's a habit that's stood me well so far.'

'Perhaps. But it also means that you look for the worst in people.'

He shrugged. 'It works for me. But, okay, I'll reserve my *jaded view* for when I meet her.'

He glanced over Leo's shoulder for any sign of Cassidy inside.

'Good. Because Elly asked me to extend an invitation to lunch tomorrow. I know from experience that it will be a low-key day so it shouldn't be a prob—' Leo frowned. 'That's the third time you've checked out the room inside. Who are you looking for?'

'Cassidy.'

Leo raised a brow. 'You invited her to the ball?'

'Yes, and I need you to take care of her tonight. Escort her in and make sure she's okay. And don't look at me like that. She's the best assistant I've ever had.'

Rather than lose the raised eyebrow, it went even higher. 'Are you sure that's all she is?'

Logan scowled. 'Now it's my turn to tell you not to go there. I'm not like the old man. I would never use my position to sleep with an employee.'

'Fine, fine.' Leo raised his hands in surrender. 'I know

you wouldn't do that. I just couldn't help but notice you looked at her a lot today. And she seems nice. It wouldn't be the worst thing in the world for you to deviate from your usual type and choose someone real.'

'Other than the fact that she works for me.'

'Lots of successful relationships start out as working ones. That doesn't make them wrong. And it doesn't make you like our father, who used his position as a power play.'

'Regardless, the only thing Cassidy and I have between us is a close professional relationship.'

So why was his heart beating hard at the thought that she wouldn't turn up tonight?

'Your Majesty, my lords and ladies.' Gerome appeared just inside the open terraced doors. 'Dinner is about to be served.'

As soon as Logan stepped inside his eyes found Cassidy in the crowded room and two things became immediately apparent.

First, that she was wearing the gown and she looked every bit as incredible as he had known she would and, second, he would need to be on his guard if he intended to keep to his word and ensure that things remained completely professional between them tonight.

Cassidy's heart hammered inside her chest, her breath locked in her throat, as her eyes fastened on Logan.

Now the idea of seeing how the other half lived and creating new memories that had propelled her into the gown and then downstairs seemed like an unnecessary risk as he cut a determined path through the crowd towards her. He had changed out of his military uniform and into a sleekly cut tuxedo and bow-tie, his layered hair swept back from his rakish features, his vivid blue eyes narrowed with irritation.

'You're late,' he wasted no time in telling her. 'Which is unlike you. I thought I was going to have to send out a search party.'

His earlier threat that he would be the one to come and find her if she didn't show up hung in the air between them.

'Sorry… Your Majesty.' She half dipped, half curtsied in the tight-fitting gown, hiding her disappointment that he had not commented on how she looked, only now realising how much she had wanted his approval when he didn't give it.

Hating the needy feeling that balled in her stomach like cooling lava, she called herself a fool and thought seriously about turning around and returning to her room.

As if sensing her desire to escape, Logan latched onto her arm. 'You only need to curtsy to me the first time you see me.'

Feeling like she couldn't get anything right, Cassidy's throat constricted. 'This is the first time I've seen you tonight.'

'Just…' He looked like he was grinding his teeth. 'You've left your glasses off again.'

Seriously, he was going to talk about her glasses? 'I already told you that I don't need them all the time. And they hardly go with the dress.'

'I like your glasses,' he said gruffly.

Suddenly aware that he was standing so close that she could scent his cologne, she shook her head, her newly straightened hair swishing around her shoulders. All she could think about was how handsome he was and the only nice thing he could say was that he liked her glasses.

Unable to come up with a single response to that, she glanced over his shoulder at the sound of a man clearing his throat. She'd been so overwhelmed at seeing Logan, not to mention the low-level hum of excitement in the room, that she hadn't even realised that his brother was standing right behind him.

'I think your glasses are very nice as well,' Leo said, casting his brother a reproving glance. 'And may I add that you look incredibly elegant this evening.'

'Thank you.' Cassidy gave him a grateful smile, which seemed to irritate Logan even more.

'I've asked Leo to escort you to the dining room this evening,' he said curtly. 'After that everyone will gather in the ballroom for the remainder of the evening.'

Fully aware of the schedule as she'd helped produce it, she nodded and made a mental note to never listen to her sister's advice again.

Nodding, as if he was pleased to have done his duty to her, he turned and strode toward the front of the room where his mother stood in a small circle of guests.

'Well…' Leo stepped forward and offered her his arm. 'That was interesting.'

More like horrible, Cassidy thought grimly. 'Actually, I'm not all that hungry.' She cast a glance toward the door she'd just come through as if to make sure it was still there. 'I might see if I can't get a snack delivered to my room. I'm sure no one will notice if I don't go through.'

'Oh, someone will notice,' Leo said with a broad grin. 'I think you're going to have to soldier on and do it now.'

Sighing heavily, Cassidy placed her hand in the crook of his elbow and let him lead her past the milling guests, who watched them curiously as they headed toward the front of the line.

Feeling herself panic at all the attention, Cassidy tugged on the former King's arm. 'Really… I'm happy to stay at the back of the line.'

Leo gave her an amused glance. 'You might be, but protocol dictates that I can't. I'm obliged to follow my brother to the table and as his special guest you're obliged to stay with me.'

'Oh, I'm not his special guest. I shouldn't even be here.'

'Probably not. But you are so my advice is to relax and enjoy it.'

Cassidy pulled a face. 'Any advice on *how* to do that when so many people are looking at me as if I've just landed from another planet?'

'When in doubt just smile and nod. It's always got me through when I've had to work a tough crowd.'

Hoping that this crowd wasn't going to be any tougher to handle than her boss, Cassidy decided that now that she was here, wearing a dress that probably cost at least her monthly rental bill back in New York, she may as well make the best of it. At least until she could slip away unnoticed and collapse into bed with a film.

The line moved sedately toward the dining room like a procession of tourists lined up to get into The Met on a hot summer day, only much better dressed.

The cavernous dining room was dominated by three rows of glittering chandeliers and two long tables set with white tablecloths and gleaming silverware. Footmen stood to attention every few metres along the wall and Cassidy forced herself to concentrate on not tripping up in her new sky-high stilettos the exact colour of the dress.

Stopping beside Leo, Cassidy followed his lead and stood behind her chair, surprised when she looked up to find Logan directly opposite her.

When their gazes collided she felt all the air leave her lungs and suddenly she was back on the mat with him leaning over her, and she had a breathless feeling he was having the same thought.

Fortunately Leo murmured for her to take her seat, breaking the connection between them, and Cassidy let out a breath, telling herself that she had imagined the whole moment.

After that the dinner went surprisingly well. Leo was great company and the never-ending relay of mouth-watering dishes left little else to do besides eat and drink.

Of course she was conscious of Logan across from her the whole time, but fortunately he didn't scowl at her as she imagined that he might after his terse greeting. Instead, his testy mood seemed to have evaporated as he conversed with the guests on either side of him. Which didn't lessen her awareness of him, but it did mean that she could begin to relax and take in the splendour of her surroundings.

When the meal was concluded, Leo directed her to the ballroom, the largest room in the palace, with rich, red-flock-covered walls and gilt-edged thirty-foot-high ceilings with cherubs holding bows and arrows chasing each other across puffy white clouds.

Orchestra music drifted through the dazzling room that was bright and airy with the wall of French doors opened to take advantage of the balmy evening. Fairy lights twinkled like stars from the manicured gardens, beckoning guests to enjoy the stone terrace and tranquil surrounds.

Cassidy caught sight of Logan at the far end of the room, surrounded by a group of glittering guests. Wondering how many of those were the single women on his mother's list, she reminded herself that she wasn't going to think about that and turned to watch the crowd that had already taken to the dance floor.

'Shall we?'

Flushed with exceptional wine and food, Cassidy pushed all thoughts of Logan and his mercurial moods to the back of her mind and took Leo's hand. 'Yes, please.'

After that the evening seemed to fly by. Cassidy felt as if she danced with every man at the ball. But it was either dance or feel out of place in the crowd of people that, after their initial surprise at finding that she worked for the new King, subtly dismissed her when they realised that she didn't have a title preceding her name. Just as his mother had implied that it would.

To be fair, some of the guests were nice. Like the Italian twin countesses with whom she had passed a pleasant half-hour talking about the tricks identical twins played as children. But it had soon became apparent just how different their lives were when they'd mentioned their summers spent in Portofino and shopping trips to Milan and Dubai. Cassidy hadn't thought that taking her nieces on the subway to Coney Island and getting to the sales early at Macy's quite cut it, and it had been a relief to accept the hand of the next man who had asked her to dance.

And it had taken her mind off the number of suitable women Logan had been dancing with all evening. A statistic she'd like to not have in her head, but which was firmly planted there by every person who commented on it whenever he came into view.

Dispirited by the fact that everyone wanted a piece of her boss, and that she was no different, she was contemplating whether to have another glass of champagne or to call it a night when Logan materialised in front of her.

'I've been looking everywhere for you. Where are you going?'

Startled, Cassidy's hand fluttered to her chest. 'I was thinking of retiring for the night.'

Looking distinctly disgruntled, he shook his head. 'Not yet you're not. You've danced with every other man here tonight. Now it's my turn.'

CHAPTER NINE

CASSIDY BERATED HERSELF when she automatically put her hand in Logan's. She was so use to doing what he asked that she didn't stop to question whether it was a good idea to dance with him, and before she could reconsider he'd swept her into his arms and out onto the dance floor.

And then she couldn't really think at all with Logan's large hand planted firmly against the centre of her back and one of hers captive in his other one as he pulled her against him.

Breathlessly aware that her composure had deserted her, she tried to stop her body from melting against his but it wasn't easy when all he did was firm his hold on her when she tried to ease back.

'Relax,' he ordered, his warm breath against her ear, sending rivulets of pleasurable pulses down the line of her neck.

Cassidy lifted her gaze to find that he was staring down at her with a dangerous gleam in his eyes. 'We're just dancing.'

It didn't feel as if they were *just dancing*, and she couldn't relax. 'I can't,' she said, wriggling a little in his grasp. 'You're holding me too close.'

'Stop trying to get away and I won't.'

Taking a breath, she did as he suggested, only to find that instead of easing his grip he inched her closer.

'I thought you said—'

'Dancing is much better when it's done in silence,' he murmured, his hand smoothing down her spine to rest on her lower back.

Her breath hitched in her chest at the caress, every one of her senses in a silent battle of wills with her self-preservation instincts. 'Your guests are already wondering why I'm here,' she said, ignoring his edict to keep quiet. 'If you don't let me have enough room to breathe, you'll start unnecessary gossip.'

And Cassidy knew intimately that gossip could destroy a person's reputation, and that Logan in particular could not afford to create any for himself. Arrantino stocks had not only started to recover once Logan had confirmed that he would become King but had bounced even higher than before.

'You have room to breathe,' he said.

Yes, she did, but every time she drew air into her lungs her breasts brushed against his jacket and it only made her want to press closer.

Realising that she would give too much away if she kept complaining, and that he was completely unaffected by how closely they were dancing, she gave up.

'Such a heavy sigh.' His lips quirked as he studied her. 'And here you looked like you were enjoying dancing earlier in the evening.'

She had been. But that was because she hadn't felt like this in the arms of any other man. Ever. 'I thought you said dancing was better without talking,' she threw back.

Logan laughed softly, the sound rumbling from his chest and into hers. 'So I did.'

If it were possible, he drew her even closer and Cassidy had no choice but to follow his lead. And then she didn't care, her body melting against his as he expertly guided her within the tight circle of his arms. He really was an exceptional dancer, his strong thighs brushing intimately against hers as he controlled their steps.

She didn't know if it was the soft music flowing over her, too much champagne, or Logan's hard body solid and strong against hers, but the intimacy of the moment took her over and dragged her into a sensual spell that made her feel dizzy.

Worried that he'd see the effect he was having on her, she ducked her face against his chest. Logan brought the hand entwined with hers in against her cheek and Cassidy had to fight the urge to place her lips against his skin.

When she felt him stiffen against her she was mortified to realise that she hadn't just *thought* it, she'd *done* it, and the tantalising male taste of his skin was exploding across her taste buds.

Jerking back, Cassidy stood mute in the circle of his arms, her eyes wide with panic.

Logan stared down at her so intently that for a moment she thought he was going to kiss her in full view of his other guests. Then he swore softly under his breath and started to lead her off the dance floor.

Stumbling to keep up, Cassidy leaned close to him. 'Where are we going?'

'Somewhere else.' His grip on her tightened as he picked up his pace.

That somewhere else turned out to be outside, down past a thick hedge of conifers to a trellised garden bed and stone steps that continued to a high brick wall. Stopping in front of a green-painted door, he flicked a hidden latch and shifted aside so that she could precede him inside.

Cassidy was immediately assailed by the soft scent of roses and jasmine that lingered in the evening air, the perfume heady and intoxicating. Breathing deeply, her eyes closed and she forgot the reason Logan had dragged her out here.

Rose bushes stood like silvery sentries around the perimeter of the small square garden, ethereally still in the moonlight.

Mesmerised, Cassidy moved from one bush to another, taking in the shape and what she could of the colour, leaning in to smell the tightly furled blossoms.

Suddenly she sensed Logan behind her, the heat from his body warming her back, even though he wasn't touching her.

'This is a Perfume Passion,' she said, recognising the flower her father had grown in their garden before their mother had walked out. 'It's a hybrid tea known for its incredible citrusy scent.'

'All I smell is you,' Logan said, his voice deep and low.

Cassidy shivered at the hunger her body picked up in his tone. She couldn't fathom that he might actually want her as much as she wanted him, and yet every feminine instinct flooded her with the knowledge that he did. It seemed incredible. Impossible. And she daren't move in case the fragile moment was ripped away from her and revealed as a figment of her imagination.

'Cassidy?'

Her name was both a question and a command on his lips, and she didn't move as he shifted closer. If she leaned back the barest inch they'd be touching, his front to her back, his hands on her body. His warm breath on her neck. Every cell in her body urged her to do it but she couldn't. She couldn't make that tiny move to show what she wanted because the fear of making a mistake overwhelmed her.

And then Logan's hands settled gently on either side of her hips, taking the decision out of her hands.

Cassidy's breath left her lungs in an excited rush. Hearing it, Logan's fingers tightened as he nuzzled her hair aside, his lips soft as he kissed the tender skin beneath her ear. 'You taste better than I imagined.'

Cassidy shivered, arching her neck to the side, a quiver racing through her as Logan's lips seared a path to the pulse point at the base of her neck. Need flooded the space between her legs and she sagged against him.

'And you feel better than I imagined.' His hands came more fully around her, splaying across her belly and coming to rest under her raging heartbeat as he took her weight back against his chest.

Cassidy's breasts ached to have him shift his palms higher, a small keening sound ripping from her throat as he kissed the base of her neck, his teeth biting gently on the tendon that joined her shoulder. Her whole body drew tight at the contact, a stab of piercing pleasure shooting from her breasts to her core as he finally moved his hands and cupped her in his palms.

Her sob of pleasure was lost as one of his hands rose to turn her chin as his mouth captured hers. Twisting in his arms, Cassidy plastered herself up against him and wound her arms around his neck, her mouth open to the delicious thrust of his tongue.

The distant sound of crystal clinking and the soft strains of the cello couldn't compete with the sound of her heartbeat in her ears as Cassidy gave herself over to the madness of Logan's kiss.

Her father's early warning to 'hold out until you know it's real' was muddled with the bizarre feeling that this *was* real, and then her sister's voice joined the mix, urging her to soak up every experience while she was here.

But neither message mattered. All that did matter was for this madness to continue. For the clamouring in her body, and the desire to touch this man, be met.

Now.

Always.

'Logan?'

His confident mouth slanted across hers, teasing her and devouring her in turn, his tongue seducing her to open and cling. Cassidy moaned and the kiss deepened until they were both panting.

Logan leaned his forehead against hers to catch his breath. 'I don't know what this is,' he murmured, his voice like velvet-covered gravel. 'And I don't care. I want you in my bed. Tell me you want to be there too.'

The raw need behind his command sent a shiver up her spine, creating a tingling sensation that spread over her skin. She did want what he wanted. She wanted to be in his bed with a desire that terrified her because she was very afraid that she wanted it too much. If it was just a matter of physical release she might not be so perturbed, but she couldn't hide from the feeling that it was more than that, at least for her.

'Cassidy?' His lips grazed her ear lobe, his warm breath sending her brain into free fall. 'Tell me.'

'Yes.' Her arms tightened around his neck as she gave herself over to a need that was greater than fear. 'Yes, I want to be in your—oh!'

Even before the words were out of her mouth he was lifting her and striding toward the entrance to the rose garden. Overawed at the powerful muscles in his shoulders that flexed beneath her hands, all Cassidy could do was bury her head against his shoulder and hang on.

Logan didn't know how he made it to his apartments without being seen by anyone other than the two guards stationed outside his door but he didn't care. He didn't care about anything right now but the woman in his arms and the ache in his body. He hadn't meant this to happen, hadn't *expected* it to happen, but now that it was he knew he needed it more than he'd ever needed anything.

'Cassidy?'

She looked up at him, her moss-green eyes soft, her body pliant in his arms. He groaned and bent to her, taking her mouth in another deep, hungry kiss.

Her fingers slid into his hair and Logan was beyond reason, completely lost to the feel and the taste of her, the soft curve of her body in his arms. The trickle of worry that perhaps he needed her just a little too much was replaced by the burning desire to strip her naked.

He released her legs so that her body slid down his, but he didn't let her touch the floor. His hands banded around her as he continued to devour her mouth, one hand sliding lower to cup her bottom, the other moving up to the back of her head, his fingers tangling in the silky mass of her auburn hair.

Cassidy writhed against him, the little sounds of pleasure coming from her lips driving his need higher.

Conceding that if he didn't leash his lust for her this would be all over in a matter of minutes, Logan dragged air into his lungs and stood her beside his bed.

She looked at him with glazed eyes and he leaned forward and took her mouth in another addictive kiss.

A little moan escaped her lips and he realised that he already loved those sounds. That he wanted more. Smoothing his hands down over her narrow shoulders, he skimmed his fingers down her arms, revelling in the way she shivered beneath his touch. She was so responsive, so expressive, and so *his*.

Suddenly impatient to see all of her, Logan searched for the zipper in her dress and eased it down. The bodice sagged to her waist, revealing gorgeous breasts cupped in a whisper of silk.

'You wore it,' he breathed, tracing his fingers gently along the delicate edge of the cup, making her tremble.

'It came with the dress,' she said, angling to get closer to him.

Logan held her back so that he could look at her. 'I know. I chose it.'

'You did?' Her eyes flew to his. 'I thought the shop assistant would have done that.'

'Not a chance, *mi amor*. I've been imagining you in this all night and reality far exceeds what I came up with.'

Her hands rose as if to shield herself, but Logan captured them in his. Then he sat on the bed and pulled her between his spread thighs.

Cupping her breasts in his hands, he watched her eyes glaze over with pleasure as the rough pads of his thumbs grazed her nipples.

The catch in her breath sent a spike of heat through his blood and he bent forward, kissing his way towards one rigid peak before pulling it into his mouth. She moaned, a soft keening sound, her hands forking into his hair, her grip urging him on.

Logan was happy to oblige her, his lips and tongue caressing each hard bud in turn as he teased her arousal to another level.

'Logan?'

She twisted in his arms, arching closer, and he gave her what she craved, unclipping the bra at the back and letting if fall away before he fully latched onto her nipple and tugged hard.

Her fingers tensed in his hair, her head thrown back as she gasped with delight.

He was delighted himself, her response ratcheting up

his own arousal until it was all he could do not to throw her onto the bed and bury himself inside her.

But he was enjoying unwrapping her too much, which he continued doing, sliding the dress down her legs so that it pooled at her feet. This time it was his breath that caught as he took in her slender legs and the pale silk at the juncture of her thighs.

A soft curse left his throat and his hands shook a little as he took her hips between his hands and eased the scanty fabric downwards.

'Logan…' Her soft plea for more undid him and he eased one hand up the inside of her creamy thigh, while the other one held her in place.

'Are you wet for me, Cassidy?' His voice was thick with need, his eyes on hers as his fingers grazed her softness.

A whimper escaped her throat and her feet shifted wider, giving him better access to her. He took it, cupping her sweet mound in his hand, the essence of her damp against his palm.

She wasn't just wet, she was fully aroused, her female scent sending his senses into a spin.

Growling softly, Logan pushed to his feet, picking her up and throwing her on the bed before she had time to draw breath.

She gave a nervous laugh and glanced at her feet. 'My heels—'

'Leave them.' He circled her ankles with his fingers and slowly parted her thighs.

'Logan, it's too much,' she said, her cheeks flushing even hotter under his gaze.

'Let me,' he said, coming over the top of her and bracing his hands on either side of her head. 'I want to taste you.'

'I don't… I've never…' her tongue sneaked out to wet

her lips and Logan kissed her as he wondered just how innocent she was.

'You mean no man has ever gone down on you before?'

She shook her head, her hair spread out on his white sheets.

'Then it will be my pleasure to introduce you to the delights of the flesh, *mi amor*,' he said, chuckling a little as she tried to grip his shoulder to prevent him from sliding down her body to bury his face between her legs.

Her gasp of shock turned to one of rapture as he swept his tongue along the seam of her lips, his hands urging her thighs to spread as her hesitation dissolved.

He took a moment to breathe her in and then he showed her exactly what she'd been missing, using every ounce of expertise he had to bring her to the brink of climax over and over before finally letting her fall over the edge into delirious oblivion.

She screamed his name as she orgasmed, her fingernails making small crescent moons in his shoulders.

Logan didn't mind. His body was throbbing and he barely gave her any time to recover before his clothing hit the floor and he'd rolled a condom over his pulsing erection.

She took him in as he came over the top of her, her hands skimming his shoulders and stroking his chest.

'I want to touch you,' she said.

'Next time,' he promised, his lips taking her mouth in a searing kiss as he positioned himself at her entrance. 'I need to be inside you too badly to wait for that.'

He stroked a hand down over her thigh and around to her bottom to angle her up to him and then he entered her on one deep, smooth thrust.

He felt her body tense beneath his, a frown forming between his eyes as he gazed down at her. 'Cassidy?'

'Oh, that feels so full,' she moaned, wriggling her hips

tentatively beneath him as if she was trying to get comfortable.

'You have done this before, haven't you?' he asked, straining to hold himself back.

'Yes.' Her gaze swept him in wonder. 'Once. But it was nothing like this.'

Once?

He wanted to pursue that incredible detail, but she'd started moving, shattering his concentration. 'Cassidy, *mi amor*, you need to relax. That's right, you're so tight.'

He groaned as her inner muscles gave around his hard length, her lower body tilting upwards as she sought to take him even deeper.

Sweat rolled down his spine as he powered inside her, swallowing her gasp of pleasure with his kiss. Sensation built like a dam about to burst as she learned his rhythm and matched him, her legs locking around his hips in an attempt to find her release. He wasn't at all sure he could hold out until she got there again, and then she did, her body exploding around his in a paroxysm of pleasure that shredded his self-control and sent him spiralling into the strongest climax he'd ever had.

Fighting for breath, Logan rested on top of her, completely shattered, a rush of pure emotion short-circuiting his brain.

Time had no meaning as his lungs worked to regulate his breathing, the soft rasps of her own uneven breaths warming his throat, her slim arms loose around his shoulders.

Sex had always been great for Logan, fantastic even, but this... What they'd just shared together was something entirely different. And for a man who prided himself on control and a keen ability to keep emotion and sex separate he'd just displayed an unhealthy version of the opposite. Because that had not felt controlled, or unemotional.

Waiting for his usual desire to remove himself immediately from a woman's arms, he was surprised when it didn't happen.

Then he heard Cassidy's soft sound of shock and knew that at least one of them was panicking.

Sensing that she was about to push him away, Logan rolled to his side and drew the length of her body against his. 'What's wrong? Did I hurt you?'

He hadn't been overly rough, but he hadn't exactly been gentle either.

Cassidy buried her head against his chest. 'No. But I should go.'

'Why?'

'Because…because… I'm in your bed.'

'Which is where I want you to stay,' he said, realising that it was true. 'Tell me how it is that you've only had sex once?'

She made an inarticulate sound of discomfort. 'Because the first time wasn't something I felt compelled to repeat.'

'Why?' Logan's muscles immediately tensed. 'Did he hurt you?'

'No.' Her voice was muffled against his chest. 'He was repaying me for giving him my study notes.'

Logan reared back to look at her. 'You bartered sex for study notes?'

'Not deliberately.' Even in the low light he caught the scarlet tinge to her cheeks. 'I thought he liked me.'

'Idiot.'

'Well, thanks.' She made to push away from him but he hauled her back.

'Not you. Him. He clearly had no idea what he was missing out on.'

'He did know because we—'

'He didn't. He obviously had no idea how to arouse you.'

Logan rolled onto his back and brought her over the top of him. She looked down at him in surprise, her palms flat against his chest, her hair a curtain framing her lovely face. 'Widen your legs.'

'Logan—'

'Do it,' he whispered, settling her thighs on either side of his hips so that she could feel exactly how much she turned him on.

'Oh!'

'Yes.'

Reaching up Logan dragged her mouth down to his, plastering her upper body to his chest. 'Let me love you again. You're so beautiful, *mi amor.*'

'Logan…' Her token resistance was lost as she gripped his face in her hands, her body supple and pliant as he showed her just how much he wanted her.

Logan woke from an almost catatonic state after a night of unbelievable sex to find himself alone. He took in the mussed bed sheets and the stream of light that arrowed between the partially closed curtains.

The whole incredible night came back to him in a rush, starting with that incredible kiss in the rose garden to the moment he'd surged inside Cassidy's body that first time. Just thinking about it sent a shaft of arousal through his bloodstream and he strained his ears to hear if she was in the shower.

Silence greeted him and he wondered where she was. On the rare occasion that he spent the whole night with a woman it was usually to wake up with her artfully displayed on the sheets beside him and ready for round two.

He frowned. He couldn't remember how many times his body had sought Cassidy's during the night but he did remember how sleepily receptive she had been each time he'd reached for her.

Hell, he'd just spent an incredible night in bed with his EA. The realisation was like a hammer blow to the solar plexus. From the moment he'd found himself attracted to her he'd planned to keep things strictly professional between them.

So much for that.

He'd been undone as soon as she'd appeared in that amazing gown in his drawing room, all his good intentions disappearing like dust in a sandstorm.

He scrubbed a hand over his face. No matter what the cause, there was no getting around the fact that he'd just made his life exponentially more complicated than it already had been.

And he'd slept with an employee. Just as his father used to do.

Leo's words bounced around inside his head. Something about Logan not being like their father because he didn't use his position as a power play with women. And his own response. *'Regardless, the only thing Cassidy and I have between us is a close professional relationship.'*

Right. Having just spent much of the night doing the most intimate things a man and a woman could do together, he could no longer lay claim to that.

And even though he hadn't used his position as her superior to get Cassidy into bed, there was no denying that he'd set aside his principles and slept with an employee.

In fact, he'd even forgotten that she was an employee. Sometime during these last few days his view of her as just his EA had transformed into something different.

He remembered her at the museum. Her warmth with those around her. Her smile. She had not only handled herself impeccably during the event, she'd added to it. He had always forced himself to only notice her professional attributes in the office, but it was clear she was much more than that. She was an accomplished, loyal woman whose commitment to her job, and her family, ran as deeply as his own.

He'd never taken the time to really know her and now he knew her a little too well. Would they be able to get their working relationship back on track? Because that was a priority. The idea of having to find a new EA as good as her didn't thrill him. But what did thrill him was the thought of seeing her again. Which didn't help.

Forcing an image of a sexy, pliant Cassidy from his mind, he jumped out of bed and trekked into his bathroom, heading straight for the shower.

A cold one.

He needed to clear his head, and lying in bed recalling every erotic moment they had shared the night before wasn't going to achieve that outcome.

The important thing to do was to set aside everything that had happened last night and chalk it up to two people who, having just discovered that they shared an intense chemistry, had given in to temptation after a particularly gruelling few days. Because he had never intended to jeopardise her position in his life and he didn't want to lose her over one slip-up.

And hopefully she felt the same way.

Hopefully she hadn't misunderstood last night and believed that sex equalled a serious relationship. It never had for him, and usually he made that clear with a woman from the outset.

So where had that speech disappeared to the night before? The same place as logic and self-control.

Slamming his hand against the controls, he stepped from the shower, shaved and pulled on jeans and a shirt.

There was no sense in putting this off. He had to find

Cassidy and deliver the news that as good as last night had been it would be best for all concerned if their relationship remained that of boss and employee and nothing else.

And surely she'd want the same thing. She was a woman who liked her i's dotted and her t's crossed as much as he did.

She was also romantic, his rational side reminded him. *Romantic and inexperienced.*

And he had been the one to shift their relationship into the personal realm when he'd danced with her. He might not have used power to persuade her into his bed but he'd known how badly she'd affected him and like a moth drawn to a flame, he'd let his libido take control.

Deciding that what was required here was calm, logical reasoning, he shut down his guilt and went in search of her.

CHAPTER TEN

CASSIDY REREAD THE letter she'd just finished typing.

It wasn't very long. In fact, it was quite short.

Should she add more?

Your Majesty,
It has been a pleasure working for you these past
twenty-one months, but I hereby tender my resigna-
tion forthwith.

Was it too blunt?

And what about the pleasure reference?

After last night she didn't want that to be misconstrued and so she deleted *'a pleasure'* for the more ambiguous *'great'*.

Then she added a couple of lines about how much she had learned, working with him, and sent it to the printer.

And even if she hadn't already been thinking of resigning there was absolutely no way she would be able to work with him after last night. Just the thought of facing him this morning was enough to make her blush.

And sleeping with her boss was not exactly what her sister had been thinking about when she'd advised her to fully immerse herself in the experience so that she had no regrets. It hadn't been what she'd been thinking either when she'd decided to attend the ball at the last minute, although she was honest enough to admit that she had wanted him to notice her as more than just his EA last night. And she *had* wanted to create some 'amazing memories'.

Mission accomplished, she thought.

Not that she regretted anything that had happened between them. How could she when it had felt so right to be in his arms? But she had to eradicate that feeling. Along with her plan to work for him for another month. Yes, she'd feel badly, not helping him settle into his new role, but after last night… She felt her throat thicken with emotion. That terrible suspicion she'd had about falling in love with him had tripled since this morning.

Just remembering how she had woken up with her body wrapped around his like Christmas paper, a smile on her face and a sense of wonder in her heart, was enough to make her break out in hives.

Last night hadn't been about love or commitment, it had been about lust and letting off steam, and she wouldn't make the mistake of thinking otherwise. And no doubt Logan wouldn't want her working for him after last night either. In fact, he'd probably be relieved to receive her resignation because it would all be neat and tidy. The way they both liked things.

'Working already.' His voice behind her sounded cool, remote. 'I'm not that hard a taskmaster, am I?'

Snapping the lid closed on her laptop, Cassidy gave a guilty start.

'It's not really work, it's—' She groaned softly when the printer started up on the bench space, drawing his attention. Before she could react Logan had crossed the room in three long strides and retrieved her letter. Scanning the page, he lifted his blue eyes to hers, his gaze glittering with an unnamed emotion that made her shiver.

'I have to say this appears to be an extreme case of morning-after regret,' he said, his voice lethally soft.

She smiled as if nothing was out of the ordinary when all she could think about was how his mouth had felt, exploring her body. 'It's not regret.' It was a simple case of self-preservation. 'I know my resignation might be a surprise, and this was certainly not the way I planned to tell you, but... I think it's for the best.'

'Do you?' He came to a stop in front of her and dropped the letter on the table. 'Exactly how did you plan to tell me?'

Shifting on her seat, she felt a pleasurable sensation pulse through her lower body, a reminder of everything they had done the night before. 'I hadn't got that far. I was still working it out. But I had already decided to resign before the ball.'

'Why?'

'Because you'll be living in Arrantino permanently and my life is in New York.'

'You could easily relocate. It's not like you have anything tying you to New York other than your sister.'

'Gee, thanks for pointing that out.'

'You know what I meant.' He ran a hand through his hair, reminding her of how thick and soft it had felt under her fingers. 'If you're worried about not seeing your family I'll happily provide you with regular trips home to visit them.'

'That's very kind of you but—'

'But this has nothing to do with logistics, does it?'

Frustrated that he wouldn't just accept her resignation at face value, Cassidy let out a controlled breath. 'I've seen you naked. You've seen me naked.' Probably not the best thing to say, given the way his eyes darkened. 'You have to admit that last night makes it impossible for us to work together.'

There was also the small situation of him having to marry and her having to be nice to a woman who would be sleeping with him every night. Something she would find too confronting for words.

'I don't admit anything of the sort. Sex, no matter how good, doesn't have to ruin our professional relationship. We're both mature adults who gave in to a moment of temptation. As long as we keep emotion out of the equation, things can go back to the way they were.'

The smile he gave her was gentle, almost tender, as if she were a small child needing to be placated.

Cassidy didn't know what made her feel worse. The fact that he could so easily dismiss what had happened between them, or the fact that she couldn't. Last night she hadn't cared that she worked for him, or that there was no chance of a future for them together, or that he would never want more from her than sex. She hadn't considered that she might already like him a little too much, or what would happen afterwards. All she'd thought about was the way he had made her feel. Beautiful. Wanted. *Sensual.*

Now she felt bereft. And she knew herself well enough to know that she would one day want more from him. So much more, and she would not let herself fall for another man who wouldn't want her back.

Determined that this time she would hold her line with Logan, she pushed her glasses closer to her face and huffed out a breath. 'I'm happy to keep emotion out of the equation,' she said, resolutely ignoring the pang in her chest that said that last night had been unforgettable. 'But I'm still resigning.'

Logan's scowl deepened, his whole demeanour one of outrage. He paced away from her, his broad shoulders rigid. 'You're being stubborn.'

Cassidy's eyebrow rose as if to say *pot...kettle* and his scowl deepened.

'We make a great team. I've never had an assistant I've worked so well with before.'

Cassidy didn't disagree with him, but knowing that her professional prowess was her most important attribute to him hurt, even though it shouldn't.

'We just need to compartmentalise what happened last night,' Logan decreed. 'Something you assured me you were extremely good at during your job interview.'

'I thought I was good at it too.' It was now very clear to her that she could strike that off her superpowers list. Or perhaps it was more that her ability, along with her intelligence, seemed to diminish to zero whenever he touched her.

'Then do it now. Better yet, come to lunch with me.'

'Lunch?' She blinked, struggling to get her head around his sudden change in topic.

'I promised Leo I would meet Elly today.'

She narrowed her eyes. 'I don't know that I should be there. I don't think it's—'

'Appropriate?' His mouth turned into a grim line. 'Probably not. But it will allow me to prove to you that we can resume a normal relationship. At the moment you're using emotion to dictate your decision and that's always a mistake.'

Cassidy frowned. 'On the contrary, I'm using logic and the knowledge that when men and women become intimate it complicates things.'

'That doesn't have to be the case if both parties are mature adults.'

'Then why have you never slept with one of your EAs before? Because I'm pretty sure there were some offers on the table.'

Logan's nostrils flared, his gaze drifting to the sofa behind her. She had the distinct feeling that he was contemplating lifting her onto it and having his way with her again. The fact that she wanted that to happen so badly only convinced her that she had made the right call. She couldn't work with him. If there was one thing Cassidy knew from a childhood full of instability it was when to cut and run. Her mother had been the first person to reject her and she had been watching people walk away from her ever since. Something most of them did with startling ease. Something Logan would eventually do as well.

'If you must know, I've never been tempted before.'

Rather than feel flattered by his soft words, a lump formed in her throat because it didn't matter how tempted he had been the night before, he still only wanted her in his life as an employee. And he would never want more than that from her because not only did she not have the right pedigree to suit his new station in life, she didn't have a pedigree at all.

She swallowed heavily, ignoring the fact that even scowling and dominant he made her feel dizzy with lust. 'I won't change my mind about this,' she declared with stubborn emphasis. 'I'm not as practised as you are in being able to move on from sex. And besides that, I want to work for someone who is less demanding than you are.'

Logan made a scoffing sound. 'You'd be bored within an hour.'

Probably, but she wouldn't give him the satisfaction of agreeing with him. It would only fortify his position. 'Believe what you want.'

'Dammit, Cassidy...' He stalked to the windows that overlooked rich, rolling green hills. 'Whether you admit it or not, your resignation is rash. This is all just a matter of self-control and discipline. We make a great team. Come with me to lunch and, if at the end of the day, you're not convinced that we can work together then I'll not only accept your resignation, I'll have Ben fly you back to New York tonight.'

Cassidy gnawed on the inside of her lip. Perhaps she should go with him if for no other reason than to prove him wrong. And, really, what was the harm? She knew she wouldn't change her mind about working for him in the future.

'This isn't a good idea,' she declared, questioning her sanity as he moved back to stop in front of her.

'Duly noted.' He adjusted her glasses on her nose as if he couldn't help himself. 'Dress is casual.'

Cassidy stared dubiously at the small red moped in the underground garage. 'We're taking that?'

Logan gave her a sexy grin. 'Not enough speed for you, *mi amor*?'

'It's not that.' She wondered what it was he was calling her and then decided that she didn't want to know. 'I'm just surprised that you would choose to ride one.'

'That's the whole point.' He swung his leg over the small contraption and balanced it between his long legs, managing to retain every ounce of his masculinity in the process. 'Sometimes, when we were younger, Leo and I would take off for a break from palace life and no one was any the wiser.'

'And security was okay with that?' She took the shiny silver helmet he proffered. 'They're okay with it now?'

'No, but they work for me. Which means they have no choice.' He grinned at her when she shook her head. 'They also know that I'm only going half an hour out of the city and I've already cleared where we're going. If something goes wrong they can be there in five minutes by helicopter. But who is going to be looking for the new King of Arrantino today, especially on one of these? Most people will assume I'm still in bed.'

At the mention of bed Cassidy's cheeks heated and she stuck her helmet on her head, accepting that he was probably right. She was accepting a lot from him lately. First the gown, then the casual outfit she had pulled from one of the designer bags in her room. And even though she intended to pay him back every cent for anything that she wore, she still cautioned herself to be careful. This wasn't a courtship by any stretch of the imagination. He wasn't in love with her, he was merely working to get the outcome he desired—which was for her to remain as his EA.

Forcing herself to not focus on the negatives and to just enjoy herself, she slung her leg over the back of the bike. Logan kicked up the stand and they zoomed out of the garage towards the rear entrance reserved for deliveries and staff.

Five minutes later they were weaving in and out of traffic and heading for the hills.

Finally dragging her eyes away from his broad back, she scanned the lush countryside rich with vineyards and orange groves.

In what felt like way too little time they pulled up outside a small house nestled behind a brick fence.

'Your brother has been staying here?'

'No. Elly lives here.' He took their helmets and slung them over the handlebars. 'Leo has been staying in a rented apartment close by. Since no one has been able to identify the woman in the photographs, her privacy has been preserved.'

'Something I'm sure she's more than happy about.'

'We will see.'

She heard the hard edge that entered his tone and placed

her hand on his arm. 'You said that Elly is an archaeologist. Is there anything else I should know?'

'She's a single mother.'

'Oh, that's hard. Do you know what happened to her husband?'

'No idea. She probably dumped him for a bigger fish.'

Cassidy frowned. 'That's terribly cynical. What makes you say that? Is it because of your father?'

'No. It's because of Leo's first wife. Anastasia was a shark with red lipstick. She wanted the power and privilege that comes with being a queen but not the everyday acts of service the role requires. When she got bored she searched for entertainment elsewhere.'

'Ah.' Cassidy remembered the stylish blonde from the time she had visited Logan's New York office. A shark with red lipstick was a fitting description; the woman's blue eyes had never been still, always sizing things up. Especially Logan. At the time Cassidy had thought that her reaction had been that of any other woman in Logan's presence, but apparently all those sexy little smiles had been a tad more targeted than that. Which was even more appalling considering she had been married to his brother at the time. 'That would have made it uncomfortable for you whenever you and Leo got together.'

'Extremely. I tried to warn him about her but he wouldn't listen and over time she succeeded in driving a wedge between us. I don't want that to happen again.'

'It doesn't mean that it will, though.'

'No. But it doesn't mean that it won't either.'

Completely understanding why Logan was preparing himself for the worst, and why he would want to protect his brother so much after having watched him battle leukaemia, Cassidy followed him as he pushed open the squeaky metal gate.

As soon as she stepped into the garden and spied the sun-flower-yellow front door, Cassidy knew that Elly wouldn't be the kind of person Logan imagined her to be.

No polished sophisticate who had money as their number one goal would have such a happy front door, or a garden grown wild with lavender and poppies, neither would she have the well-worn gardening shoes placed haphazardly beside the front door that signified that she wasn't afraid to get her hands dirty.

'I know you're anticipating the worst, but Leo comes across as a smart guy,' she offered, hoping to reassure him as she stopped beside him on the veranda. 'I'm sure he knows what he's doing.'

'Marrying Anastasia goes against that theory. And they say that love is blind. Today I plan to make sure he hasn't made a second mistake before this relationship goes any further.'

Cassidy swallowed at the laser-like intensity behind Logan's blue eyes, seriously glad that she wasn't the one in the firing line. 'And if you decide she's not good for him?'

'This time I'll make sure he listens.'

'Just…' Cassidy waved her hands between them wondering if he would welcome her counsel.

'What?' he bit out with barely concealed impatience. 'You've never been backward in giving me your opinion before.'

Actually, she had, but that had usually been to do with the women he'd dated and she'd determinedly told herself it was none of her business.

'Just watch the, you know, juggernaut face, it's very intimidating.'

Both exasperated and fascinated by his EA, who apparently was determined that she was not going to be his EA for much longer, Logan found himself tense up as he waited for the door to be opened.

He wanted this to work out for his brother and he hoped Leo was right about Elly because Anastasia had made him miserable, and as far as Logan was concerned, Leo had suffered enough in his life. On top of that, these past few days had shown him how much he had missed his brother's friendship and he didn't want to lose it again so soon.

Being back home, he had come to appreciate how unfulfilled his life in New York had been, driven by making deals and moving from one success to another without really taking the time to celebrate any of it.

He glanced at Cassidy as she bent to stroke the fur of a giant ginger cat. The large feline wove between her ankles, rubbing its scent on her and purring with delight at the attention.

He knew how it felt. Right now he wanted to ditch lunch, bundle Cassidy up, stick her on the back of the moped and haul her off to the closest bedroom.

Usually after he'd spent the night with a woman he was unaffected by whether he saw her again or not, but the thought of not seeing Cassidy, of not touching her, made his gut tighten with an emotion that felt peculiarly like dread.

But he was going to have to push that aside if he was serious about fulfilling his promise and proving that with a little self-control and discipline they could easily get their relationship back on track.

Looking at her now, her gorgeous curves encased in denim and a purple gypsy blouse that he was almost certain was concealing a black bra, he wasn't at all confident that he could—or that he even wanted to.

'Hello! Welcome!'

A petite dark-haired woman and the mouth-watering aroma of homemade bread and tomato sauce greeted them.

Elly's brown eyes were open and friendly and she was dressed as casually as he and Cassidy were. Score one for Elly, he thought, and then caught the cynical thought before it could progress any further. *Possibly* he was still a little jaded from his past, and *possibly* he did need to let that go and move on at some point.

'It's so nice to meet you both.'

Cassidy greeted the other woman with a natural exuberance he just didn't have, kissing her warmly on both cheeks. This in turn seemed to relax Elly and Logan masked his scowl and tried to play nice.

Fortunately Leo came up behind the woman and placed a hand on her shoulder.

'Right on time,' he said, easing the rising tension between them all with grace and aplomb.

It was a trait he was going to have to cultivate in his new role, Logan thought grimly.

And then a small ray of sunshine stepped out from behind Leo's legs with large unwavering eyes in a small fey face surrounded by clouds of dark hair.

'I'm Skylar,' she said, sticking out her hand for him to shake. 'I'm six years old. Are you Leo's brother?'

'Yes.' He found his throat had closed over and had to clear it before he could go on. Leo had sent him a text explaining that Skylar had no idea that they were from the royal family and would he mind playing along with that. Having wondered if that had been a ploy of his new girlfriend's, Logan felt a wave of shame flood him.

If the colourful array of flowers in the well-loved garden hadn't served to convince him that he was using a crooked lens with which to view the world, then this intelligent eyed child had finished the job.

Feeling unmoored for the first time in his life, he was

at a loss as to how to proceed when Cassidy tucked her hand into his.

'Yes, his name is Logan, and I'm Cassidy,' she answered. 'What grade are you in at school?'

'One.'

'And what's your favourite subject?'

'Reading.'

'Ah, mine too.' Cassidy laughed. 'Ever read *Fantastic Mr Fox*?'

'Yes, twice.' Skylar beamed under Cassidy's warm interest.

'That's one of my favourites too,' Logan said, vaguely remembering that he had enjoyed the antics of the wily fox raiding Farmer Boggis's hen house. 'What?' He gave Cassidy a superior look when her eyes went wide. 'You're not the only bookworm in the house.'

Skylar giggled and ran off, muttering about books, and Elly warned them that they had started something they might regret.

Leo stepped back for them to enter the house and Logan followed everyone into the cosy cottage awash with multicoloured cushions on the sofa and quirky prints on the walls.

Elly moved to the table set with a candelabrum and ceramic bowls filled with olives and dip and picked up a bottle of wine just as a timer went off in the kitchen.

Slightly flustered, she glanced around and Leo gave her a nod. 'I'll do the wine…you check the chicken.'

Elly's face immediately softened and she let out a slow breath of relief.

Leo touched her face so briefly that if Logan had blinked he would have missed it, but he hadn't and he felt a tug inside his chest at having witnessed the tender moment.

Cassidy shifted beside him, a dreamy smile on her face,

and he realised with a pang that this was what she most likely wanted from a man.

Love.

Probably a family too.

The whole concept was so foreign to him that he was relieved when Skylar danced back into the room with an armload of books and readily sat down to view her offerings.

Slightly embarrassed that he was using a child to mask the raw emotions that seemed keen on piercing his skin, he soon got caught up in the relaxed atmosphere and started to enjoy the afternoon.

'Thanks.'

Logan glanced away from where Skylar was teaching Cassidy some sort of game on the outdoor patio. He was quite sure his EA knew how to play it already, but was indulging the high-spirited child.

'What are you thanking me for?' he asked, taking in his brother's relaxed demeanour.

'Meeting Elly and Skylar on their level and not bringing your prejudices to the door.'

Logan shifted uncomfortably, well aware that if Cassidy hadn't spoken to him about his 'juggernaut' face before Elly had opened the door, the outcome of the day might have been very different. 'I did bring my prejudices to the door,' he admitted with a wry grimace. 'Cassidy made me leave them there.'

Leo laughed. 'I knew I liked that woman. I'll be sure to thank her in our wedding speech.'

Logan shook his head. 'You're that serious about Elly?'

'I gave up the crown for her, didn't I?'

Logan sighed heavily. 'You did. And I'm man enough to acknowledge when I'm wrong.'

'So no warning?' Leo asked bemusedly.

'No warning,' Logan grouched. 'She seems great. And it's good to see you happy.'

'And you.'

Logan frowned. 'What do you mean?'

Leo shrugged. 'It's been a long time since I've seen you without your phone glued to your ear or pushing another deal through. It's a nice change.'

Before Logan could fully process his brother's observations Skylar's clear voice called out to them. 'Who wants to play hopscotch?'

Hopscotch?

Leo laughed at his flummoxed expression and Logan elbowed his brother in the ribs.

'I'd love to,' he said. 'And so would Leo.'

Leo elbowed him back and placed his glass of wine on the table. 'Prepare to have your arse whipped,' he promised.

An hour later, with Skylar victorious, Logan downed a glass of cold water as Cassidy came up beside him at the kitchen bench. The sun had started to lower in the sky, taking some of the heat out of the air.

'Skylar's really tired. It might be a good time to head back,' she murmured.

Logan nodded in agreement, dragging her delicate scent into his lungs and wanting nothing more than to tug on her ponytail to bring her mouth to his. He hadn't touched her all day but now he wanted to. Badly. And he didn't care if that broke his promise or not. Having her as his EA was suddenly far less important than having her in his arms.

After saying their goodbyes Cassidy settled on the moped behind him and put her hands around his waist, and Logan knew he wasn't ready to return to the palace, or his new life, just yet.

CHAPTER ELEVEN

'WHERE ARE WE?'

Cassidy glanced around at the small car park high up in the hills overlooking the Mediterranean. The late afternoon sunlight turned the blond streaks in Logan's hair to gold before he covered the thick layers with a baseball cap he'd grabbed from under the seat of the moped.

'It's called Gran Mundo Lookout. It's one of the most beautiful places in Arrantino. Let me show you why.'

Conscious that they were not the only people on the gravel trail, Cassidy ducked her head and clung to Logan's hand as he led her along the path.

'Relax,' he advised. 'You're very expressive and you look like you you've just robbed a bank, which will make anyone watching us nervous.'

'But what if you're recognised?' she hissed under her breath.

'Most of the people here are tourists who wouldn't have a clue who I am. I'm not worried. So you shouldn't be either.'

Unconvinced, because it was her nature to worry, Cassidy tried her best to look unconcerned. Logan might be right about the tourists not recognising him, but he clearly didn't understand how appealing he was *as a man*, and she'd already noticed a couple of women giving him covetous glances as they crunched along the path.

'*Gran mundo* means great world,' he explained as they rounded a corner and Cassidy let out a reverent breath as the leafy foliage they'd passed through opened up to reveal an endless rugged coastline dotted here and there with colourful fishing villages nestled along the coast like jewels hanging from a golden chain.

'Wow,' she murmured softly, taking in the terraced vineyards and the ancient buildings that looked like they might topple from the rocky cliff face and straight into the azure sea at any moment. 'It's gorgeous.' She turned her face to his with delight. 'Thank you for bringing me here.'

'It's my pleasure.' His voice had a rough edge that instantly sent spirals of need cascading inside her.

All day he had been a perfect gentleman, not touching her, as he had promised, and it had driven her insane. Especially when he had allowed himself to be coaxed into a game of hopscotch by a playful six-year-old. Before long they had all been playing the game, Leo and Logan naturally turning it into a testosterone-fuelled competition of who could best the other.

'What are you grinning about?'

He stepped closer to her, a certain glint in his eye heating her blood even more.

'I was remembering the game of hopscotch after lunch. It was nice of you to indulge Skylar. Especially since you had already read her favourite book to her before lunch.'

Logan shrugged. 'I like her. The kid is so precocious I might offer her a position on my special council one day. To say that Leo will definitely have his hands full with that one is a gross understatement.'

'So you think that he and Elly might work out?'

He saw the impish grin that crossed her face and tugged on the end of her ponytail. 'Do you want to hear me say I was wrong?'

'Yes.' Her eyes sparkled. 'It would be such a novelty. But truly I completely get why you were worried. I feel the same way about Peta. That day everything went wrong in your office I was reeling from the shock that she was engaged. I never imagined that she could trust someone enough to marry him after everything she's been through. It seems like such a leap of faith, but the fact is she's more of an optimist than I am. She thinks love is worth the gamble.'

Something in her eyes, a shadow of sorts, poked at the hard, solid barrier around his heart. 'Maybe she's right.'

'You're agreeing?' She gave a startled laugh, shaking her head. 'Now I've definitely heard it all.'

Logan moved closer so that he was blocking everything from her view but him. 'Want to hear something else I might have been wrong about?'

'What?'

Her voice was breathless with anticipation. 'That we'd be able to resume our normal working relationship after last night.'

'You don't think we can?'

'No.' He took another step closer, effectively caging her in against the wooden safety barrier. 'Do you?'

'No.' Her throat bobbed as she swallowed. 'But I already knew that because… I… No, I don't think we can.'

Logan tilted her chin up so that her eyes met his. 'You were going to say something else. What was it?'

'Nothing.' She shook her head emphatically. 'But I know I can't work for you and I don't want you to try and change my mind because I always cave in to what you want.'

'I don't intend to try and change your mind.' He slipped his hand around to cradle the nape of her neck. 'And now that we've established that you no longer work for me, I don't have to worry about breaking any more rules with you.'

He nuzzled a few loose strands of her hair away from her neck, bracing his legs wide as he leaned in to kiss her.

She immediately opened to him, her small hands warm as she flattened them against his chest.

A low moan escaped from deep inside his chest as she responded to him, her hands moving up over his shoulders, her fingers tangling in the hair at the base of his cap. Feeling her unrestrained response, Logan put his arms around her waist and gathered her up against him.

The kiss went from 'exploratory' to 'get a room' within seconds and it was only a deeply ingrained sense of decorum from years of looking over his shoulder that had him pulling back.

Without her glasses Cassidy's green eyes were like luminous pools of phosphorescence. Unable to hold back, he dipped his head and kissed her again. This time when he came up for air she leaned her forehead against his chest, panting softly.

'I thought you said this was just a matter of self-control and discipline,' she said breathlessly.

'It is,' he said against her ear, absorbing her delicate shudder deep inside his body. 'But I'm all out. You?'

When she glanced up at him he read the answering response in her diluted pupils and this time he didn't need her verbal okay. It was written all over her gorgeous face. 'I'm not sure I ever had any.'

Cassidy glanced around at the front of the secluded sandstone building Logan had pulled up in front of. She was already having doubts about the intelligence of agreeing to sleep with him again but it was so easy to stem the trickle of unease.

He made her feel sexy and irresistible and she was simply intoxicated by the thought of exploring the chemistry between them once more. Reality would intrude at some point and she'd deal with it then but for now…

She glanced over as Logan secured the bike beside the brick wall. 'I thought we were going back to the palace?'

He pulled his helmet from his head and stowed it with hers on the bike. 'You know when I said that a king rarely has any privacy? At times it will feel so oppressive it will be claustrophobic. But right now I have a moment. A weekend. And I don't want to spend it at the palace where I'll be available to anyone who wants me. Tonight I'm going to turn off my phone and do what I want to do.'

'You make it sound like it will be the last time that can ever happen.'

'It won't be the last—it is possible to sneak away now and then, and even the King gets holidays—but the weight of responsibility will never be far away, and I'll always be on call.'

'So what is this place?' She looked up at high arched windows that denoted the buildings of Moorish heritage.

'My cousin's apartment. He's in Tahiti, surfing, right now so he won't mind if we use it.'

'He might not but I can't see your security detail letting you stay here without first making sure it's secure.'

'I know.'

Just then the ancient wooden door to the interior garden opened towards them and two soldiers with machine guns strapped across their torsos stepped outside.

'All clear, Your Majesty,' the female soldier said, taking the lead.

'Thank you. I'll let you know tomorrow when we're ready to return.'

Moving with a lightness that belied the weight of their heavy-duty equipment, the soldiers left them alone.

Curious to see what a surfer's place would look like,

Cassidy followed Logan along a stone path dotted with green ferns into an elevator that took them to the top floor. The apartment didn't disappoint. Low sofas in burnt orange, dark square tiles on the floor, a magnificent view of the white yachts in the harbour from the arched windows. When she looked closer she could see that all the appliances were state of the art, and ready on command, as evidenced when jazz music filtered into the room through hidden speakers at Logan's voiced request.

'Do the curtains also open and close on command?' she asked, moving into the kitchen and perching on the edge of a wicker stool.

'Of course.' Logan popped the cork on a bottle of wine he'd pulled from the wine fridge. 'My cousin loves his gadgets.'

He poured them two glasses and raised a toast. 'To secret rendezvous.'

Cassidy's heart did a mini-somersault inside her chest, her gaze dropping to his mouth.

The air between them became charged and Logan slowly lowered his glass to the bench top. Then he rounded the counter and took hers from fingers that had turned nerveless.

Without preamble or finesse he lifted her onto the counter and reached up to drag her mouth down to his.

Cassidy felt like her body went up in flames, her fingernails digging into his thick, soft hair, her moans trapped in her throat as he fed her kiss after kiss.

'Por Dios, Cassidy... Mi hermosa mujer... Mi amor...'

Logan's litany of Arrantinian love words tightened her nipples into unbearably aching peaks.

Feeling wanton and unlike herself—or maybe more like herself than ever before—she raised her arms and dragged her blouse up over her head, letting it flutter to the counter behind her.

Logan's eyes were hooded as he watched her, his gaze hot as it travelled from her face to her collarbone, his fingers trailing gently after, raising goose bumps wherever he touched her.

'Take your hair down,' he encouraged, his tone low and deep.

Cassidy did, letting the soft waves fall down around her shoulders, relishing the way he hissed out a low breath before hands forked into the mass as he pulled her lips back to his.

Hot liquid need pooled between Cassidy's thighs and she shifted restlessly on the counter, needing more.

Reading her perfectly, Logan pulled his mouth from hers and buried it against her neck, licking and sucking at her skin.

Burning up with need, she suddenly felt self-conscious sitting in the bright sunlight in only her jeans and a black bra. But then he looked at her with such undisguised hunger it made all her inhibitions dissolve to dust. 'You have too many clothes on,' she murmured, tugging at his T-shirt.

Obliging her, he reefed it over his head with one hand and she immediately smoothed her hand over the pelt of thick hair on his chest.

He groaned huskily, bending to her once more and trailing hot kisses down between her breasts.

Breathless, she cried out in pleasure as his lips crested one breast and sucked her nipple deeply into his mouth.

'Logan.' She gripped his wide shoulders, dazed with rapture as he removed her bra and feasted directly on her naked flesh, his lips pulling first one peak into his mouth with wicked skill before moving to the other and then back again.

Delirious with wanting, all she could do was hold on, barely aware when he picked her up and carried her to the sofa. He placed her on it and stood in front of her, unbuckling his belt, his blue eyes so hot they threatened to incinerate her.

Feeling more daring than she ever had before, Cassidy leaned forward and brushed his fingers aside. 'Let me.'

He went still, every one of his senses homed in on her trembling fingers as she released his zipper and pushed his jeans and briefs down his legs. He was gorgeous. So perfect she felt her heart constrict. Reaching out, she enclosed the long, hard length of him in her hand, her eyes finding his to gauge if he was enjoying her touch.

His chest moved in and out like a set of bellows, his eyes half-lidded as he gazed down at her.

Turning her attention back to his thick erection, she leaned forward and greedily flicked him with her tongue, fascinated by the low growl that emanated from deep inside his chest.

'Cassidy...' His fingers tangled in her hair and she looked up at him. 'Stop torturing me, *mi amor*.'

So turned on it was shocking, Cassidy slid his long length between her lips, completely lost to everything but pleasuring him.

What felt like seconds later, Logan released her hair and shuffled her back. About to complain, Cassidy fell silent at the feral glitter she saw in his eyes.

He reached down and nearly tore her jeans in half as he yanked them from her body. Then he was on her, his fingers sliding between their bodies, parting her swollen folds before he drove them deep inside her body.

Cassidy nearly blacked out at the pleasure, only dimly aware that he had sheathed himself before he'd moved between her thighs and opened her to the hot, hard plunge of

his body. Each powerful thrust moved her closer and closer
to the peak of pleasure until the only thing she could say
was his name over and over as her body splintered into a
thousand pieces.

Minutes felt like they turned into days as she lay there,
gasping for breath. Logan reached around her back and
gathered her up against him. Cassidy looped her arms
around his neck, her limbs the consistency of overcooked
spaghetti.

'Damn.' He pressed his forehead to hers. 'I didn't mean
that to happen.'

Cassidy blinked up at him. 'You didn't?'

'No.' His brow puckered. 'I meant to at least make it to
the bedroom.' He feathered light kisses across her eyelids.
'But you affect me so badly I have no control where you're
concerned. How hungry are you?'

'You mean for food?' She was so full after the enormous lunch they had not long eaten that she didn't care if
she didn't eat for a week.

A slow grin crossed Logan's face. He stood up and
reached for her hand, pulling her to her feet and giving
her a quick, blistering kiss. 'Neither am I.'

'Tell me about growing up in Ohio.'

Logan pushed the midnight feast of olives and cheese,
which they had assembled after raiding his cousin's lar-
der, onto the floor and stretched out on the bed beside her.

She rolled her eyes at his unabashed nudity and fixed
the sheet tighter beneath her arms. He hid a grin, knowing that all he would have to do to make her soft and begging was to drag that sheet down and take one of her lovely
breasts into his mouth.

Deciding that he could forgo the pleasure of her body

for at least another ten minutes, he played with a strand of her hair instead.

She glanced up at him, her long lashes causing soft shadows to fall over her cheekbones. 'What do you want to know?'

'Anything—' *and everything* '—you want to tell me.'

She started talking about the weatherboard house she had grown up in on the outskirts of a small town called Sherwent Creek, her mother walking out on them when she was fifteen and what that had meant to them all. 'My sister and my father really suffered after she left. It wasn't long after that my sister fell pregnant, then my father, who had already been struggling, completely fell apart...' Her voice grew quiet. 'Being the oldest, I did my best to cook and clean and make sure Peta was okay, but she wasn't interested in me being a replacement parent and for a while we fell out. Then she had the twins and that was when things really got tough.' She winced and peered at him sheepishly. 'Sorry, you were probably wanted to hear about the tourist attractions rather than my life story.'

Logan brushed her lips with his. 'If I want to know about the tourist attractions I'll visit there myself. It's you who interests me. What happened next?'

'Well... Peta is quite shy and the gossip and derogatory comments she received, having the twins so young, made all of our lives miserable. Peta drifted for a while, barely making ends meet. I got a job to help out with the bills but...' She hesitated and Logan sensed she was holding something back but didn't want to push her. She blinked as if to clear her memory.

'It got so bad that our father eventually relocated us to another town. We packed up the station wagon one night and drove all through the night. Amber and April were only young at the time.' She gave a soft laugh at the memory. 'Anyway, it was a little better after that but not great. Eventually Peta moved out and I stayed to take care of our dad.'

'What happened to him?'

'He died in a car accident.'

'I'm sorry, *mi amor*. And your mother? Did she ever return?'

'No. Having kids didn't suit her. I have no idea where she is now.'

Logan felt the pain of every word she spoke like a lash abrading his skin. He wanted to grab every one of those people who had made Cassidy's life a misery around the neck and squeeze. Hard.

Unable to do that, he pulled her unyielding body against his and looped his arm around her waist. 'Then what?'

She laughed softly. 'You really want to know everything, don't you?'

'I'm greedy like that.'

Loving the way he was able to make her smile after such a gruelling story, he encouraged her to go on. 'So what's next? Was that when you moved to New York? Came to work for me?'

'Yes.' A fleeting smile crossed her face. 'Once my father passed away I moved to New York to finish my online course and Peta moved in with me. After that I needed a well-paid job and walking into your building was definitely a case of being in the right place at the right time. I never expected to get the job but just as I handed my résumé to your receptionist she became violently ill. You had a Chinese delegation waiting to receive their building passes, as well as a persistent paparazzi guy lurking around, asking questions about you. It was Todd Greene, I think.'

Logan's lips twisted into a grim line. 'Don't talk to me about him. The guy has a vendetta. He tried to get a press pass to the coronation yesterday too but I had him removed. Anyway, go on.'

Cassidy shrugged. 'There's not much else to tell. I happened to know how to use the computer system you used so I printed the passes for the Chinese delegates and phoned your HR department. Your HR manager was in a flap because you'd just fired your last assistant and demanded a replacement asap. She interviewed me on the day, did a security check, and I was hired two days later.'

'Much to everyone's relief. You know you're amazing, right?' He kissed her shoulder. 'And utterly beautiful.'

'Don't say that. I don't need those kinds of compliments to feel secure.'

At her nonchalant comment Logan's eyebrow went skyward.

'I don't,' she persisted.

'That's because you don't believe it,' he said shrewdly. 'But you are beautiful, Cassidy.'

'I'm not.' Her eyes wouldn't quite meet his. 'My sister is the beautiful one. You haven't met her but—'

'I'm sure your sister is quite lovely, but we're not talking about her. We're talking about you.' He tilted her chin up so that she was forced to look into his eyes. 'And you are gorgeous. Gorgeous eyes. Gorgeous nose.' He kissed each attribute he labelled. 'Gorgeous chin. Gorgeous neck.' His voice became a sexy murmur. 'Gorgeous collarbone. Gorgeous—'

Cassidy squealed as he slid lower down her body. 'I get the picture!'

Rising up to loom over her, his biceps braced to take his weight, he locked his gaze with hers. She touched his face, her fingers stroking over his stubble, her eyes soft. For a moment he heard nothing but the sound of his own heart beating and the echoes of forever in his head.

'When you look at me like that,' she whispered breathlessly, 'I feel like anything is possible.'

CHAPTER TWELVE

THIS TIME WHEN Logan woke up, Cassidy was beside him, her arm flung across his abdomen, her leg draped over his thigh, and for someone who was always eager to move on from a woman he'd slept with he was hard pressed to explain this sense of belonging he felt at having her nestled beside him.

He knew it was very early because no light appeared around the blinds on his windows, or it was very late. He couldn't tell. He'd lost all sense of time after he'd made love to her again, more slowly this time, wanting to eradicate all the hurts she'd experienced as a child.

He moved a strand of her hair away from her face and thought about all the reasons why it was a bad idea to continue seeing her and couldn't come up with any, not now that she no longer worked for him. Since they were both single, there was no reason they couldn't continue an affair for as long as it lasted.

Other than the fact that Cassidy seemed more determined to get away from him than to stay with him but maybe that was only because she didn't know how he felt about her.

Which raised the question—how did he feel?

He liked her. He was insanely attracted to her. But it felt like more than that. She was the smartest, sweetest, mos' caring woman he'd ever met. He loved it that she matche him in so many ways. In the boardroom, the bedroom and even on the gym mat. If he ever lost his fitness edge, he knew she'd cut him off at the knees, and the knowledge that he could bend her but not break her was extremely appealing.

He also wanted to protect her and take care of her. And that was definitely new. He'd always avoided engaging his emotions with women in the past. Sex had always been just sex, but he was struggling to think of it that way with Cassidy.

What would she say if he asked her to stay on in Arrantino? If he told her he wanted to continue seeing her? It wasn't that much of a stretch. He could set her up in an apartment not unlike this one. He could get her a local job so that she was free to see him after work and on weekends.

But would she go for that?

And did he really want it? The fact that he was even considering doing all that to keep a woman in his life seemed crazy. But the alternative was that she fly back to New York, probably as early as tomorrow, and while he might not be one hundred percent sure about what he *did* want, he knew what he *didn't* want and that was for her to leave.

He liked waking up with her lying in bed beside him and he wasn't ready to say goodbye to that. And he knew she liked being with him this way. It was in every soft smile that she gave him, every tender touch.

He blew out a breath and contemplated the unpainted beams that crisscrossed the ceiling.

Unused to wanting something more with a woman than a good time, he found himself once again in the unusual position of not knowing how to proceed.

Cassidy stirred beside him, rubbing her calf along his 'eg, and he immediately thought about one way he could ~oceed—and a much less complicated one at that.

Shelving his vacillating thoughts with a much more pleasurable objective, he was about to roll her onto her back and press her into the mattress when he heard the first thump on his cousin's door.

Frowning, he didn't move just in case he'd been wrong when three extra-loud thumps followed.

Gently untangling himself from Cassidy, he murmured for her to remain asleep and rolled to his feet.

Given that he hadn't received much sleep the night before, his body wasn't impressed with being dragged out of bed as dawn touched the horizon and he padded grumpily downstairs to the front door.

'Your Majesty. It's Lukas.'

His head of his security?

Opening the door, Logan took in his grim demeanour. 'Your mother sent me.'

Instantly on high alert, Logan barely showed a flicker of emotion. 'Is she okay?'

'The Queen is fine, sir. But there's been a stir. In the news.'

A sense of dread even worse than when Leo had called washed over Logan. 'What kind of a stir?'

'The press have certain information.' He could tell his head of security was trying to be diplomatic and Logan strode over to the kitchen and switched on his phone.

A million messages pinged into the receiver, but he bypassed those and pulled up an international news site. A picture of Cassidy and himself at the lookout yesterday, his arms caging her in, her face turned sweetly up to his, was the first image that greeted him. The next ones were much more revealing.

'Logan, what is it?'

He heard Cassidy pad up behind him, leaning in to get a look over his shoulder before he could stop her.

She gasped and he turned to find her fingers covering her mouth.

He glanced over her head at Lukas. 'How bad is it?' He knew Lukas would have already fully apprised himself of what had happened. 'And don't pull any punches.'

'A journalist, Todd Greene, has published an exposé on your relationship with Miss Ryan. He's included information on her family and interviews from her home town.'

Logan took one look at Cassidy's stricken face and frowned. 'This photo was taken yesterday. How can that be possible?'

'From what our intelligence agency has been able to ascertain, Greene had a local source. Someone who worked at the museum and was at the opening you attended last week talked about seeing the two of you together. It seems that Greene sniffed out the story and has been lying in wait to get photographic confirmation ever since.'

And Logan had given it to him.

He felt the rise of bloodlust in his veins and wasn't sure how he managed to not put his fist through a wall.

He glanced over to find Cassidy on her phone, her face chalk white.

Doing what he did best, Logan went into damage control. 'Cassidy?'

He had to say her name twice more before she registered that he was talking to her. He gripped her shoulders in his hands. 'Don't read any more. I'm going to fix this.'

'How?' her lower lip trembled and she staunchly bit down on it. 'You can't fix it. It's all true. Oh, God, he has those photos of me.' She hid her face in shame and Logan glanced at her screen to see an artless photo of a girl in cotton underwear that had clearly been taken years earlier.

'I sent it to a boy in the hope that he would like me. I never thought you would find out. I never thought *anyone* would find out. He promised that he and his friends had deleted the images...'

'God dammit,' Logan swore fiercely in the face of her open vulnerability. It was his fault that everyone knew about her past because anyone who came into his life was put under the microscope. 'You should have told me about this before now. I would have—'

What? Wrung the guy's neck along with that of every other person who had ever hurt his woman?

He ground his teeth, furious that someone would invade her privacy. Only just coming to understand how much he thought of Cassidy as his. Unable to process that right now, he turned his attention to what he needed to do next. 'Forget the photo. I'll fix it.'

She shook her head, barely listening to him. 'I need to call Peta.'

'It's the middle of the night in New York. Don't call yet.'

'Oh, no, the twins...' Her eyes scanned her phone. 'That bastard even interviewed their lowlife father!'

Wondering if she was about to be sick, Logan gave her a shake. 'I'll fix it.'

'You can't fix it.'

'I can. And I will.'

Oh, God, he was furious with her—and who could blame him after seeing *that* photo flashed all over the media with the caption *The King's New Sleaze*?

Bile rose in her throat. This was awful. Horrible. The worst possible thing that could have happened to either of them. And yet she couldn't blame Logan for being angry because he had probably thought that her past was as pristine as the women on his mother's marriage list. A list she knew she'd never make in a hundred years.

'What are you going to say about the two of us?' she

asked hoarsely. 'Because I don't think *no comment* will cut it.'

'I'm going to close it down before it grows any more legs. You need to stay put and not get involved.'

Cassidy's stomach dropped into her toes. She supposed closing down whatever this was between them was the most obvious solution, and why wouldn't he take that route? She would have been leaving soon anyway. And probably the sooner the better because while she hadn't meant this to happen, her tarnished history had put Logan's kingship in jeopardy. And he was furious about it. Which she completely understood. He'd come to Arrantino on the back of one scandal—not to get involved in another.

And while logically she knew that it wasn't all her fault she couldn't bear being the reason someone was publicly slated. Just as she had been.

Dismayed, the threat of tears backed up in her throat, and she stared at the floor. 'I need to get home. I need to be with my family.'

'You need to stay here and trust me.'

'No.' She shook her head, everything inside her going ice cold. The last thing she needed to do was stay here and make it worse. She'd acted rashly by sleeping with him and now she'd face the consequences.

She crossed her arms over her chest. She'd indulged in a silly affair, *'put herself out there'*, and brought public shame on herself and her family again. And on Logan. 'I'm not waiting around for you to do anything. I want to go home. Now.'

'You're overreacting.'

'I'm *overreacting*?' She stared at him. 'My family name has been dragged through the mud for the world to see, you're being compared to your father, Leo's relationship is back in the news and you think I'm *overreacting*?'

'I know how bad this is,' he growled, dragging a hand through his hair. 'That's why I have to go. I have to fix it.'

'I knew this was a bad idea.' Her voice was a thread above a whisper, but he heard it.

'What was a bad idea?'

'Us.' She glanced around his cousin's apartment at the still full wine glasses on the bench, the uncorked bottle. She felt like soiled goods all over again. 'This.'

She had known it would be a mistake and she'd done it anyway so she had no one else to blame but herself.

Cassidy shook her head. What they had was a first-class mess. 'It doesn't matter now. Go.' She waved her hand in the air. 'I know you're desperate to get this under control.'

'I am. I will. Then we'll talk about what happens next.'

As far as Cassidy was concerned, she already knew what happened next.

'Your Majesty, I'm sorry to interrupt but—' Lukas stepped back into the room, his eyes on Logan '—Her Majesty is on the line.'

'Fine.' Taking a deep breath, Logan turned back to Cassidy.

Unable to stop herself, Cassidy reached out and pushed a lock of his hair back from his forehead.

'Wait for me.'

She shook her head. 'This isn't my home.'

Tension was stamped all over his handsome face. 'Lukas, I want you to personally take Miss Ryan back to the palace and make sure she's secure. Do not let anyone see her enter. I don't want to fan any more flames about this until I have it under control.'

Cassidy swallowed heavily. Of course he would be ashamed for anyone to keep associating them together when he had to correct this latest disaster. Her father had felt the same way when he'd returned home from work, asking if it was true that she had sent revealing photos to a boy at school. Having tried to weather the storm of her mother's desertion and Peta becoming a teenage mother, her mistake had been the straw that had finally broken the camel's back. And it only made her more resolved about her next move.

'Your Majesty.' A secret service agent in a black suit stopped beside him. 'The helicopter is ready when you are.'

Logan nodded, his eyes never leaving her.

Close to tears, Cassidy sniffed, her hungry gaze sweeping his face one last time, committing every one of his beautiful features to memory.

'Go,' she whispered. Go, before the hot tears scalding her eyes leaked out and revealed what she had only, in this awful moment, come to fully understand. That she did love him. Completely, and against all common sense.

She also knew that he needed to go into damage control for his family. That he would do his best to stifle this latest scandal and protect them. And she would do the same for him, and for her family.

She'd go home.

Logan paced his office, his shoulders tight, the muscles in his back aching. This had taken hours to pull together. Hours to ensure that every international outlet had agreed to pull the stories about Cassidy and her family in exchange for a bigger story.

Once that was done he'd put the world on notice.

Okay, his methods hadn't been entirely conventional, but neither was Todd Greene's revolting exposé.

But now he was drained and exhausted. He didn't think he'd fought for anything harder, or longer, than he had to ensure that Cassidy's decision to sleep with him did not completely destroy her reputation, or that of her family. He knew how important that would be to her. He knew how upsetting if he failed.

But finally it was done. His team had pulled off a miracle—for the most part.

The only tiny element of doubt in the whole thing was how Cassidy would react to the method he had used to close everything down. How she would react when he told her, and whether he could convince her that he'd done the right thing.

He'd never been this uncertain of anything in his life and he hated the voice in his head that said he'd overstepped. That this could backfire sensationally on him.

As his mother had angrily promised that it would. She didn't agree with the strategy he had come up with. In fact, she had turned around and walked out after she'd heard it, telling him that he was just like his father.

That had hurt.

But he hadn't let it sway him. He *was* like his father in many ways, but he knew he'd never betray the woman he had given his heart to. He'd never betray his family by turning his back on them. That was where they differed entirely.

They also differed in that Logan faced his problems head on and made decisions quickly to rectify them. It was what he did best. He only hoped he had made the right one this time.

With a few members of his team finishing up, Logan called Margaux into his office. She had done an amazing job of pulling various source materials together and he'd likely offer her the position as his private secretary when everything had settled down. 'Margaux, it's two in the morning. You need to go home. And don't rush in tomorrow. In fact, I'm fine if you want the day off. But tell me, has Cassidy called the office?'

'No, sir. Not that I'm aware of.'

She hadn't called him on his cell phone either. She was probably asleep.

In his bed or hers?

'But Gerome did leave a message earlier to say that he had taken care of Miss Ryan's request.'

'Request?' A cold feeling of dread chased away the anticipation firing his blood, everything in him going still. 'What request?'

'Apparently Miss Ryan left the palace some hours ago.'

'Left the palace?'

'Yes, sir. She wanted to be taken to the airport, so Gerome arranged a car. Is there something wrong, sir?'

Given his plans, yes. 'You should have told me earlier.'

'I'm sorry, I only checked the message five minutes ago.'

Logan dismissed her and turned toward the window, staring out at the dark night sky. She'd left, after he'd specifically asked her to wait. It didn't make sense. Why would she have done that?

Apart from the obvious—to get home.

This isn't my home.

Logan's jaw clenched. Well, it damned well was going to be if he had any say in it.

'Your Majesty?' Jason, his head of PR, spoke quietly behind him. 'If Miss Ryan isn't here, do you want us to pull the—?'

'No.' Emotion churned through him. Emotion mixed with a good deal of anger that she hadn't trusted him enough to sort this. 'Leave everything in play.'

A grim smile twisted his mouth.

In his country they had a saying he'd long lived by: *Al hombre osado la fortuna le da la mano.*

Fortune favours the brave.

He certainly hoped that held true because he had a feeling he would need it now more than ever.

CHAPTER THIRTEEN

'I can't believe it. They're still outside.'

Cassidy buried her head under her pillow against the evening sun streaming in through her back window as well as against her sister's voice.

'You should probably close the blinds,' she croaked. 'I've heard the paparazzi have telephoto lenses and if they come over the back fence they'll get what's called the money shot.'

Peta glanced out the window, a frown marring her brow. 'They wouldn't dare. Dan would take them out at the knees. He's already nearly come to blows with several of them out the front.'

Cassidy didn't want to hear that. The last thing she wanted was for Dan to get into trouble because of her.

It was all because of her.

She'd arrived home on a red-eye flight from Arrantino and found Dan waiting to pick her up. It had been such a relief to see him that she'd promptly collapsed in his arms and cried her heart out. All during the flight home she hadn't let herself think about actually having left Logan but as soon as she'd arrived on home turf it had become real and tiredness and emotional overload had overwhelmed her.

Dan had ushered her into his jeep and gunned it for the house, covering her with his jacket as they'd pushed their way through the mob of journalists outside her tiny Brooklyn home. The only upside, Peta had said, was that a few of their neighbours were loving every minute of the notoriety, dressing up and parading around just to see themselves on camera. Causing a distraction.

And telling the press that neither she nor Peta had ever been 'any trouble'.

If only that made her feel better.

'You're going to have to get up. You haven't eaten in twelve hours.'

And she might not eat ever again. It seemed like a viable solution to fixing the hole in her heart. Not to mention her reputation. Within twenty-four hours she had quit her job, slept with her boss, and become internationally unemployable. Quite a feat really, but not something that would look good on any future job applications. 'I'll get up soon.'

Peta perched on the end of her bed. They'd talked a little the night before, and Cassidy had apologised profusely, but her sister was holding up better than she'd thought she would be.

'I don't believe you,' Peta said. 'The girls will start to know that this is more than jet-lag if you don't show your face because it's not like you not to be able to pull it together.'

'I know.' She never let anything get to her, or at least to let it show that it got to her, but she had no superpowers left. She was like Superman without his cape, or Batman without his tool belt.

Of course she knew she'd be all right. She knew once the dust settled, life would return to normal and she'd be able to push her feelings for Logan to one side and move on. It's what she did best. But she could see by the look on her sister's face that she was going to have some trouble convincing her of that.

'Sorry.' She pushed to a sitting position and shoved her

tangled hair out of her face, grabbing her glasses from her nightstand to put them on before picking up her phone.

'No you don't.' Peta grabbed her cell from her. 'You've done enough Internet searches for the time being. It will only depress you.'

Knowing her sister was right, she subsided back against her pillow.

'I'm just so sorry you got dragged into it,' she said in a small voice.

'Don't sweat it.' Peta put on a brave face. 'And none of this guilt. I might not like having my life splashed all over the papers, but I've never lied to the twins about where they came from. They know their father abandoned them.'

'Yes, but now all their school friends will know. And your work.'

'We'll deal with it just the way we've always dealt with it. We'll start again.'

'But what about Dan?'

'He already knew everything, of course, but he said that he'd stand by me. He said he'll go wherever the girls and I go.'

'Oh, Peta.' Cassidy had to fight back a wave of tears. 'I love you so much.'

Peta hugged her tight, stroking her hair. 'Half the reason this has been such a big deal is because of my wild teenage years. Seriously, you have to stop blaming yourself for everything that goes wrong.'

'You weren't responsible for that awful photo of me everyone is laughing at.'

'You were only eighteen, and a little too trusting at the time. And you could have been wearing a bikini. Really, Cass. No one will care in a day or two. Maybe a month.'

Cassidy tried to smile. She knew someone who would care. Logan.

'You'll see I'm right,' Peta said.

Cassidy tried to smile. 'I hope so.'

'The only question is what you do with yourself once that happens.'

'Move to Siberia.'

Peta laughed, wiping away a tear that had leaked out of Cassidy's eye without permission.

'I thought I'd cried out every tear in my body last night.'

'Unfortunately we produce more.'

Peta touched her forehead to Cassidy's. 'You're in love with him, aren't you?'

All the night before Cassidy had denied having any feelings for Logan, but she didn't know why she'd bothered. This was her sister, after all. 'Yes,' she said simply. 'Silly of me, isn't it?'

'I think you've always been a little in love with him,' Peta said softly. 'You never let a single person criticise him in your presence. It was as if the man really did walk on water.'

Hearing that only made her feel more miserable. 'Which means you were right to be worried. Something happened and it was my heart that was broken after all.'

'Maybe his is too. Maybe he loves you back.'

Cassidy sniffed and wiped her nose with a tissue. 'No. Desire isn't the same as love and that's all he feels for me.'

'Maybe you're wrong, maybe—'

A knock on the door startled them both.

'Sorry to intrude, ladies.' Dan poked his head around the door. 'But the twins just pulled this up on the Internet. It's an official palace statement. And apparently you can't find a mention of Peta or the girls on any of the main news sites. And believe me, the twins have searched every site known to man.'

Cassidy's heart beat out a slow, sad tattoo inside her

chest. So Logan had closed it all down. She was glad. She only hoped the fallout on his side was somewhat mitigated by the lack of information out there now.

Peta took the laptop Dan held out to her and started to read, a strange smile curving her lips.

Cassidy gave her a quizzical look. 'What does it say?'

'It's a private statement from the King, explaining that his relationship with you is new and deeply private. He's asked that the media respect your personal space and said he will prosecute any individual or group harassing his fiancée. It then says—'

'Fiancée?' Cassidy frowned. 'Are you sure you read that right?'

'I do know how to read.'

Cassidy held out her hand. 'Let me see that.'

She scanned the article, noting the official Arrantino seal and Logan's scrawling signature at the bottom of the letter. Then her eyes went back to the word *fiancée*.

'It must be a misprint,' she murmured. 'He must have meant assistant, or ex-assistant. He's probably furious with the error.'

Both Peta and Dan stared at her.

'Is it possible he thinks you're his fiancée?' Dan asked carefully.

'No.' Cassidy thought back to their last interaction. His anger with her and his intention to close everything down. 'No.' She shook her head. 'The concept is ludicrous.'

'Aunty Cassidy?' One of the twins poked her head around the corner of the door. 'Since you're awake we wondered if you wanted a cup of tea.'

Cassidy swiped at the tears on her face and gave her niece a hesitant smile. 'Thanks, April. That would be lovely.'

'And there's a man at the front door who wants to see

you.' Amber nudged her twin out of the way. 'He looks sort of like the King of Arrantino, only way hotter.'

Cassidy felt goose bumps run up her arm, but immediately discounted that it was Logan.

'It's probably a hateful reporter,' Peta bit out.' I hope you didn't let him in.'

'No. He's waiting on the doorstep.'

'I'll handle it,' Cassidy decided, pushing out of bed and throwing a ratty old sweater over her singlet top and boxer shorts. She was tired of being the victim in this scenario. She'd said she was taking charge of her life and so she would. Starting with the hateful press. 'They need to understand that there's no story here and there never will be.'

Marching through their shambolic living room, she wrenched open the door. 'You have some nerve. Do you—?' The words instantly died on her lips as Logan turned back from scanning her street.

His blue eyes, surely brighter than they'd ever been before, grimly took her in from her awful bedhead right down to her bare toes.

Cassidy swallowed, wondering if she was dreaming.

Logan scowled. 'You didn't wait.'

She was so stunned to find him on her stoop she nearly fell sideways as he swept passed her and into her living room. Cassidy followed, finally managing to unstick her tongue from the roof of her mouth. 'What?'

Logan eyed her coolly. 'You said you'd wait.'

'Cassidy...' Peta's tentative voice came from the kitchen doorway, and trailed away as she recognised Logan standing like a conquering warlord in the middle of their tiny living room. Wearing a dark suit, and with legs braced wide apart, he looked magnificent.

'Your Majesty.'

Her sister dropped into a wonky curtsy, which made the twins, who were stood just out of sight, giggle.

'You must be Peta,' Logan said, managing to soften his features when he looked at her stunning sister. 'It's an honour to finally meet you. Please accept my heartfelt apologies for what the press has printed about you. I've done everything in my power to ensure that you, and all of your family members, will not be bothered again.'

'Thank you.'

Peta looked like she was about to apologise to Logan in return when Cassidy gave her a look.

'I'll just give you two a minute,' she said, backing out of the doorway and closing it behind her.

Reminded of just how Logan had tried to solve the problem, Cassidy frowned. 'I'm not sure you solved anything. In fact, you've no doubt made things worse.'

Logan turned the intensity of his gaze on her, which made her horribly aware of exactly what she must look like.

'You will not be bothered by the press any more, because I'm assigning bodyguards to all of you.'

'Bodyguards?'

'Yes.' He let out a breath. 'It won't be for ever. Just until the press understand the full consequences of hounding your family for information.'

'Okay, well, that's very nice of you, but not really necessary. When everyone realises that there's no story to write about, they'll disappear. Which would probably happen a lot quicker if you hadn't actually shown up here today. The paparazzi must have gone crazy when you drove up the street.'

'My men cleared them out first. Although there is no doubt they will go crazy when they learn I'm here.'

'If you leave quickly enough, they won't.' Suddenly she realised that he *was* here and she had no idea *why*—unless it was just to apologise in person. 'Why are you here? It's nice of you to apologise to my sister in person, but a phone call would have worked just as well.'

'Not from my perspective.'

'Well...' Starting to feel nervous now that the adrenaline rush of having him in her home had worn off, Cassidy fidgeted with her shirt. 'You've said your piece so you can go.'

'I haven't said anything.' He gave her a hunted look and ran his hand through his hair. 'I need you to come back to Arrantino.'

'Why? If you're looking for a replacement, Margaux will be perfect. She knows everything.'

'I know. She might even eclipse you in some areas.'

Cassidy force a smile, trying not to let him see how much that hurt. 'Great. Excellent.'

She moved to straighten the twins' homework, which had been left haphazardly on the coffee table. Anything other than having him see how upset she was.

'The problem is,' Logan said softly coming up behind her, 'she's not you.'

Swallowing heavily, Cassidy straightened and turned to face him. 'That's nice, I suppose, but I can't come back to work for you. Is that why you're here? Because I thought—'

Logan clasped the tops of her arms, staying her words. 'That's not why I'm here. I don't want you to work for me. Did you not read the notice I put out at all?'

His eyes met hers, the usual arrogant sparkle in them missing. Cassidy swallowed heavily. 'Of course I read it. And I suggest you fix the typo pretty quickly if you haven't already.'

'It wasn't a typo.'

'You referred to me as your fiancée—ah!' Cassidy nodded, finally catching on. 'Clever.'

Logan frowned. 'What's clever?'

'Your strategy.' She nodded, wishing he'd used the phone instead of coming in person because she was struggling not to wind her arms around his waist and lean into him. She had thought that with time she'd get over never seeing him again but with him here now, larger than life, she knew that had been a fool's dream. 'Rather than deny that we had a fling, you're trying to make it look more serious so that the scandal factor is removed. But, honestly, with my history I wouldn't have gone with that, not to mention that your mother—'

'Cassidy.' He gave her a little shake. 'Be quiet.'

She blinked up at him, not sure if she should be offended or not.

'Sometimes you talk too much. The notice isn't a strategy. It's a plan. A plan you would have known about before the statement was released had you done what I asked and stayed at the palace.'

'A plan?' Her brow furrowed, her brain sluggishly stuck on how good it felt to have him touching her. 'I don't think—'

Dios mio!' His hands lifted to her face as he brought her body up against his. 'How I convinced myself for two years that I didn't want you I don't know.'

Instant desire slammed through her when he kissed her, her hands gripping his shoulders as she held onto him.

'Logan…' She was panting as she pulled back from him. 'You can't kiss me any more. It feels too good and I—' She shook herself out of his arms, shocked at how close she had come to revealing how she felt about him. The words *I love you* had been about to tumble from her lips.

'*Mi precioso amor*, look at me.'

Cassidy shook her head, resisting the hand beneath her chin as he tried to get her to look up at him.

'Don't hide from me,' he rasped. 'I don't ever want you to hide from me because I don't ever want to hide from you.'

Confused, she risked a glance up at him. The look in his eyes made her breath catch. 'You don't have to hide from me.'

'Good.' His hand stroked her hair back from her face. 'Because I love you and I want you to come back to Arrantino with me, as my Princess, not my EA.'

Cassidy blinked up at him, her brain still on a go-slow. 'You love me?'

His eyes scanned her face, his thumb tracing over her lips. 'So much I feel like it wants to burst from me.'

'But you don't do love. You said—'

'I've said a lot of things in my life that turn out not to be true. Love always seemed like a burden that was best avoided and I arrogantly assumed that I had control over how I felt. But I don't...' The emotion in his eyes was spellbinding. 'What I feel for you is beyond logic and control. It's like a part of me is missing when you're not beside me.' His smile turned soft. 'You make me smile even when you're not there.'

Cassidy felt tears well up in her eyes, spilling down her cheeks. 'Logan, I...' Clumsily she reached up and pulled his head down to hers, half laughing and half crying as she kissed him. 'Do you mean it?' she whispered. 'Do you really mean it?'

'You doubt me?'

'No.' She shook her head, a glorious laugh leaving her throat at his affronted look. 'I don't doubt you. I love you back.'

Her arms tightened around his neck as he lifted her off the floor and her legs wound around his waist. 'I love you so much I can't stop crying. But you know that I'm not princess material. That I'm not suitable. That photo—'

Logan made a dismissive sound. 'That photo is nothing.'

'I'm sure your mother doesn't think so. If she knew you were here—'

'She knows. And she will come round as soon as she gets to know you and realises that you're the most suitable woman in the world for me. You and no one else, *mi amor. Eres todo para mi.*'

'What does that mean?'

'You are everything to me.'

'Oh, Logan, I feel like I'm dreaming.'

His brow rose with mocking humour. 'And I'm not even half-naked.'

'Do not laugh about that,' she admonished. 'I felt so embarrassed to walk in on you half-dressed...not to mention totally aroused! I think it changed everything for me.'

'That's only fair because you have changed everything for me. You have made me a better person. A less cynical person, although I'm sure I'm not completely reformed.'

'I don't want to reform you. I just want to be with you.'

'Even though your life will never be your own again?' His expression turned serious. 'Because the life of a monarch is not for everyone.'

'I know that.' She stroked the rough stubble on his jaw. 'I'm not afraid of hard work and as challenging as it might be, as long as you're beside me I know that everything will be okay.'

'Then be with me, Cassidy.' His hand spanned her face. 'As my partner in life, as my Princess, as my wife.'

Bursting with the kind of happiness she had never expected to find, least of all with a man, Cassidy smiled giddily. 'Your wife?' She tightened her legs around him and heard him groan.

'Yes, it's the only role I'm willing to allow you to have in my life.'

Not waiting to hear her response, Logan kissed her with all the patience of a man hanging on by a thread.

'Aunty Cass—oops!'

'Oh, my stars, I told you two not to go in there,' Peta hissed at whichever twin had just opened the door.

'I need my homework. I didn't know they'd be fooling around like you and Dan do.'

When her sister squeaked in dismay Cassidy half groaned and half laughed. 'This is my family,' she said. 'Warts and all.'

Logan released her enough to let her feet slide to the floor. 'Your family is my family now, *mi amor*. They're perfect. Just like you.'

Cassidy didn't think it was possible to fall any harder for the man holding her so strongly in his arms, but she did then.

EPILOGUE

THE DAY OF the wedding dawned bright and blue. The vintage car had just dropped Cassidy at the entrance to the gothic cathedral in the centre of Trinia and the streets were lined with people waving banners and calling her name.

Cassidy had to blink back tears as she waved at everyone in return, her throat thick with emotion at the outpouring of support for her after the harrowing media scandal two months earlier.

Behind her Peta fanned out the train of her wedding dress, while the twins straightened her long veil.

'You look awesome, Aunty Cassidy,' April murmured, her wide smile full of joy, her hair fashioned in tiny plaits interspersed with white flowers.

'Like a real-life princess,' Amber agreed.

'You do,' Peta agreed, coming to stand in front of her, her soft lilac bridesmaid's gown the same shade as the twins'. 'You couldn't look more perfect, which is a surprise considering that your groom rushed the wedding.'

Cassidy grinned from behind her veil. Logan had told her in no uncertain terms that he didn't want to wait to make their relationship official and that he considered two months a lifetime to make her his.

Secretly she'd agreed, but she had wanted to make sure that his mother was completely on board with everything before the wedding went ahead. Family had always been the most important thing for Cassidy, as it was for Logan, and she'd done everything that she could, followed every royal protocol, to prove that she was worthy of him.

That had paid off this morning when his mother had stopped by her room with two footmen in her wake carrying a very old, very intricate chest. Inside was a diamond teardrop tiara that had taken Cassidy's breath away.

'This was my mother's tiara,' she said. 'And her mother's before her. Since I didn't manage to have a daughter, I would be honoured if you chose to wear it today.'

Cassidy had felt herself choke up as she'd lifted the spectacular piece from its velvet bed. 'It's I who am honoured,' she said, biting her lip to stop the tears from falling.

Logan's mother had shaken her head. 'None of that. You'll ruin your make-up.' She had patted Cassidy's arm. 'I knew my son was enamoured of you very early on, but I didn't think you would fit. I was wrong. And one should never be afraid to admit that. Especially when you make my son so happy.'

'He makes me happy too,' Cassidy had said.

'As it should be. And now I will leave you to prepare for the day ahead. But perhaps one night in the near future you could take a stroll with me around my rose garden. I'd be very pleased to show it to you.'

Cassidy had coloured at that, fervently hoping that there were no cameras in the rose garden to reveal exactly what had happened the last time she had been there.

Now she stood at the bottom of the stone steps, staring up at the towering church spire, her stomach alive with butterflies.

Suddenly she wished that Logan was beside her because she couldn't help feeling intimidated by what she was about to enter into.

As if her sister sensed it, she touched her arm. 'Don't

stumble now, Your Highness,' she warned impishly. 'You have every camera on the planet aimed at you.'

'Thanks for reminding me,' Cassidy complained, her fingers trembling as she lifted them to smooth down her veil in the light breeze.

'Seriously, Cass,' her sister began softly. 'I know the King makes you very happy and if anyone deserves it you do. You've helped me out more times than I care to remember and now it's my turn to return the favour.' She held her arm out for Cassidy to take. 'Lean on me if you need to.'

Cassidy had asked Peta to walk her down the aisle and now she was very happy that she had. 'Thank you.' She placed her hand on her sister's arm. 'I love you.'

She turned one last time to wave to the crowd, before straightening her spine and gazing up at the entrance to the church.

The twins preceded her, scattering rose petals as they slowly made their way through the wide doors and up the aisle. Cassidy followed, with Peta beside her, her eyes riveted to the tall, handsome man waiting for her. He looked solid and steady and full of love as she made her way to him.

Barely noticing anyone else in the packed pews, she smiled up at him as Peta took her hand and laid it over his.

Logan gave her a slow grin. 'You look incredible, *mi preciosa*, but for a minute I thought I was going to have to send out a search party.'

Cassidy felt her whole body relax at his teasing tone, her heart overflowing. 'Not a chance, my love,' she whispered back. 'I'm yours for ever.'

* * * * *

COMING SOON!

MILLS & BOON

Coming next month

BEAUTY AND HER ONE-NIGHT BABY
Dani Collins

Scarlett dropped her phone with a clatter.

She had been trying to call Kiara. Now she was taking in the livid claw marks across Javiero's face, each pocked on either side with the pinpricks of recently removed stitches. His dark brown hair was longer than she'd ever seen it, perhaps gelled back from the widow's peak at some point this morning, but it was mussed and held a jagged part. He wore a black eye patch like a pirate, its narrow band cutting a thin stripe across his temple and into his hair.

Maybe that's why his features looked as though they had been set askew? His mouth was...not right. His upper lip was uneven and the claw marks drew lines through his unkempt stubble all the way down into his neck.

That was dangerously close to his jugular! Dear God, he had nearly been killed.

She grasped at the edge of the sink, trying to stay on her feet while she grew so light-headed at the thought of him dying that she feared she would faint.

The ravages of his attack weren't what made him look so forbidding and grim, though, she computed through her haze of panic and anguish. No. The contemptuous glare in his one eye was for her. For *this*.

He flicked another outraged glance at her middle.

"I thought we were meeting in the boardroom." His voice sounded gravelly. Damaged as well? Or was that simply his true feelings toward her now? Deadly and completely devoid of any of the sensual admiration she'd sometimes heard in his tone.

Not that he'd ever been particularly warm toward her. He'd been aloof, indifferent, irritated, impatient, explosively passionate. Generous in the giving of pleasure. Of compliments. Then cold as she left. Disapproving. Malevolent.

Damningly silent.

And now he was…what? Ignoring that she was as big as a barn?

Her arteries were on fire with straight adrenaline, her heart pounding and her brain spinning with the way she was having to switch gears so fast. Her eyes were hot and her throat tight. Everything in her wanted to scream *Help me*, but she'd been in enough tight spots to know this was all on her. Everything was always on her. She fought to keep her head and get through the next few minutes before she moved on to the next challenge.

Which was just a tiny trial called *childbirth*, but she would worry about that when she got to the hospital.

As the tingle of a fresh contraction began to pang in her lower back, she tightened her grip on the edge of the sink and gritted her teeth, trying to ignore the coming pain and hang on to what dregs of dignity she had left.

"I'm in labor," she said tightly. "It's yours."

Continue reading
BEAUTY AND HER ONE-NIGHT BABY
Dani Collins

Available next month
www.millsandboon.co.uk

LET'S TALK
Romance

For exclusive extracts, competitions
and special offers, find us online:

facebook.com/millsandboon

@MillsandBoon

@MillsandBoonUK

Get in touch on 01413 063232

For all the latest titles coming soon, visit
millsandboon.co.uk/nextmonth

MILLS & BOON

THE HEART OF ROMANCE

A ROMANCE FOR EVERY KIND OF READER

ODERN

Prepare to be swept off your feet by sophisticated, sexy and seductive heroes, in some of the world's most glamourous and romantic locations, where power and passion collide.
8 stories per month.

STORICAL

Escape with historical heroes from time gone by. Whether your passion is for wicked Regency Rakes, muscled Vikings or rugged Highlanders, awaken the romance of the past.
6 stories per month.

EDICAL

Set your pulse racing with dedicated, delectable doctors in the high-pressure world of medicine, where emotions run high and passion, comfort and love are the best medicine.
6 stories per month.

rue Love

Celebrate true love with tender stories of heartfelt romance, from the rush of falling in love to the joy a new baby can bring, and a focus on the emotional heart of a relationship.
8 stories per month.

Desire

Indulge in secrets and scandal, intense drama and plenty of sizzling hot action with powerful and passionate heroes who have it all: wealth, status, good looks…everything but the right woman.
6 stories per month.

EROES

Experience all the excitement of a gripping thriller, with an intense romance at its heart. Resourceful, true-to-life women and strong, fearless men face danger and desire - a killer combination!
8 stories per month.

DARE

Sensual love stories featuring smart, sassy heroines you'd want as a best friend, and compelling intense heroes who are worthy of them.
4 stories per month.

To see which titles are coming soon, please visit

millsandboon.co.uk/nextmonth

JOIN US ON SOCIAL MEDIA!

Stay up to date with our latest releases, author
news and gossip, special offers and discounts, and
all the behind-the-scenes action
from Mills & Boon...

 millsandboon

 millsandboonuk

 millsandboon

It might just be true love...